Amends

A Novel

Dale J. Moore

Published by Northern Amusements, Inc., LaSalle, Ontario.

Amends / Dale J. Moore - 1st Edition Trade Paperback

ISBN 978-0-9868534-1-8

This book and others by Northern Amusements are available in electronic format. Visit your e-book stores or our web site at:

www.northernamusements.com

e-Pub version
ISBN 978-0-9868534-2-5

Cover by Ami Moore

Edited by Maureen P. Moore

Author photo by Linda Moore

Printed and bound in the United States and/or Canada.

Dedications

To Linda, for her love and ongoing encouragement of my writing endeavours. She makes me look forward to whatever comes next in our adventure together.

Prologue

The merits and drawbacks of gun control had never received serious thought in his mind. Six feet away, mesmerized by the barrel of a pistol fixed at his head, he quickly settled on a position for gun control, what little good it did to alleviate his current predicament. There was no escape from the gun-wielding messenger of death. He possessed no martial arts or other combat skills to reverse the situation in a quick and decisive manner. No superpowers lay dormant awaiting his command to act. He knew not how to sway his captor to forgive and forget.

He'd heard time slowed in moments like this, perhaps the reason why people saw their life flash before their eyes with detail previously lost to faded memories. In all likelihood, he deserved this fate. What goes around comes around, his mother always said. And while someone had died at his hands, he'd done harm in possibly worse ways, leaving souls ravaged by his indiscretion, self-preservation, or sense of sport. He'd left a trail of damage that he'd never stopped to contemplate prior to three weeks ago. Now, with a bullet in his immediate, and likely short, future, he wondered: aside from the holder of the gun, would the other people in his life feel he'd done enough to make amends?

0 Billboard

Three weeks earlier …

The new billboard on the 405 elicited a reflective grin on his thirty year-old face. A woman with a near perfect smile consumed the left side of the roadside advertisement. On the right, a catchy slogan, 'Smile like a STAR! Call Dr. Yugo Farr,' followed by a phone number and address. The word STAR glittered with the mid-morning sun breaking through the early-morning haze.

It didn't seem that long ago that he'd deployed a similar tactic. He brushed back a lock of his wavy, dirty-blond hair and looked in his rear-view mirror. *Could it be six years already?* But this billboard had flaws. The phone number was much too small and lacked a catchy or memorable set of digits – it looked like a random string of numbers. And the good Dr. Farr should have picked a perfect smile. The driver could see two glaring deficiencies, one in spacing and one in alignment across the uppers. As a renowned maxillofacial surgeon, he considered himself a stickler for detail and a gap of one thirty-secondth of an inch between the maxillary central incisors was the dental equivalent of the Grand Canyon. But he realized most passing drivers would not notice, their gaze more likely to ogle the nice rack that lay below the imperfect smile. Another novice mistake. Only the face or a partial of the face should show. He bet half the drivers wondered if Dr. Farr's profession was dentist or plastic surgeon. He laughed thinking about how many calls Yugo would get for boob jobs, this was LA after all, and doubted this new upstart represented a threat to his thriving practice.

Simultaneously, his cell phone vibrated and Bluetooth jingled. Without glancing at the caller ID, he pushed the button on his earpiece.

"Dr. Tre Brightman."

"Tre, Steve Jones calling."

"Steve, good to hear from you. Is my deal finalized yet?"

"He turned it down. Wants two-fifty more."

"Fine, tell him to find another buyer who'll give him two-fifty more."

The caller remained silent.

"Look, Steve, you know it. I know it, and he knows it. I'm the only buyer he's got. Nobody else is even interested in a dump like his in a low-rent district like it's in. It's purely a tax write-off for me, but it's not cost justifiable unless I get it at this price. I'm not going any higher."

"He's losing money on the deal, Tre."

"That's the gamble of real estate these days, Steve. We both know he can't wait another six months for a deal to come along. He either loses a bit on my offer or a lot by losing the place to his creditors."

"Did anyone ever tell you that you can be ruthless?"

Tre grinned. "It's business, Steve. Nothing personal against the guy. Maybe next time he won't get in over his head. I'm actually doing the guy a favour." He paused for a moment. "Look," he paused again, letting his conscience be heard. "To prove I have a heart, throw him a bone. Offer him fifteen more and tell him to take it or leave it."

"I'm not sure he'll see you as benevolent with that revision."

"That's why I pay you that big fat commission, Stevie-boy. Spin it however you like, but get this deal done by tomorrow at noon or it's off the table. Period."

"Got it. I'll get back to you later."

Tre added a stern quality to his voice. "Tomorrow by noon, Steve. No later."

"On it. Talk to you before noon tomorrow."

Tre pressed the off button on his earpiece.

"Prick," he said out loud, tossing his phone onto the empty seat beside him, wondering why he paid Steve so damn much money and had to tell him how to do his job. Tre had found the property and pretty well brokered the entire deal himself. *Mental note – get new commercial real estate agent.*

Tre made a quick, but illegal, left turn and pulled into the gated entrance to his Beverly Hills office. Retrieving his phone from the passenger seat, he touched an app and a bar code appeared. Placing the phone up to the proximity reader, the two black iron gates parted slowly. As he waited for the gates to open completely, he glanced around.

"Shit." He shut off his car and got out, leaving the door ajar. "Hey, you!" he hollered at a homeless person sleeping in the corner where the garage met the office building. The lump didn't move. Tre walked over to within a couple of feet and yelled again. "Get up!" He debated kicking the heap for signs of life, when a man emerged from under a pile of plastic shopping bags and the tattered remnants of a blanket.

"I'm sleeping," came the gravel throated response, followed by a disturbing hacking sound and the launch of a ball of phlegm flung to within six inches of Tre's designer shoes.

Tre looked down in disgust. "Not here, you're not!" Reluctantly, Tre reached down and grabbed the man by his soiled jacket sleeve and yanked the vagrant to his feet.

"All right, all right. I'm leaving." The man pulled up his pants, wiped his dirt smeared nose on his sleeve, and snatched up the bags containing his life's possessions. He looked at Tre like a great oppressor, made a horrible retching noise with his throat, and sent another phlegm ball flying. Tre lurched, but the missile struck his pant leg. Pissed off, Tre cursed, pushed the man to the ground, and walked back to his car. He sat on the seat, door still open, and pulled an interior cleaning wipe from a small canister under the seat and extracted the disgusting mucus from his clothing. He closed the door and glared at the homeless guy once more gathering up his bags.

Fortunately, Tre sat in his car, which always made him feel better. Car? This wasn't just a car. The driving machine was a Mercedes SLK-55 Class Roadster, with performance package. An eight cylinder, 355 horsepower two-seater chariot of fire. Fire Opal to be precise, the manufacturer's name for the colour shrouding his driving machine. The hot LA days necessitated the Orient Beige-coloured interior. He didn't have kids to drip chocolate ice cream on the seats, but he almost threw one Hollywood starlet out on her ass for dropping her bright red lipstick on the seat. If he'd already slept with her, and if those lips didn't look so enticing, he would have stopped, given her a fifty, and sent a cab to pick her up.

"Good morning, Dr. Brightman!"

His buxom brunette front desk assistant flashed her pearly whites at him. He admired the fabulous job he'd done on her teeth. Of course, she'd done a few fabulous things for him too to help reduce her cost. He didn't consider it paying for sex, but helping out a damsel in distress.

Some men are leg men. Some men focus on breasts. Others fixate on a woman's butt. Tre was an eye guy. His friends all thought him crazy. To him, the other features had their own merits and seductive powers, but a woman's eyes told her story. As someone once said, and he'd read the debates about who it was or wasn't, the eyes are the windows to the soul. He wasn't so sure it was the soul he was seeing. To him, the eyes let him sense their personality and thoughts. A portal to their persona. And looking into Katie's brown eyes, he saw a Pink song – crazy, energetic fun, but a chilling darkness lurked somewhere below the facade, waiting to erupt or lash out.

"Good morning, Katie," and he air-kissed her cheek in passing.

She wrinkled her nose at the all too familiar fake kiss. "Your ten-thirty isn't here yet."

He looked at his cell phone. Ten-twenty. In spite of the incident outside, he'd arrived in his comfort zone. Tre hated getting to the office more than fifteen minutes early, and scolded himself if ever late. Ten minutes provided him enough time to use the washroom and start a bottle of vitamin-enriched water.

"Thanks. Let her sit until ten-forty, then come get me."

"Got it. The usual."

He detected some sarcasm, sending an uneasy smile across his face. *She'd worked for him for too long.* Nothing made him more uncomfortable than someone knowing his habits and apparently despising them. He made a mental note to put an ad online tonight for a new receptionist. With the benefits he offered, he'd have his pick and a replacement for Katie by the end of the week. He'd send her off with a good reference in hand, of course. C'est la vie.

Scrubbing thoroughly as he finished in the washroom, he remembered his patient list for this morning and his face lit up. His first. Not his first patient, nor his first lover. His first success. Tre had encountered difficulty getting his practice established in LA, including some ugly battles with business partners. His big break came when today's client, Marla Main, walked through his door subsequent to spotting one of his billboards. Perhaps glided through his door was more appropriate. He wasn't in the luxurious digs he now occupied and it was a miracle she'd entered the office at all from its outward appearance; clean and professional looking, but far from upscale. Tre recognized Marla immediately at the time. She'd achieved moderate success in a sitcom, and had moved onto movies, always in a small supporting role. He loved her acting, even in those dry, predictable, half-hour travesties to intelligence. Her movie roles at the time usually meant somewhere south of two minutes of actual screen time. The day they met, Marla was a black haired, hazel eyed, former teen model, with attractive but not stunning beauty. She didn't possess large breasts or big flowing hair, and entering his office she could have been any girl from the Midwest. Her body was tight like her acting. Down to earth, at least back then, her fresh energetic eyes retained traces of youthful innocence. Marla was Tre's first real Hollywood star client, even if C-list back then by most people's standards. She and Tre hooked up a couple of times early on, definitely in the category of searing fling, not romance. He worked on her teeth for a few months, transforming her mouth into a thing of beauty at considerable expense to the young up-and-comer. She had a nice smile before, but he'd made it full and alluring.

Her new smile and short stature landed Marla her next role as the feisty, rebellious young daughter of one of Hollywood's biggest, and shorter, leading men. The movie launched her Hollywood star. Her on-screen time quadrupled, she stole most of her scenes, and the part garnered an Academy Award nomination for best supporting actress. She didn't win, but the nomination opened the floodgates to lucrative offers. While filming her next flick, an offhand mention of Tre's name in an interview to a women's magazine had the same effect to his practice. They lined up at his door. To the relief of his hygienist at the time, who also worked the front desk and as his assistant, he could finally hire a full-time receptionist and a full-time assistant.

Tre now employed three people at his office. Katie, for now anyways, the Jekyll and Hyde of emotions; Wendy, his new-to-Los Angeles dental assistant; and Cassy, his girl-next-door hygienist. He paused as he tried to recall the name of his first hygienist – no luck. From his recall, she was nothing to stare at and he'd never had any interest in her romantically, if you could call any of his relationships romance. In most cases, he could find something in any woman that attracted him. But then again, back then he wasn't very active sexually. He'd just moved to town and was still getting over leaving …

"Cassy!" His current hygienist bolted out of a nearby room and right into Tre. Consumed by thoughts of his past as he made his way back to the small kitchen to fetch his water from the fridge, he'd stepped blindly into the hallway. They collided, and he gripped her arms to keep her from falling. He looked in her eyes and his lit up. Her lustrous brown eyes showed a fascinating depth. In fact, she was the only hygienist, short of what's-her-name at the start of his practice, that he hadn't gotten into bed. And definitely not for the same reason. Cassy's long brown hair, when free from its bun and hairnet, shone brighter than his Fire Opal Mercedes. A perfect complexion and nice healthy figure added to her allure. Her smile, not one of his, also sucked him in. It wasn't perfect like the ones he manufactured, but its appeal unmistakable. He wouldn't touch it for the world. Then there were her eyes! He'd never seen eyes like hers. They radiated trust and kindness, with the warmth of a crackling fire in winter. Some women's eyes screamed mysterious, devilish, or oozed of sex appeal. Cassy's eyes soothed and welcomed him.

Tre made a few unsuccessful passes at Cassy early on. She'd discouraged every attempt with a casual and polite demeanour. Their relationship stayed professional, albeit politically incorrect. It evolved to him making an incredible and ridiculous pass once a week, usually on Wednesday mornings, and her replying with a witty rejection that kicked his ego to the curb. It got to the point where he looked forward to Wednesdays, developing an atrocious pickup line the prior night in anticipation of what she'd come up with to shoot him down. The guys teased him about not getting into her pants, due to his otherwise stellar track record. Tre told them he had too many other irons in the fire to spend energy chasing anyone. Other than Cassy, his cockiness knew no bounds in the past few years when it came to women.

"Sorry, Cassy," he said as he held her.

"My fault, boss," she replied.

"You have to learn to stop throwing yourself at me."

She leaned in closer to him. "You are hard to resist …"

Tre stammered, caught off guard. "Really?"

She laughed and pulled away. "No, just messing with you, boss. Unlike most of your girlfriends, I don't start my day with a handful of pills with a scotch chaser."

"Ouch. And for the record, only forty-seven percent of my lady friends start their day that way, so using *most* is an exaggeration!"

"Whatever you say, boss." She turned and hurried off to get ready for Marla's cleaning.

He had tried to get Cassy to call him Tre, but gave up. She called him boss, and sometimes Dr. Brightman if upset. Most of the time upon telling women to 'call me Tre', they took it as a personal invitation. Not with her. He grabbed his water, and looked at his watch. Ten thirty-five. He'd told Katie to get him at ten-forty, but it was Marla after all. He took a quick drink and entered the reception area.

"Marla! So good to see you."

"Tre, looking as good as ever."

They exchanged a brief hug. He inhaled her perfume, recognizable from their times of intimate involvement. More memories, until he looked into her eyes. They'd changed. A barrier stood in the way, limiting the reach of his inward gaze.

"I just saw your latest movie the other night. You put on a great performance. I have to say I jumped out of my seat when you thrust the dagger into your lover's heart."

She let out a warm laugh. "Don't worry, darling. I wasn't thinking of you during the scene. More my agent, that money-sucking leech." She frowned at the thought.

His young assistant had entered the room and stood by patiently.

"Wendy here will take you to start with a few x-rays, and then Cassy will do your cleaning. I'll see you in about thirty or forty-five minutes to let you know how everything looks in that famous mouth of yours."

"Famous thanks to you, Tre."

Flirtatious words, but her eyes said otherwise. He admired Marla's butt as she followed his assistant out of the room. During recent visits she'd treated Tre like nothing ever happened and he was just her dentist. They'd both gone their own ways years ago, so he didn't expect any flirting. She'd married an actor as famous and rich as her. Their rare appearances together led to a paparazzi frenzy fuelled by an insatiable tabloid market.

Pleasing every starlet, single or otherwise, that came to him to get a smile like Marla's contented Tre after she'd moved on. All eager to make it, they didn't limit their ambition to the casting couch. It made for great, short relationships. The ones who didn't become famous, which was most of them, would sometimes blame his work for their lack of landing jobs, instead of their cardboard acting skills, and would want nothing to do with him afterward. And the ones who did become famous, like Marla, didn't want their red carpet photos with their dentist. No ties. Just the way he liked it.

"Tre, you have a call," his receptionist Katie nervously interrupted.

"Take a message," he replied.

"He says it's urgent," she responded, fidgeting.

Tre didn't have many male patients. He could count them on both hands.

"Okay," and he reached for the wall-mounted phone that came in handy while he worked. "Dr. Tre Brightman here."

"You're ruining my life," an altered voice came across the line. Even through the digital disguise, Tre could feel the anxiety in the words. "You piece of slime. Confess to what you've done, or I'll kill you."

"Who is this?" Tre asked, thinking as he finished that it was a stupid question. Who would use a voice altering device and then give up his name?

"You'll know my name when I carve it in your chest if you don't stop doing what you're doing."

Thinking it was a joke by one of his buddies, Tre shot back a smart reply. "But the cops will know you did it if your name is on my chest."

"Shut up, asshole," the voice angrily replied. "On second thought, just leave LA or I'll kill you."

1 Start Up

Six years ago Tre Brightman had arrived in LA, naïve and full of dreams, although his dreams didn't include the big screen like many newcomers to Tinseltown. After taking off the summer following graduation to drink beer and contemplate life, he needed a fresh start and moving to the City of Angels was as radical as he could think of. With his degree from the University of Louisville Dental School underarm, he approached bank after bank to secure the least overpriced, but still undersized loan to start his practice. He'd sunk every penny of that loan – a loan in addition to his school loans – into setting up the practice. Tre spent twice what he would have needed back home in Michigan, even with refurbished equipment. It still wasn't enough money to float a new business in LA. So he made calls to some of his fellow grads to lure a partner. Most had already established themselves, with the few months' head-start on Tre. Finally, he found George Smiley. A great name for a dentist, but not Tre's first choice for a partner. His fourteenth choice, actually.

George Smiley proved an adequate dentist, settling firmly in the middle of the bottom half of their graduating class. Right out of college, he'd moved into work in his father's dental practice right in Louisville. No capital outlay and a good way to hammer down some of those school loans – except George didn't have any school loans since dear old dad had footed the tuition and George had lived at home while going through college. So basically, George was socking away the dough, gaining experience, and inheriting his father's clientele.

Tre felt a nibble during the first call to George, and subsequent to a little persistence, and discussion on independence, they formed a partnership. The fresh infusion of cash allowed Tre to stay ahead of the bills and do some modest advertising. They had picked up some clients, but it was slow. They started with a hygienist, a dental assistant, and a receptionist. The hygienist left after bouncing a paycheque, leaving the men to use a temporary employment agency to bring in a hygienist when needed. It meant scheduling that work on particular days to maximize the profit from those procedures. While difficult dealing with a different hygienist every time, it proved an effective cost-cutting measure. They had to let the receptionist go due to lack of business, doubling up duties as the dental assistant took over the receptionist duties. She appreciated the additional work; the days dragged on horribly with the limited clientele. It wasn't long before George had tapped out his reserves, refusing to get a business loan. And George Sr. wasn't on great speaking terms with his truant son, let alone lending terms. After only six months in business, George asked out of the partnership. Tre put him off for one month, and the terms of the separation agreement George had signed without reading carefully deterred him another month. Finally, enough was enough. George took the twenty-five cents on the dollar return on his investment per the agreement, or at least the first of twenty-four monthly payments of it, and ran back, hat in hand, to George Senior. The parting was inimical, with loud ugly exchanges between the two young dentists, one in front of one of the few regular patients they'd landed. The two Georges filed a lawsuit a year later, once Tre's practice had taken off, but it was tossed out of court due to Tre keeping up the monthly payments per the agreement.

With George's departure, Brightman and Smiley began looking for a new partner, having lost its Smiley. During the interim period, Tre had made a friend in Bobby Cassidy, an orthopedic surgeon that he'd met in the nearby fitness centre. Bobby gave Tre a low-interest long-term loan that Tre spent to put up his billboard, a simple sign with a perfect smile filling the top two thirds. Underneath, in bold letters, read his name, an easy to remember, almost musical phone number, and address in Beverly Hills. A last-ditch, last dollar desperation hail Mary to save his practice. If it didn't work, Bobby would never see a dime repaid on the loan. Bobby knew but didn't care. He'd write if off if he had too.

The ad generated modest traffic flow to his small practice, allowing Tre to keep up his payment to George and juggle late payments to his debtors and vendors. The debt load proved unsustainable with the current stream of income. He needed a partner and took the first candidate that came through the door with the ability to borrow money. The new cash flow and some back payments backed off the debt hounds, while allowing him to give his poor dental assistant slash receptionist some back wages and a small raise. Tre convinced his original hygienist to come back on a cash-in-advance basis, which worked better for both of them. He'd grown weary of dealing with the habits of a new hygienist every few days. Tre paid back half of Bobby's billboard investment in a lump sum too, even though he didn't have a payment owing for another month. Tre had struck a similar deal with Dr. Lionel Ramsey to the one he had with his first partner, although Lionel read the contract and negotiated better terms, by a fraction.

Tre still performed some creative accounting, juggling bill payments to keep any one creditor from getting too demanding. Very conservative, Lionel kept demanding to see the books. Tre complied by showing a more optimistic set he kept on the side. With the practice apparently now breaking even, Lionel invested more money into the business, upgrading some of Tre's initial equipment with newer, more expensive versions, and coughing up money for an additional two billboards. While Lionel was cautious, his wife was as prudish a woman as Tre had ever met. In the dead of summer, the lady wore full sleeve, turtleneck tops and floor length boring black dresses. She might as well have worn a habit. Her eyes emitted venom every time she exchanged glances with Tre. Those hateful eyes left little doubt how she felt and Tre wondered how much of her daily energy went into despising him.

Tre dated his dental assistant-slash-receptionist a couple of times. Strict dinner-and-a-movie stuff, with no kiss goodnight. It was more a mutual break from the daily suffering of a failing business than dating. Misery is forgotten by company.

The day Marla Main came into Tre's life, it changed. She'd tried to get into a string of Hollywood's premier dentists, but upon finding out the rates, she began searching for an affordable option. She spotted Tre's billboard and after talking to his receptionist about pricing, booked a consult. The talented but under-noticed Marla Main and Tre hit it off immediately. They started dating as soon as he started working on her teeth – although the term dating implied old fashioned courting. They just had sex – no dinners or movies involved. One night after hours, returning to retrieve a gift he'd bought for his wife but forgotten at the office, Lionel found Marla and Tre having sex in the office. Lionel wrestled with telling his uptight wife, but decided to let it slide as he'd never had an ounce of problem with Tre up to that point. The second time Lionel stumbled across them in the act however, he went straight home and told the prudish one. She made her husband put his foot down. After all, Tre and Marla weren't even married. She expected everyone to save it for marriage, like she had. So Lionel issued an ultimatum – Tre had to break it off with Marla or else. Tre took the 'or else' and severed the partnership, buying out Lionel for thirty-two cents on the dollar of his initial investment. Lionel got very little for the tens of thousands he'd invested in new equipment and nothing for the large sums invested in billboards, leaving him bitter. At the insistence of his wife, he sued. And lost.

Within three months, Marla had made it big, dropped Tre's name in the magazine article, and there was no looking back for the young Dr. Brightman.

2 Busted

Three hours after receiving the phone threat, it still bounced around Tre's mind. It sounded real, but was it? It definitely put him off his game. Not his dental work, mind you, that bordered on automatic. He'd seen two new aspiring actresses for initial consultations without flirting, on his behalf at least. Entering the kitchen to grab another bottle of water, he saw Cassy smiling at her e-reader. She laid it down when her eyes detected him.

"Are you sick today?" Cassy asked, with a sincere look of concern.

"No, why do you ask?" Tre bent down to grab the coldest bottle from the back of the fridge.

"Wendy told me you ignored the advances dripped all over you today by our newbs," she replied.

"Newbs?"

"New patients."

"Oh, yeah." He paused, still lost in an old thought. Recomposing himself, he replied, "Maybe I'm turning over a new leaf? Did you ever think of that?"

Cassy laughed so hard, that if eating, her food would have projected across the room.

Tre looked disturbed by the reaction. "Is it that bad?"

"Let's put it this way. You'd have to turn over the whole tree." She smiled at her own joke. Her expression morphed to disgust and she put up her hands in front of her chest, palms forward. "You do not pay Wendy enough for what she has to witness every day. Thank God I'm a hygienist and I don't have to witness those women drooling all over you, and you reciprocating with clever, witty come-ons."

"You think my come-ons are clever and witty?" He grinned from ear to ear, pleased she thought so.

"That's not the point, Dr. Brightman."

Ouch. That hurt like his mother yelling at him as a kid when she'd use his first and middle name to summon him.

"Well, thanks for your concern, Cassy, but I'm fine. Just have my mind on other things."

"Can I go for today?" she asked. "I checked, and there aren't any more cleanings scheduled."

"Sure. I've got a few hours off too, so I'm going to hit the gym."

"You did remember that I'm leaving at two tomorrow, right?"

"Two … yeah, sure. No cleanings after two?"

"None. I'm heading up home for the weekend and will return Monday afternoon."

"Sure. See you tomorrow."

"See you later," she answered as she flicked off her e-reader and slid it in the side of her voluminous purse.

He watched her walk out of the room. He liked her eyes, but even in scrub pants her butt looked great.

Goodbodies gym was a short walk from Tre's office. Most days, he'd leave his schedule open for an hour or more in the early afternoon to workout. An advantage of being the boss was the flexibility to make his own schedule. The split allowed for early evening appointments, often more convenient for his clientele. His elongated midday break also allowed for a quick liaison as well, if one of his patients just couldn't wait. And the early evening appointments allowed him to send the staff home and 'entertain' in his office.

Tre had developed a few friends at the gym, all men oddly enough. He didn't need to trawl for hook-ups at the fitness centre, like many men had become accustomed to doing. Bobby was the first real friend he'd made in LA. The orthopedic surgeon had been paid back many times for his kindness of floating the billboard money. Tre put Bobby's loan first, even ahead of the legally obligated payment to George Smiley. On a handful of occasions early on Tre set Bobby up with his female overflow, or Tre had arranged double dates. Bobby had met his wife Jenny via one of Tre's setups. Tre never told Bobby that his fate lay in a coin flip. Inadvertently, Tre had double booked two gorgeous women one night, and decided to take both girls out. He couldn't decide whether he'd rather pursue Jenny or the other girl, whose name escaped him, so he flipped a coin. Heads Jenny, tails what's-her-name. Tails it was, and tail he got. Lucky for him he thought at the time, as Jenny had old-fashioned morals and restrained Bobby until their wedding night. Bobby had actually been the lucky one.

Tre had met Jack and John, so-called identical twins, in a game of pickup hoops. He didn't like the term identical twins because in most pairs he'd known, and these guys were not the exception, they shared many similar experiences, but each one made their own course in life. The brothers ran a small but comfortably successful private detective agency. Most of the cases entering their door were of the domestic variety. It was Hollywood after all. Next to lying, cheating was the most popular vocation. Acting sat a distant third.

Twenty minutes of weights preceded another twenty on the treadmill, set on extreme hills. Following a seven minute cool down on the bike, Tre headed to the half-court basketball floor. An inside court was perfect for the LA summers, allowing for players to work up a sweat without burning in the afternoon sun. Tre would often come in the evenings and just shoot balls for an hour at a time, like back home in the high school gym.

With Bobby, the four of them played pickup at least twice a week. The other three guys were already shooting around, waiting for their fourth to arrive.

"Tre, man!" Bobby greeted his best friend with their four-part handshake. Regular handshake, thumb-wrap, finger lock, and forearm shiver as they did a quick man-hug.

Jack thrust a ball into Tre's chest the second the hug had ended. "Who's stuck with you today, Doctor Love?"

"Sorry about your luck, Jack. You're the poor sap."

"Great. Remember to give me the ball every once in a while, leather hog."

John stepped forward with a coin. "Jack, call it for possession."

"What's better, Tre, head or tail?"

Tre laughed. "You should be happy with either, Chewbacca."

"Thanks for your support, partner. Let's go with heads."

John watched the toss coin fall to the court. "Tough luck, big brother. Tails. Our ball."

The game was always a battle, no matter the teams. Tre always enjoyed them most with the twins on opposite teams, watching them beat the crap out of each other rather than him. When one of them drove the basket, they drove it like encased in a Hummer. After splitting two games to fifteen, with two points for a three-pointer and one for all other baskets, they paused for a drink break.

"I got something to ask you guys," Tre spoke, looking at the two detectives.

"Sure, but we can't help you if you got crabs from one of those starlets of yours," Jack laughed.

"Thanks, but nothing as tragic as that," Tre said, an uneasy smile crossing his face. "I got a death threat this morning."

"Pissed off husband?" John asked.

"That's what I'm thinking, how'd you guess?"

"Do you really think most dentists get death threats?" John answered.

"Suppose not," Tre replied, wiping his brow with one of the fitness club's small white towels.

"If I were you, I'd be more worried about crabs," replied Jack.

"Sounds serious enough to me," Bobby objected. "I mean think about it. Maybe this guy is afraid of losing his meal ticket. He married a starlet, she has a pre-nup, and he loses everything if she just walks for another guy."

"Like I'd run off with any of them. They're mostly self-centred, plastic dolls," Tre responded.

"So Tre likes to play with dolls," Jack said.

Concerned, Bobby replied. "But this guy doesn't know that. He just knows Tre's making his wife happy and he's not."

"I just don't see it," Jack said. "Aside from Marla Main, most of the starlets Tre sees rate as wannabe's or at best C-listers. If they're married, I'd bet it's to some rich Hollywood exec who has his own money."

"So money's not a motive," John stated.

"Agreed," Jack said. "So the caller is likely just pissed off. He'll cool down in a day or two, if he hasn't already. These execs aren't the type to bother whacking a guy like you. In our experiences, they're all bark and no bite."

"So what do you suggest?" Tre asked.

"First, stop dipping your feather in the married ink well," Jack answered. "And call us if the guy calls back. We can get all over it like hair on a gorilla. If the guy is serious, we can find him and give him motivation to back off," and he slammed the basketball to the floor with both hands.

"I doubt that will be necessary," Tre stated. "It's got to be a prank or some guy blowing off steam, like you said." He looked at Bobby. "Remember when you pranked me about Marla Main? You jerk."

"Hey, it was funny." Bobby began speaking with a bad German accent, repeating his pretend threat from a few years ago. "Stop making Marla smile, or I'll bust your pearly whites, Brightman."

"You sound like a drunken Arnold Schwarzenegger," Jack chuckled.

"It was only funny because you called from your office and I could tell it was you, you idiot," Tre replied.

"Let's finish the game. My legs are stiffening up," Bobby said.

The tie-breaker ended with Tre hitting a three-pointer from the corner, after John thought he had the young dentist boxed in at the baseline. Exchanging customary excuses and digs, the men grabbed their stuff and headed for the showers. Ten minutes later, Tre re-enacted the four-level handshake with Bobby as they bid adieu.

"Don't forget about tonight," Bobby told him.

"Tonight?"

"You forgot, didn't you? Dinner at eight. Jenny's friend. Ring a bell yet?"

"Oh yeah. The blind date. Why is Jenny trying to set me up anyway? I get lots of action."

"She wants to set you up with a nice girl."

"But I like naughty girls."

"Nice girls can be naughty when they want to be. You know women; they always think you're unhappy if you're not in a serious relationship or married."

"Then I am obviously very, very unhappy," Tre grinned as he patted his friend on the shoulder. "I'll be there to meet June Cleaver, don't worry. I know if I don't show you won't get any for a week."

"A week? I should be so lucky."

"What's this girl-next-door's name anyway?"

"I think Jenny said her name was Sandra."

"All right, then. I shall see you, Jenny, and Sandra at eight."

Walking back to his office, Tre felt invigorated from the exercise, and relieved from his discussion with the P.I. twins. He entered his office to a smiling Katie, who nodded in the direction of the waiting room. Spotting the curvaceous bottle blonde sitting, he turned and walked her way. A short red skirt barely covered her long silky legs and matched her red nails and lips.

"Rachel! So glad to see you," and he placed his duffle bag down and gave her a Hollywood hug.

"You look just yummy today, Tre." She nibbled on his ear, releasing a steamy breath into it. His skin tingled as he backed away.

"I'm just going to stow my bag, and my assistant Wendy will come get you when she's ready to set you up in a room."

She licked her lips and replied. "I'll see you in a few."

Tre looked at the young vixen. *Man was she hot.* And married. He came back down to earth. Scooping up his bag of sweaty attire, he looped around the reception area toward the side entrance that led to the secured parking lot. He flung open the door and marched through, pressing his trunk release as he did. The top was up, so the trunk looked deceptively large. With care, he stowed his duffle, knowing that dropping the roof later would consume much of his trunk storage space. Closing the trunk, he realized his sunglasses sat on his head. He liked them for the walk to the gym, but wouldn't need them for the rest of the day. Walking around the driver's side to stow the sunglasses, he spotted a scratch in his baby's paint. But it was no minor scuff. He backpedalled from his vehicle. His jaw dropped. Etched into the Fire

Opal paint was a single jagged word – 'asshole.' That's what his mystery harasser had called him.

"Shit! I'm going to kill that ..." He stopped in mid-sentence and covered his mouth in horror. How did the bastard get into the parking lot? He wondered if Mr. Rachel Legs-up-to-here had driven her and lurked in the parking lot, ready to attack. Tre turned and strode to the door, stopping a few feet short to turn and activate the car alarm. It still worked – he must have forgotten to set it after the confrontation with the homeless guy this morning. Now he was mad at himself. He re-entered the office, his heart beating through his shirt. Flustered, his hand shook as he grabbed a Gatorade out of the fridge. He drank the entire contents in an attempt to settle his nerves. Deciding on his next steps, he returned to the reception area.

"Katie, get me Jack or John Gordon on the phone." He took the call in his office and explained the latest incident.

"How about I swing by tonight and look over the surveillance footage of the garage? I can also check the phone system for the death threat caller." Jack's concern came through the phone.

"Sounds good. I'll owe you one."

"We'll call it even for your game winner today. I've rubbed it in John's face all day the way you got out of his shadow in the corner."

"That was sweet, wasn't it?" Tre replied, smiling to himself as he relived the shot.

"I can't come by right now, but how about 7:00 or so?"

"Can you make it 7:30? I'll be with a patient and the girls will have left for the day."

"With a patient, huh? Is that what the kids are calling it these days? You dog, you. 7:30 it is. See you then."

Tre felt some relief, knowing Jack would investigate. Bobby had told Tre stories of the twins' cases, portraying both as intelligent and clever, and he knew first-hand their brick house physiques. Tre proceeded to step two – confronting his current patient.

Tre composed himself a little further before heading into room three where Rachel waited.

"Hi, Rach. I assume Wendy has taken good care of you."

"Yes she has. Any chance of getting her to join us some night?"

Tre hesitated at the thought, then set his mind back to his mission. Using a dental mouth mirror and explorer he started examining her teeth.

"Perhaps. Did your husband drop you off today?" He pulled back for her to answer.

"No way. I always plan my appointments to coincide with Frankie being out of town." She tugged on his shirt and he slipped closer to her.

"How long's he gone for?"

"Why, are you looking for a double-header, so to speak?"

"No, just wondered if he ever came back early."

"What's up with you, Tre? You've never been nervous about hooking up before. Did you get caught by a jealous boyfriend?"

"No, not at all. Just being careful."

"That's what condoms are for. Don't worry. Frankie's in Paris at the film festival. Saw him last night at a pre-awards gala. Tonight was the ceremony." Rachel glanced at her watch. "Well, I'm sure it's over by now, with the time difference. And tomorrow he's got interviews with French television lined up. So," – and she ran her foot up the inside of Tre's thigh – "there's nothing to worry about."

"That's good to know. Now let's get back to work." At least that crossed Frankie off the list.

It was 6:30 p.m. when Katie popped her head in and said she was leaving for the night. Tre also told Wendy she could go too, since he'd finish in less than ten minutes. She offered to stay, but he declined the help. He walked Wendy to the front door – she didn't have a car – and locked the door behind her. He shut off half the lights in the reception area and set the alarm. Returning to room three, Rachel had made herself at home. She'd closed the blinds and stood stark naked, except for her four-inch heels, which made her legs look even longer. He checked his watch. The restaurant was a few short blocks away. No need to rush. Jack wouldn't knock at his door for an hour. An hour to do his own knocking … boots that is. Or at least four-inch heels.

3 Dinner

Jack had conveniently arrived ten minutes late. Convenient for Tre, as his game had gone into overtime with Rachel. Steering Jack to the utility room that housed the surveillance and phone equipment, Tre headed to the shower. One of the smartest things Tre did with his office remodel was installing a shower. A large shower with a bench seat. Although tonight's activities with Rachel were confined to room three, many evenings with other women were capped off in the steamy glass enclosure. On this night it came in handy to clean up after Mrs. Legs-up-to-here had left for the night, apparently quite satisfied with the visit to the dentist.

He glanced at his Ironman watch as he scrubbed his hair. Fifteen minutes. She'd taken longer than he thought, and for some reason he felt annoyed by it. As of late, his trysts hadn't left him feeling as satisfied. Maybe it was all in his head. Gorgeous women and great sex – so why did he feel grumpy afterward, instead of satisfied or victorious? Maybe the death threat and talk of staying away from married women had thrown him off tonight. *But why had he felt this way the past few weeks?* Maybe he needed to slow down for a bit. Or a few days anyway. He looked again at his watch. Shutting off the water and grabbing a towel, he told himself that miss girl-next-door blind date wouldn't mind him showing up five minutes late. Jenny would keep the young lady company, doubtless giving Bobby the evil eye that Tre was late.

A beautiful night greeted Tre outside, accentuated by an almost cloudless sky. Unfortunately, living in Los Angeles, the glow of the lights in the heart of the city tended to obscure the stars at night. He didn't miss the warm muggy summer nights back home. Or the mosquitoes.

Tre gave Bobby's name to the maitre'd, who in turn nodded to a nearby waiter. The waiter donned a casual dress code compared to many of the area restaurants, and the gentleman snapped up a menu and headed off toward the waiting party of three. Tre was impressed at Bobby scoring a table in the front bay window area; he knew B- or C-listers gobbled up these tables on most nights yearning for the paparazzi to spot them and snap their beautiful faces. The fringe actors hoped their photos would make the cut if the A-listers locked themselves inside for the night. The real stars of course would tuck themselves away in a private dining room, or at a swankier restaurant. But Tre had to admit, gazing about, this was an elegant establishment.

Bobby stood upon sight of his friend. Tre could see Bobby's wife Jenny, her tense impatient grimace replaced by a triumphant smile upon sighting him. His date for the night sat with her back toward him. At least her hair looked nice.

"Tre, Man," said Bobby, followed by the ritualistic handshake.

"Will you boys ever grow up?" Jenny mused.

"Not if we can help it, dear," Bobby replied.

Tre stepped around Bobby and gave Jenny a hug. "Nice to see you again, Jen." He turned to look across the table.

"And you already know Cassandra," Jenny said.

Tre's head jerked back and his eyes opened wide.

"Cassy? I didn't … I mean I wasn't …"

"You weren't expecting me? I thought you knew," his hygienist apologized, nervously folding her cloth serviette.

"Bobby!" Jenny stood, hands firmly on her hips in an 'I'm going to kill you' stance. "Didn't you tell him?"

"I heard you say Sandra," Bobby shrugged.

"Cassandra. I told you Cassandra. *Ca Sandra*. And I specifically said from Tre's office. Do you ever listen to me when I'm talking?"

"I wouldn't answer that if I were you," Tre interrupted. "There's no right answer to that one."

"I'll just leave. I'm sorry to put everyone out like this." Cassy stood up from her seat, placing her now severely crumpled napkin on her plate, head down in embarrassment.

"No, no, it's cool," said Tre. "Bobby here just mixed the message up a bit. Sit down." He motioned toward her seat with his hand. He bent down to catch her eyes. "Please?"

Cassy glimpsed his eyes, the sincerity obvious. She sat, placing her napkin back over her lap, trying to press the wrinkles out of it.

Tre waited for Jenny to sit before seating himself. "To tell you the truth, I'm relieved it's you and not some hideous blind date."

Cassy looked at him, wondering if a compliment lay buried somewhere in that sentence.

"So … nice place, huh? I know how to pick 'em, don't I?" Bobby said, trying to break the awkwardness he'd created.

"When it comes to women, you certainly do." Tre lifted a glass of wine that had awaited his arrival, with a gentle tip in Jenny's direction.

"To Jenny," Bobby added, and a round of glass clanging followed.

"I've eaten here a few times," offered Tre. "It was very good. Not sure why I haven't come back more often. It's only a few blocks from the office."

"Maybe *because* it's only a few blocks from the office," Cassy replied.

"You mean don't piss in your own backyard," Bobby remarked.

"Bobby! We're eating dinner. Can you keep the crude remarks tucked away for a while?" Jenny said with a glare.

"There's no food on the table. Unless you count these breadsticks," Bobby replied. "How about this. You don't run through your own flowerbed."

"I'm not sure how either of those makes any sense," Tre said. "I think I just go to other restaurants."

"You mean those starlets like the ritzier places," Bobby smiled.

"Some do. Some can't afford them. I don't think though that Cassy came to dinner to hear about my escapades."

"Escapades," Jenny started. "That's what men get to call it. If a woman runs around like that, she's called a slut."

"No doubt there's a double standard," Tre agreed. "But I would never call any of my lady friends that."

"I agree with Tre on that one," Cassy chimed in. "I've never seen Tre treat any of his conquests with disrespect." A devilish smirk came across her face, inciting a response from Tre.

"Conquests?"

"What else could they be?"

"Dates."

"Dates?" Cassy rested her forearms on the table and clasped her hands together. She leaned forward and looked straight and unflinching into Tre's eyes. "A date is meant to be a way to get to know someone. Find out what makes them tick. Whether you have anything meaningful in common. Understand their hopes and dreams. Look for that elusive chemistry. See if you get that tingly feeling being with them, and if you feel empty when you're not. Discover if that person makes your heart pound out of your chest."

Tre continued to stare into Cassy's eyes well after she'd finished. He hadn't noticed, but he'd drawn closer to the table to focus on those dark brown glossy jewels. She sat back, tucking her serviette onto her lap. Tre took a deep breath and likewise sat back in his chair.

Bobby lifted his glass to salute Tre. "Your dates skip all that other crap and go right to the hearts pounding part, eh, buddy?"

"You know how to kill a moment, don't you, Bobby," Jenny told him.

"What?"

The waiter rescued Bobby from his own obliviousness, dropping off a basket of assorted warmed breads. "Are you ready to order yet, sir?" the waiter asked Bobby.

"Give us a few more minutes, please," Bobby replied, picking up the menu again.

"So, Tre," Jenny said, "where is it you're from in the first place? I know you've told me before but I don't remember. Somewhere in the Midwest, isn't it?"

"A small town in southern Michigan called Monroe. About ten to fifteen miles from the Ohio border, depending on where you are in town."

"Cassy's from the Midwest too. Indiana, isn't it?" Jenny smiled, pleased with herself, obviously aware of the connection but pretending not to be.

"Yes, Jen. Anderson, Indiana. Small industrial town north of Indianapolis. Before my folks packed it up and moved out here to Monterey." She sighed. "Anderson, Indiana. Sometimes I miss it."

"I've driven through it," Tre replied.

"Likewise for your hometown. I've stopped in Monroe on my way to a Tigers game. Did the outlet mall thing."

"They had big plans for that place when they built it. So much for the saying 'build it and they will come'. I'm more interested in the baseball game though. Are you a Tigers fan?"

"Yeah. My dad's doing. I could never figure out why as a kid. They were just awful in the nineties when I was young. The whole family made the trip to a game in '99, the last year for Tiger Stadium to host games. I didn't get it at the time. It was run-down and the washrooms scared me. The field was pretty though. I remember the cross-cut grass and balls flying into the stands all around us. We sat upper deck, first base side, not too far from home plate. My mother scolded my father the next day for getting seats where we could get hit by foul balls."

"You had to stay alert anywhere close to home plate in the old park." Tre looked at Bobby. "No screens in the upper deck back then. I don't know how many times I saw people attended to after being struck by an errant baseball. I caught a few back there too." Tre sipped on his water. "Did your dad take you to a lot of games?"

"Once or twice, most years. It was too long a drive for us kids to go more than that. He'd have gone everyday if he could. Back in the 760 AM days he could get every game on the radio, no matter where he travelled in Indiana, Michigan, or Ohio. It had a strong signal. I'd heard of people picking up games in the southern states and in Northern Ontario."

"I remember going on road trips as a kid and my father listening to the west coast games late at night as he drove."

"Did you and your father go to many games?" Cassy asked.

"From the time I was about four or five, until I finished high school, we'd go to at least five games a year. We'd always go on a giveaway day. We'd often get five buck tickets in the bleachers and I'd get a duffle bag, or glove, or bat. He'd score the game while I ran around the old benches in the outfield stands. Finally, I graduated to better seats, where we weren't 440 feet away from home plate."

"Do you still go with him when you're home?"

"No." Tre made his reply quick and succinct.

Cassy looked at him, confused by his abrupt response. "Oh, I'm sorry. I didn't realize your father had passed away."

"He hasn't," Tre said, looking up. "I just haven't made it home much since I left high school."

"Your poor mother," Cassy sighed. "She must miss you something awful!"

"I call. Every weekend."

"It's not the same," Cassy replied.

"It's complicated," Tre answered.

An awkward silence told Cassy the subject was closed.

The active two-way conversation had come to an abrupt end, like the brilliant and excited fireworks sparkler that flares, then instantly stops, leaving a momentary blinding darkness. Bobby took the pause as a cue to speak. "You guys and your Tigers. Dodgers all the way. When was the last time you guys won anything? Eighty-two?"

"Eighty-four," both Cassy and Tre replied, exchanging a smile afterward.

"And we made the series in oh-six and in twenty-twelve," Tre added.

"Whatever. Dodgers rule."

"The Dodgers haven't won since eighty-eight," Cassy replied. "And only then because former Tiger Kirk Gibson stepped up."

"Dodgers are still better," Bobby whimpered. He was about to continue when he caught a look in his wife's eyes telling him with no uncertainty to zip it.

Cassy smiled and placed her napkin on the table. "Excuse me. I need to use the ladies room. Care to join me, Jenny?"

"Yes, thank you," Jenny replied, picking up her clutch purse from beside her chair. Cassy stood waiting for her. "Go ahead, dear. I'll be right behind you."

"Okay." Cassy smiled and walked away.

Jenny came over to Bobby and leaned over. "Stop interrupting them. Can't you see they're getting along, but you keep butting in?" She whacked his arm with her clutch purse and left to catch up to Cassandra.

"Owww," Bobby said once she escaped earshot. He turned to Tre. "You guys go on for like ten minutes without me saying a word, and I get smacked for stepping in when your conversation goes down a sewer."

Tre grinned and patted his buddy on the arm. "Jenny's just trying to be a good wingman, that's all. You remember, don't you? Be there if anything goes wrong, but otherwise stay out of the way."

"That does bring back some memories," Bobby laughed. "Guess I'm just rusty, that's all." He paused to have a drink of wine. "So what do you think?"

"Of?"

"Of Cassy, you idiot."

"She's nice. But I liked her before."

"No. You wanted to jump her before."

"Maybe when we first met, but I haven't given shagging her much thought since. Yes, she's nice. Much deeper than the women I'm used to spending time with, mind you."

"And that's a good thing?"

"Yes, that's a good thing."

"Great. Jenny will be happy, which means I might get some tonight."

"Might get some what, Bobby?" The girls had already returned. Tre stood as the ladies neared their seats. He kicked Bobby in the leg to also stand. Tre scooted around Bobby and pulled out Cassy's seat for her.

"Might get some shrimp as an appetizer," Bobby replied as Jenny sat.

"But you don't like shrimp," Jenny said.

"I just thought you might enjoy some. You know, since we don't get it that much because I don't like it."

"That's sweet. Thanks, hon," Jenny replied, reaching across the table to hold his hand for a moment. Sitting back, she turned to Tre. "So on the walk back, Cassandra told me she's an avid hiker."

"Is that so?" Tre asked.

"Yeah, it's a bug I developed as a teenager. I used to go to camp every summer for a week or two, and did the whole survival thing with the Guides. I got in with a group in Anderson that used to take off once a year on an excursion. Canoeing in northern Ontario, hiking in the hills of Tennessee, and other things that made me feel alive. But I loved the hiking trips the most."

"Where do you like to hike around here?"

"I go to Griffith Park. Did you know there's fifty-three miles of trails, horse paths, and fire roads to hike? I've covered all of them," she said sporting a proud grin for her accomplishment.

"Impressive," Tre grinned. "I've gone up there running a few times. I didn't realize there were that many trails."

"Great scenery, isn't it? I love it when I come across a deer, quail, or fox."

"And a good workout, with the hills," Tre replied.

"Yes, it's great for the calves."

Bobby looked like he was going to speak, but caught Jenny's look out of the corner of his eye and bit his tongue.

Cassy continued. "My favourite place to hike though is Big Sur. Breathtaking trails amongst those giant redwoods, trickling creeks, and amazing panoramas …" Her voice trailed off as she closed her eyes to revisit the images in her mind. She took a deep breath and flipped her eyes open. "Being there refreshes and invigorates me more than anything else."

"Sounds amazing," Tre said, admiring her passion.

"You've never been?" Cassy looked surprised. "You've lived in LA six years and never gotten up there?"

"It's not like it's as close as Griffith Park."

"Well, you've just got to get up there. It's truly spectacular!"

The waiter arrived to take their orders, and once his little black flip pad was satisfied, he departed to place their orders. Cassy took a sip of water in advance of asking Tre another question.

"So you like to run?"

"I do, but I can't run as much as I'd like. I blew out a knee at the end of my senior year in high school." Just talking about it caused an instinctive rub of his left knee. "I have full range of motion, and it's plenty strong."

"But?" she asked.

"But it can't hold up for more than ten or twelve miles. Any more and it swells up like Bobby's head after he wins at our two-on-two basketball games."

"Funny," Bobby responded, wanting to add a retort, but not wanting Jenny's wrath.

"The knee doesn't seem to slow you down much," Cassy added, applying a smirk to her face.

"I think that was a dig," Tre smiled as he spoke, "but I'm not quite sure."

"You know," Jenny said, concerned the conversation was going to take a bad turn, "you two should go for a hike sometime. Like maybe this weekend!"

Cassy and Tre looked across the table at each other, both feeling the pressure of this proposal.

"Maybe some other time," Cassy answered. "I'm off this weekend to Monterey to visit my folks."

"Yes, maybe another time," Tre smiled with relief. He disliked feeling pressured into things, even if it sounded like a good idea. It was always much better if it was his idea, reminding him of a T-shirt that Bobby had given him that simply said, 'Everyone is entitled to my opinion.'

Bobby started to speak, but paused at the sight of the waiter arriving with their food. The waiter circled the table, gently and correctly serving the entrees to the group. Confirming another round of drinks was required, the waiter politely bowed and backed away from the table.

"As I was about to say …" Bobby again started to speak.

"This must be important," Tre said. "I mean for you to not dig into your food as soon as it's served." Tre's comment evoked smiles from the rest of the table.

"As I was about to say, before being so rudely interrupted, don't you have that thing in San Francisco this weekend, Tre?"

"That thing?" Tre asked.

"You know. That dental thingy. Conference or whatever it is." Bobby winked at his best friend.

"Oh, yes." Tre replied, placing his serviette on the table. "Conference of Oral Western Surgeons, or COWS."

"That sounds made-up to me," Cassy replied. "I saw the flyer. I mean COWS? Who would name a dental conference COWS?"

"It's better than the old name," Tre said. "It used to be called the California Oral Conference, or COC. Sounded like a porn convention."

"I see your point," Cassy grinned.

"So my point," Bobby added, "was if Tre is driving up that way this weekend, maybe he could give you a lift."

Tre looked at his former wingman, not certain of this particular setup attempt.

"I wouldn't want to impose," Cassy said, shyly looking down at her lap.

"You're not going to make the poor girl spend eight hours each way crammed into a bus with a bunch of strangers, are you, Tre?" Bobby knew Tre too well.

“No, of course not. It’s on the way to San Francisco. It would be great to have some company. You’ll have to pack light though – I don’t have much trunk space.”

You’d have thought Jenny was going to jump up and high five Bobby for his brainstorm. Tre was certain he’d setup his former wingman for a rewarding night. Cassy’s eyes lit up.

“Thanks, boss … I mean Tre.”

“No problem,” Tre smiled, aware of her use of his first name. “I’ll get Katie to cancel my afternoon appointments so we can get an early start.”

“Oh, by the way, Tre,” Jenny said to him, “I wanted to thank you for calling ahead and getting this window table for us. I feel like royalty sitting up front. It’s funny to watch gawkers go by trying to guess who we are. I’ve even seen a few photographers snapping our picture.”

“Yes, Tre,” echoed Cassy, “these are great seats. Like front-row at Comerica Park.”

“Thanks,” Tre said. “However, as much as I’d like to take credit, it wasn’t me.” He looked over at Bobby.

Bobby put up his hands. “Not me. Maybe they just had an opening and like to keep the front filled so the place looks packed from the street. You know LA. Everyone wants to go where it’s impossible to get in, just so they can say they did.”

The sound of screeching tires grabbed their attention. They all turned to look outside. A black SUV had slammed on its brakes, laying a nice patch of rubber in the process. Dressed entirely in black and wearing a mask, the driver jumped out holding a small canister high in one hand. With the other hand, he sparked a long lighter, like one used for grills and set the canister ablaze. The masked person took two quick steps and launched the flaming projectile toward the window.

Tre sprang up and hoisted his chair in front of him, like a matador wielding a cape. The Molotov cocktail shattered the bay window, causing panicked patrons to scream. Through the commotion, Tre lunged with the chair, redirecting the ball of fire to the ground. Chairs, tables, tablecloths, meals, and cutlery flew in every direction as the diners scrambled out of harm's way. Screeching tires rose above the clamour and chaos, as the assailant sped off. Tre tossed his chair aside, as he confirmed Bobby had grabbed Jenny and Cassy and led them away. Tre dumped their pitcher of water to douse the smoldering fire bomb and cut off the source. Flames were already eating away two tablecloths nearby. Tre kicked one of the tables into the other, knocking them both over and creating one ball of fire on the floor. He turned quickly to another table and yanked the tablecloth out from under the glasses and utensils, with nowhere near the delicate precision of a magic trick. He located two more unspent water pitchers and dumped their contents on the balled up tablecloth. Spreading the large damp fabric sheet in front of him, and looking somewhat like a flying squirrel, he leapt on the tablecloths burning on the floor. The moisture of the cloth, coupled with the smothering and rolling action of his body doused the flames.

4 Dessert

Dinner had not ended as anticipated for Tre, although not too far off metaphorically. He expected it to go down in flames, but not real ones! He'd assumed his 'nice girl' blind date would turn out to be some desperate, homely tree-hugger that only a mother could love and that he'd have to pretend to enjoy spending time with for Bobby's sake.

The police allowed patrons not seated in the window area to leave the restaurant within thirty minutes of their arrival at the incident. The others had to wait for the police to take their statements. Tre described the arrival of the black SUV and specific details of the events. He chose to leave out any mention of the prior threats against him. As soon as the police would let them go, his feet would hustle him to the office and Jack for an update on what the detective may have found on the surveillance tapes and phone records. Tre had felt some initial resentment to Bobby for trapping him into driving Cassy to Monterey – he *never* went to dental conferences – but after the fireball in the restaurant, he was glad to leave LA for a while. Maybe the lunatic would back off after a weekend absence.

Cassy was the last of the four to give her statement. She smiled, joining the others outside on the sidewalk.

"I've never had to give a statement to the police. That was exciting!"

Tre smiled, recalling all the trouble he'd gotten into in his youth.

"Jenny. Bobby. Thanks for inviting me." He stepped forward and hugged Jenny. The ceremonial handshake with Bobby followed, while the girls just grinned at their adolescent behaviour. Tre turned and looked at Cassy. "Thank you for a lovely date. I have to say it was unique." He extended his hand to shake hers, which she softly did. "I'll see you in the morning, Cassy. Don't forget, pack light."

"Thank you. I'll see you tomorrow. Me and my small travel bag."

Jenny stood, arm locked with Bobby's, watching Tre walk away in the direction of his office. She turned to Bobby and whispered to him so Cassy couldn't hear.

"Let's get Cassandra home. I'm going to model that new Victoria Secret nightie that I've saved for a special occasion. And I've got a feeling it's not going to stay on too long."

Back at the office, Tre came across a note from Jack.

CALL ME WHEN YOU CAN. NOT URGENT, BUT WANT TO UPDATE YOU.

To Tre the message sounded like Jack had come up empty. Regardless, he found Jack in his cell's contact list and called.

"Jack. Tre. What's up?"

"Got the perp on the video. Did you piss off some homeless guy recently? That's what this guy looks like. Some bum with a bunch of bags that he set down before keying your car with the tab of a beer can. At least that's what he scratched your ass with – I mean the word ass with. He found a sharp stone to write 'hole' after it."

"Shit! Yeah, I had a run-in with this guy outside the gate this morning. No doubt he snuck in as the gates closed."

"At least that means it's not the same guy who threatened you on the phone."

"Did the phone turn up anything?"

"No, not yet. I'm going to have to go to your provider, but I'm not optimistic. These calls get placed from untraceable sources in most cases, like pay phones in a bar, an unregistered cell, or some such thing. It will be close to a week before I get anything back, and as I said, it won't lead anywhere unless the guy is a total moron."

"Thanks. Any advice?"

"Short of leaving town, you mean? Maybe you can keep your fly zipped for a while. My hunch is still a pissed-off husband. That's the normal scenario."

"Thanks, but the second option sounds like cruel and unusual punishment. I am going away for the weekend though, so maybe that will be long enough for this guy to forget about it."

"Maybe. I'll keep working it though."

"You just want to run up my tab," Tre joked.

"That too. John mentioned his wife Deanna needed some dental work, maybe even braces. Maybe we can trade services."

"Sure, that'll work. Call me this weekend to let me know how it's going."

"Look on the bright side," Jack offered. "The threat and the scratched car had no connection. That means the guy hasn't escalated yet. If he'd done two things to you within a few hours I'd be sure we had a psycho about to act on his threats. Now, I'm not so sure."

Tre bit his lip on the phone. His silence tripped him up.

"What are you not telling me, Tre? And don't bullshit me," his buddy chided him.

"Tonight at dinner. Some guy threw a Molotov cocktail through the window of the restaurant, right where we sat."

"And you think it was meant for you? Any celebrities nearby?"

"A few."

"Maybe one of them was the target."

"I doubt it. Someone called the restaurant and had us moved to a table by the window."

"Not good. It means the guy knows your itinerary. He may be watching you right now. I think you should get out of there right now. He's still trying to scare you or he would have tossed an explosive through that window and finished the job then and there. No sense taking any chances though. Leave your car and walk out the back. Find a nearby hotel and spend the night there. I'll come check the office out before you open up tomorrow then stake it out. Maybe we'll catch the guy lurking about. Leave the lights on when you leave. If you are being watched, he may just think you've gone to the back."

"Got it. I'm heading out the back now."

"Good. Stay on the phone, but stay alert of your surroundings. Walk like a man with diarrhea trying to find a bathroom."

"Nice visual."

"John's got some good connections on the force still. We'll find out if they have any clues from tonight's restaurant drive-by. You gave the police your statement?"

"Yes. We all did."

"Good. Tell me anyway."

Tre spent the next few minutes repeating his statement to Jack, all the while speed walking to a nearby hotel. His eyes scoured the rapidly passing environs with a nervous glimpse at anything that moved. He confessed to Jack that he hadn't mentioned the phone threat to the officer, even though he suspected the two were related.

"Thanks for the detail, Tre. That's helpful. Now stop by an instant teller and take out your daily limit. Pay for the hotel with cash, and try to avoid showing ID if you don't have to. In the morning, I'll meet you at your place. Take a cab past your home and look for me parked out front. I'll give you a thumbs-up if it's okay to stop. If I'm not there or don't signal you, keep going in the cab. Have the cab stop a few houses past yours, pay the driver with cash, and walk the rest of the way. I'll cover you while you pack, then we'll head to your office."

"Got it. Pay cash for everything. Do you want to know my hotel for tonight?"

"No, don't tell me. By the way, where are you off to for the weekend?"

"Monterey, then San Fran."

"You're not taking one of your starlet patients with you are you? And not a married one, I hope."

"Do you think I'm an idiot – don't answer that," he laughed. "No, I'm taking Cassy from the office."

"Finally going to nail her, are you?"

"No, it's not like that. Bobby suckered me into giving her a ride."

"Yeah, sure. Anything you say. I'll talk to you tomorrow, bud."

"Later."

5 Rescheduling

Tre's watch alarm sounded disturbingly early. At least for him six A.M. was early. He was used to starting in the late morning, after a long night, and enjoyed avoiding the morning rush hour. Stretching, he lay there momentarily disoriented trying to remember whose bed he occupied. Just as the summer sun can dissipate a heavy morning fog, the memories of last night dispersed the fog in his brain. He realized he'd spent the night in a hotel at Jack's advice. Sitting up in the hotel bed, he recalled the crazy night before. *Hey, the whole day was crazy.* Death threat, run-in with a homeless guy who keyed his car, great sex in the office, a pleasant dinner, finding a truly interesting person existed right under his nose, the attack at the restaurant, then scurrying through the streets like a fugitive seeking some sanctuary from his pursuer. He felt grimy and in need of a shower. He smelled the front of his shirt. Confirmed. Tre wanted to wash the odour, and most everything about the prior day, away. He debated taking a shower in the hotel, at his place, or the office. He didn't like showering and getting back into yesterday's clothes, so no hotel shower. His place fell off the list next. Jack said quick packing and out. No time for a shower there. He'd have to tough out his own personal flagrant aroma for another hour, or however long it took to take a cab to his place, pack, and get into the office. Fortunately, it was early and traffic shouldn't pose a problem yet.

"Jack here," answered the recipient of his call as Tre tucked in his shirt and slipped on his shoes.

"I'm just heading out the door to call a cab. I should be at my place in twenty minutes. Are you there yet?"

"Yes, I'm sitting outside. I already searched your place and all is clear."

"What do you mean you searched the place?"

"I checked all the doors and windows for booby traps, then went inside and checked everything over. You know, looking for exploding appliances and toilets."

"Exploding appliances and toilets? Seriously?"

"Appliances, yes. Toilets no. I've seen a fridge rigged to blow upon opening. Some chef in Malibu, if I recall. Made a hell of a mess. I guess an exploding toilet would too. Balls to the wall, so to speak."

"Funny," Tre sarcastically replied. "Is that how you get business? Go around scaring people to hire you? By the way, how did you get into my place? I never gave you a key and don't leave one around in a flower pot or under the mat."

"Don't you read any detective stories? We all know how to pick locks. It's the second thing we learn in Detective Academy."

"I'm afraid to ask. What's the first thing you learn?"

"How to comfort women after you tell them they have a cheating husband. They love immediate revenge."

"Nice. And you call me a gigolo."

"I'm just providing a service," Jack laughed. "See you in twenty minutes."

Tre was unaccustomed to paranoia, but on this day felt it like a three hundred pound monkey on his back. Tre's herky-jerky looks out the windows must have led the cab driver to believe Tre was hyped up on something, like speed or a dozen Red Bulls. He hadn't felt this much anxiety since … well, for a long time.

Stopping a few houses past his own, per Jack's instructions, Tre handed the driver his fare and a generous tip, then, still nervous, stepped out of the taxi. He'd seen Jack's black SUV – not dissimilar to the one from last night – as the cabbie approached his address. His anxiety eased with the sight of his friend, although truth be told, even he had trouble telling Jack and John apart. It was easy if you saw them write. John was a lefty and Jack a righty. From what he'd read, Tre knew this was a real anomaly. The twins had explained it to him a few months after they'd starting playing hoops together. John was actually ambidextrous, not a lefty. As kids, their mother and father always sat Jack to the left of John. At the dinner table, on the couch watching television, and in their car seats. When items were placed between the two of them, Jack always got them first, as he just had to extend his right hand to grab them. John, however, had to reach across his body with his right hand, and thus was slower. At the time, John looked noticeably smaller than his older brother. The doctor said it was normal in twins for one to act more assertively, although not so much in identical twins. Tired of getting beat to the draw by his brother, and sharing the same competitiveness as his sibling, John started using his left hand to grab for things. Initially, he wasn't as quick with his non-dominant appendage, and Jack still prevailed. Over time, though, John's theory paid off. Soon his left reflexes became just as quick as his right, and not too much longer after that, he developed the necessary strength in his left to win his fair share of the spoils.

"Thanks a lot for coming, man," Tre said, exchanging a jive shake and short embrace.

"No sweat. I've kept watch and no one's come near the place. I'll go in with you and stand guard at the door while you pack, but you shouldn't worry. Most of these guys, and even their hired thugs, don't like to do anything in daylight."

"Thanks. I'll be quick."

Tre watched Jack re-check the door before allowing entry. Once inside, Tre became methodical and efficient. He had thought through his wardrobe on the cab ride over and packed with haste for the entire weekend, grabbing a hoodie for the cooler nights up the coast and in San Francisco, should he decide to head up that far. It wasn't like he was going to the convention Bobby used to set him up. He did love the atmosphere of San Fran and hadn't visited there in almost a year though, so he could use a night in the City by the Bay.

Tre looked at his duffle bag for the gym. He'd really like to get a workout in this morning before heading to the office. Instead, he stuffed a running shirt and pair of shorts in his weekend bag. He didn't like using hotel fitness rooms, finding the equipment inferior to his club and the rooms ill ventilated. A run along the piers would give him his exercise fix, and proved a good way to meet someone and work up an appetite for dinner and afterward. Tre zipped up his travel bag and hustled down the stairs.

"Ready?" Jack asked, stepping away from his window outlook.

"All set."

"Okay, let's get you to your office. What time are you leaving for San Fran?"

"One, at the latest. First order of business is to reschedule some appointments."

"Sooner the better," replied Jack. "Give John and me the weekend, and we'll have a firm list of suspects, if we haven't nailed the guy by then."

"Thanks. I'll pencil Deanna in for top of the line braces."

The drive to Beverly Hills was slower at this earlier time of the morning, but with Jack behind the wheel, Tre felt safer about going to the office. Tre stood a few inches shorter than the six-foot-four detective and Jack packed a good thirty pounds more of solid muscle. Tre looked fit. Jack looked tough. Ruggedly tough. The kind of tough that, coupled with a menacing glare that transformed his handsome face into cold stone, could scare the crap out of most people.

Arriving at the office, Jack parked on the opposite side of the street, strategically located to watch the front entrance. They both exited the SUV and crossed the road, Jack insisting he check out the place before Tre went about his business. Securing the front door by checking for trip wires, Jack allowed Tre to wait inside the lobby while the private detective scoured the dental office for any sign of trouble.

Five minutes later, Tre received the thumbs up and Jack took his station curbside in his SUV.

The office was quiet. Tre never arrived ahead of his receptionist. Never. He often stayed after everyone else had left. That was different though. On those nights, he'd have finished an affair with a patient and was happy to relax alone, relishing the encounter. He'd never experienced a silence like this in the office. Eerie. The air conditioning hadn't kicked in yet. No phones rang. No clacking of keys on Katie's keyboard. No television rambling in the background to occupy waiting patients.

He couldn't wait for Katie to arrive and reschedule his day. *Katie – he was going to fire her today, wasn't he?* That would have to wait too. He couldn't deal with a crying receptionist today, and if there was one thing he knew about his Jekyll and Hyde assistant – she didn't handle a crisis well. Tre flipped through his appointment book for next week, looking to see where he could reschedule patients. Nothing. When did he last have a week as busy as next? Katie knew better than to book so many appointments in a week. Another reason to can her, next week. For now, he had to decide – early morning or later into the evening. He ruled morning out – he hated working earlier than ten. And his staff would be pissed to work past six. But he was the boss, so evenings it would be. He ran through the names of his afternoon appointments. Too bad, he thought. His last appointment was Kelly Treemore, a dancer on 'Dancing with the Celebrities'. Her moves were always memorable. Always scheduled for Friday nights, her checkups didn't end until Saturday around noon at her place. What a shame.

Tre's body shouted at him for water. He could go all day without food, but his body needed water. He always drank two or three bottles of water, vitamin enriched water, or Gatorade as a precursor to starting his work. Tre went to the small lounge, happy to have the silence broken by the slight hum of the refrigerator. He grabbed the handle but paused, recalling Jack's story of the exploding chef. Surely Jack had checked the fridge. He opened the door, relieved to still be thinking, and extracted two bottles. Sticking one between his body and left arm, he cracked open the other and drank half without taking a breath. In an instant he felt better. A flash came to him as he walked back to the front reception area to make his rescheduling calls. He grabbed the yellow pages and opened them up to dentists. Turning a few pages, he came across the F's, and a half page ad for the man on the billboard on the 405. Dr. Yugo Farr. The same smiling, large breasted woman adorned the yellow pages. On the other side of the ad appeared a picture of Dr. Farr himself. A smile came across Tre's face. This guy would do. He wasn't good looking. No threat to steal his clientele. Tre was in a generous mood. He'd refer all of today's appointments to the young, struggling dentist. Maybe just the break the guy needed. Maybe not all appointments. He'd call Kelly Treemore and reschedule.

"Hello. Is Dr. Farr available please?" Tre asked the fellow dentist's receptionist.

"Yes, may I ask who's calling please?"

"Dr. Tre Brightman. I have some referrals for him."

The receptionist didn't put him on hold, and left part of the phone mouthpiece uncovered, allowing Tre to hear her talk to her boss.

"It's Dr. Brightman! He's got some patients for us!" Her excitement sounded clear even in her whispered voice.

"Thank God!" Dr. Farr said not as quietly in the background. "Give me the phone." His muffled voice now came in loud and clear. "Dr. Brightman. So good to meet you. I've heard such wonderful things about your work."

"You're very kind, Dr. Farr. By the way, is Yugo Farr your real name?"

"No, it's actually Ken Rottenberger."

"Understandable. Yugo Farr is catchy," Tre replied, but thinking the name was a tad too corny. "Say, I need you to help me out. How's your appointment book for today?" Tre could tell from the earlier murmurs that the schedule was as open as an ugly guy's dance card. He could hear Dr. Farr flipping some pages for effect.

"I've got a few open slots. You know, late cancellations."

"Sure, happens all the time," Tre responded, remembering the code phrase from his startup days. Even if his calendar looked as bare as the desert, as it often was back then, he always had his receptionist make it sound like she performed miracles to move appointments around to accommodate the caller. "I've got five appointments that I need some help with. I can get my receptionist to email you their particulars, once she gets in for the day."

"Sounds good, Dr. Brightman. Why don't you give me their names and numbers and I'll take the work of calling them off your hands. It will allow my receptionist to find the best times for each of them."

"Great," Tre replied. He began reading the names and phone numbers off to Dr. Farr, who kept interrupting with comments about which show the actress starred in, who she dated, or what the latest tabloid had to say about her. Tre rolled his eyes. This guy would without a doubt scare Tre's patients right back to him – he had nothing to worry about. Finished relaying the contact information, Tre repeated his appreciation. "I really am grateful for your help in this emergency."

"Everything okay?"

"Yes, just leaving town for the weekend on short notice."

"Death in the family?" Dr. Farr asked.

"Not yet."

6 The Drive

By the time Katie arrived to start her day, Tre had re-arranged the entire stock room in a futile attempt to take his mind off his tormentor and to burn some built-up nervous energy. He'd thought of going to the gym for a workout, but Jack had quashed that idea. Aside from the first time he and Katie had gotten naked together, Tre was never happier to see her. It was good just to have someone else making some noise in the office. His feeling of relief didn't last long. Not only did she make noise, she made too much noise. Like a kid on a temper tantrum, she slammed her purse into the filing cabinet then rammed it shut with such force that the metal in-box on top rattled off its perch onto the tile floor, spewing the morning's files and their contents all around her chair. Still sitting in her chair, she bent down to pick them up, but just stopped and buried her head in her hands. Tre really wasn't in the mood to empathize with someone else's problems today.

"What's wrong, Katie," Tre said, sounding more agitated than sincere.

"I knocked over some files," Katie replied.

"So you did. Let me help you pick them up." Tre moved around the counter and knelt down to begin picking up errant papers. He handed a dishevelled pile to her, still sitting in the chair. Bending over, her cleavage almost jumped out of her top. Tre scooped up some more papers and file folders, and turning to hand them to Katie, realized she'd gotten down on her knees beside him. He looked at her face – she looked like hell. *Hadn't anyone ever told her the virtues of waterproof mascara?*

"I miss you, Tre," she said, trying to wipe her running blue-black mascara, but instead smudging it across her face. She reached out and held his hand.

"Okay," Tre answered, "what's this really all about?"

"Jimmy," she said. "He's being a jerk."

"Is he cheating on you?" Tre asked, wondering why it would upset her, since she'd cheated with him a number of times, and heard she had another guy on the side too.

"No, worse than that," she sobbed, further smearing her makeup.

"He left you?"

"No, he asked me to marry him," she cried, throwing her hands down at her side.

"Oh."

"I don't know what to do."

"Did you say yes?"

"I said I'd think about it," she said, standing up and crossing her arms in an odd look of defiance.

"I see," Tre said, picking up the last misplaced file and also standing. He handed it to her. He felt sorry for what's-his-name. Getting the nerve to propose and being told she'd have to think about it? That was as good as her saying she just wanted to be friends; a knife to any man's heart.

"You see, I've still got feelings for you."

Now those were some of Tre's least favourite words. He liked his women with no strings attached. One of the things he liked about married women – they weren't looking to settle down and have kids, at least not with him. He instinctively took a step back.

"I appreciate the sentiment, Katie. Really, I do. I'm just not the marrying, or even the living together to see how it works out, kind of guy most girls dream of. I'm still out there, doing my thing."

"Stupid me. How could I expect you to want to be with me when you're surrounded by these glamourous movie stars all day and night?"

She made a point. But she was no ugly duckling herself. She just wasn't famous like some of his patients, and that may have played on her self-esteem, especially at this moment.

"You're a great girl. Beautiful and sexy. Johnny's lucky to have you."

"Jimmy."

"Jimmy's lucky to have you. I'm just not ready for anything serious."

She leaned forward and gave him a hug. "Thanks, Tre. You know how to cheer a girl up. Excuse me while I go clean up."

Tre stepped aside and let her pass, relieved he'd gotten out of that one. He'd faced similar situations before and often ended up getting hit with a handbag or dodging a nearby object hurled his way as he grabbed his stuff and ran for the nearest door. This went rather well in comparison. Maybe his day was turning around already.

As he tried to square the pile of papers retrieved from the floor, Cassy came walking through the front door. He looked up and stared. Her smile was amazing, and not just from a dental perspective. She looked like she was walking on a cloud, which struck a stark contrast to Katie and her rain cloud.

"Good morning, Tre," she said cheerfully.

He again detected the use of Tre and not the typical Boss, or more serious Dr. Brightman greeting.

"Good morning, Cassy," he replied. He looked at a small tote bag flung over her shoulder. "All packed, I see."

"Yep. Excited to hit the road."

Katie returned, her fresh makeup returning her face to normal except the betrayal of red eyes. "What time's your bus, Cassy?"

"I'm not taking the bus anymore. Tre's driving me." She turned to him. "What time *are* we leaving?"

Katie's eyes glared at Tre, and her face burned red. She burst into tears and ran into the back.

"What's wrong with her?"

"Jamie."

"Who?"

"Her boyfriend."

"You mean Jimmy."

"Yeah, whatever."

"Did he hurt her?"

"Worse. He asked her to marry him."

Cassy shot Tre a nasty look. She hesitated for a minute, as if thinking about giving him a speech on the blessed vows, but instead she ran after Katie.

Calm had finally been restored, and their first patient of the day had arrived. Their first of only two. Tre had suggested Katie take the rest of the day off. She mumbled something about that being exactly what he wanted and stormed away. Tre shook his head and vowed once again to never get into a long-term relationship. When she settled down again, Katie did thank Tre for clearing his calendar on his own, and not making her call all of his disappointed clients. She flashed a grateful smile to Tre for letting her call Kelly Treemore, since Katie was such a huge fan and Kelly never objected to talking about herself. At length.

By eleven fifteen, the second client had paid her bill and walked out the door. Tre had given Katie a reassuring hug, and escorted her out the door, locking it behind her. He gave Jack a little wave through the glass door. Tre went to his office and stripped off his smock. He finished his vitamin water and tossed it in the recycle bin that Cassy had put in his office. He went to the lounge and grabbed a few more drinks for the road.

"Ready to go?" Tre called out loud, not sure where his travel companion had gone.

"Ready to go," she called back, coming out of the women's washroom. Tre stood with his mouth open. Cassy had gone into the washroom his dental hygienist and come out a transformed woman. She wore cute little heels and a short, but not too provocative or skanky jean skirt. A light coloured blouse flared open just enough at the top to look alluring without over-revealing. She'd become the hot girl-next-door. She noticed his look.

"What?" she said, beaming.

"Nothing. You look good."

"Thanks," she said, casually dismissing his flattery outward but loving it inside. "Is my tote small enough to fit in your trunk?" She held out her bag for him to see.

"Perfect. You pack light."

"I'm a nature nut, remember? Can't carry too much into the woods."

"Right." He held the door to the garage open for her.

"My God! What happened to your car?"

"The wrath of a homeless guy."

"I guess that will cost you a fortune to have repainted."

"I'm sure it will," he said, opening the trunk and placing her bag neatly to one side. "Lots of room." He closed the trunk and walked around to open her door. "Maybe I'll just leave the car as is. I'll be able to spot it more easily in parking lots."

"I'm sure there are just tons of Fire Opal SLK-55's in your neighbourhood in Van Nuys," she laughed as she sat in the car.

Tre walked around to his side and got in. As he buckled up, he replied. "I'm impressed you know the colour of my car."

"It's the colour I'd pick, if I could afford one of these beauties. Of course, I'd get one without 'asshole' carved in the door. At least they'll know you're a dentist."

"Ouch!" Tre looked over his shoulder to back out of his parking spot. He found the app on his phone and the gates to the garage opened.

"It's true. All the dentists that I've worked for have been assholes."

"You realize you just called your boss an asshole."

"If the car fits…"

"Funny."

"You're a good boss, actually. You just act like an ass sometimes."

"So I'm not an asshole, I just act like an ass sometimes."

"Yeah, that's about right."

"Belay that thought." Tre picked up his phone as he pulled to a stop just beyond the closing gates. "Jack? Tre. We're all set. Thanks for everything."

Cassy could hear Jack's voice, sitting so close in Tre's roadster.

"I'll follow you to the 405, then peel off. Call me if you need anything, and I'll call if John or I get any solid leads. Have a good trip, buddy."

"Thanks, Jack. Later." Tre ended the call and put his phone to vibrate.

"What was that all about?" Cassy asked.

"Nothing."

"Wasn't that Jack, your detective buddy?"

"Yes, it was."

"Was that him parked across the street this morning?"

"Yes, it was."

"Why is he watching you? Is it about last night?"

"Yes, but it's nothing for you to worry about. Okay?"

She looked at him for a few seconds. She started to speak, before deciding to let it go. A few minutes later, true to his word, Jack's shadow disappeared as they veered off onto the highway.

"So which way are you taking?" Cassy asked, settling into her leather seat.

"Are you in a hurry?"

"No, not at all. I called my folks and told them I had a lift and not to wait up. But of course my mother will."

"Of course," Tre smiled, remembering the nights his mother would lie awake until he got home late from a party or from a night out with friends. She'd have some excuse for staying awake, like heartburn or the neighbour's dog woke her. "I thought we'd scoot across the Ventura Highway over to the Coastal Highway, and follow it all the way up."

"That's going to add a lot of time."

"I didn't think you were in a rush?"

"I'm not. And I love tripping up Highway One."

"Good. Me too. Although I haven't made the entire trip in one day."

Cassy reached over and almost touched the radio. Stopping, she asked, "Do you mind? Not that I don't enjoy the conversation, but I love music."

"Help yourself. I have it programmed to skip classical and country stations."

"Fine by me, and I would have added rap to that list."

"I don't mind a bit of rap. Guess I've gotten used to it in the clubs. Every song gets remixed with a dance or rap sound and pumped through their sound systems."

"I'm not much of a club person, as you may have guessed."

"I assumed," Tre smiled as she continued to scan stations, bypassing several songs he would have stopped at. "Most nature freaks aren't into that scene."

"So now you're calling me a freak," Cassy laughed.

"If the hiking boots fit," Tre replied.

Cassy laughed briefly, but stopped suddenly as her ears tuned into a song. "U2. Love U2." She started humming along to 'Mysterious Ways' and tapping her hands on her bare legs.

"What's your favourite U2 song?" Tre asked.

"'One.' Without a doubt. Love the lyrics. I heard it kept the band from breaking up. I just think of all the music that wouldn't exist if they had broken up in 1990. What's your favourite?"

"I like 'One', but mine is 'With or Without You'."

Cassy smirked, and Tre caught it. "What was that for?" he asked.

"Seems like an appropriate title for a die-hard bachelor, that's all. Although," she paused briefly. "I'd have thought that 'I Still Haven't Found What I'm Looking For' would be your fave."

"Very funny. If you want to hear more U2, there's a small box of USB sticks under your seat. There's a red one labeled U2."

She found the case and opened it, revealing close to a hundred of the sticks. "Beats lugging around CD's. You'd have to fill your trunk with CDs to get this much music in your car."

"Trunk's too small," Tre laughed. His vibrating cell phone interrupted him, and he read the caller ID. "Excuse me. I've got to take this."

Cassy nodded agreement.

"Steve. Tell me some good news." Tre nodded and smiled. "What did I tell you, Steve? The guy was out of options. That's the way you play hardball, my man. You earned your commission today. Have a good weekend!" Tre tapped his cell to end the call. "Sweet!"

"Good news, I take it?" Cassy asked.

"Yes, ma'am! I've been working on acquiring some investment properties. I just snagged a nice parcel for half of what it's worth from some down-on-his-luck schmuck."

"I feel sorry for the guy," she frowned.

"What?" Tre took his eyes off the road for a second and looked at her. Returning his gaze to the pavement in front of him, he replied. "It's business. Besides, you heard me. The guy was out of options. My deal helped him out."

"How did you help him by giving him half what it's worth?"

"Simple. Bank was about to foreclose on him. He would have lost everything in 60 days. I gave him enough to appease his creditors. That's the risk you take in real estate. I could end up in the same spot a year from now if I can't fix it and flip it."

"Is everything a game to guys?"

Tre smiled and glanced at her again. "Pretty much. Shallow, right?"

"I was thinking immature."

"Maybe, but, and you may find this a surprise, but dentistry is not the most exhilarating job in the world."

"You seem to have fun with it."

"See. That's my point. You need to have fun, no matter what you're doing. My dad always told me he didn't care what I did for a living, as long as I worked hard at it and enjoyed doing it."

"Your dad is wise. I can't believe you haven't talked to him in years."

Cassy's comment was greeted with an awkward silence. Tre's grin had slipped away. "Sorry, I should have realized it was a touchy subject from last night."

"Hey, don't worry about it." He looked in his rear-view mirror. "I'm going to pull over up here and grab some more drinks." He looked in his mirror again.

"Thirsty or just wondering about the black SUV that's been a few cars back for the last twenty minutes?"

"Pretty and observant. Let's just see what he does when I pull in." Tre flipped on his turn signal and pulled into a small roadside plaza. He checked his mirror, while Cassy looked over her shoulder. The black SUV didn't turn. Tre breathed a sigh of relief.

"This incident last night has you a little shaken hasn't it? Do you think that was meant for you at the restaurant?"

Tre parked the car and shut off the engine. He turned and looked at her, as if about to say something. Looking into her innocent but concerned eyes, he refrained. "No need to worry, just some unfounded anxiety."

She stared in his eyes and could see something wanted to get out. “Whenever you’re ready to let it out, I’m here to listen.”

Surprise crossed Tre’s face. He’d grown accustomed to his ‘dates’ not caring about his personal life. Sure, they would feign interest during dinner, but he knew they weren’t listening to him. He looked down, as if ashamed he couldn’t, or wouldn’t, tell her.

“Thanks,” was all he said. Tre turned and stepped out of the car. With a hand on the window, about to close the door, he leaned back in. “I’m sorry. What would you like to drink?”

“Aquafina, if they have it. Otherwise Dasani, thanks.”

Tre nodded and closed the door, hearing her hit the power door lock as he turned away. She watched him through the windshield as he stretched his back and looked around, trying to act nonchalant while looking for a sign of a black SUV. A few minutes later he reappeared from the store, a bottle of Gatorade and Aquafina in one hand while he tore a chunk of a pepperoni stick off in his mouth with the other hand. Once again, he paused and perused the surrounding area. She flicked the door locks open as he approached.

“Here you go,” he said as he sat down and handed her the water.

“Thanks. No pepperoni stick for me?”

Tre looked startled. “Really?” He leaned forward and towards her, which surprised her.

She swore he was going to kiss her.

Instead, he reached behind, pulling a crumpled brown paper bag out of his left back pocket. “I’ve got more.” He held out the bag to her, folding down the rim to expose five more sticks of purported pepperoni. "Want one?"

"I was just kidding, but sure, I'll try one." She examined them for a moment, then plucked the one in the middle.

"You've *never* had a pepperoni stick?"

"Is that so odd? I bet most of your starlets haven't tried one either."

"You got me there. I guess they're more of a guy thing." He set the bag holding the remaining product between them, looked over his shoulder, and backed out.

While he'd taken care of his business in the store, Cassy had rummaged through the collection of music on memory sticks. She held one up in the air. "May I?"

"Absolutely."

She could see him listening intently, patient as he waited to hear the first chords of music so he would know what she'd selected. Within a few beats, he smiled as the sounds of Muse filled the car. "Good choice."

"Katie has some of their tunes on her Ipod. She played them on our trip south down the coast a few weekends ago."

"I didn't know you two hung out."

"We don't really. It was fun though, except ..."

"Except what?" Tre asked.

"Except it seemed she spent most of the time talking about you."

"She hates her boss, does she?"

"The opposite, actually. She's got this great guy, and she's still thinking about you. I just don't get it."

"You don't get that someone would be interested in me?" He smirked.

"No, that's not what I mean." She gave him a soft punch on the arm. "I mean, I see it all the time. Women have great guys who adore them, and they're stuck on some fantasy guy that doesn't know they exist or a ship that's long since sailed."

"I know what you mean. I've seen it plenty of times."

"I don't think I'll ever understand. If someone betrayed me, or told me it was over, I'd know their heart wasn't in it as much as mine and I'd move on."

"What if the guy was a really, really, really great guy?"

"Like you, you mean?" She laughed. "You have a lot of upside, but it'd still never happen if you cheated. For me anyway."

The sleek Fire Opal automobile cruised down the highway, the two passengers moving in their seats to the tunes, yet neither feeling comfortable enough to sing along. The drive had turned from city, into farmland, and now into coastal highway. No matter how many times she'd taken this drive, it amazed her. The view still took her breath away. Maybe because she hailed from the Midwest. Maybe because of her love for nature. Maybe because it reminded her of the drives she took with her parents when she first moved to California. Whatever the reason, she held out her arms to behold the goosebumps on her arms.

"Cold?"

"No, not at all. Just caught up in the view."

"Yes, I know. It's hard driving and keeping my eyes on the road at times." He looked at her smiling.

"Eyes on the road, remember?"

He turned back to the curving road in front of him. She opened the box of music.

"What are you looking for?"

"That's for me to know and you to find out," Cassy teased him.

"I haven't heard that expression in years."

"My dad says it all the time."

Tre looked at her fingers as she flipped through the box.

"No peaking," she cautioned him.

He turned his eyes back to the road.

A minute later they both sang along to a song from the Barenaked Ladies, and talked about hearing BNL songs back home growing up. Time and coastline passed briskly by. The conversation and company complemented the enjoyment of the scenery for Cassy. Tre was surprised that they already approached San Luis Obispo. Pulling in for gas, they decided to grab a bite to eat too. During dinner, Cassy talked Tre into stopping at Big Sur for a short hike. They still had a few hours of driving up Highway One to get to the park, but that would preserve enough daylight for a decent hike.

As they meandered up the coast toward their next stop, Cassy brought her knees up to her chest and gently placed her bare feet on the front edge of her seat.

"I haven't had a good hike in Big Sur since last fall. It's so beautiful at that time of year. The trees are so …"

BANG!

Tre tightened his grip on the steering wheel as the car pulled hard to the side. Cassy grabbed for the front dash as the SLK-55 jerked toward the shoulder and Tre guided it to a gradual stop. Cassy sat panting, one hand on her chest.

"What was that?" she exclaimed.

"Flat." He looked around and in his rear-view, checking to see if he'd pulled far enough off the road to fix the tire unimpeded. He opened his door and stepped out. Cassy followed suit on her side.

"Thought so, but wasn't sure. Thank goodness it happened where we have a nice wide shoulder to change the tire! There are a lot of places with nowhere to go on this road if you need to pull over. At least not without your butt sticking out onto the highway. Do you need a hand changing it?"

Tre's eyebrow rose at the offer, one he'd never get from any of his other dates, that was for absolute sure. "No spare in this car," he replied. "But thanks for the offer."

"Oh yeah, small trunk. So what do we do?"

"There's a repair kit in the trunk. Should be good enough to get us to Monterey, since we're not going much more than fifty."

She watched him as he pulled out the few bags they had and extracted the repair kit. He crouched down at the tire and read the side of the can.

"I didn't think guys read instructions."

"True in most cases, like putting stuff together. When it comes to this car though, I always follow the book. I know this car isn't expensive by LA standards, but it is to me. My mom would tell you it cost more than their first house."

"You've heard that one too? I got that line when looking at the cost of college."

"A dental hygienist program is only two years. It couldn't have cost that much."

"It didn't. But I wanted to go into Med school. Same as you – seven years."

"Really? I would have never guessed. You seem so content doing what you do."

"What do you mean?"

"I've known a lot of people that had to settle and they usually end up hating what they're doing for a living."

"All the woulda-coulda-shoulda's … it's all about attitude, I guess. I'm happy with what I'm doing. And my life is about me, at least right now."

Tre looked at her, wondering what precisely she meant.

Cassy saw Tre's perplexed look, so she changed the subject.

"I suppose you won't want to stop for a hike now."

Tre looked up at her and saw a glimmer of a pouting lower lip. Just a glimmer though, not the over-the-top, spoiled brat act that his dates would dramatize when they weren't getting something they wanted. And if they didn't get it, he'd witness stomping or screaming or some other behaviour you'd expect from a three-year-old, not a grown woman.

"There!" Tre smiled as he stood up and looked at the no longer flat tire, gleaning satisfaction from his first use of a repair kit. "I don't see why not? We're only going to pull off the main road a few hundred yards and park the car for an hour or two. It shouldn't make a difference in this flat holding."

"Thanks, Tre. You'll love it!"

7 The Hike

Tre thoroughly enjoyed the drive, and not just because he loved cruising in his sports car. He couldn't remember the last time he shared so many genuine laughs in the company of a woman. She definitely differed from the women he'd typically accompanied. Perhaps the common Midwest experience struck a chord and provided the relaxed feeling and fresh outlook. Whatever the reason, he felt like he was smiling from the inside out.

The car parked, Cassy slipped on her sandals and waited at the trunk for Tre. She scooped out her bag and pulled out a pair of socks and Nike hiking boots.

"How'd you fit those in that little bag?" Tre asked in disbelief.

"I don't have size twelves like you have," she laughed.

"Thirteens, but who's counting?"

"I told you I pack light. These boots are more important to me than packing an extra outfit or two."

"I'm used to travelling with women who think ten pairs of shoes is packing light."

"Not this nature girl." She looked at his feet as she put her bag back in the trunk. "I hope you don't intend to hike in those sandals."

"Nope, but all I've got is my running shoes. At least they're my training shoes and not my basketball shoes."

"Stop yapping and let's go," she teased him. "We'll be touristy and take the Valley View trail and cut over to Pfeiffer Falls. The normal trail is still under repair from a fire a few years back. This route's about three miles with a rise of about two hundred feet. Should take just over an hour for us, since we're both in good shape." She looked toward the ocean at the fading sun. "And at this time of day we won't have to worry about getting behind a group of kids."

Tre double knotted his sneakers and tossed his sandals into the trunk as he closed it. "Let's go. Daylight's burning!"

"All right, Jack London, let's go." She laughed at her own literary reference.

The hike invigorated both of them. A hike always had that effect on Cassy. For Tre the hike made up for his missed workout, providing him a great opportunity to stretch the legs and get some exercise. The destination proved worth the trip. The looming giant redwoods impressed with their fortitude, stature, and girth. Tre soaked up every bit of the fantastic surroundings. And as incredible as the view was along the way, it was eclipsed by the vantage point at the peak of the trail. Cassy had packed a small sport bottle and topped it up with Gatorade. She took a drink and passed it to Tre. They stood side by side at the outlook, just staring at Pfeiffer Falls and the surrounding valley. She rested up against him and gently put her arm around his waist, leaning her head on his shoulder. He enjoyed the softness of her touch. They remained silent, watching, time irrelevant. The arrival of a group of four hikers broke their solitude. She pulled her arm away and stepped to the side.

"I guess we should be heading back," Cassy said, looking up at the setting sun. "Besides, we want to get ahead of these guys for the return trip."

"You're the hike-master." Tre gave a mock salute.

Back at the car, Cassy sat on a low curb and slipped off her boots. Tre had removed his runners in favour of his sandals. He handed Cassy her casual footwear. She slipped them on and stuffed her socks into her boots. Tre extended his hand to give her a boost from her low sitting position. She accepted, but he caught her off guard as he yanked her firmly from her roost. She flew off her seat and up against him. He held her for a minute, looking into her eyes. She smiled at him, wanting to kiss him, but at the same time not wanting to – yet.

"Shall we go?" Tre asked.

She cleared her throat. "Yup, let's go."

Tre guided his roadster out of the parking lot and down the small road leading to the highway. He pulled onto the road, not a car in sight in either direction.

"I almost forgot!" Cassy excitedly flapped her hands like she was attempting flight. "Pull off the road up here at the bend." She pointed across the road to a wide shoulder built for parking and as a lookout. Tre followed her instructions.

"What is it?" Tre asked.

"McWay Falls. See over there?" Cassy pointed off the cliff toward a small cove on the beach. She hopped out of the car to get a better view and Tre joined her. “I must have seen this place twenty times, and it’s as beautiful as the first,” she added.

Tre gazed at the magnificent vista. The sun lay low on the horizon, a sliver of its reddish-orange hue glimmering across the water below the thickening clouds. The nearly new moon rendered no additional illumination, the thin slice obscured by the gathering grey aerial masses. The water shimmered aquamarine, in spite of the reduced sunlight. A focused waterfall poured its contents directly onto the beach lying about eighty feet below. The ocean waves lapped gently against the shore, sometimes daring to extend far enough to reach the outpour from above, other times shying away to retreat at the thought. A large rock sentinel guarded the scene, accompanied by a few pines that somehow grew out of the formation to serve as lookouts. He imagined the scene hypnotic on a sunny summer afternoon, as it looked inviting even in the dwindling light and darkening clouds.

“I absolutely have to come back here during the day. It must be stunning then,” Tre said in amazement. “Hell, it’s stunning now!”

“Definitely worth the trip,” Cassy added, snuggling up to Tre’s arm.

“Can you get right down there on the beach?”

“Yeah. Most people don’t bother, and the park management really discourages it. They want it left pristine for all to enjoy. It’s also a tough climb and not safe due to crumbling rocks. Much easier to reach by small boat or kayak, but even then the waves can throw you onto some pretty nasty rocks. I went down there once, but it felt like violating nature, if you know what I mean. I’m happier viewing its beauty from up here.”

They stood there locked in silence, admiring what remained of the view as it succumbed to nightfall.

"Shall we go?" Tre asked, checking the sky.

"Are you in a hurry to meet my parents?" Cassy laughed as she separated from his arm.

Tre blushed, a rarity for him, as he strode a few steps to the passenger side and opened the door for her. Closing the door after her, he walked around the front of the car, pausing again for a final glimpse at the falls. Closing the door behind him, he took the sunglasses out of his hand and put them away.

"No need for those anymore today," he said.

"Guess not. I think we can officially say the sun has set. Do you think we need to put the roof up?"

"I like the top down. If you put your window up, it will block some of the breeze. But I'll put the roof up if you like."

"No, I'm good," she replied, deciding not to put up her window.

Tre backed up slightly, turned the car to allow a view of oncoming southbound traffic through his windshield, then looked over his shoulder for other northbound travellers. Some of the highway turnouts or lookouts made it difficult to re-enter the highway and a quick glance didn't provide sufficient awareness. Most cars weren't going very fast, but there wasn't much warning when one would be upon you either, with all the turns and obstructed views. After waiting for a few cars to pass in the opposite direction, he scooted across to the north-bound lane, throwing a few bits of gravel with his tires.

They'd driven a while when Cassy reached under her seat and pulled out a light windbreaker she'd stashed there after their hike. She used it cover her legs. Tre clipped along, modestly above the speed limit. Definitely not racing. The winds picked up and the breeze into the car chilled the compartment. Rain seemed inevitable. Tre noticed goose bumps on Cassy's bare arms.

"Caught up in the view?" Tre asked.

"Cold," Cassy replied, arms folded across her chest.

"Let me pull over and I'll put the roof up."

"It's only a few minutes to the Bixby Bridge," she noted, rubbing her arms to warm them. "We can pull over there, enjoy the view, and put the roof up."

"There won't be much of a view with this sky. Are you sure you can wait? I don't want you turning blue."

"Yes, I'm fine. I'm going to throw this on in the meantime."

"How'd you fit a jacket in that little bag?" Tre asked with wonderment.

"I told you I'm a light packer. This jacket folds up into a little square and tucks into its own hood." She folded it back up to illustrate it to Tre. "Of course, I can fold it up tighter with a flat surface to work on."

"Of course."

Cassy laughed at Tre and opened up the jacket again. "The only downside is the wrinkles it gets if you keep repacking it without wearing it." She slipped off her seat belt and started to put the jacket on. She easily slid her right arm into the sleeve. Tre looked at her as she pushed her chest forward to slide her arm into the left sleeve. She zipped her jacket and spread her arms out to show it off.

"Tada!" she exclaimed.

"You sure you don't want me to pull over?" Tre queried again.

"No, it won't be long." As she fumbled to re-buckle her seat belt, she stopped and sat up quickly. "Look! Just up ahead is the Bixby Bridge."

BANG!

The car lurched violently to the left. This time the trouble came from the front driver's side. They drove on a section of road that hung precariously on a cliff embracing the ocean. Tre attempted to steer the car back to the slim right shoulder, but it didn't respond. He tried braking, receiving a feeble response out of them. The car shot between a large boulder and a section of abused guardrail. The damaged front driver's wheel clipped the edge of the rock formation and sent the car onto its side, twisting through the air. The air bags deployed as it soared off the precipice and toward oblivion below. Tre looked at Cassy, whose eyes filled with horror. Centrifugal force pushed her body away from him and the car - he realized she hadn't finished putting her seatbelt back on - and tethered by his own seatbelt, he hopelessly lunged to clutch her arm as she flew out of the rapidly falling car. His airbag further restricted his reach. Lacking impediments such as a seatbelt, side window, or roof, her airbag coupled with gravity to catapult her from the vehicle. Tre looked toward the darkness where she had gone, but her last point in the air spun out of view. He turned to face his own destiny. Everything crashed to black.

8 It's Like Awaking From a Dream

Tre woke to a slow steady beeping sound. Eyes closed, he reached for the nightstand where his Ironman watch served as an alarm clock. It wasn't there. Brushing his hand in search pattern circles, he discovered his nightstand wasn't there either. Where was he? A brutal jackhammer-like pounding in his head screamed encouragement to his eyelids to remain shuttered. He dreaded the thought of light or any other optical inputs putting additional demands on his throbbing brain. Worst hangover ever. No wonder he couldn't remember where he was. His eyes remained firmly shut. Tre strained to gather his thoughts and attempted to persuade his eyes to open. No luck. He felt numbed pain in different parts of his body, mostly on his left side. Did he do something stupid like get thrown from a mechanical bull last night? He must have gotten wasted to get dragged into a country bar – or she must have been very, very tantalizing. He hoped she was worth it. The best solution was to open his eyes and find out where he was and who he'd spent the night with. As much as light penetrating the membrane of his eyes concerned him, he knew he'd have to open them eventually – even if simply to find the bottle of Tylenol and go back to sleep.

Tre attempted to rub his eyes to pry them open. Problem was only his right hand responded. The left was somehow stuck. He prayed the beauty from the night before hadn't gotten kinky and handcuffed him to the bed. Once was enough for that – he found it very discomforting to lay disabled and vulnerable. His right wrist rubbed both his eyes and he slowly cracked them open. The amount of white that greeted his eyes did little to convince them to open fully. Adjusting his vision, Tre was stunned to find himself in a hospital bed. How rough did it get last night?

He inched his way to sit up to observe he lay in a private room. Relieved that it wasn't intensive care, his head throbbed as he tried to pull himself upright. He touched his right hand to his temple and found it wrapped in some type of bandage. Now he wished he simply had a hangover. Tre's left arm lay in a sling – no – he looked further, one of those immobilizer contraptions held it in check. *Great, what else did he break?* He held up his right arm and bent it a few times, followed by stretching all the still-attached fingers. His right leg responded and he pulled back the sheet to watch his toes wiggle upon command. A further tug on the blanket exposed the left leg to the knee. Limited to the use of his right hand, he struggled to flip the sheet all the way off his leg. He bent his left leg successfully, but when he tried to flip the sheet off with his leg, he felt the extra weight. He frantically kicked at the sheets a few times. The blankets responded to expose a foot encased in a small ankle cast.

A nurse entered the room, pulling a cart behind him.

"Good morning, Mr. Brightman!" the nurse proclaimed in a voice too cheery for Tre's new- found predicament. "Glad to see you're awake. My name is Wayne and I'll be here until three to assist you in any way you need. There's a little buzzer strapped to the side of the bed if you need anything."

Tre looked at the buzzer tied to the left railing of the bed. He reached for it, only to let out an agonizing wail as he rolled onto his immobilized shoulder.

"Sorry," Wayne apologized. "I didn't notice they hooked it up to the wrong side." He unknotted the cord and gingerly maneuvered it over Tre's head to the other side and re-secured it.

"Where am I?" Tre asked.

"West Hollywood Medical Center," the nurse replied.

"How'd I get here?"

"Accident, I think."

"Good to know I didn't do this on purpose."

Wayne snickered. "That's the attitude! Nothing cures what's ailing better than humour. And you need a sense of humour, because I bet you have to go to the bathroom."

Tre gave him a puzzled look.

"Do you want me to take you into the bathroom, or do you want a bedpan and sponge bath?"

If Wayne were a Wanda, Tre might have enjoyed the second option – minus the bedpan. But he wanted to see how bad things really did hurt, and trying to move seemed the best way to find out.

"I'll get up."

Wayne lowered the right railing and stood at the ready. Tre slid his right leg off the bed. It didn't touch the ground. Not even close.

"Hold up, Mr. B.," said Wayne as he held up his hand like a crossing guard. "Let me lower the bed. I don't know why they put these things up so high. There, try it now."

Tre's right foot still dangled slightly. He started to slide his left leg over, but felt a tugging pain up his left side straight to his shoulder.

Wayne caught the wince. "Let me just help you sit up first. That shoulder probably feels like dead weight right now." A few seconds later, and with Wayne's help, Tre sat up on the edge of the bed, both feet on the ground, though far from feeling firmly planted. His head felt light and still throbbed.

"Just sit for a few seconds and let the blood catch up with you."

Wayne was right again. After a minute, Tre felt much better. The nurse had positioned a wheelchair and locked the wheels.

"I'd rather walk."

"I'm sure you would. But my boss gets upset when a patient hits the floor like a ton of bricks."

Tre's head finally cleared enough to get a close look at his male nurse. The guy looked more like a lineman than a nurse, at least the stereotype Tre had in his mind. He doubted anybody would escape Wayne's grasp, but nodded agreement. With his right arm around Wayne's broad shoulder, Tre stood. At least he thought he stood. It looked more like a drunken lean. Again, the blood rushed to Tre's head, and he felt relief that his butt sat securely deposited on the wheelchair.

"You all right?" Wayne asked, not even puffing at the effort of moving Tre's six-foot-two frame.

"Never better," Tre laughed, feeling fortunate his ribs only ached in a few places. "Looking forward to a man helping me take a dump."

"It's one of my job's many rewards," Wayne replied sarcastically, inducing a chuckle from his patient. "Second only to sponge baths of octogenarians – male or female."

"A lovely visual. So how do we do this?"

A few minutes later, Tre had successfully used the toilet and, in spite of Wayne's threat, had moved himself to his wheelchair, where he washed himself. The light-headedness had dissipated, but he encountered pain in the shoulder from maneuvering in the wheelchair as he washed up. He hollered out to Wayne that he had finished, and the nurse came in, scowling at the sight of Tre off the toilet by himself.

"Remember what I said about my boss getting upset if you crack your melon on the floor?"

"Yes, but …"

"No buts." Wayne sternly stared him down. "I don't care if you don't like it," he said pointing a firm finger at him. "Until I feel you are safe to move around on your own, you don't move around on your own. Got it?"

The intensity in his nurse's eyes told Tre to shut up and nod sheepishly. Wayne went around to the handles of the wheelchair and pushed his patient back toward the freshly changed bed. Tre moved much better now, and Wayne did less lifting and more guiding.

"How's the pain, on a scale of one to ten?"

"You know, I've always hated that question. I have one friend who thinks jamming a finger playing basketball is a ten on the pain scale, and another that I'm sure you could run over in his SUV and he'd say it's a two."

Just then Bobby knocked on the open door.

"We were just talking about you," Tre exclaimed.

"Is he the ten or the two?" Wayne asked.

"The ten," Tre responded.

"Good to know I'm a ten," Bobby smiled.

Wayne just smirked. "You never answered my question, Mr. B."

"Four, with six on the horizon."

"Got it. I'll be right back with something for that."

Bobby watched Wayne leave, the nurse's hulking frame consuming much of the doorway.

"So that's what NFL players do after they retire," Bobby said.

"Pretty imposing figure, isn't he? Seems like a good guy though," Tre replied.

"Is he …"

"No, I don't think he's gay. But what would that matter?"

"Well, the bathing, etcetera." Bobby scrunched up his face in disgust.

"I don't want any guy bathing me, gay or straight. But it is his job, so if it comes to that, I'll grin and bear it."

"Bare it, for sure. I suppose you don't have a choice." Bobby obviously fixated on the mental image. He blinked hard, attempting to snap himself out of the trance. "So how are you feeling? You don't look so bad."

Puzzled, Tre replied. "I don't look so bad for what?"

"For what happened. You know, for being in a wreck."

"My car? I totalled my car?"

"Don't you remember?"

"No." Tre closed his eyes, trying to find some images of the incident, or some misplaced memories. "No, I don't remember."

"You went off a cliff on Highway One on your way to Monterey. Flipped a whole bunch of times. Everyone says it's a miracle you walked away. Well, not walked away," and he motioned at Tre's injuries, "but survived, period."

"Highway One? Monterey? What was I doing up there?"

Bobby hung his head for a long time. When he looked up, tears streamed down his face.

"What?" Tre asked, for the first time seriously worried about something other than not playing hoops for a few weeks or his car suffering irreparable damage.

"Cassy. You were taking Cassy to her parents."

"Cassy." Tre paused. "My hygienist." He closed his eyes and images of her smiling and laughing in the office came flooding back in. He recalled seeing her attired in a jean skirt and how happy she looked that day. His heart pounded and his eyes remained closed.

"It was north of Big Sur, near the Bixby Bridge."

Tre remembered the darkness and got goose bumps as he recalled a chill setting into the air. Cassy was putting on a jacket – some little thing she'd unfolded from her purse.

"The police think you blew a tire, lost control of the car, and went over the cliff."

"I remember scattered fragments. A loud noise. The car pulling hard and it flipping." His eyes still riveted shut, his whole body shuddered.

"What?" Bobby asked, holding the arm of his shaking friend.

Tre's eyes abruptly popped wide open. "She hadn't put her seat belt back on. She flew through the air." He closed his eyes and broke out in tears. "Bobby, she flew through the air. I reached for her but she was gone."

"I'm sorry, Tre."

Silence held a tight grip on the suddenly small hospital room, loosened periodically by a few sniffles from the two men.

"There he is!" came a voice from the doorway. It was Jack. Or John. Then another figure emerged from the hall. It was both brothers. "Feelin' okay, bro?"

"Fine," was all Tre could muster, as he and Bobby both tried to secretly wipe their tears.

"Well you look like shit on a stick," one of them replied.

The other agreed. "Jack talked to the doctor hoping they could do something about your ugly mug, but he said your face somehow escaped injury so you're stuck with it."

At least now Tre knew which twin was which. "Thanks for your support. How long have I been in here, anyway?"

"Today's Friday, so what's that? Five days?"

"Seven, it would be seven," Tre corrected.

"Five. They didn't find you until Sunday morning," Bobby added. "Where they found you, they had to arrange for an airlift out of the canyon. You got back to L.A. late in the afternoon."

Jack's inner detective needed to know, so he asked the difficult question: "So what happened, man? They say you lost control of your Mercedes. I don't see it happening. I've seen you drive that baby of yours. You handled that sweet ride like another natural born appendage."

Tre smiled and tried to no avail to sit up, instead wincing while he spoke. "I'm not sure. It's still coming back to me."

"Let me get that," Bobby said, and he used the side bed controls to tilt up the head of the bed for Tre's comfort.

"Thanks, Bobby," Tre acknowledged. "Like I said, I'm not sure what happened. We had a flat earlier, but on the passenger rear."

"Where did that happen?" John asked.

Tre could see Jack and John slip into detective mode, no doubt adding to his bill. "Big Sur area. Near the Michelle Pfeiffer Park."

"Michelle Pfeiffer, eh?" Bobby laughed. "It's Julia Pfeiffer Burns State Park."

"Give him a break, he's probably concussed too," Jack laughed.

Tre continued. "I used the repair kit and the tire seemed fine. Cassy … we stopped for a hike in the park. The car was running fine."

"Do you remember anything unusual? Did you swerve to avoid a rock or animal?"

"No, I don't remember anything like that," Tre shook his head.

"What about the noise?" Bobby asked. "When you told me the story a few minutes ago, you mentioned a loud noise."

"I was likely thinking about the flat tire."

"No, I don't think so. You said you heard a loud noise, lost control of the car, and it flipped."

"Yeah, that's right!" Tre sat up a bit more. "There was a bang. But a second flat?"

"Seems unlikely," John said. "I think the wreck arrived back here today, so we'll see what we can find out later."

"It's possible," Jack added, "that your friend had a hand in this."

"What friend?" Bobby asked.

"Remember, Tre's death threat last week," Jack replied. "We've worked on tracing the call and the SUV from the restaurant."

"You never told me you thought they were connected!" Bobby bitterly complained.

"I thought it was a prank, but Jack convinced me it was worth looking into. I haven't talked to you since then."

"Well you could have called," Bobby replied.

"What are you, his mother?" John teased.

"Speaking of parents, how are Cassy's doing?" Tre asked.

The three men looked at him. They'd never known him to express such concerns.

"They're in shock," Bobby replied. "Jenny talked to them on the weekend. They alerted the police that you were missing. In fact," he continued, "you may owe them your life. When they found you, you'd lost a fair bit of blood out of that coconut of yours. Someone said if you'd laid undiscovered another eight to twelve hours you'd either be dead or extremely brain damaged."

"Like he's not brain damaged already?" Jack joked.

"Funny," Tre responded. "I'll keep that in mind." Tre paused. "I've really messed things up this time."

"It's not your fault … likely," replied Jack.

"I've done a lot of stupid things over the years, but this tops them."

"Just be quiet," Bobby hushed him. "You heard the man. This wasn't your fault."

"Maybe," Tre replied. "Bobby – can you hand me that pad of paper and pen?"

"Sure," and his friend grabbed it from the bedside table up against the wall.

Tre wrote some names down. "You're going to have to earn those braces for Deanna," he said to John. "Can you get me addresses and phone numbers for these people?" He handed the folded paper to Jack, who flipped open the note and looked it over. "I guess you lost all your contact information when you lost your phone in the crash."

"True, I did. It's amazing all the information I had on that phone when I think about it."

"Just get a new one and you can sync it to the backup on your computer," John replied. "You do have a backup on your computer?"

"Yes, I do. Good idea. But sadly the people on that list weren't in my phone," and he reached to get the note back. He scribbled 'last known address' on the page and handed it back to Jack.

"Sure, what's it about, if you don't mind?"

"Just some people that I've lost touch with that used to be important to me."

"Tomorrow okay?"

"I don't think I'm going anywhere today."

"For a few days, I'd say," Bobby said.

"I'd say one more day and Tre will be climbing the walls to get out of here," John stated.

"Agreed," replied Jack. "FYI, Tre. You're on John's team for hoops this week."

The men all laughed.

"So has it been a steady stream of women up here?" John asked.

"You're my first visitors that I know of."

Bobby patted Tre on his uninjured leg. "Jenny and I stopped up here yesterday, but you were lights out. The nurse said they hadn't seen any other visitors during the day."

"Thanks, Bobby. I hope you weren't blubbering over the sight of me."

"I protected you from Jenny. She's torn between hurting you and feeling sorry for you."

"I can understand. Feel the same way myself," Tre said through a guilt ridden grimace. Changing the subject, he added, "So no other visitors?"

"I wouldn't worry about it," Jack responded. "Most of your lady friends are celebrities, and they hate going to hospitals unless it's a photo op visiting some other celeb or checking into rehab."

"And, in spite of what we think, you're just not famous," Bobby replied.

"Thanks for making me feel better," Tre groaned.

Jack fumbled with the piece of paper Tre had handed him, unfolding and folding it over and over.

"What's the problem with my list?" Tre asked after the fourth or fifth re-fold.

"I just don't get it. I recognize the names from you talking about them, usually after we've had too many brews."

"And?" Tre asked.

"Why now? I mean, from what you've said, you haven't talked to, emailed, or even friended them in Facebook. So why now?"

"You know, I've been this carefree spirit all my life, avoiding any commitment other than my job. I've screwed over some people, big time."

"It's L.A, man. Everyone does it." Jack replied.

Tre continued. "It doesn't make it right. And this stuff I did before I even got to L.A."

Jack nodded in acknowledgement.

Tre sat up slightly, propping his right elbow on the bed rail and using it for support. "I know that psychologists would say it takes time to reflect and make life changing decisions, or at least tell me to sleep on it." He pensively looked around at his friends. "Don't you ever think about things you've done, or not done when you should have, and just wished that you could go back in time and fix them?" His friends all looked reflectively at the floor. "I don't have a time machine, or a DeLorean. I can't go back and prevent the car crash. I can't go back and undo all the other things I've screwed up in my life. The misery I've put people through. So reflect? I don't need time to reflect. You know me. I don't dwell on shit, I just do it. I make decisions and run with them.

Well I've decided. It's time to fix what I can. It's time to make amends."

9 Fragments

Two days later, Tre got nurse Wayne's okay to move around without help. Weaning himself off the pain medication was one of his goals; he hated taking pills. He disliked not feeling in control, and that was exactly how this medication made him feel. And he liked, perhaps needed, to feel in control. Maybe another change he'd have to make in his life.

"I'm getting out of here today," Tre announced during his blood pressure test.

"I rather doubt that," Wayne replied.

"They can't keep me here."

"That is correct, unless I get the doctor to declare you mentally unstable."

"You wouldn't."

"You're right. I wouldn't. But you shouldn't leave. You still have concussion-like symptoms."

"Concussion-like. But not definitely a concussion."

"Technically, you're correct. But you've had trauma to your head. You should rest."

"You should know me better than that by now, even if it's only been two days since I came to."

"So why are you in such a hurry to get out?"

"I've got to fix some things."

"Some things aren't fixable."

"Which makes it more important to fix the ones that are."

"I suppose that makes sense."

"Where are my clothes?"

"The ones you were wearing were trashed. The 'ten' brought some clothes by before you came around. If he wasn't with that hot wife of his, I'd think he had a thing for you."

"It's just the way he is. The opposite of me."

"Well, they say opposites attract."

"Thanks for that, Wayne. I will miss your words of wisdom."

"Am I interrupting something?" Jack had entered the room with a small manilla envelope in his hand.

"Wayne was just giving more sage advice. Do you have my list for me?"

"Yep. Piece of cake to find these people. I almost feel guilty for charging you my usual fee."

"Then why don't you give me a break?"

"Because you're a dentist. You have a licence to print money."

"Oral surgeon."

"Dentist. Oral surgeon sounds dirty to me. And I don't want to associate you with porn."

"Can I just have the list?"

Jack handed it to him. It had a bill stapled to the front.

"Very subtle."

"Thanks. John's idea."

"Thank him for me. Can you just charge the card I have on account with you from the real estate gigs?"

"Sure thing. How much tip should I add?" He smiled. "Just kidding, buddy."

Tre smiled at his friend prior to browsing the list. "Thanks. This is great. I've got a couple of other things I could use help with."

"Ka-ching! You're going to get our customer of the month award."

"First, can you buy me a car? Has to be automatic though, unfortunately. Won't be using a clutch for a while. Maybe a red Mustang convertible. I don't want to spend too much. I'll likely get rid of it as soon as I can get back to driving a stick."

"Okay. What else?"

"Pack a bag for me."

"Why don't you get Bobby to do that? He's more the motherly type."

"Nice. I'll remember to tell him that you called him a 'mother'. I need one other favour too. Get a hold of Katie in my office. Tell her I'm taking indefinite leave, but I will pay her full wage the entire time I'm off. Ask her to reschedule regular checkups, say two months out. For all other appointments, have her refer them to Dr. Farr. He's another guy that I'm going to make rich."

"Got it. I assume you want the car today?"

"How'd you guess?"

"Climbing the walls, remember? Oh, I almost forgot the other reason I came by. The police have your car and are going over it. They found some suspicious metal fragments in the driver's side tire, or what was left of it, and some scoring on the axle. They're going back out to the site tomorrow to pick up the pieces they left behind. They just thought it was an accident or mechanical failure when they recovered the car, so they weren't as thorough as if it were a homicide."

"But now they're ruling it a homicide?"

"Not yet, but it seems likely. So I don't disagree with you slipping out of town tonight. I doubt anyone set out to kill sweet, innocent Cassy. You were obviously the target, and since they know you're not dead, they may try again."

"Your bedside manner needs some work."

"Do I look like a doctor?"

"Good point. So I'd like to get out of here by three or four. Can you make that work?"

"If you take care of the paperwork, John and I will take care of the rest."

"Thanks."

"No problem. You better tell Bobby what you're up to. You know how Mother worries."

10 Getting Out

Nurse Wayne walked into Tre's room, hunched over as he pushed a wheelchair that looked like a doll stroller under his massive frame.

"Are you sure about this?" the nurse asked his patient.

"I can't stand hospitals. And I'm bored."

"Lots of people don't get many visitors. It's nothing personal. They can't stand hospitals."

Tre smirked. "Is the wheelchair really necessary? You've seen me motoring around here all day."

"Motoring? Scootering, maybe. Motoring, no chance."

"Funny. Just get me out of here." Tre reluctantly sat down. Wayne handed him the overnight bag Bobby had dropped off containing a change of clothes then released the brake and quickly spun the wheelchair around toward the doorway.

"Do you jerk all your patients around like that?"

"Just the stubborn ones. Where's your mother?"

Tre laughed. "Bobby's at work. Jack's picking me up in my car."

"Thought it was totalled?"

Tre sighed at the memory of his Fire Opal SLK-55. "It was. New car."

An empty elevator opened and Wayne flipped the wheelchair to do a wheelie to cross the threshold.

"Owwww!"

"I am so sorry." Wayne feigned sympathy, before laughing. "I hope you didn't get yourself another sports car with a tight suspension or every bump on the road is going to feel that way."

"Don't worry about me, I'll be fine."

They'd reached the exit and through the glass they could see Jack standing beside a black Mustang convertible.

"I see him," Wayne said as Tre began to point.

They patiently exited the automatic revolving door, a feat made to look easy by Wayne. Five feet out the door Tre started to stand up, stopped by a heavy hand on his shoulder.

"Not so fast, dentist boy. Have to follow protocols and set the parking brake before you get up."

Jack stood nearby chuckling and clutching a set of keys and an envelope.

Tre felt the slight jerk on the wheelchair as Wayne locked each wheel. Tre stood and hobbled over to Jack, grabbing both items from his hand.

"Thanks. Car looks black to me though. What do you think, Wayne? Is that a red Mustang convertible?"

"Definitely black."

"Red Mustangs are for chicks," Jack replied in defence.

"He does have a point, Mr. B. Ladies look mighty fine driving a red Mustang."

"Just thinking resale," Tre replied.

Jack held his hands up in surrender. “Whatever you say, Tre.”

Tre handed the envelope to Wayne. “A little something for your help. I would have given you cash, for wheelchair driving lessons or bedside manner training, but didn’t know if you could take it.”

“I take cash, Visa, and Mastercard,” Wayne laughed as he opened the envelope. He pulled out a gift card. “What, no thank you card saying how much you’ll miss me?”

“Like hemorrhoids, I’m sure,” Tre answered. “And I don’t need a hug goodbye.”

“Do I look like your mother?”

“But seriously,” Tre reached up to put a hand on Wayne’s shoulder, “thanks for taking care of me and helping me get all the paperwork done to get me out of there.”

“No sweat. Take care, Mr. B. If I ever need a root canal, I’ll look you up.”

“You can’t afford him,” Jack said.

“It’ll be on the house,” Tre replied. “But if you want freezing…”

“Revenge for the wheelchair ride, got it.”

“Later.”

Tre limped around to the driver’s side.

“Do you honestly think you can drive with that ankle cast on?” Jack spoke over the roof of the sportscar.

“No sweat. The boot’s on the left foot and no clutch. I’ve driven a stick in big winter boots. Should be easy.” Tre opened the door and maneuvered himself behind the wheel of his new car. He slid the sling off his left arm and stuffed it between the seats.

Jack opened the passenger door and hopped in beside him.

"What are you doing?" Tre asked.

"How do you expect me to get back to the office?"

"Oh, right. I'm so focused on getting out of town that I wasn't thinking."

Tre made minor adjustments to the seat and mirrors before putting the key in the ignition. He stopped short of turning the key, remembering to put on his seat belt. Jack followed suit. Turning the key to start the car, a blaring sound system greeted his ears.

"Good sound, huh?" Jack hollered over the thunderous music. "I got the premium sound system installed. You know, for resale," he smirked.

"Great," yelled back Tre. He put the car in gear, glanced over his shoulder, and pulled away from the hospital pickup zone. Just then the song on the radio hit the chorus and Tre realized the tune playing.

'Crawling from the wreckage, crawling from the wreckage, into a brand new car…'

Tre pushed off the radio.

"What? I thought you loved Dave Edmunds."

"I do. Just can't take that song right now."

"Oh, right. Didn't think about that."

Tre focused on the traffic in front of him.

Jack looked out his window, humming and patting his leg.

After a couple of minutes, Tre had had enough. "Can you stop?"

"What?"

"You're still humming 'Crawling from the Wreckage' and tapping to it." Tre looked at his friend. "Never mind," and he pushed the radio back to life, turning it down a notch or two as he did so.

'I'm on the highway to hell …'

Click.

"What station do you have on? I mean, Dave Edmunds followed by AC/DC?"

"I forget the number, but they're the one with the slogan, *We Play Anything*."

"For now they're going to play nothing. Why don't you tell me the latest news?"

"Not much to tell. Oh, shit! That reminds me." Jack popped open the glove box and retrieved a cell phone. "They found this yesterday at the scene. It doesn't power up, but the SIM card is still intact. You can just get a new phone, plug that little sucker in it, and you're good to roll." Jack held the phone out to Tre.

"Put it back in there for me, will you?" Tre motioned to the glove box.

"Sure, just remember to get the new phone today. We'll call you as soon as we hear anything."

"No, you won't."

"Yes, either John or I will, promise." Jack looked at Tre wondering why the lack of trust.

"No, I didn't mean that. I mean I'm not getting a new phone to take with me. I don't want interruptions while I'm on the road."

"What? Are you on a mission from God? Like the Blues Brothers?"

"I just need time to my own thoughts. I got a few calls at the hospital from reporters this morning. They dug up my connection to Marla Main from some old story when I went to one of her openings as her escort. I saw a few in the reception area as we came out, but they didn't recognize me from Jack, so to speak."

"Parasites. So how am I to get a hold of you?"

"I'll call you. Might pick up one of those disposable phones, or call from pay phones."

"Do they still have pay phones? I mean, other than in malls."

"I'll figure something out, Jack. I need time to think. And I'm tired, so I may rest at odd hours of the day if I need to. Besides, I'm bringing my laptop, and I'll check my email – no Facebook, just email."

"Okay, it's your call. If you need anything – I mean anything – call me or John. Day or night. Got it?"

"Got it. Thanks."

Tre pulled his new black ride up to the curb in front of the small store-front detective agency. Jack got out of the car and closed the door. He reached through the open window and they exchanged a thumb-wrap handshake.

"Keep in touch. If you don't call for a few days we'll worry. And Bobby will go crazy if he doesn't hear from you."

"I'll call him now. When I call you from the road, let him know, so he doesn't piss himself worrying."

Jack laughed and pounded on the roof of the car. "Godspeed."

11 The Twins

John Gordon never thought he'd end up a private detective in LA. He and Jack both wanted to be cops like their father, and his father before him. And they had suited up for the force, for a while. Raised in and around Sacramento, they'd always succeeded athletically. They led their high school football team to a couple of titles, Jack as quarterback and John his favourite passing target. Occasionally, they'd switch positions, which would mess up some teams when suddenly the quarterback started throwing with the opposite hand. John had more of a tight end build than a receiver, but his coach wanted to take advantage of his deceptive speed.

They'd both received scholarship offers, a couple of low rated Division One teams, but mostly Division Two. Many had offered the same deal to both boys, hoping to entice them to come together. The hearts of the twins, though, lay with policing and they both enrolled in the academy. To their father's surprise, however, they went to Los Angeles to train instead of staying in Sacramento. John wanted to stay at home, but his brother could be persuasive.

While in the academy, the twins moonlighted as bouncers at an LA hotspot. The job provided some spending money and allowed them to get off their hot dog and mac and cheese diet. Both street-smart, they firmly kept things in order at the club. Of course looking an intimidating presence at six-four two-fifty helped too. And the club gave them 'uniforms' – shirts so tight that their chests looked ready to rip the material apart if they flexed, a la The Incredible Hulk.

The club provided Jack and John their first detective gig. The owner, Lance Stone, was convinced his wife was cheating on him while he worked. Of course the club owner cheated on her practically every night with some short-skirted patron, yet he couldn't handle the thought of her messing around. So John and Jack got a few nights off to follow the suspected cheating wife. Hard to refuse at triple pay, even if morally John knew it was a farce.

The first night, Friday, passed mostly uneventful, aside from Jack spilling his Gatorade all over his lap and the passenger seat. They'd parked across the street, a few doors down from the Stone residence. A girlfriend of Mrs. Stone's stopped by around eight, clutching a movie rental. With his binoculars, John could make out the cover as 'Pretty in Pink'. Jack teased him the rest of the night about knowing chick flick movie covers. The glow of the television lit up the front room through the thin, drawn curtains. The visitor left around two A.M, looking a little tipsy but not out of control. Minutes later the lights went out and no further movement occurred at the house until Lance pulled into the drive about 3:30 A.M.

The second night, Saturday, was a complete snore-fest. No visitors. Mrs. Stone moved from room to room, every light in the house appearing on. Again, Lance pulled into the drive around 3:30 A.M.

The third night of their stakeout, though, things turned interesting. Sunday night around eight, the same girlfriend arrived. All the lights inside the house glowed brightly. As she got out of her car, she once again clutched a movie.

"'Pretty in Pink', again," John said.

"Maybe they didn't finish it the other night," John replied.

"Maybe."

Within minutes of the girlfriend entering the house, all the lights dimmed, and the glow from the television reappeared in the front room.

"I think we need to get a better look," John motioned with his binoculars.

"Why? Can't you see the movie from here? You could always rent it yourself, you know."

"I think they're up to something."

Jack sat up from his slouch. "Shit! They're likely slipping out the back and hitting the town. We should have had eyes on the back door too!"

"Maybe. I'm going to sneak up to the front and look in. You can go around back. Check the windows on the way around to see if there is any sign of them."

"Got it." Jack stuffed his cell phone in the back pocket of his jeans and got out of the car. John watched his brother slip across the street and toward the house. John followed suit a minute later. As he crossed the street, he could see Jack hop the fence into the backyard. Getting a look into the front windows would prove trickier due to lack of cover. There wasn't much traffic on the street, and no pedestrian traffic on the sidewalks. He strolled by the house. The front room on the right lay in darkness. Even from the sidewalk directly in front of the house, he couldn't see anything more than from their parked vantage point. He walked past the house then darted into the bushes separating the Stones' home from its neighbor. His phone vibrated. He flipped it open.

"Nothing back here. No sign of movement on this side of the house. Jack out."

John closed his phone and chuckled to himself at Jack's manner on the one-sided call. Too many espionage movies for that one. Crawling on his elbows across the lawn, John approached the window of the light-emitting room. Looking out to the street for passersby and not seeing any, he raised his head up to peek in. The television beamed a solid blue screen. The movie had apparently ended. Looking around he saw no movement – until he saw the couch. His eyebrows instinctively rose. There in front of him, Mrs. Stone and her visitor lay nude, embracing. No, kissing. And doing much more. Tempted to keep watching, he refrained and dropped down to the ground. He crawled back to his prior spot of cover, stopping to sit up and take a few deep breaths. Getting to his feet, he crossed the street and walked back toward the car. He flipped open his phone to call Jack just as it vibrated.

"Report, John. Any action?"

"Oh, yeah. There's action alright."

"Ten-four. What's the plan?"

"Rendezvous at the car and I'll debrief you of the op." John smirked as he used some of his own spy-speak.

A minute later, Jack opened the passenger door and sat down.

"What's up, little brother?"

"They're lesbians."

"She's married to Lance. She can't be a lesbian."

"Okay, they're bi-sexual. Better?"

"And you know this how?"

"I saw them at it."

"Oh, this I've got to see!" Jack put his hand on the handle to open his door. He felt John's hand on his shoulder.

"Rent a porn. Leave these ladies to their privacy."

"But…"

"Just leave them be."

"But …"

"Jack – I said leave them alone."

Jack saw the look in his brother's eyes. John normally wasn't intense outside of sports, but his eyes burned tonight. When they had that look, Jack knew to back down.

"Fine," Jack replied. "What do we tell Lance?"

"Nothing. We do this a few more nights to make him happy and pad our wallets a bit more, then we tell him that his wife is not seeing any other men."

"Isn't that taking advantage and twisting the truth a little, honest Abe?"

"It's an appropriate twisting. It's not like Lance is a saint or anything."

Following their report out to Lance, he gave them their pay and a generous bonus. He also referred them to a few of his associates over the next four or five months. In that span, they'd graduated from the academy and started their full time jobs as police officers. Both enjoyed the work immensely, until that unforgettable, steamy hot night in July.

While Jack got paired with a seasoned veteran of ten years to ride with, John got partnered with a young female officer named Deanna Flores. The force usually didn't pair up two rookies, but in summer a lot of seniority cops took vacation with their kids. And since Deanna Flores graduated at the top of their class, she received a command in lieu of letting a cruiser sit idle. The city also sought good publicity by parading to the press a female, Hispanic to boot, top graduate afforded such opportunities.

As John and his partner approached the scene of a robbery in progress, the burglars burst through the front door. The crooks stopped on the porch, startled at the sight of the two officers. The taller of the two robbers panicked and shot her in the abdomen and the head. John hit the shooter with a kill shot, while the other bandit tossed his handgun and put up his hands. John radioed for backup and an ambulance, but went into shock as he held his torn-off bloodied shirt sleeve firmly against the stomach of Deanna to prevent her from bleeding out further. He spent the first three days in her room with her, as she lay in an induced coma. For the next five weeks, every waking hour away from the job he spent at Deanna's side. John knew that he and his partner had approached the scene by the book and had suffered an unfortunate outcome. Regardless, he couldn't get the guilt out of his head in spite of clearance from Internal Affairs. He'd found himself drawn to her more each day they worked together, but didn't realize how deep his feelings ran until he held her almost lifeless body in his arms, frantically praying out loud for her to hold on. He debated whether it was guilt or love. Eventually, he reconciled it was both.

After twelve weeks, Deanna came out of her coma, with John the first person she saw when she opened her eyes. After those twelve weeks, John's heart was no longer in his work. Jack knew it too. They quit the force and started their own private detective agency. Within six months, John married his former partner Deanna, with Jack the best man. She also left the force, and often assisted with stakeouts when the load required. Jack often teased John that he'd rather have Deanna backing him up, for she was a much better shot than John, with scores from the academy to back up the ribbings. Deanna gave up the field work two months after their wedding, after a devastating miscarriage. John didn't mind leaving all the field work to Jack, and soon became more comfortable working in the office, doing internet searches and all the adminis-trivia of running a small business.

Jack, on the other hand, thrived in the field.

12 Messages

Tre felt anxious to get on the road, but a steady throbbing in his temple told him otherwise. A less noticeable ache emanated from his left shoulder, still in a sling and now adjusting to the confines of the form hugging bucket seat of the new Mustang. He drove back to his place to crash for a few hours. Not wanting to think of rest as a sign of weakness, he justified the break as showing wisdom to head out after rush hour subsided. He'd frequently checked his rear-view mirror the entire trip, looking for suspicious black SUVs. He wished Jack rode shotgun, keeping a watchful eye out for any unwanted company. None followed him, that he could tell, but he didn't have the trained eye of a detective. Regardless, enough paranoia remained in his banged up skull that he parked one block over and cut through the back way to his place.

Climbing his back fence should not have provided a challenge, but a sling and an ankle boot on the same side will restrict anyone's athleticism. Now very athletic, not many of his peers, or his parents, would have guessed through his early high school years that Tre would do well in sports. He always did the bare minimum to get through gym class, preferring to spend his after school time reading or doing extra science experiments. To his school coaches, he was just another gangly uncoordinated kid who would take more work than he was worth. Tre always did fine at his fitness tests; he just didn't have any drive when it came to sports. He didn't care if someone stole the ball or puck from him in gym class games, be it basketball, soccer, or floor hockey. He held no passion for sports. His dad took him to Tigers games as a kid, and running on the old Tiger Stadium bleachers, examining the architecture like it was a Knex set, or simply eating, held more interest for Tre. His father never got upset with Tre for his lack of interest, instead enjoying spending time with his son, even when it meant following the sprite around the bleachers and missing the game action.

One day it all turned around. On a rainy, blustery fall Saturday morning, the velocity of the wind shook the colourful autumn leaves from their summer homes to their winter resting place. Stuck inside, Tre searched the television channels for a science show he liked. To his surprise, the show dedicated itself to the science of sports. It had segments on the myth and the science of the curve and knuckleball pitches in baseball, the arc and rotation of a basketball shot, and kinetic energy behind a slapshot in hockey. He had always thought of sports as trivial games, never realizing the science at work in each sport. He gained an immediate appreciation for sports, and a desire to learn more about them. Armed with this new information and curiosity, Tre began putting more attention into how he played the games in gym class, and the added focus brought with it a healthy dose of passion. He hated if someone took the ball away in basketball before he could complete a shot and measure how successfully he had mastered the proper angle, force, and spin of his shot. That led to added aggression while playing, and began to get him noticed in gym class. It also helped that his body began to fill out. Finally, in his senior year, a coach convinced him to try out for the basketball team, which he made and became a starter by the third game of the season. He'd turned down similar offers for participation in other sports, preferring to keep much of his time dedicated to maintaining his stellar grades.

So the science and mechanics of hopping a fence needed re-evaluating based on the handicaps imposed on his left side. Tre resorted to a move that resembled the Fosbury flop, rotating his body horizontally over the wooden fence. Though successful in a results sense, the movement certainly lacked grace and would have received no style points if judged. Landing with a thud he winced, quickly brushed himself off, and proceeded inside to catch some sleep.

8:00 illuminated Tre's alarm clock as his eyes opened from his cat nap. He soon realized it had exceeded a cat nap. Daylight flooded his bedroom. He'd slept right through to the next morning. And without taking the prescribed oxycodone. Tre had heard a few nightmarish stories from his Hollywood lady friends about oxycodone abuse and addictions they'd witnessed firsthand on the set. Actors and directors experiencing complete meltdowns that led to tabloid fodder. With his disdain for taking pharmaceuticals anyway, it would take extreme pain to pop one of those.

He desperately wanted a shower, but heeded his nurse's instructions and washed up instead. Feeling somewhat, but nowhere near fully refreshed, he dressed and stuffed a second bag with a few more items of clothing and another pair of shoes. He appreciated that Jack had filled a bag and put it in the car earlier. Tre just wasn't sure how long he'd be gone, and didn't want to have to stop to buy new clothes or do laundry. Plus the Mustang's trunk looked the size of a medium storage locker compared to his Mercedes roadster's boot. He grabbed his wallet and Jack's list of addresses and phone numbers from the nightstand then tucked one into each back pocket of his Guess blue jeans. Downstairs, he instinctively headed to the kitchen to grab a bottle of water from the fridge. Remembering Jack's story of the exploding refrigerator, Tre opted to buy some water on the road. A look around the kitchen and his eyes caught the timer flashing on the microwave. The last time he'd heated food, he stopped it short of the full cycle and it still flashed fifteen seconds. In itself this wasn't significant, but it did cause him to think about checking his cell phone for messages. He'd planned on cancelling his land line for months and had never gotten around to it. At least it would come in handy to call and retrieve his cell phone messages. He had three.

'One of your friends registered you at a major department store and your name was drawn as a winner of a trip to Cancun.'

"Yeah, right." He hit the delete button. The next message sounded odd and disturbing.

'Goodbye … goodbye … goodbye … goodbye …'

All clips from songs: 'Hello Goodbye' by The Beatles, 'Goodbye Yellow Brick Road' by Elton John, 'Kiss This Thing Goodbye' by Del Amitri, and a few others. An anxious feeling crept in and sent shivers down his spine. He saved the message and with trepidation played the last one in case it held another clue as to the sender.

'Hello, son. It's your mother. I thought you were going to call on Sunday? Hope everything is okay. Love ya!'

While replaying the second message for the fourth time, he pressed the 'more information' key. Tre checked the date and time of the message and a shudder of fear ran through his veins.

It had been placed within minutes of his accident. Tre vomited.

13 The Road to Recovery

A sudden urge to get out of his home overcame Tre after the ominous voice mail. He nervously scribbled a note to report the call to Jack and John, then felt certain he wouldn't need a piece of paper to remind him and crumbled the slip and tossed it on the counter. The date and time couldn't be a coincidence.

He checked the timer for the lights, set the alarm system at the back door, then scurried to exit via the front door ahead of the alarm delay. The thought of scaling the fence again was too much. He hoped his paranoia was unfounded, but the 'goodbye' message jingled through his mind. Once outside, he placed his bag down, and locked the deadbolt. He scanned the area for suspicious vehicles before awkwardly ambling down the stairs to the sidewalk. Briskly as possible in his condition, he walked around the block to his awaiting car. He popped the trunk and tossed the second bag in beside the one Jack had packed. He got in his car, and with a sigh of relief slipped on his sling and buckled up. Tre's trip would take him north, then east. For today, he'd head north, up the west coast. He'd laid it out in his head, but plugged his first destination into the GPS, just in case. Besides, with his head injury, he might need some help as the day wore on.

Getting out of Los Angeles and through the mountains on Highway 5, he settled into the flat drive north. The mountains continued to his left. If he didn't know better, he'd never suspect that an ocean lay not far beyond. His pain remained quite tolerable at this point, and he kept the radio volume down as a precaution to further migraine-level headaches. Late morning meant early afternoon in the Midwest. He hit the satellite radio preset and listened to the Detroit Tigers day game.

The baseball game wasn't as good a distraction as he had hoped, and Tre's mind wandered while he drove. A smile covered his face as he recalled hearing the great Ernie Harwell's trademark calls near the end of his stellar career. His favourite Ernie call came when a batter took a third strike. Ernie's voice rang out with an exuberant, 'He stood there like the house by the side of the road and watched it go by'. Classic.

Behind the wheel gave Tre a certain freedom of spirit, something he remembered talking to Cassy about on their ill-fated trip. He thought back to how he got started in LA. His first hygienist came to mind, then Cassy and her innocent smile. Tre thought of the other women he'd employed – he'd never hired a male. He wouldn't have hired Katie if his first choice hadn't suddenly died the day before. Strange how things work out sometimes. He thought about Katie, fondly at first, and then about the last day he'd seen her at work. How he'd planned to fire her prior to the death threats, and how she cried until calmed by Cassy. It was likely a good thing that he hadn't canned Katie, as she and John's wife Deanna had become somewhat tight and that may have messed up his relationship with the twins. Then where would he go now for help?

Driving on, the faces of his many patients formed a collage in his mind. Faces came to mind, however sometimes names didn't follow, forgotten or discarded. Even some of the ones he'd slept with slipped his mind. Who was he kidding? Many of the names of women he'd slept with slipped his mind. *Did that make him a horrible person?* It certainly meant that he often went through the motions, never wanting nor needing anything more. It certainly didn't make him a saint, but doubted that it damned him to eternity in hell either. Though some of his forgotten dalliances may have thought otherwise. Enough to kill him though? Not likely. He hoped.

He snapped back to the here and now. His GPS flashed information at him. His planned turn to Highway 46 approached quickly. From there his route would skirt the edge of the foothills of the San Benito Mountains, finding a path through them and over to Highway 101. It was his plan, but as someone once told him, plans were made to change. He kept going; his GPS wasn't happy as it tried to recalculate his route back to Highway 46 with every exit he passed. Eventually it gave up and settled on Tre's new intended route through Coalinga to Highway 198 and through the heart of the mountains. Cassy would have liked the views. And he wanted to avoid what he thought of as the most disturbing sight he'd seen in California – the massive cattle farm. Hundreds, no thousands, of head of cattle crammed onto a barren section of land. He'd grown up around smaller farms where cattle roamed grassy fields. He didn't recall seeing any grass on the farm that lay ahead. If he cut off the road earlier, he'd spare himself the reminder and could stomach eating beef that night. Perhaps he was too idealistic. Perhaps.

The slow drive over the mountain took much longer than he'd thought. The highway, if you could call it that, wound like a lazy river as it sought its way through the mountain ridges. He'd kick himself now for picking such a route if he'd been in a hurry. As it was, he only fought fatigue, not anger.

Reaching San Lucas, just short of the 101, he pulled over for gas before turning into a local stop for a bite to eat. His mind was tired from all the thoughts exercising his brain more than from driving. The food perked him up, but also gave new life to those words and images racing around in his head. They would certainly not rest until he had fed them appropriately, and it would take more than food.

Tre activated the voice feature on his GPS, and to his relief, the commands that guided Tre sounded much more human than the first version he had owned. The early GPS voices often sounded like mindless fembots from a cheap science fiction movie. Hours later, and now late afternoon, his navigator gave her last command of 'turn left in fifty feet,' into the driveway of his first destination.

Tre sat quietly. He summoned courage, an oft avoided need. Accustomed to running instead of dealing with anything too serious, he discarded that option today. Out of the car, he approached the front door of the small home, built as a vacation cottage. A mixed bag of housing styles populated this neighbourhood in Monterey. Larger modern homes replaced some cottage-style houses, at the expense of two or three of the smaller predecessors. Still, somehow it worked in this seaside town.

Pushing the doorbell, he felt it resonate through his body, like it hit a nerve. He stood in silence, holding a small bouquet of deep-crimson roses. The flowers shook in his hands, the petals clinging to their stems for dear life. He waited. A tiny drop of perspiration trickled off his brow onto the hand holding the roses. Still no answer. He rang the doorbell again. And waited. At last he heard a noise from inside, but it wasn't footsteps. A tan tabby peered through the left sidelight window. It looked at Tre for a few seconds, then lost interest and wandered away.

The cat's solo trip to the door alluded to an empty home. Tre hobbled back to his black Mustang. He laid the bouquet gently in the back seat. He typed 'Cannery Row' into the GPS, figuring he'd grab a bite to eat and try again later.

The section of Monterey made famous by John Steinbeck's novel was a far cry from the way the author had seen it in his time. The canneries had long since shutdown, as of course had the whorehouses. In an attempt to capitalize on the novel, the town renamed the area in the late fifties, and it had become gradually more commercialized. An aquarium added in the mid-eighties became a popular draw. The area was touristy, yet in a quaint way. Over-the-top would likely not work in this peninsular town. Venturing into one of the few stereotypical souvenir shops to kill some time, Tre found the usual assortment of trinkets and t-shirts, most looking like the manufacturer replaced 'Los Angeles' or 'San Francisco' with 'Monterey.' He never bought anything at these places, not feeling the need to possess a keychain or towel to remind him of his journeys in life. And he had no one to buy for. He had no one. His mind began racing again and his temple began to throb. His feelings did him no favours. He'd probably overdone it already today. A short rest would do him good. With lunch only a few hours in the past, dinner could certainly wait. Back to the car for a nap. Out of necessity rather than desire, he bought a brightly coloured towel with an ocean panorama. It would serve as a blanket for today. This time he'd set the alarm on his watch – waking tomorrow was the last thing he needed. Not wanting to, but feeling it might relieve the pain cascading down his entire left side and slow down his rampaging thoughts, he popped an oxycodone and washed it down with water.

Two hours later the beeping watch awoke Tre. He sat up, but lay right back down. A disturbing disorientation inflicted his mind. His mind felt not his own, instead as if controlled by some unseen force. The oxycodone. Tre had avoided all types of narcotics, even when he'd blown out his knee. Aspirin or ibuprofen was the most pain relief he'd ever taken. Similar to the stories from his Hollywood girlfriends, a few of his fellow dental students got hooked on various narcotics while pulling endless all-nighters cramming to keep their marks up. Tre had witnessed their downward spiral and couldn't understand how they could let that happen to themselves.

Tre's cousin was the foremost example that came to his mind when he thought of someone losing it to drugs. Three years ahead of Tre in school, his cousin had started up a dental practice in a small Midwestern city. After a skiing accident shredded his shoulder, Tre's relative went from morphine to cocaine, finding the white powder much easier to obtain. Obtain anonymously especially. The coke though led to other uncontrollable desires, and the authorities arrested the dentist six months later for raping female patients who were under the effects of gas. His dental assistant, and lover, acted as a willing accomplice and they likely would have continued to get away with their molestation of clients if they didn't get sloppy. One day, after snorting copious lines of cocaine off the bare chest of a knocked- out victim, they both passed out naked on the floor. The patient awoke horrified at her state of undress and the sight of her passed-out abusers. A line of coke still lay on her chest, unsnorted, and a discarded used condom lay on her abdomen. Tre's cousin went through a very public trial that made state headlines for a few months. National headlines followed the verdict putting him away for a long time. Tre would have quit dental school over the matter if not convinced of alternatives by a close friend.

Tre liked control of his life, his mind, his situation. This little white pill had taken that from him, temporarily. The lack of control terrified him. Other people probably took it for that very reason. His buddies had accused him of being a control freak a few times, and he'd always taken it as a compliment to his command of his environment.

He tried to reset his alarm, but wasn't really sure he'd done it correctly. He closed his eyes again. Another hour had passed when his watch alarm sounded. Tre's mind remained groggy, but improved. He tried to justify the trade-off in his mind. Loss of control for relief of the pain. He'd really needed something to slay the pain. Something to forget *his* pain. Something more than booze. The aching disappeared, replaced by a hunger. He'd spotted a nice looking place on the wharf and, tidying himself up in the rear-view mirror, he set his sights on a steak dinner. Waiting for his meal to arrive, Tre glanced through a local newspaper. He couldn't focus on anything he read. His brain still wasn't working on all cylinders - or was the paper a diversion? An object to keep it preoccupied from the failures he attempted to bury in the dungeon of his mind. And to suppress the image of Cassy's horrified look as she slipped from his view and his grasp, into permanent darkness.

The steak arrived prepared to perfection with a well-dressed baked potato. He left the al dente vegetables sitting after the first bite. He paid the bill and wandered around the area, looking in store fronts without seeing anything. Tre admitted to himself it was a stall tactic, and got back in his car to return to the cottage-like home just east of Washington Park.

The routine on arrival played out eerily similar to the earlier stop. The pause, the approach to the house, and the triggered nerves. The roses once more shook, as if a brisk breeze blew around his hand, or an unseen force tried to wrestle the flowers from his grip. This time the door opened. A middle-aged man with greying hair looked him over. The man had never met him, but knew who Tre was.

"I'm not sure this is a good time, young man."

A voice approached from the inside hallway. "Who is it, Lawrence? Are you expecting someone?"

As the woman stepped into the doorway, her face went pale and her mouth hung agape. She stood momentarily speechless. Momentarily.

"You have a lot of nerve showing up here!" she yelled as tears flowed down her now reddening cheeks. She'd come to the door with a mop in her hand, which began to lurch around. "You killed my daughter. My little baby girl."

Tre held the bouquet forward. "I just …"

She pushed past her husband, snatched the flowers, and threw them on the ground. She furiously stomped the life out of the roses, still gripping the mop, which bobbed up and down like dreadlocks on a runner. Her puffy, aching eyes looked up, right into Tre's heart, ripping into it. Frozen, Tre stood defenceless. The tightly gripped mop reared back and laid a resounding blow to the sling on Tre's already injured left shoulder. As he grabbed his arm in pain, a second blow landed on his right hand as it nursed the first assaulted area. She pulled the mop back for a third strike, but her husband pulled her back and engulfed her in a tranquilizing hug. Blurrily, she looked into her partner's eyes. He released her and she ran crying into her home.

"It's not a good time, Tre. She's not ready." He closed the door.

Tre remained bent over, a few paces from the welcome mat, and feeling quite the opposite. In spite of the physical abuse on his already injured body, the most pain he felt tore at his heart. He didn't expect forgiveness. He didn't know what to expect, but it wasn't this. *But why shouldn't he have expected this?* He'd driven the car that led to their daughter's death. Who else could they find to hold responsible, even if an accident? A rocky launch on his journey to make amends.

He gingerly knelt down, wincing as he cleaned up the remains of the roses, the last thing she needed to see on her stoop to remind her of his visit. He had limped about halfway back to the car when he heard the door open behind him. He looked over his shoulder to see Cassy's dad. The man approached in silence, perhaps trying to get out of earshot of the house.

"I'm sorry for my wife's reaction."

"It's understandable. I'm sorry for making her think of the accident."

"Trust me. We haven't stopped thinking about it, and never will. Her mother is truly heartbroken. I thought losing Cal was hard. This is worse."

"Cal?"

"Cassy's brother. He was killed in Iraq while serving."

"I'm sorry. She never told me."

"Cassy took it very hard. They were very close. Only fifteen months apart. She was a senior in high school. He went right into the army out of school. I tried to talk him out of it, but he wouldn't hear it. Cassy barely passed that last year. Kicked her grades and any chance of a medical career to the curb, although truth be told, we would have had to take a second mortgage on this place to pay for it." He paused, looking down at his feet. "So it's just not a good time. I'm not sure it ever will be. I do thank you for coming by though. As hard as it is for us to see you, I'm sure it was tough for you."

"Thank you, sir. Someone told me you instigated the search that found me, and I otherwise might have bled out and died. So thank you for that."

Cassy's father nodded silently.

"I just wanted to say that it was an accident," Tre continued. "The front tire blew and I couldn't control the car. The second worst feeling in my life, next to finding out Cassy …" Tre choked back the tears.

Cassy's dad hugged Tre, causing additional pain to his shoulder but relieving some of the pain in his heart.

"It's all right, son. We're all just looking for closure." He separated from Tre, keeping a hand on each shoulder. "We just need to do it on our own. So, in respect of Cassy's memory, please don't come back here."

Tre nodded, and he watched the man walk back into his house. Wiping tears from his cheek as he limped back to the Mustang, Tre hoped he had just experienced the most painful, least satisfying stop on his trip.

14 The Dentist's Wife

Not up to any further driving and with night settling in on the coast, Tre found a hotel in Monterey. After tossing and turning for a few hours that felt like a few days, Tre relented and swallowed an oxycodone. And slept. He needed the sleep and couldn't slow his mind down without help.

His morning shower revived his body and his mind. He still saw Cassy's mom crying whenever he closed his eyes, and as a result, he suffered the sting of shampoo hitting his peepers as they remained open during his shower. A small price to pay.

Mid-morning arrived by the time he got on the road. His black car's interior was already heated up from the brilliant morning sun, in spite of the moderate morning temperature. He'd have to thank Jack again next time he spoke to him. But that wouldn't be this morning. Tre felt no need for an update, and the wacko 'goodbye' message could await investigation. He likely should have told Jack about the call by now, but simply wasn't in the mood. His next destination felt more important right now. Sacramento. More precisely, El Dorado Hills, California. He'd never gone there. El Dorado Hills, that is. He'd seen Sac Town. Once. Tre debated stopping in San Francisco for a day. Or two. He loved that city, at least to visit. He didn't think he could live there. It just seemed like a difficult commute. Funny, him living in LA and thinking somewhere else had a difficult commute. He opted not to stop, or even go through the Golden Gate city. Instead, he would take the six-eighty around it, east of Oakland. He wasn't in a hurry, but knew that he shouldn't put things off either, no matter what he feared at his destination.

Topping up the 'Stang, he stocked up on some healthy drinks and some not so healthy, too good- looking-to-resist, home-made pepperoni sticks. He plugged the address into the GPS – the dental office of Meagan Winters.

A long time had passed since he'd seen, or even thought of her. At one time, it was all that he could do not to think of her. He pondered on how the importance of things, and people, could change so quickly and dramatically. Sometimes by our own hand, other times completely out of our control. It was why he never understood suicide. He knew that often medical conditions triggered the fateful event. Simplistically, he didn't get how someone could become so obsessed by someone or some moment that they would kill themselves rather than living without somebody, or without that feeling. After all, a person's life was within their own control. They made decisions every day that either increased or decreased their ability to control their destiny. If people took the time to inform themselves of the consequences of their decisions, making decisions became easy. In his life, he had called the shots, most of the time anyway, and he steered his life as he chose. He was beginning to understand, perhaps, what others less fortunate than him went through on a daily basis. It was hard to make correct decisions, he supposed, if your mind suffered from clouds and lacked clarity. These relentless images pursuing his every thought acted as a stick stirring the bottom of a muddy pond, making it impossible to see clearly to the bottom. Perhaps that drove people to make bad decisions, and some went to the extreme of suicide. They just couldn't take the murkiness anymore.

Tre tried to observe everything that went by the windows, directing his focus outward and away from the dark thoughts trying to drag him into that cloudy water. It seemed to work. His trip took him around San Jose, north over the Benicia toll bridge and east on the I-80 to Sacramento. Near the capital city he spotted one of his all-time favourite road signs. It was located at the beginning of US-50, as he veered off I-80. The sign listed distances to three cities. Placerville 46, South Lake Tahoe 107, and Ocean City, MD 3073 miles. Initially, Tre thought the picking of this east coast city was some engineer's wacky homage to their home town, but it was actually a reaction to a similar sign first erected in Ocean City at the other end of US-50. Over a few beers on his previous visit to California's capital, he'd been told the story behind the sign. Originally, it was a smaller black sign and held the single destination of its eventual end in Maryland. But the sign kept disappearing, a novel keepsake for roadside bandits. He was also told that the traffic engineers decided if they made it much larger and added the other cities to the sign it would appear a less tempting target. Unfortunately, when the sign came back, the manufacturer had mistakenly reversed the last two digits, so the distance from east to west showed 3,073 miles, in contrast to the 3,037 miles from west to east. The mistake was caught, after erecting the sign, and an overlay was nailed on the sign to correct the mistake.

For Tre, the sign meant he had twenty to twenty-five minutes to his destination. He glanced at the time. Food first. He better not try this whole amends thing on an empty stomach, the pepperoni sticks long gone. His stomach rebelled against the thought of fast food, so he pulled into a sit-down restaurant just off the highway in Rancho Cordova, a few miles east of downtown Sacramento. Normally impatient with slow service when he ate alone, it didn't bother him today. He'd picked up a USA Today and read it as he waited, although the restaurant lighting didn't make it easy. Why places like this didn't have different lighting for afternoon dining, he never knew. It was great atmosphere for a romantic dinner but sucked for lunch. Tre never had dessert with lunch, but his subconscious was intentionally delaying him with an order of pie. Almost an hour following his arrival, he exited the eatery and immediately flipped on his sunglasses to the outside glare. Coming out of dim lighting in midday felt like a laser trained on his retinas. Back in his car, he took a swig of Gatorade, only too late to realize the afternoon heat on his black Mustang had warmed it somewhere just short of boiling. He opened the car door and spit it out, but the damage to his taste buds had been done. He took the bottle, and an unopened bottle of water, and tossed them in a nearby garbage can.

He started his car and cranked up the air, stepping out and closing the door for a minute to let it cool down. Tre thought again about his request for a red Mustang, and how it wouldn't get so hot. Back in the car he activated the voice commands of his GPS, pulled out of his spot, and executed a tight turn out of the parking lot.

Guided by his electronic navigator, he'd barely reached the foothills when directed to exit US-50 for the city streets. A small strip mall right off the highway held Meagan Winters's dental office. Conveniently located, he supposed, for the suburbanites who travelled into Sacramento for work. As he sat stopped behind a car in the right lane, his GPS repeated to him 'turn right now' at an annoying frequency. After the fifth or sixth reminder, he unplugged the persistent prompter. Tre glanced across his dashboard to the plaza on his right. Something looked unusual about the plaza, but he couldn't put his finger on it. The traffic cleared and as Tre guided his Mustang around the corner, it came to light. There were no cars. Not in front of the pizzeria, the Laundromat, or the pharmacy. As he got further down the road leading into the plaza, he did see some cars – police cars. They blocked the three entrances. Tre scanned the storefronts, and right beside the dental office he sought out, was a bank. Police officers stood on the sidewalk comparing notes, surely from a midday bank robbery. They'd likely sent everyone home for the day, aside from a few witnesses probably subjected to questioning inside.

Tre pulled out the folded paper with Meagan's information and plugged her home address into his re-activated GPS. Nothing in El Dorado Hills went in a straight line, or flat. Without a navigation system, he'd never find his way. Assuming her hubby would also have been sent home, since they shared a dental office, he wished he had a cell phone to call and announce his pending arrival.

The roads snaked up the side of a rocky urban hillside, leading him to the front of Meagan's house. A red Jeep sat parked dead centre in a four car driveway, with the driver's side door open. The position made it impossible for another car to park without one set of wheels going up on some piece of landscaping, even if mostly rock and stones.

He drove just past her place and stopped, yanking on the parking brake as he shut the engine off. He'd no doubt that left untethered his car would roll about two hundred feet and barrel into the living room of some less fortunate soul with a modestly poorer view than Meagan's. Her house stood near the peak of the web of streets covering this Sierra foothill. Stucco houses provided the norm in this exclusive neighbourhood, mostly soft colours that fit nicely with the natural look of the terrain. No wartime brick boxes in this summit paradise, a far cry from Monroe, Michigan. No sign of siding either. Or plain cement driveways – all coloured and textured. There was a hefty price of quality and standards to pay to live in this suburb, and he doubted many of the residents cared or had any financial concern. Meagan's home didn't look any more lavish than the others, at least from the front with three large arches over rounded windows with custom drapery concealing the inside. A beautiful two-storey home.

Tre wanted to go around back and check out the view, as he could see Folsom Lake in the background. The back yard would provide a view of Folsom Prison, the jail made famous by Johnny Cash. The song jingled in his mind and he found himself humming it aloud. But since Meagan shared this dwelling with her husband, a knock on the front door would be a more appropriate, and safer, entrance. Of all the ways he could imagine dying, mistakenly shot by an ex-girlfriend's husband did not appear high on his list of life exit strategies. Caught in bed maybe …

Although he refused to accept the pain, the drive had an ill effect on his booted foot. With a noticeable lilting to the left, he made his way up the driveway, confident his fortunes would fare better than at Cassy's parents. He'd soon prove himself wrong.

The front door to this hillside palace stood wide open. He cautiously approached, hoping nobody came to the entrance armed with a Swiffer. Tre stood in the doorway for a few seconds, debating if he should just walk in. Then the 'mistakenly shot' headline flashed through his mind, so he sought out the doorbell. He pressed it. Nothing. He pressed it again. Still nothing. He wondered how someone could own a house worth two million, give or take, and not have a functioning doorbell. Surely they could afford an electrician.

Tre leaned through the imaginary plane of the door and called inside.

"Hello … anyone home?"

He waited. He got no reply and heard no sounds of movement inside. He took another step inward, so that he now stood on the floor mat inside the house.

"Meagan? Are you home?"

Still no reply. The Jeep sat out front, door open. Certainly she was home. Then again, maybe it was the hubby's Jeep. *But what guy buys a red Jeep, unless he's doing it for resale?* He took another two steps inside so he now stood on an intricate marble floor in a two-storey foyer larger than the apartment that he and Meagan had shared in their last year of dental school. That was when cosy was fun, and not a statement of financial status. This house definitely reeked of financial status. He could see clear through the house to the back deck, though 'deck' seemed entirely inadequate. Back home, a deck meant a wooden structure stuck on the back of a raised ranch, usually large enough for a grill and maybe a small table for four. Maybe patio was a better term for this house. Through the floor to ceiling windows that blanketed the back of the house, a negative edge pool shimmered as it appeared to flow into the lake on the horizon. Breathtaking luxury. It surprised him to see a staircase down about halfway to the back of the house, as he assumed most houses in this area were built on solid rock. The advantage of living on the edge of the cliff, he supposed.

To his left, an ornate spiral staircase carried its wrought iron railing up to the second floor, where presumably the master bedroom lay. He called Meagan's name again and intently listened for a reply. With the amped up focus, he heard sound upstairs, although it wasn't voices. Sound carried through these open layout homes. Calling again, he gazed at the stairs in front of him. He didn't do stairs so well these days. He slowly ascended the winding hardwood steps, one at a time, sounding like the peg-legged villain in an old movie. Step, clop. Step, clop. An anchor would have been easier to haul up these steps than his ankle cast, provided of course his left arm was unburdened of its elbow hammock. Each step zapped his energy as he compensated for the agony. Fortunately the railing rose with him on the right, as he required the extra leverage by the time he reached the climb's mid-point. After calling two more times en route to the summit – and this indeed felt like a climb up Mount Whitney – he stopped summoning her. Suffering a mortal gunshot at the hand of her husband had fled his mind, replaced foremost by pain, then by nostalgic images of their time together.

Tre had left Meagan. Without notice, without provocation, without explanation. He simply left. She never knew why. He wasn't sure he knew. He'd never felt closer to claustrophobic. He couldn't explain why. He moved on without much additional thought of her. Every so often, he'd wake in a sweat, induced by a passionate dream that recalled their best of times together. There definitely were good times, and big dreams. She always wanted a big home on the water, although her descriptions back then placed her palace in a more remote location. Her desire for a mansion in the woods always baffled him, as she was as big a city girl as he'd ever known. Of course, he was from a small Midwest town, so Toledo seemed busy to him back when they were together. She would have never guessed six years ago that he'd be happy in LA. They both appeared to have drifted from their earlier dreams, but both had achieved career success and some measure of wealth. That was enough for many people, including him, until recently.

Finally reaching the upper landing, Tre bent over to catch his breath, still relying on the railing for support. He stared at the ankle boot and cursed its existence. Straightening up, he looked around. The noise came from the bedroom at the back, likely the master overlooking the lake. He called her name again as he entered the room. Two suitcases lay open on the bed, one fully packed but not yet zipped closed, the other with room for only a few more items. Meagan hurriedly emerged from a large walk-in closet, wearing a black skirt and bra, and trying to fold a grey skirt while squeezing a couple of blouses under her arm. Shimmering from the sun shining through the balcony doors, her silky brown hair fell just to her shoulders, a good foot shorter than the last time he'd set eyes on her. Time had no effect on her figure, still looking as slim and fit as he remembered. She pushed the folded skirt into the suitcase, and placed on the bed the blouses from under her arm. She lifted one up in front of her to fold it.

"Oh, shit!" she cried out, pulling the blouse to her chest as she finally noticed someone had entered her room.

"Hi, Meagan."

"Trevor? What the hell are you doing here?"

He hadn't heard his birth name in some time, other than from his mother on their regular calls. He'd become Tre just prior to graduating, and his diploma held his adopted name. He'd forgotten that she called him Trevor. In fact, she refused to call him Tre after he had it officially changed. She understood his reasons for changing his name, but didn't like the name Tre. Meagan said she didn't want to marry someone whose name sounded more like a hip-hop star or gang member than an oral surgeon. He accepted she wasn't going to change what she called him, and it wasn't worth the fight.

"I wanted to stop by to apologize," he sheepishly said.

"What? Are you serious? After all this time you decide to apologize?"

"I know. It's long overdue."

"Major understatement, Trevor. But I really haven't got the time right now for you to make yourself feel better."

"Yes, I see you're packing. Going on a vacation?"

"Something like that." She zipped up her two bags and yanked them off the bed into an upright, pulling position. "Grab one and help me get it downstairs."

"I would but…" and he pushed his left arm forward to show the rose-battered sling.

Meagan looked him over. He looked like shit. Not only was he banged up from head to toe, but his face looked out of sorts, as if suffering from sleep deprivation. "You look like hell. Never mind," and she brushed by him, one of her large roller bags bouncing over his booted foot. Tre yelped.

"Sorry," she said as she continued without slowing. Tre followed her out to the hallway. She parked one bag while collapsing the handle on the other and scurrying downstairs with it. Through the large window over the entrance, he could see her hoist the bag into the back of the Jeep. She ran back into the house and up the stairs. As she got to the landing, she looked at Tre.

"You really couldn't have picked a worse day."

"I know, you're in a hurry."

"You have no idea."

"I just wanted to explain and say I'm sorry."

Movement outside caught Meagan's eye. "Shit." She looked around, suddenly extremely agitated. Frantically, her eyes darted around.

Tre had no idea what he had done. She stood in front of him, her second suitcase upright with one hand on the handle. Her eyes still moved around, and he could tell her mind moved much quicker. She'd moved hurriedly before, but now she seemed panicked. The colour had escaped her face. He limped over in front of the stairs to see her vantage point. Perhaps her husband had pulled in the drive and she was concerned they would look guilty of rekindling an old flame. Activity stirred out front. A few sedans had pulled up. If he didn't know better, he'd swear they were police cars.

"You came here looking for forgiveness, right?"

"Correct. What's going on?"

"You are about to be forgiven."

"But I haven't even explained myself…"

"No need. Besides, I don't have time. Or time to explain myself now."

Tre looked perplexed.

Meagan picked up her suitcase like she was going to make a run for it. Instead, she surprised him with her next maneuver. She hoisted her suitcase in front of her chest, which in itself seemed no small feat based on what he'd seen her toss into it, and double clutched it. She looked deep into his eyes. He'd studied eyes for years, and he'd never seen a pair express the emotion like hers at that moment. A sorrow the likes of which he'd never felt in his life passed between them.

"Now you'll need to forgive me."

"For what?"

"This." With the entire force of her strength, Meagan heaved the bag straight at his upper body. He had no time to react sufficiently to catch it, let alone cease its momentum. The weight and force of the bag plunged Tre backward, not so much staggering as thrown, down the circular staircase. Her eyes had disappeared behind the suitcase as it assaulted him. His eyes closed as his head crashed against the wrought iron railings, consciousness rushing away with the light. His limp body continued an erratic bounce down to the base of the stairs in the expansive foyer. Tre's body lay on the marble floor, the suitcase covering his lower legs. As he lay there, two undercover police officers burst through the door, guns drawn.

15 Aftermath

For the second time in a week, Tre awoke without a clue where he was, or how he got there. Again, his head throbbed as he attempted to allow light into his eyes. Cracking his eyelids open, his mind paused to focus, then he violently sat upright. The bars of a jail cell surrounded him, and through those bars he saw an angry looking man who looked to have the strength, and desire, to pull limbs from Tre's body like a tormented child abusing a Barbie doll. Self-preservation in mind, Tre scooted back on his cot as close to the wall and as far from this disturbing onlooker as he could get. With sudden instinctive self-preservation movements, his body screamed a reminder to his brain of its recent duress, buckling him over in agony. His ribs ached in ways he'd never experienced. He didn't remember getting beaten and kicked. *What did he remember?* Then it came back to him. Meagan pushed him down the stairs. No, she threw a suitcase at him, which caused him to fall down the stairs. Another aborted attempt to sit up straight forced his eyes closed in pain. A tear crept out of his left eye. He could hear Jack and John teasing him – beat up by a girl. Aside from the ribs and a renewed throbbing in his melon, his left arm felt okay, considering. Same with his left foot. Wiping the tear off his cheek, he could feel the swelling on his face. He looked around for a mirror, but there was none. He felt around his face.

His left ear had a small bandage and gauze over it. His left cheek had swollen, and his lower lip was slit – on the left side. Between the two accidents, the entire left side of his body was in tatters, while his right side remained unscathed.

"Brightman," a voice summoned from outside his cage.

Tre hesitated, glanced up cool as a cucumber, acting accustomed to jail. His first time behind bars, he already hoped it would be his last. In front of him stood a man in a cheap and wrinkled suit, emitting the aura of a police detective and not a lawyer.

"Get up, Brightman. We've got some questions for you." An armed uniformed officer unlocked the door and opened it.

Tre's slow movements to stand resembled an arthritic old man. A walker would complete the image.

"Can you speed it up a bit? I got lunch in two hours," the detective said sarcastically. "You better keep an eye on him, Reynolds," the detective said to the officer, "he might try and make a run for it." He laughed at his own joke. As Tre crossed the threshold of his cell, the officer slammed the door of bars shut.

Tre flinched with the noise, but kept moving in the direction signalled by the detective. Exiting the cell area, he led Tre into an interrogation room, complete with a large mirror on one wall. Tre sat down and looked up, wondering who watched him.

The detective turned his armless steel chair around backward and sat down. He opened a folder in front of him and held it at an angle to prevent the prisoner from seeing the contents. He focused on the pages inside the folder, not looking up at Tre.

"Dr. Tre Brightman. Van Nuys, California. You've got a whole bunch of letters after your name." He closed the folder and slammed it on the desk. "Do you think that makes you important?" He glared at Tre with his best bad cop glare. Tre almost laughed.

"No, sir."

"Hmmph," the detective grunted back. "You must be quite pleased with yourself. You slept like a baby. Over twelve hours, aside from what looked like a nightmare near 4 A.M. I would have kicked your ass earlier, but the doctors ordered us to let you sleep. Just as well. Gave us time to dig up clues and witnesses."

"For what?"

"Shut up. You've had a busy week." He paused for effect and glared again, which forced Tre to hold back another chuckle.

"Something funny?"

"No, sir."

"So here's how I put it all together. Tell me when I go off track. You and Dr. Winters were in this together."

"In what together?"

The detective bolted up off his chair. "Did I say you could talk?" Another glare.

"No, sir."

"As I was saying, you and Dr. Winters were in this together. I'm not sure how long you've planned it, but that doesn't matter. That will come out later I'm sure."

"Planned what?"

The detective stood straight up, clenching the top of his steel chair so tight that veins popped in his hands. "Shut up, Brightman. Hell, they should call you Dumbman. You seem pretty stupid to me."

Tre leaned back, away from the aggressive stance of the detective. He decided to remain quiet and let the idiot finish his story.

"So you two planned this together, being old flames. I guess the spark re-ignited, huh, Dumbman?" The detective backed away from the table, grasping the folder in his hand and waving it around. "Part one of your plan is to get rid of your girlfriend and make it look like an accident. You pick a spot on US-1, and coaxing your girlfriend to undo her seatbelt, ditch your car. She dies and you're free to pursue your relationship with Dr. Winters." The detective stopped to read his suspect's face. Tre greeted him with a dumbfounded look. "What's the matter, Dumbman? Cat got your tongue? Making you squirm, aren't I?"

"I …"

"Did I ask you to talk?"

Tre looked at the detective, amazed at the total fabrication spewing from his mouth, but deciding to stay the silent course.

"Where was I? Oh, yeah. So now you've got to get rid of your sweetie's hubby, let me see … Dr. Hfuhruhurr."

Tre burst out laughing. "You mean like in 'The Man with Two Brains?'"

"What!?" the detective yelled at him.

"Never mind. It's Dr. Hafur."

"Whatever. You killed him."

"Meagan's husband is dead?" Tre leaned forward in shock.

"Good bluff, Doc, but I'm not buying it. Your girlfriend couldn't do it herself, so she asked you to do it. Once her husband was out of the way, you two could run off together. You met her at her office first thing this morning. She started work before her husband, so she let you in the back. You waited until after lunch, then you popped out of the closet and stabbed him eight times." The detective turned as he finished his story, smiling at the two-way mirror, pleased at his summation.

Tre sat in the chair, stunned. His mind reeled over the possibility of Meagan killing her husband. The rest of the allegations were the wildest thing he'd ever heard. The detective turned back to Tre.

"You're not such a smartass since I busted your ass, are you?"

"I'm just not sure where to begin. It's all so outrageous."

"Tight as a drum, I think."

"For starters, Cassy and I were not dating. I don't have a girlfriend."

"Lie. The LA police have witnesses that saw you two cosy as could be hiking." He opened up his folder. "She was pretty. Why would you want to get rid of a pretty girl like that?"

"I didn't. We weren't dating. And it was an accident."

"Lie. You killed her."

"And I haven't seen Dr. Winters in years."

"That doesn't mean anything these days. Between cell phones and computers. You were probably sexting her all the time, and video porning each other."

"Video porning? Is that really a thing? Sounds made up. And I just got into town yesterday afternoon. I checked out of my hotel in Monterey in the morning. Did you check the hotel?"

The detective looked down and flipped through his papers in his folder.

"And why would she push me down the stairs if we were running off together?"

"She saw us closing in on the two of you. She needed a distraction to get away, and you were it. Partners in crime double-cross each other all the time."

The lack of progress that he made with the detective frustrated Tre. "Okay, why would I possibly wait in the closet all morning, then jump out after lunch and stab the guy? Why wouldn't I just shoot the guy first thing when he arrived for work? And why do it at work where there's potential for witnesses?"

"Don't try to worm out of this! So maybe you were at the hotel and didn't arrive until later. That's why you killed him after lunch."

"But why would I stab him?"

"Crimes of passion are often done with knives."

"But I never met the guy."

"You weren't passionate about him, you idiot. You were passionate about his wife."

"But I didn't kill his wife out of passion."

"Shut up and sit down."

"Where am I anyway?"

"In a police station, you idiot!"

"No, where? I didn't think El Dorado Hills had a big police station."

"They don't. You're in Sacramento."

"Why?"

"We know how to handle the tough crimes with murdering scum like you."

Silent, Tre sat looking at the crazed detective. Realizing the guy was hellbent on his story, Tre spoke.

"I want my phone call."

The detective slammed the folder down on the table. "Fine." He picked up the folder and with a childish outburst, stomped out of the room.

With his one call, Tre called Jack. Well, John, actually. Their phone voices sounded similar, aside from their greetings. Jack answered with a simple "Jack here," while John answered more professionally, "Gordon Detective Agency, John here."

"Tre – I just saw your picture on the news! How the hell did you end up accused of killing your dentist friend up near Sacramento? Jack's freaking out. Are you okay?"

"What! They've given my name and photo to the news? And I didn't kill my dentist friend. Her husband is dead. They think she and I were in on it together."

"Sounds like you need a lawyer more than a pig needs mud."

"You got it. I need you and Jack to get some alibi statements for me too. Go to the hotel I stayed at last night, I mean two nights ago, the restaurant that I ate at that day, credit card receipts with date and time, whatever you can dig up as proof I wasn't here to kill anyone."

"Got it. I'll call Ezra to get you sprung okay? He's got a partner, Maury I think, in San Fran that can likely get over there in a couple of hours. Hang tight."

"I'm not going anywhere."

"Hey, almost forgot. We've been dying for you to call. Remember the metal fragments in your tire? They were from a shell casing from a high-powered rifle. Looks like someone shot out your tire."

"I didn't see anyone around," Tre replied, searching his memories of the seconds before the crash.

"You wouldn't have. They would have shot from quite a distance with this kind of rifle, like a sniper. But it wasn't an accident. Someone did try to kill you."

"Great. Well, not great that someone tried to kill me and cost Cassy her life, but at least it's more evidence against Detective Idiot's case."

"The LA police have some other startling new evidence too. Do you recall us mentioning the scoring on your axle? They confirmed that someone sabotaged the brake line on your car."

"So they rigged my brakes and shot at me?"

"I guess they made contingency plans. Jack wants details about the whereabouts of your car every minute of the forty-eight hours prior to the crash, as he figures your brakes would have failed sooner if done earlier than that. He thinks the saboteur turned off your car alarm and tampered with the brakes in your garage before the homeless guy played etch-a-sketch on your paint job."

"And that's why the alarm didn't sound when the jerk keyed my car."

"Exactly. Jack's got photos of the sabotage and the bullet fragments with him en route and the Sacramento police should be getting them soon as well. I'll get a collaborating statement from the LA police and fax it up to the Sacramento police."

"Jack's coming up here?"

"Yeah. He's flying up this afternoon. He said something about you buying him a truck. Do you know what that means?"

"It means my bill has already paid for Deanna's braces, and he's running a new tab."

16 Background Check

John Gordon had met Tre through the gym. Jack and John used to play one on one until they came across Tre and Bobby doing the same one day. After playing a few spirited games, they turned it into a regular thing. Jack and Tre immediately became best buds, both very personable, A-type personalities. John was the same before his partner's accident. Bobby could play aggressively on the court, but most would call him laid-back otherwise.

John wore the label of geek in the Gordon Detective Agency. He'd spent countless hours on cases searching the internet to decipher the important, true information from the rest of the crap. This proved an arduous task when it came to the interesting mix of people that resided in and around Los Angeles. A lot of superficiality, in the people and the internet wake they left behind them.

Since Jack remained single, he often asked John to do background checks on his dates. John would shake his head, but did it anyway. A couple of times the intel dug up by John proved invaluable prior to his twin's dates, such as the statuesque female police officer that Jack had met at the shooting range. She had that leg over leg walk like Catwoman, and she'd tempted Jack by sliding a picture into his locker of her in a black, skintight, leather outfit. Jack's eyes almost popped at the sight of the picture. John's instinct though set off alarms, although Jack claimed it simple jealousy over the thought of him getting a chance to score with such a vivacious woman. An hour before Jack's date, John broke the news. This leggy temptress almost killed a man she'd taken home and talked into a little, not-so-good-natured bondage. The man never filed a complaint because he was a fellow police officer and didn't want to live with the harassment for the rest of his career. Unfortunately for him, buddies do talk, and this poor sap ended up with the nickname Dave the Slave.

Another close call was the rich Hollywood socialite. Jack's eyes lit up with dollar signs over the money in this young lady's family. An introduction to her came via his date for the evening at a movie premiere. His date didn't seem to notice, but this other woman had come up from behind him on a couple of occasions and grabbed his ass or pressed her bra-less body up against his side. If Jack hadn't arrived with a date, he would have no doubt gone home with this other lady. He had to pull her hand out of his pants pocket to retrieve his keys to drive his actual date home. She called his date the next day and got Jack's number. He'd gotten her voice mail but hadn't called her back. John did some digging and found out she'd tragically tried to kill herself four times – after each relationship she had had dissolved. Daddy's girl didn't handle rejection very well. Jack was grateful to pass on her and spare any guilty conscience afterward if it didn't work out.

They, however, had never run a background check on one of their friends. It didn't seem right. Until today. Tre's run-in with the law could have far reaching implications for their friend. While it felt like an invasion of Tre's privacy, John had to follow Tre's trail for the past few days, and if time permitted, he'd dig deeper. After all, something John dug up might lead to information related to the allegations. Or it would come in handy to know if Tre's past had potential to discredit his reputation or sabotage his position. While he wasn't preparing evidence for a court case, John knew it always best to get out in front of any possible criminal investigation. Lord knew how easily information got twisted, so it was best to know the truth before the tabloids, or police, painted a different story about Tre Brightman.

Foremost to his surprise, at first glance anyway, John found that Tre's trail terminated six years back – to his arrival in Los Angeles. The brothers knew Tre had come from Michigan, but preliminary searches showed no trace of Tre back there. But it had gotten late and his eyes were as tired as his brain. Queries to look into tomorrow, when revitalized by a good sleep. The immediate concern was the past few days, and John tracked back a few months. John assembled a nice list of highlights about Tre for those months:

- He'd had no contact with Meagan via phone, email, or social media. In fact they didn't even have any common friends.
- Receipts collaborated Tre's stops, with dates and times clearly showing his location far from the dental office when Meagan snapped.
- Twelve confirmed sexual encounters – clarification – twelve different partners, several of which involved multiple encounters. Twelve confirmed, they'd have to get a full list from Tre.

- The Santa Monica Young Leaders scholarship was founded, and funded entirely, anonymously by Tre. The third recipient was named last month.
- Aside from his residence, Tre owned four homes during the past year. He'd already flipped two of those. The other two were in the midst of renovations by contractors.
- He was the landlord of three apartment properties with a total of twenty units. He'd evicted two tenants in the past three months, one of which got in Tre's grill on two occasions before the tenant totally trashed a two bedroom unit with the help of fifty friends. Most rooms had obscenities scrawled on the walls in crayon (not easy to remove or paint over). The other tenant moved back to Montana, failing to land paying acting jobs.
- He made a $10,000 contribution to the local Republican candidate. The next month he did the same for the Democratic candidate.
- He'd attended three movie premieres. One date was a shoo-in for a Razzie later in the year, looking infinitely better than her acting.
- His winning percentage for their basketball games stood at sixty-two percent, highest of the four participants.
- Tre had one speeding ticket, for twenty-two mph over the limit, the day he bought his Mercedes SLK-55 Class Roadster. Which was lucky, according to Jack, the passenger at the time, who noted Tre had the car travelling significantly faster, well into the triple digits.

The research was a good start, with the first two items the most important, and taking the bulk of the day to confirm. The information would at least clear Tre of the current charges, and John plugged it all into an email with attachments, and sent it off to Jack for when he arrived in Sacramento.

Now if he could just find out why Tre Brightman didn't seem to exist until six years ago.

17 Good Cop

Six long hours in his cell preceded Tre's escort to meet his lawyer, his pace slowed due to his recent stuntman routine down the stairs and the lack of any painkillers. As the door opened and he stepped through, Tre felt relief to see Jack standing beside his lawyer.

"Man, am I glad to see you!" Tre hugged his private eye friend.

"Maury Montcalm," the lawyer extended his hand.

"Pleased to meet you, Mr. Montcalm."

"I picked Jack up at the airport, and we had a good talk on the way here."

Tre turned to Jack. "I thought prisoners were limited to one visitor?"

"They are, when one of the visitors isn't good friends with the chief of police," Jack grinned.

"Working the connections. Should have known," Tre replied.

"So," Maury started, "between the two of us, we've convinced the good chief that you were not found at the scene of the crime and there is no physical evidence to link you to the scene. Second, the detective's theory and your supposed motive have no merit. Third, we have produced evidence clearing you of any wrongdoing in your unfortunate crash. And finally, we have proof of your whereabouts at the time of the stabbing."

"Great! So let's get out of here!"

"Soon enough. Your friend Jack told his friend the chief that you'd be glad to help them out by answering some questions. They hope that perhaps their suspect let a clue slip to you that might help them track her down. As your lawyer, I of course have to advise against such a thing. It is up to you."

"Sure, as long as it's not the same idiot as before."

Jack smiled. "You're safe. My brother told me about your earlier encounter. That was one of the conditions – no bad cop routine."

"All right. Let's get to it so I can get out of here."

Jack opened the door and motioned to a detective waiting outside.

"Detective Willoughby. Sorry about earlier. My partner's a little over zealous at times. He's shook up a bit about this one. She really did a number on her husband."

"So I heard from your partner."

"What did the perpetrator say to you?"

"She said it was a bad time."

"I bet it was," the police detective replied.

"I just thought she meant her husband was coming home. Maybe he was the insanely jealous type. You know, fly off the handle and snap."

"I think she's the one with the temper."

"I'm having a hard time believing it."

"Why did you drop by her house to see her, anyway?"

"I went by her work first, but the parking lot was all blocked off. I reckoned a bank robbery, since I saw one next to their office."

"I could see how you'd assume that."

"So I went by her house, assuming she'd gone home early. Jack had given me both addresses, just in case. I came here to apologize to her."

"For what, if you don't mind?"

"We lived together our last year of school. I dumped her on the last day of our dentistry program. Truthfully, dumping is too nice a word. I just up and left. No explanation. No forwarding address. Just gone."

"Ouch. You're lucky she didn't hunt you down and kill you."

"I definitely deserved it the way I treated her." Tre put his head down, shaking it. He let out a huge sigh. "But she didn't have a violent bone in her body back then."

"Any idea what changed?"

"I hadn't even talked to her since then, until of course I saw her at her home. The reasons that I can think up are pretty lame, like stress from working with her husband, another dentist. And dentists have horrible suicide rates – I guess some people just take their work too seriously, or get bored with doing the same thing all the time."

"You're right, they do sound lame," the detective replied.

"Maybe I left her totally jaded. I hope not, but I could have."

"You do think a lot of yourself, don't you?" Jack smirked.

The detective ignored Jack's remark. "Well she did attack you the other day, a good sign of some pent-up aggression toward you."

"She didn't attack me."

"She pushed you down the stairs!"

"It was self-defence."

"You attacked her?"

"No, that's not what I mean." Tre paused for the right words. "She saw you coming and needed to use me as a distraction to get away."

"She could have taken you as a hostage."

Jack laughed. So did Tre, who responded, "I would have gotten in the way more than helped as a hostage. If you didn't notice, I can't move too fast these days."

Willoughby nodded. "Did she say anything about where she might be headed?"

"No."

"Any ideas? Favourite vacation spots?"

"She used to like Florida, but we vacationed on a budget back then."

"What about relatives or friends?"

"I don't mean to be rude, officer, but like I said, I haven't had contact with her in six years. I couldn't tell you if her folks are still alive. And any mutual friends we had, I left them behind too."

"Sounds like you were running from something," the officer replied, leaning forward on his chair.

"I was. It's called commitment. And I haven't stopped to look back for six years."

18 Out of the Big House

Walking out the front door of the police station, Tre thanked his lawyer. So did Jack. Not that Maury Montcalm had much to do, but Jack always felt these things went smoother just by having a lawyer around. Kept things from taking a turn in a bad direction and they could quickly.

Upon opening the door, a sudden throng appeared that surprised all of them. Reporters and their crews surrounded them like ants to a dropped Cheetos.

“How did you get out when they had such an airtight case against you?” A lady yelled as she shoved a microphone into Tre’s face

“Did you pay off someone inside to get out?” yelled another reporter.

Maury then earned his money. Firmly, but gracefully, he stepped in front of Tre and blocked their access to the former suspect.

“Mr. Brightman has been cleared of all charges. He wasn’t even in town when this horrible event took place. He was merely a victim of bad timing and circumstance. Now, if you’ll respectfully excuse us, Mr. Brightman is injured as a result of this terrible ordeal.”

Maury reached back to put his arm around the shoulder of his client, and nodded to Jack. The private detective moved in front of the pair and, with shoulders spread and square, ploughed through the crowd. Despite a few voiced complaints no one followed them.

Arriving at the visitor parking lot, Maury released his arm from around his client and turned to face him.

"Thanks again, Maury. I have to say I was impressed with how you shut up those vultures."

"That's why you pay me the big bucks, Mr. Brightman."

"Unlike some people I'm paying" – and he looked at Jack – " your services are worth every penny."

Tre and Jack watched as Maury got in his car and drove off.

"So. Where to?" Jack asked.

"I need to get some meds from my car, find a hotel, and crash for sixteen hours."

"And after that?"

"Keep moving down my list. Which means I have a bunch of driving ahead of me."

"Are you sure you're up to it?"

"Are you Jack or Bobby?"

Jack punched Tre's arm. "I'm not acting like your mother. Just a friend."

"Yeah. I'm up for it. After sixteen hours of sleep, I'll be up for it."

"My flight back isn't for three hours. Do you want to grab a bite?"

"Sure. I'm starving now that you mention it, and I shouldn't take those meds on an empty stomach."

"Cool. And I need a lift to the airport. I forgot Maury picked me up."

"No problem. Did you forget your wallet and I need to buy you lunch too?"

"No, don't be ridiculous. Besides, I'm on the clock so I'm going to expense you for it anyway."

"Good to hear. At least then I can write it off."

"All right, let's go. Where's your car?"

"Around back. They towed it down here as evidence. Hopefully they didn't tear it apart looking for a murder weapon. I hear they don't bother putting them back together when they do that."

Jack provided protection for Tre around the side of the station, but this time Tre walked in front. Jack felt pain just watching Tre walk – the man was seriously banged up.

"Are you sure you're okay to drive?"

"Drive, yes. Walk, not so much."

Tre maneuvered himself into the low-riding seat of his Mustang. Sitting didn't feel a whole lot better, but there was no way he'd let on to Jack. He buckled up and they drove off to find a restaurant.

"You should know a good place around here, growing up in Sacramento. Or do you only know the clubs?"

"Maybe next time we'll hit the clubs. Yeah, I know lots of places to grab some grub." Jack motioned with his hand. "Up here a few blocks. I'll tell you where to turn. It's not far."

"Just don't pick a roadhouse. So no Hooters."

"It won't be Hooters," Jack replied. "Say, did I ever tell you about my Hooters episode?"

"Can't say you did. Bad experience?"

"Let's just say a different experience."

"All right, I'm interested," Tre laughed.

"They turned me down for a part-time job when I was in school."

"Too young?"

"No, I was in college. Before the Academy."

"Didn't know you went."

"One semester. But that's another story. Or two."

"So why'd they turn you down? No bartending experience?"

"They discriminated against me."

"Because you were in school?"

"No. They said I didn't look right in the uniform."

"What?"

Jack smirked. "Yeah, I showed up for my interview in a uniform that I borrowed from a female acquaintance."

"You didn't!" Tre exclaimed.

"Did. Those orange shorts look stretchy, but they squeezed in the wrong spot."

"I'm getting nauseous just imagining it."

Jack continued, "And that tank top was tight at the waist and saggy up top," as he cupped his breasts.

"What possessed you to do that?"

"My friend got fired, so it was my way of protesting."

"Why did they can her?"

"At the time, she told me it was because she repeatedly turned down advances from her boss."

"That's bad!" Tre shook his head.

"Would be if it had a grain of truth to it. I found out later she was drunk on the job – for the third time."

"So you protested for nothing."

"Not entirely. She was grateful. And I did get to wear women's clothes."

"You're one sick dude. And don't ever show me any photos if they exist."

"There are photos, but I claim they're John."

Tre laughed. "I'll have to be sure to ask your brother about that next time I see him."

"Speaking of John, he's on the cut brake line like lint in my navel. He called to say the closed circuit televisions in your garage didn't show any signs of someone tampering with your car brakes. He said he winced when he saw the 'asshole' incident, though."

"So a dead-end?"

"He's going to run down the list of other places you'd parked to see if any cameras might have caught some evidence. John's usually very thorough but it's still likely a long-shot, so don't hold your breath."

"I figured as much," Tre sighed.

"Speaking of dead-ends, John's researched your former partners," Jack added.

"That'd be a long time to hold a grudge," Tre replied.

"Some think revenge tastes sweeter when it's not expected," Jack responded.

"The Klingons say something like that," Tre smiled.

Jack ignored the reference and continued. "Regardless, George Smiley and Lionel Ramsey both had alibis. Ramsey's on a European vacation with his wife, and Smiley never left Louisville."

"Thanks for checking. I never would have thought of them as possibilities. Good to know John is thorough."

"Turn here," Jack said, motioning to his right.

Jack looked in the rear-view. Someone followed them. Actually, it looked like two someones. A van plastered with the markings of a local television station, and an innocuous blue sedan.

"Pull in this lot here," Jack directed.

Tre guided the car to a stop, but was slow to get out of the vehicle due to his pain. A female reporter rapidly approached him, her long hair blowing across her face as she tried to keep it back with the hand holding a microphone. Her cameraman struggled to keep up while settling his gear on his shoulder.

"What do you know about Dr. Winters? Rumour was you were part of a love triangle?"

"Just ignore them, Tre. Let's go eat."

Tre paused for a second after closing and locking his door. He looked up at the cameraman, then the reporter.

"I knew Dr. Winters many years ago, but we haven't stayed in touch. As my lawyer told you, I was a victim of bad timing and circumstance."

The reporter looked at Tre with pleading eyes.

"Come on, you can give me a better quote than that. Please?"

"Okay, how's this. I hadn't seen her in six years, and she pushed me down her stairs. Better?"

"Thanks! We can use that." The lady reporter beamed like she had an exclusive.

"Lord knows what they'll turn that into," Jack chuckled. Imitating a reporter, Jack raised the pitch of his voice and did an awful female impersonation. "When asked if he thought Dr. Winters was a crazy maniacal killer, he replied …" – and lowering his voice pretending to be Tre – "she pushed me down her stairs."

Tre sighed. "You're right. I should have just shut up."

Jack looked around for more reporters. No sign of any.

Tre found the restaurant's food tasty. Then again, Tre was so hungry that he'd have thought shoelaces with spaghetti sauce a delicacy.

"So John did a background check on you," Jack informed his pal.

"He what?"

"He had to dig up all this information, and thought it best to get the scoop on you in case a skeleton lurked in your closet that the police might hold against you."

"And?"

"And what?"

"And what did he find?"

"Yeah, right. Well, he just got started, and he had to produce a full workup of your whereabouts for the prior seventy-two hours, so John didn't get too far. Plus he ran into a dead-end."

"Six years ago, right?"

"Right."

"I told you, I ran away from commitment." Tre's hands tensed as they leaned on the table, his fingers laced.

"I heard that. We just don't know where you ran from."

"Whatever. It's not important." Tre looked intensely at Jack. "I'm out and that's all that matters."

"Your call, bro."

They polished off their entrees in silence. As he finished, Jack flipped open a folded piece of paper.

"You know, John did find out some cool stuff about you. Like the scholarship fund you started."

Tre looked surprised. "How did he find out about that? It was supposed to be anonymous!"

"It's John, man. What can I say? The guy's a star on digging up shit like that. You shouldn't feel embarrassed. That's a great thing you're doing."

"Thanks. You don't understand though. When you have money, if people find out you give it away, there's an unending stream of people trying to get some from you."

"Wouldn't know about that problem. Not that we're starving or anything, but you know, there's a lot of competition in our business."

"Sorry, didn't mean to sound like a snob."

“No sweat. Hey, talking about the background check, John said you had a tenant trash one of your rentals because the guy was so pissed off at his eviction. Think he’d be crazy enough to try and kill you?”

Tre stared straight ahead.“Hadn’t really thought about it. Didn’t he move to Montana or somewhere?”

“That’s the other evictee. Moved to Great Falls. John’s trying to trace down the trasher.”

“Speaking of leads,” Tre remembered, “one of you guys should check out my cell phone voice mail. There’s a message that’s made up of the word goodbye from all different songs.”

“You mean like one of those old radio contests? Those were so cool!”

“Well, this isn’t cool, just creepy.”

“Did you call home and get it from the road?”

“No, it was there the morning I left. It was time stamped about the time of the accident.”

“You’re right, creepy. But perhaps a good lead, and we could use one. I’ll get the recording and see what John can do with his digital do-dads in the office. He’ll be salivating over the chance to pull the recording apart, sound by sound.” Jack looked at his watch. “I better get heading to the airport. Those TSA lines can take forever sometimes.”

Pulling out of the parking lot, Jack thought they picked up a tail. The same blue sedan as earlier, it appeared. He wondered why the reporter didn’t just run up and accost them like the other one did. They didn’t seem to worry too much about privacy.

As Tre made his way out of the city and toward I-5 and the airport, Jack pretended to play with his phone while intent to keep an eye on the side mirror.

"Must be a killer app to keep you this quiet for so long."

"Just checking who's playing tonight."

"For five minutes? You've got the attention span of a flea. What are you really doing?"

Jack acknowledged he'd been busted. "We picked up a tail. Another reporter I'm sure. I'd like you to slow down, then pull over so I can confront the guy, or girl. Can't tell with the tinted windows."

"Won't they just give up after a while?"

"You don't know reporters very well do you? They're a persistent bunch. If I don't confront them now, they'll follow you to your hotel tonight and ambush you. Or worse, later after you're all hopped up on pain killers."

"Okay. Slowing down."

"That's it. He's a lane over, but the gap's closing. Slow down so you don't make this light. I'll jump out and give him a piece of my mind."

Tre did as instructed, and before the car had come to a complete stop, Jack had bolted out the door heading toward the blue sedan. The trailing car had stopped suddenly, realizing that his prey had detected him. As Jack neared the back bumper of the Mustang, a loud noise rang out, followed by the tail light smashing.

"SHIT!" Jack yelled out, and ducked down at the side of the car. He jumped in the door that he'd fortunately left open.

"Drive, Tre! Drive!"

Tre hit the gas hard as a second bullet pierced his back window, exiting the vehicle through the driver's side back window. Tires squealing as it left rubber on the road, the Mustang called on every one of its horses to bolt away from the curb lane. Not the same feel as his Mercedes Roadster, but it did the trick. The light switched to green halfway through the intersection, Tre swerving to avoid a Jeep making an advance left turn. Jack yanked his swinging door closed, then turned to view the road behind them. No sign of pursuit.

"Just keep driving fast!" Jack hollered over the racing engine.

"What the hell was that about??" Tre yelled, adrenaline pumping through his aching body.

"My guess is that wasn't a reporter," Jack replied.

"No shit, Sherlock."

"Maybe your friend is back."

"I thought he'd give up with me being crippled."

"Apparently not."

"Did you get the plate?"

"No, the front one was obscured. John hasn't even come up with anything yet, so this guy knows a thing or two about staying invisible."

"So what do I do now? Are you calling the police?"

"When we're safe. He's long gone from the scene by now and I've got no plate number for them to track."

"How are we going to be safe? He knows what I'm driving and must know the plate since he tailed me so long."

"Ditch the car."

"But I just bought it! I'm not going to total it."

"I didn't say total it. I mean drop it off and get some new wheels."

"Buy another car? You're costing me a fortune!"

"Get a rental for a few weeks. And make it less noticeable, like a Ford Focus or Dodge Caravan. A vehicle that there's a million of on the road. So no yellow Camaro or orange Challenger."

"You're killing me. A Ford Focus? You're going to destroy my rep."

"Seriously? Your rep? Have you looked at yourself lately? You look like interns practised on you and failed. Or mortician apprentices. Let's recap, shall we? Death threat, drove off cliff, tossed down stairs like a rag doll, thrown in jail, and now shot at. I think obscurity is what you're looking for, bud."

"Yeah, I get it. I'll find a car my mom would be happy driving."

"That a boy," and Jack slapped him on the shoulder. "Something with a five-star crash rating that Bobby would think you're safe in."

"I don't think Bobby would think I'm safe unless I'm in a Humvee, and they aren't too inconspicuous." Tre laughed, then realized it hurt far too much.

Turning into the airport, Tre finally eased up on the gas pedal.

Jack looked at his watch.

"I've still got a bit of time. Let's swing over to the long term rentals and drop this pony off. The car rentals are just across the road. Then you can drop me off at the terminal."

Per Jack's plan, they soon pulled up to the terminal in a new, black Ford Fusion, one of at least twenty Tre had seen in the rental lots. He received the okay from Jack to upgrade from a Focus to a Fusion. It wasn't as bad as he'd feared, at least from an accoutrements perspective. The satellite radio would come in handy where he was headed. He'd just have to get used to the reduced horsepower. He hoped for no more flying bullets to flee from.

Tre slowed the car as they neared the airport terminals.

"Which airline, bud?"

"First terminal will do. Thanks for the lift."

Jack got out of the car, but stopped short of closing the passenger door. With his forearm on the roof of the Fusion, he leaned in to talk.

"Take it easy on those meds, Tre."

"Sure thing, man," Tre said, dragging out the word 'man' in his best pot-head impersonation.

"Funny. And here," Jack reached into his duffle bag and yanked out a Lakers hat. "Wear this for the next twenty-four hours. You're less likely to be recognized by reporters and your stalker friend."

"But I hate the Lakers!"

"I know, you've told me you wouldn't be caught dead in a Lakers hat. Well, you might be caught dead without it. So suck it up for twenty-four. And stop sounding like Bobby! In a couple of days you can go back to wearing your Tigers hat, okay?"

Tre straightened up out of his self-pitying slouch. "Yeah. Forget I mentioned it."

"John's probably already dug up a fist full of leads for me to run down tomorrow back in LA. We'll track this guy down." Jack slammed the door and pounded twice on the roof of the car. Tre looked over his shoulder and pulled away from the curb.

"And keep in touch!" Jack hollered after Tre, hoping he'd heard, and would.

19 Return to LA

The line through the Sacramento airport TSA checkpoint was short in comparison to LAX. Re-buckling his belt, Jack looked around. A newsstand store stood straight ahead, the divider between the two wings of the small terminal. A good mystery might help pass the time while he waited for his flight, for boarding to complete, and of course during the flight. He wasn't a big reader like John, but then he wasn't the stay-at-home type like his brother had become since his marriage. Grabbing a book by an author whose name sounded familiar but wasn't a household name, and a protein bar, Jack headed to his gate.

Typically, he stuck to conventional mysteries and thrillers. 'Ubiquitous Medical' was different from his normal read in that it took place in the near future, but it was on earth, so it wasn't too science fictiony for him. No aliens and laser cannons. Jack had fallen deep into the story and in no time the pre-boarding announcement came over the public address system. The wrapper of his protein bar made a decent bookmark, and he closed the novel and slid it into an outside compartment on his duffle bag.

Jack looked around the assembled passengers. The usual group of travellers. The frequent flyers stood patiently, with their economically packed bags and efficiency in their procedure – knowing exactly when they'd board, where to line up, and how to avoid the infrequent flyers that had a tendency to get in the way. The families tried to keep the little ones occupied using every trick in their parenting arsenal, before giving up and resorting to candy to pacify their offspring. And of course, the couples on a getaway weekend to LA cuddled, excitement beaming from every pore. He looked at them and pictured John and his wife. But then, John would have to leave his comfortable little world, and that wasn't apt to happen anytime soon. The power of love was a phenomenon that Jack certainly didn't understand. His brother's swift metamorphosis was beyond his comprehension. Ever since John's wife's shooting, her recovery, and their marriage, his brother had been a changed man. And not for the good in Jack's mind. They were twins – how could John seem so different now? Sure, his brother *seemed* happy. But was he? His 'twinsinct', as he called it, told him no.

After the accident, Jack completely understood his brother's desire – no, need – to leave the police force. Jack, however, was reluctant at first to quit and start the agency. He never let his brother know that though. He still missed the police force at times, primarily during idle time between cases. Jack got bored easily when he wasn't in the field. He couldn't understand how John could contently sit at a desk all day. Four years ago that would have never happened.

Jack handed his ticket over to the gate agent for scanning, smiled at her, then proceeded down the jet bridge. Waiting in line to cross the threshold into the plane, Jack wondered if his brother had finished changing. He hoped the religion thing turned out to be a phase, or would at least remain a hobby and not a devotion. Prior to John's wedding, neither of them had stepped inside a church since childhood. John's wife was a good Catholic girl, going to mass regularly, and initially had to drag him to church. After a few months, Jack could tell that his brother enjoyed the Sunday outing and it had become a highlight of his week. Jack thought for certain that John's life had become so boring that getting out of the house to help seniors at the retirement centre to go to the bathroom would have sounded exciting. But as Jack kept reminding himself, as long as his brother was happy, and they could spend time together at work, he was happy.

Settled into his seat on the plane, Jack took his new book out of his bag and slid it neatly into the seat-back pocket in front of him. He'd buckled up, forgetting the empty seat beside him, when a young woman informed him she needed to get by to take her seat. Jack unbuckled, and stepped into the aisle to let her slide in. Sitting back down and re-securing his seat belt, he exchanged smiles with the lady.

"I'm Jack."

"Paula. Nice to meet you. Jack."

He examined her face, her hair, her look. An innocence surrounded her. She looked comfortable with who she was, something that many women seemed to struggle with at her age. She kind of reminded him of Cassy, rest her soul.

"Going home to LA, Paula?"

She smiled. "No. I'm going to visit my older sister."

"First time?" Jack could see she looked excited.

"Yes! I'm a little nervous. First time flyer."

"Nothing to worry about. Just think of the number of flights every single day around the world, and how often you hear of a problem? You have a better chance of winning the lottery."

"I suppose you're right. I'm a little afraid of LA, too. It's such a big city. Do you live there?"

"Yeah. I'm originally from Sacramento, but left to join the police force."

Her eyes reflected a new sense of security.

"How long have you been a police officer?" Her eyes fixed on his.

"I'm not, anymore. My brother and I started a private detective agency."

"That's cool! Is it like in the books or movies?"

"Sometimes. But the bills get paid by a lot of domestic intelligence."

"You mean catching cheating spouses?"

"Simply put, yes. Those assignments are usually pretty dry, although occasionally I have an angry husband to deal with."

"I'm sure it's more exciting than you make it sound."

"Not really."

"That's okay. I like a guy who's a little modest. Too many guys are just hot air."

Jack smiled an acknowledgement. He watched as she bent over to tuck her purse under the seat in front of her. Her top rode up her back, revealing the top band of her black lace underwear. She was noticeably fit. Bobby wouldn't like her though – too small up top for his taste. Paula sat up, holding an unseen object in one hand and brushing her hair away from her face with the other.

"You up for a game?"

Jack looked at the plastic cube she held, filled with bright green cards. "What kind of game?"

"It's a game I play with my sister when she comes home. The card gives a situation and you have to answer with what you'd do. It's a lot of fun!"

He wasn't much for that kind of game. Sounded like a girl's pyjama party-type game. "I probably won't be very good at it, I'm afraid."

"You don't need to be afraid."

"I didn't mean I was afraid to play."

"Sure you did. Most guys are intimidated to play this kind of game. They say it's too girly, when they really mean they'd rather have a sharp stick pierce their eye than have to reveal any true feelings, even to their best friend."

"Have to say that you're pretty close on that summary."

"So you won't play."

He smiled at her as the flight crew announced the boarding doors had closed and that everyone had to shut off their phones, ipads, e-readers, walkmans, and eight-track players, or put them in airplane mode. The passengers chuckled.

"I didn't say that. I said you were right about guys not wanting to show feelings. I'll try it."

"Goodie!" she screeched.

"But if I start to cry, it's entirely your fault," Jack joked.

"Suck it up, big guy. Here's your first question. What do you most worry about?"

"Losing my hair."

"Seriously? Didn't picture you as totally vain," Paula stated.

"So I'm somewhat vain, but not totally, is that what you're saying."

"All guys are somewhat vain. Women even more so. Is losing your hair the answer you're sticking to?"

"Why, are there points for good answers?"

"No, just curious."

"Seriously, what I'm most worried about is my twin brother."

"There's another one just like you?"

"Not anymore. He's changed a lot," Jack sighed.

"Got a girl, I assume?"

"Are you a psychologist or something?"

"No. But if you ask nine out of ten guys why their best buddy changed, they'll say a girl."

"And the tenth guy?"

"Likely will say the guy's gay or some other macho excuse to wash their hands of it."

"How old did you say you are? There's not a fifty-year-old hiding in there, is there?"

"I have a big sister who's taught me a lot."

"Right. So is it my turn to ask you a question?"

"Okay. Take a card. If you don't think it's relevant, pick another one."

Jack looked at a card. "You're not still in school, are you?"

"No."

"Good." He put the card back in the deck and grabbed another as the engines roared and the plane started its takeoff. She leaned back and closed her eyes. Her hand found its way over to hold his. Her nails dug in as they lifted off. He put the card down and put his other hand on top of hers. "It's okay. We're good now."

She opened her eyes, but didn't move her hand, just relaxed the grip. "Thanks, Jack."

"No sweat, Paula. Here's your question. What's one thing you've done that you'd like to erase?"

"Bobby Murphy," she said without a second thought.

"Bad relationship, I assume?"

"The worst. Seemed like such a nice guy. Turned out to be into all kinds of insane drugs, had a bad temper, and beat me up one time."

"I'm glad it was only one time. I've never understood women that get beat up by their guys and don't just leave."

"I'm sure it's complicated for many of them. And you're a guy. It's different for guys."

"I suppose. Still glad you were smart enough to get out."

"Me too. Give me your card back." She pulled a new card from the cube. "Do you believe animals have emotions?"

"Now that's the type of question that I'd thought these would be. Pass."

"Pass? Why don't you give it a shot?"

"Okay. Sure. I've had dogs that definitely had feelings. Do I think frogs or rats or snakes have feelings? Don't know and don't care."

"See, you do know how to express your feelings."

"Does that mean that I get a pretty pink sticker?"

"Hush!" She playfully smacked his arm. "Give me another question."

"What fear would you like to conquer?"

"Twenty minutes ago, I would have said fear of flying."

"And now?"

"Thanks to you, I have to think of something else." She closed her eyes to think. "Falling."

"What do you mean falling? From a tree? A ladder?"

"Falling from a height. I have this recurring dream that I'm up high looking over a park. Sometimes I'm on a ledge, other times I'm on a balcony. But I always feel my balance going, and I'm about to fall. So I stay away from the edges of things. Especially if there is a park nearby. Sounds stupid, I bet." She looked over at Jack. His face had gone white and expressionless. She shook his arm. "Are you okay, Jack?"

Jack snapped out of an apparent trance.

"Oh, yeah. Sure."

"Did I say something?"

"Yeah. You hit a nerve."

"I'm sorry. Did someone you know have an accident and fall?"

"No. It's a little embarrassing …"

"You're already playing a chick game, how much more embarrassing can it get?"

Jack leaked an abrupt smile. "I have a very similar dream. Nightmare. But mine is with stairs. I'm at the top of a staircase, looking down when I lose my balance and fall. Next thing I know, I'm looking down at my dead body at the bottom of the stairs."

"That's awful. When did you have this dream?"

"I have it about once a month. Every month since I was twelve or thirteen."

"Did you have a fall back then?"

"No. I don't know why I started having it. So now I never go down any staircase where there's more than nine stairs."

"You mean you count the stairs on any staircase you take?"

"Yes."

"Every staircase."

"Yes."

"But only going down, and not up?"

"Yes."

"Wow. Sorry I hit a nerve."

"It's okay."

She held his hand tightly, reassuring him. "I guess I won't be inviting you over to visit my sister in LA."

Jack gave her a puzzled look.

She gave an awkward smile. "Third floor walk-up."

20 Moving On

A few oxycodone and twelve hours of sleep later, Tre woke up in a hotel in Truckee, California, a small city just west of the Nevada border near Reno. Determined to get out of Sacramento and at least headed in the right direction for his next destination, he'd fought off steadily increasing pain, fatigue, and dusk long enough to get a few hours out of Sac-town, as John and Jack often called it. He woke refreshed, the haunting flashbacks missing from the night. The second (or was it third?) oxycodone did the trick. At least it did the trick for his injured mind; a calculated trade-off for the discomfort of the temporary loss of control that lingered like a tequila hangover. The control eventually returned, but unfortunately, so did the aching in his body. Pain ripped at his side like a dagger as Tre gingerly sat up on the edge of the bed. Banged up ribs were a bitch to get over, a long forgotten lesson from high school basketball. Carefully, he reached toward the nightstand and grabbed the close-to-empty pill bottle. Just one. To take the edge off.

The shower felt equally good and bad. Soothing to some parts of his ailing body, but smarting whenever he twisted or moved the wrong way. Like when he tried to wash his back. Or front. Or had to pick up the soap when a sudden twinge jerked the bar from his hand. It felt good to abandon the sling for a while, even though it meant wrapping his foot in the plastic hotel laundry bag from the closet hanger. Turning off the flow of overhead water, Tre stood behind the tacky striped curtain debating if towel drying was the way to go or if he could avoid some pain by just letting the air dry him. In compromise, he sloppily spread towels on the bed and lay down on them. A few well planned wriggles, a flip and a few more wriggles, and he was dry. Dry enough, anyway.

Tre flipped open his laptop, stuffed in his mobile internet stick, and waited for the computer to fire up. Open to his favourite map app, he plugged in his destination. He picked a target stopping point for tonight. He'd have to take it easy. Eight to ten hours of driving, tops. Nothing like the cross country marathons of his past. Not this trip. Maybe by the time he headed back, he hoped. Tre picked West Wendover, Nevada as his next layover, as he conjured up in his mind that he'd rather sleep in the Silver State than in the Beehive State of Utah.

Topping up the Fusion, although the miserly vehicle had used a scant few bucks' worth, he also picked up a package of donuts and a few Gatorades for the drive. Some comfort food mixed with fuel for his body. He wondered if Red Bull and oxycodone cancelled each other out.

Three hours or so into his journey, and with half the donuts plundered, Tre felt the need for some substantial food. Something that might actually help him recover more than powdered miniature donuts. In a truck stop near Winnemucca, Nevada, he popped another pill as he headed in to eat. The open-faced turkey sandwich with gravy and peas hit the spot, and readied him for another solid stretch of driving. He checked his watch. Should make West Wendover before 4 P.M. with a little speeding and light traffic.

The second pill of the day, and probably the turkey, made him a tad drowsy. He bought a couple cans of Mountain Dew at the truck stop, just in case, even though carbonated beverages didn't usually make his diet unless a vessel for alcohol. The caffeine boost had run out a good two hours short of West Wendover, and with his eyelids failing to cooperate, he barely made it off I-80 and into Elko, Nevada. Not knowing the town, Tre followed his instincts and correctly ended up in downtown. Needing to park the car, he pulled into an open angled spot just in front of a bank, and opposite a grand old courthouse. Thank God all he had to do was pull in straight and not have to parallel park. He would have patted himself on the back for driving with his eyes closed if he didn't expect it would hurt like hell. The car placed into park, Tre fell asleep almost instantly, although not planning to do so.

A disoriented Tre jumped in his seat at the sound of a slamming truck door. He quickly realized where he was and how he got there. He rubbed his hands up and down his face a few times to wake up before blinking a half dozen times to enable him to focus on his watch. Two hours lost. He'd push darkness to get to West Wendover. Perhaps with some more food – and without a pill – he'd have the energy to finish his planned route for the day, even if he got in a bit later than expected. *Nothing went as planned these days, so why should he get hung up on it?*

Tre normally didn't eat with the senior discount group, but he wanted to get back on the road. Locking the rental, he laboured across the street to snag dinner. A pleasant middle-aged brunette, chewing on a wad of gum the size of a tennis ball, greeted Tre. Not good for her jaw, he thought. Presumably trying to quit smoking, or fighting off cravings until her next break.

"How's this, hon?" She led him to an austere table for four in the middle of the room, complete with simple wood chairs.

Tre looked around. "How about one of those booths? I'm a little banged up and could use the padding."

"Sure thing, hon." She weaved between tables. "How's this one?"

"Great. Thanks."

She handed him a menu. "My name is Peggy. Our special today is rib-eye steak, served with mashed and a vegetable medley for $9.99. Unless you don't order before four-thirty, then it's $15.99. Can I start you with a drink?"

"Just water, thanks."

"Sure. I'll be right back with your water."

Tre looked around. A grey hair fest. Or white hair. Or whatever you call it when women dye it and it comes out that silver with a slight blue tinge to it. And a lot of plaid long sleeve shirts or light jackets – it was hard to tell in some cases. For certain, different from the kind of crowd that he dined with in LA. Then again, dinner cost the same as a single cocktail in LA, or less.

When he ate alone, Tre would spend the whole time he wasn't eating playing on his phone, either on the latest app he'd downloaded, checking out the news, or hitting the sports apps hard. But no phone today, so he people watched. They all looked happy, listening and talking to each other. Real conversation. Some of them even chatted between tables. Everyone appeared to know each other, as this wasn't a big town. In LA, people stuck to themselves. Dating couples exchanged conversation in LA, but on most of his dates, the women just wanted to talk about themselves and their careers. They didn't care what Tre had to say, and he could tell when he talked that his dates were more interested in looking engaged than truly participating in the conversation. They wanted to talk about themselves then get him in the sack. It had never bothered him before. Never. Before.

Tre glanced out the window to the street. The courthouse architecture intrigued him. Pillars in front and some ornate carvings on the top. He loved old buildings and wished he'd brought along a camera. He didn't even have his phone to take some pics. Across the street stood the bank, which he would have expected to have grand architecture as old as the courthouse. Instead, the financial institution looked built in the seventies. Early eighties perhaps.

Peggy stopped by with his water. "Ready to order, hon?"

"Sure, I'll take the special."

"Good choice. How would you like it?"

"Medium rare, please."

"Got it." She stuffed the order pad in her apron. "Just passing through, I assume? I'd remember you, for sure." She gave him the once-over.

"Yeah. What time's everything close around here?"

"We don't roll up the sidewalks at five, if that's what you're asking."

"Sorry, didn't mean to imply anything. Just asking."

"The bank's open till six. Seen you staring at it earlier."

Tre didn't reply when she was expecting one.

"Okay then," she said, disappointment in her voice at the lack of chatter. "I'll get Max to work on that steak of yours. Shouldn't be long, so you can get on your way."

He'd apparently done something to upset her. Maybe only the rude customers didn't engage in a bit of social niceties in Elko. He looked back across the street at the bank, but lost his focus and just stared into space for the longest time. He wasn't thinking about anything, but thinking about everything. Kind of like when you dump out a thousand-piece puzzle onto a table. Everything that you need lies in front of you, but none of it makes sense yet. Peggy crossed his line of vision to break his meaningless gaze.

"Here you go. Medium rare." She looked across to the bank to see what he stared at. Nothing that she could tell. "You got some business at the bank? Couldn't help but noticing you staring."

Tre looked up, surprised by her comment. "No," he stuttered slightly. "My car's parked over there."

"Ain't nobody going to steal it if that's what you're worried about!" She looked at him with a hint of disgust. "Anything else I can get you? Another glass of water?"

"No. Thanks." Tre looked down at the greasy steak. "Looks great, thanks." He lied. It looked like it would clog his arteries, provided he could convince his taste buds to let the meat pass into his stomach. Rescued from a frozen bag, the vegetable medley didn't impress. He stuck his fork into the steak and cut off a piece with a sliver of fat attached. Closing his eyes in preparation for the worst, the flavour pleasantly surprised him. The potatoes were quite tasty too – much like his mother used to make.

Down to his final few bites, minus the veggies which remained untouched after an exploratory taste, Peggy came by and slapped his bill on the table.

"Whenever you're ready."

He noticed the 'hon' had disappeared. Whatever, he thought. Taking the last bite of steak, he flipped the serviette over his plate and stood up. Too quickly though, forgetting how stiff he got sitting still. He stopped and grabbed the top of the booth divider. After catching a breath, he walked to the register and waited. He glanced across the street at his car in front of the bank. The walk looked longer after the recent blast of pain. From the front register, he could see the detail in the engravings of the courthouse much clearer. He turned back to his car, spotting a pickup angle-parked very close to his driver's side door, creating a pickup sandwich with his Fusion wedged in the middle. It was hard enough getting in and out of the car, let alone contorting his already distorted body to enter.

Peggy came to the register as he once more stared at the bank. She shook her head and grabbed the credit card and bill out of his hand.

"It was very good, thank you."

She feigned a smile. "Oh, thank you. I'll be sure to tell Max in the back." She handed him the credit card slip.

Tre wrote in a very generous tip for the ten dollar meal, tore off the top copy, and slid it back to Peggy.

She gave a real smile this time. “Why, thank you very much! We don’t get many decent tips at this time of day,” she said as she looked around at the seniors.

“No problem. It was a good meal.”

She nodded appreciatively, her demeanour suddenly reversed. He turned and pushed on the door to leave. On the sidewalk, he glanced down the street to get his bearings on how to return back to the highway. Upon looking both ways, he began to cross the street to his car. Traffic was jammed up a bit, as a police officer stood talking to a driver who’d double parked in the next block. Within ten feet of his car, Tre double clicked on the car door opener. Squeezing to get in, and cursing about it, he paused for a second to contemplate taking another pill. He almost hadn’t made it here to Elko without the eyelids betraying him. Tre didn’t think it wise to push his luck again. He carefully leaned into the back seat and zipped up his carry bag which contained the pills. He’d find it harder to reach back and grab one while driving if the bag was zipped. Less temptation, he reasoned. He pushed the key into the ignition to start the car and took care to back out of the parking spot, wary of the nearby pickups. Straightening the wheel, he stopped the car to catch what remained of the box of donuts as they slid off the dash. The late afternoon sun had heated the donuts to the point they needed tossing. He looked to the sidewalk, but no sign of a trash bin, so he leaned forward and placed them on the passenger side floor. He had yet to straighten up when he was startled by someone opening his back passenger door! Tre turned to see a woman flipping a pink plastic mask onto the seat beside her, and pulling what looked like a wool cap off her head, allowing shoulder length brown hair to escape.

The woman looked as surprised as Tre. Then a second person flung open the front passenger door and jumped in. The man pulled off a ski mask as he sat down, barking an order as he did.

"Let's go, Tommy!"

The man in the front looked over when the car didn't move.

"Oh, for Christ sakes! Who the hell are you?" The man looked around the street.

Tre sat tongue-tied.

"Shit!" the man yelled, reaching into the pouch of his hoodie. "Drive!" The man screamed, waving a gun at Tre's face. The uninvited passenger tossed a couple small bags into the back seat to his accomplice. The bank alarm sounded.

"Now, asshole!" The gun clicked, ready to fire.

Tre cranked the wheel and pounded on the gas.

21 The Getaway

The opportunity to test the power of the rented Fusion hadn't presented itself. He had beaten the hell out of his Mustang after the shooting in Sacramento. That scared him. This terrified him. The bank robber held his gun low, so it wasn't so visible to ongoing traffic, but Tre was painfully aware of its proximity even without seeing the weapon. The woman in the back hardly looked like the criminal type.

"Turn here. Onto I-80 West."

Tre obeyed, veering onto the ramp, not speaking. In the rear-view mirror, he could see the woman counting the haul.

"Not as good as West Wendover, but pretty good," she said to her accomplice.

"Not now!" The man raised his voice to his accomplice, displeased with her reference to a prior job. "Just put it all in two bags so we can carry it."

"Got it," she replied back

"Where to?" Tre asked.

"Just shut up and drive. I'll tell you when to turn."

The hum of the Fusion's engine was the lone sound as they sped out of town. The man would look in the side mirror, followed by a stare out the back window, and a glance forward, and then repeat the whole cycle. Ten miles out of town, Tre received his next direction, taking a ramp to a side road, followed by a turn onto another less travelled, heavily tree-lined road.

"Couple hundred yards more, then turn right," the man motioned ahead, waiving his pistol in a way that increased Tre's anxiety. He could see an overgrown gravel driveway or old road at the aforementioned point on the horizon. Tre slowed the car as he approached. As he turned, a grey F-150 lay ahead, just out of sight from the main road.

"Stop here!" The man startled Tre, who hit the brakes hard, causing the rear passenger to bounce up against the front seat.

"Shit," she yelled. "Watch what you're doing, asshole!"

"Don't you want me to pull up to the truck?" Tre asked as they had stopped a good fifty feet from the pickup, and in sight of the road.

"No, here's fine." The man punched open the glove box and rifled through it, spilling the limited contents on the floor in the process. "Hand me the guy's bag from the back seat," he asked his partner in crime.

"Well, what have we got here? Oxycodone … this will do just fine." He clutched it in his hand and turned it to read the label. "Dr. Tre Brightman. Sweet! We got ourselves a doctor as a hostage."

"Check his wallet," the woman said. "He's likely got a couple grand in cash."

"Hand it over, Doc – but don't try anything."

Tre reached into his back pocket and silently handed it over.

The man flipped open the wallet, yanked out a wad of cash, and fanned it out to get a rough count. “Maybe seven hundred. Not great, but not bad,” he turned to tell his partner.

“Take his cards too,” she replied.

“Not worth the hassle. Too easy to track us when we use them.” The man turned his attention back to Tre. “Get out of the car. Keep your hands where I can see them when you get out – above your head.”

As Tre stepped out of the Fusion, the bank robber kept the gun trained on him. His kidnapper jumped out, bellowing more instructions.

“Put your hands on the roof!” The man holding the pistol hustled to stand in front of the car.

The woman had grabbed the bags out of the back seat and walked around to the trunk. “Anything in the trunk, Doc?”

“Nothing.”

“Not yet anyway,” the man laughed loudly. “Here,” and the man tossed Tre the pill bottle.

“Thanks,” Tre replied. “I could use one.”

“Not one, pal. All of them.”

Tre gulped. He unscrewed the top of the bottle and looked in. Rough count of eight left.

“They won’t kill you – not enough of them, I don’t figure,” the man said at Tre’s hesitation. “But you’re the doctor, I’m sure you know better than me.”

“I’m an oral surgeon.”

“Whatever. I’m sure you still know all that shit. Just take the damn pills!” Once again he waved the gun around.

Tre complied and swallowed them each individually. Seven, actually.

"Great. Now strip."

The woman giggled. "How about I put some music on the radio and have the good doctor do a slow strip for me?"

The man laughed. "Love to dear, but time's a-tickin'," and the man tapped his watch with his gun. "Go pop the trunk for me."

Tre stood on the old road, wearing nothing but what nature provided. Instinctively, he covered his crotch.

"Don't be shy, Doc." The woman teased him.

"I've got to agree with her this time," the man replied, almost reluctantly. "Hands in the air.

Tre slowly raised his hands above his head.

"Hello, Johnny!" the woman blurted out. "Has that thing been surgically altered by one of your doctor friends?" She motioned to the man. "Baby, did you see this?"

Her partner looked disturbed by her reaction.

"Mine's about the same," he stated, attempting to act nonchalant.

She smirked. "If you say so, baby. But his is limp right now."

"Whatever," he replied, his tone echoing his distaste in the topic. "It's how you use it that matters."

Under her breath she replied, "If you say so."

He popped the trunk release and lifted it open. Still upset with his partner, he scowled and barked another order at Tre. "Just get in there. Now!"

"Careful," the woman said to Tre. "Don't want to get that thing caught when we slam the trunk."

Tre stumbled as he tried to lift his leg. The pills had kicked in faster than he thought they would. He fell forward, banging his head on the side of the trunk. For a few seconds, Tre laid top end in the trunk, with his butt sticking up in the air.

"Shit! I think I'm gonna be sick," the man muttered.

"I'll take care of it." The woman stepped forward, with a bit of spring in her step. Lifting his left leg and flipping him over, Tre landed firmly in the trunk, with only his right foot sticking out.

The man leaned into the trunk and ripped out the trunk release.

"Gimme one of them empty bags."

She complied. The man took a few twenties from Tre's cash, stuffed it in one of the bank money bags, and tossed it in the trunk.

"Sweet dreams, Doc." He slammed the trunk. "Grab his clothes and bring them to the truck. But give me his wallet." He took the wallet and chucked it into a nearby bush.

"We just leaving him? Won't he suffocate?"

"He won't run out of air. Besides, he's our diversion."

22 Captured

A cold hand touched Tre's neck, sending a violent shiver down his spine. Impulsively, he grabbed for the hand. The hand pulled away.

"Freeze!"

Tre tried to open his eyes, to no avail. They resisted as if sewn shut. What the hell was going on now? And why was he so cold? He tried to lift his head. It fell right back down, hard, onto an unforgiving surface.

"I said freeze!"

"I am freezing! Where the hell am I?"

"Good try, but you're the one who's going to be answering questions, not me."

Tre recognized the tone of a police officer. And an unhappy one at that. *This waking up from a comatose state has got to stop.* Faced again with trying to recall where he was, it started to come back to him without the benefit of open eyes to get his bearings. He remembered seeing that idiot bank robber's stupid grin before the lid of the trunk shut him into darkness. Feeling exposed, he assumed the fetal position and covered his private parts.

"Can you give me my clothes? Or a blanket? Anything? Please?"

"Get out of the trunk first!"

"But I'm naked!"

"Good. It will be harder for you to conceal a weapon."

Tre pried open one eye with a finger. Lots of flashing police lights in the background, and two large figures looming in front of him. "Yes, officer." He wasn't actually sure how to get out of a trunk, having never done it. The mass of oxycodone he'd taken swept away any capability to rationalize. At first he stuck his left leg over the threshold. Realizing it hurt like hell and sensing a strong possibility that he would shred his penis on the trunk release, Tre fell back down to regroup. Suddenly nauseous, Tre slowed his breathing to avoid vomiting.

"I think I'm going to puke."

"I don't give a rat's ass," the officer coarsely replied. "Just get out of the car."

Tre's scrambled brain tried to focus, barely able to recall falling into the trunk, more or less, which he now attempted to re-enact in reverse. Backing his way out, he cupped his privates as he crouched then stepped out, ass sticking high in the air. He heard some disgusted groans from behind, but continued his exit. As his first foot hit the ground, he discovered the medication still held his balance hostage, and he fell, ass-over-tea kettle. More groans.

Then Tre puked.

"Someone throw something on this guy. I'm going to lose my lunch too if I have to look at that much more."

Wrapped in an emergency Mylar blanket within minutes, they stuffed Tre headfirst into the back of a police cruiser, headed away from his scene of vehicle imprisonment. He still could hardly keep his eyes open and the blanket closed, doing nothing for his modesty when sitting down. He passed out.

"Get out!"

Tre's eyes responded, attempting to penetrate the darkness of his still shuttered lids. He could have slept for ten hours for all he could tell, but assumed he'd only taken the short ride back to Elko. Shifting his weight to slide across the seat to get out, the silver emergency blanket inconveniently adhered to the cruiser's seat material, exposing his manly parts to an unexpected cool evening draft. He freed the blanket from the sticky grip of the car seat and modestly re-wrapped his midsection. Forcing his eyes open, the bright lights illuminating the vehicle alarmed Tre. An officer held the cruiser door open, ready to secure Tre into custody. He placed his bare right foot on asphalt, and hesitated to once again yank at the metallic blanket to re-secure coverage. Suddenly, he became aware of additional eyes on him. He heard a female voice corresponding with the officer waiting beside the car.

"Listening to the police band again, Molly?"

"Just trying to get a scoop, Tom."

"I know, you're trying to make a living. No bother to me, but" – and he looked over at the nearby door – "you better ask your questions fast, 'cause the ER guys will send you away in a heartbeat."

The reporter looked at the ER doors part and a team scurrying toward them. "Is that one of the Piggy Bank Robbers?"

"You better believe it. I'm sure this one will lead us to the other two."

"Can you tell us the culprit's name?"

"Molly, you know we can't release that to the press at this time. But we found him buck naked if you want to report that."

Tre reached across his body with his right arm, and pulled his aching left leg out to stand. As he did so, he stepped on a dangling corner of the metallic blanket and lost his balance. Tre crashed to the parking lot surface, head smacking on the hard black pavement. The lights went out. Again.

Tre sensed relief to wake up and not see jail cell bars. Instead, blinding white everything greeted him. Partially sitting up, his reflexes forced him back down quickly as pain ripped through his abdomen. He grabbed at the hospital gown, which in some ways he liked less than a jail jumpsuit due to the drafts and dangling participles. He must have slept a long time, the effects of the oxycodone gone from his once again clear mind.

"Brightman. Good to see you've re-joined the living, you miserable piece of scum!" A guard reacted to Tre's upright posture.

"What happened to me?"

"I wish I could say I beat the crap out of you," the guard smiled. "But you had your stomach pumped to get all that Oxy out of you."

"Oh..."

"Take a piss now if you're going to need one in the next ten hours. I've got to haul you back to the station. I'm sure the detectives have lots of questions for your sorry ass."

Tre stood up wincing and heeded the advice. Part way to the bathroom, the guard tossed something to him. Tre reached out to catch it, exposing his backside to the world as his gown opened with his movement. The object unfurled in mid-air – a colourful jumpsuit.

"Move it, Brightman! Haven't got all day."

At the Elko station, they led Tre into a room for questioning. At least he didn't have to sit in a cell again, at least not yet. Two detectives walked in the room.

"Oh, shit," Tre whispered.

"What's that, Brightman?"

Tre looked at the detective. It was the dufus detective from the Sacramento police department."I said nice to see you again."

"Wasn't me, stupid. It was my twin brother in Sacramento. He's told me all about you, Dumbman." The detective grabbed the metal chair in front of him and spun it around backwards. He put his left foot on it and leaned over to put his elbow on his elevated knee, trying to strike an imposing figure. Sadly for the detective, his foot had landed half onto the seat of the chair and upon shifting his weight, the chair flew out from under him, spilling his large frame onto the floor.

His partner laughed. Tre refrained with all his might.

The detective bounced up, pride injured but temper intact. "I bet you want to know how we know who you are?"

"I assume you found my wallet …"

"Listen! Keep your mouth shut and just let me think you're stupid. Or do you want to open it, and confirm it?"

"I …"

"Shut up until I ask you to talk!"

"You keep asking me questions," Tre replied.

"They were rhetorical questions, you freakin' idiot. And you know how I know you're a freakin' idiot? And that's another rhetorical question. We know because who uses a car rented in their own name as a getaway car at a bank robbery?"

"Two bank robberies," the other detective chimed in.

"Yeah, two bank robberies. What kind of idiot uses a rental car in their own name to rob two banks?"

"A big idiot I suppose."

"So you admit it!"

"I don't admit anything. I agree that an idiot would use a rental car in their own name to rob a bank."

"Two banks," the other detective repeated.

Tre smirked. "Two banks. But I didn't rob any banks, that's why the car is rented in my name."

"Good try, but we found you naked…"

The other detective chuckled.

"We found you naked without your clothes on in the trunk of your getaway car."

"Good thing you didn't find me naked with my clothes on."

"What? Never mind. You were found in the getaway car."

"They forced me at gunpoint to drive them."

"They forced you at gunpoint to drive a getaway car at two bank robberies. Sounds lame."

"One bank robbery. I drove the getaway car at one bank robbery."

"So you admit it!"

"At gunpoint. I drove the getaway car at gunpoint, yes."

"Good try. Here's how I see it went down." He smacked down his clipboard on the metal desk. "Your killer girlfriend from Sacramento was holed up in West Wendover."

"Who?"

"Your girlfriend," the detective paused to flip over a few pages on his clipboard. "Meagan Winters, your girlfriend."

"What are you talking about?"

"The female suspect. Five seven, brunette, one hundred-and-twenty to one hundred-and-thirty pounds, shoulder length brown hair. Sound familiar?"

Tre thought about his female abductor. He supposed her build was similar to Meagan when he saw her the other day. Shoulder length brown hair too. It wasn't too big a reach.

"It wasn't her."

The detective turned to his partner. "I told you he'd say that, didn't I? They always protect the woman, even after drugged and stuffed in a trunk naked." He turned his attention back to Tre. "Where was I? Oh, yeah. You get out of jail in Sacramento because your high priced lawyer buys your way out of my brother's airtight case against you."

Tre smiled, but quickly wiped it away to avoid antagonizing the detective.

Pacing, the detective continued his tale. "In West Wendover you rob the bank there, just after the local casino deposit. Your lady friend staked it out the day before to maximize the haul. Her and the as-yet-unidentified third suspect enter the bank wearing pig masks."

"Get it, Piggy Bank Robbers," the other detective noted.

"You're waiting around the corner in your black Fusion, and swoop in to pick them up as they exit the bank with their payload. Then your gang has the balls to do it again here in Elko." He stopped to pick up his clipboard "Sound about right, Brightman?"

"Sounds all wrong to me," Tre replied.

"And we have lots of evidence," the other detective said. "We matched your licence plate to the getaway car on the bank's exterior camera footage."

"I told you, they held a gun to me and made me drive them."

"Liar! We can't see that in any of the footage."

"And we found a brochure to the hotel in West Wendover in your car."

"Planted, obviously. I've never been to West Wendover."

"Again with the lies! Then explain why there was a bag of money in the trunk of the getaway car with you? A bag from the bank you robbed in Elko. Your cut I imagine."

"Planted, obviously. Let me guess, there was about a hundred bucks in the bag?"

"Yeah, but you would have known that."

"And how much did they get away with from the bank?"

"Two banks," the other detective reminded them both. "About two hundred thousand from West Wendover and eighty thousand from Elko."

"And my cut is a hundred bucks?"

"That's why they shoved you in the trunk – because you complained about your cut."

"You are definitely related to your brother."

The detective smiled at first, then thought about it.

Tre leaned back in his chair. "Can I have my phone call now?"

"You better call your lawyer. This is what they call airtight."

"Twenty minutes," Tre replied

"What do you mean, twenty minutes?"

"Twenty minutes after my lawyer shows up, I'm out of here. Then maybe you can focus on catching the people who robbed the bank."

"Two banks," the other detective re-iterated.

"Two banks," Tre chuckled.

23 Lawyered Up

Jack peered out the porthole window in the regional jet that brought him to Reno from his home base in LA. A sunny day in "The Biggest Little City in the World." Two flights north for the private detective in a three day span. Not a habit worth forming, although his return flight from Sacramento was eventful, meeting Paula. He'd had the pleasure of rendezvousing with the eternal optimist for lunch yesterday. He felt a good vibe with her so far. She was fun to hang with, and somehow she made him feel like a better man when around her. So he had reason to feel somewhat ticked off at Tre for causing a cancelled dinner date. But it paid the bills.

Walking through the small airport, Jack thought about Tre's mystery stalker. Jack could tell his brother's mind was distracted lately, even if nothing was said. He knew his brother. But he'd never known John to find only a modicum of information in the amount of time they'd had the case. Little nuggets here and there; no concrete leads to hunt down. A few insignificant insights into Tre's background, but nothing useful for the case, or even dirt that he could use as trash talk playing hoops.

Jack had lived in Sacramento much of his life, but had never heard of Elko, Nevada. He had to look it up on the map to know which airport to fly into. He could have saved a few bucks flying into Sacramento and doing the extra drive, but Tre was paying, so what the hell. Besides, the airfare paled in comparison to what Tre would dish out for Maury's return engagement as legal advisor. Jack looked at his watch. Forty-five minutes before Maury's plane landed. Enough time to grab a beverage enroute to securing the rental car.

With Maury in tow, Jack guided the rented Escalade (again, Tre was paying) toward Elko and their encounter at the local jail. Getting Tre out this time would prove trickier and take more than showing receipts, Maury explained, but still very achievable.

"Man, am I glad to see you!" Tre stood up, his right arm up prepared to embrace his friend. His damaged left arm remained handcuffed to the steel interrogation desk.

"Hey, this ain't no conjugal visit," Jack replied. "We've got to quit meeting like this, though."

"I didn't do anything … "

"And now you are going to keep nice and quiet, Mr. Brightman," Maury abruptly cut in. He turned to the police detective leaning up against the side wall. "I'd appreciate some privacy with my client now," and he motioned with his head for the man to take his leave.

It took Tre about thirty minutes to recall the events from the time he dropped Jack off at the airport, up to the most recent interrogation.

"Two banks you say." Maury circled the two towns in his notes. The lawyer reached for his phone and pulled up a mapping application.

"There's no way Tre had the time to get to West Wendover and back, based on the times he gave us," Jack said, defensive of his friend.

"Can't use that tactic. No way of saying exactly when Tre arrived or left anywhere. Not to say we couldn't eventually prove it, but that's too hard and would likely mean a court date and witnesses."

"So what, then?"

"Let's see … first, you'd have had to travel from Sacramento airport to West Wendover." He typed in the start and destination. "About 535 miles. Then back to Elko." Maury's digits plucked away. "Another 108 miles or so. That would put your trip at about 643 miles minimum."

A light went on for Jack. "I get it now. The odometer of the car. Brilliant, Maury!"

"I must be still groggy, because I don't get it," Tre apologized.

"Your car is a rental. They record the mileage when you leave the airport."

Maury continued, wanting to take credit for his thought. "So I bet your car has no more than about 450 miles on it, including your kidnapping after the second bank robbery."

"The police will have impounded your car, and had it towed here."

Maury motioned to the detective standing outside the room and followed him out to discuss the release of his client. Jack stayed with Tre.

"What's it feel like to have your stomach pumped? Always wondered," Jack asked.

"I don't recommend it, although I don't remember a thing. Just have the wrenching abdomen as a souvenir. Sorry to make you travel all the way up here for this."

"No problem, man. What are friends for?"

"Does that mean you're not charging me then?" Tre quipped.

Jack grinned. "I'd love to do it gratis for you, but you know John. He does the books and makes me give him receipts for everything. He says I need to bill every possible hour of my time."

"Wish I had a twin to blame things on," Tre mused.

"No you don't. You'd still be in jail in Sacramento if you did. That detective would have concocted some story of your twin doing the killing for you, so you'd have an alibi."

"You're right about that. His brother fell from the same tree."

"And they both hit their heads on a rock when they landed. They're both bright like an Amish light bulb."

Tre laughed, then winced at the reminder of his recent stomach flushing.

"You're a wreck, Tre." Jack glanced up as a shadow filled the frosted glass door. "I've seen cars come out of a demolition derby looking better than you do. And I'm talking about the losers!"

Maury waited for the officer standing guard to open the door. The lawyer smiled as he entered, which the friends took as a good sign. "You are free to go, Mr. Brightman. I've told them that if they get their obnoxious detective to apologize to you, that you would gladly sit down with their sketch artist so they had some real clues to chase down."

"Thanks, Maury. I owe you, again."

"Mr. Brightman, can I make a suggestion?"

"Sure."

"I'm not sure what the purpose of your trip is, but I understand it to be some kind of crusade you've undertaken."

"It's …"

Maury raised his hand and cut Tre off. "You've mistaken me for someone who cares."

A snort blurted out from Jack, before he covered his nose and mouth. Maury gave Jack a quick look of disapproval then continued. "I don't care if you are out to save the world. And I'm not a doctor, so don't presume this is medical advice. What I do suggest, is that you go home, recover for a while, pay my bill, and then, and only then, if you think your mission is that critical to your well-being, resume it by all means."

The lawyer slid his notebook into his satchel, closed it, and reached out his hand to shake with Tre. "While I always welcome your business, I'd appreciate not hearing from you for a few weeks."

"Thank you," Tre replied. "I'll try to stay out of trouble." He felt back in sixth grade talking to his minister.

"And Jack," Maury said, turning away from Tre. "Why don't you make sure our dentist friend makes it home safely?"

24 Breakdown (Go ahead and give it to me)

Tre's armour was cracked, and Jack almost convinced the dentist to ride back with them to Reno for a flight back to LA, following the advice of Maury. Almost. Tre relented for about fifteen seconds, before he reminded Jack that they each had a rental car and Elko had no rental car drop-off. Besides, Tre would delay Jack and Maury while he worked with the sketch artist, and that would translate into Jack missing the night's last flight out of Reno. Aware that Paula was leaving LA the next afternoon for her home in Sacramento, Jack knew a delay like that would mean he'd miss her altogether.

Watching Maury and Jack exit the police station gave Tre a sense of relief. Despite Maury's recommendation, and Jack's offer, there was no way Tre was giving up on his journey of amends. Going back to LA would mean starting all over again, especially from a mental perspective. He wasn't sure his resolve would persist if he took a time out. His body may appear broken, but his resolve was not.

Waiting for the sketch artist, Tre stepped outside and called for a refill on his Oxy script. After the literally gut-wrenching experience, there was reluctance to get back on board the Oxy train, but the aches from his subsequent adventures compounded the crash pain. He needed medicine stronger than off-the-shelf pain reliever.

Two hours later, the completed sketches looked pretty good to Tre. Quite reasonable resemblances. There was no point driving on tonight, as day had given way to night. He'd get a good sleep, pick up a refill for his prescription, and head east after sun-up.

The morning sky was bright and cloudless. Tre would have battled the blaze of the rising sun piercing the horizon had he arisen and began driving at the planned time. Instead, his still tired eyes would view a more forgiving mid-morning sun. He'd slept more in the past few days than he could remember, but still felt spent. A nervous chill shook Tre as he approached his car sandwiched between two all too familiar black SUVs. He looked around the lot to see three more black SUVs of various shapes and sizes. He told himself it was his imagination trying to best him – or was it his conscience? Regardless, he strapped himself in and backed the car out. He didn't notice the young lady waving him down.

In less than an hour, Tre had refilled his prescription (and taken one), and had covered a good thirty miles of eastward bound interstate. With the radio cranked up to a great new tune, it surprised him that he even heard the gurgling sound in advance of the engine cutting out. The car began to coast energy-less in his hands.

"Shit!" Tre screamed as he pounded his palms on the wheel. Looking around, he guided the powerless vehicle onto the shoulder. A car whizzed by with blaring horn, upset with Tre's maneuver.

Frustrated by the dead vehicle, Tre flopped his head back hard against the headrest. A couple of transport trucks rumbled by close, vibrating the frame of his car. In frustration, he again pounded his hands on the wheel, this time without any expletives.

Before he could get out and assess the problem, or attempt to flag down help, a black SUV pulled up behind him. Tre hoped it was help. He sat up to see clearly out the rear-view mirror and let out a sigh of relief seeing a woman behind the wheel. She flipped up her sunglasses and hopped down from her lofty perch. He moved his gaze from the rear-view mirror to the side mirror and noticed her shapely legs below the cut of the SUV's black door. As she walked closer, he looked up.

"Katie?" he said out loud as he opened the door to greet her.

"It's me! In person." She did a little pirouette that twirled her sundress around and upward, revealing more of her glistening legs.

"What are you doing here?"

"In a bit. What's wrong with your car?"

Tre looked her over, still puzzled by her presence. "Not sure. Just happened and haven't even taken a look yet."

"Do you know anything about cars?" Katie asked him.

"No."

She laughed. "So what do you expect you'll find?"

"Don't know. Just seems like the guy thing to do." He looked at Katie. "What about you? Know anything about cars?"

"Not really. I know how to call AAA."

"It's a rental."

"Okay, we'll call the rental company. Tell them where to pick it up."

Tre continued to stare with disbelief that she stood in front of him. "So?"

"So why am I here?"

"And how did you know where I was?"

"Why don't you get in and I'll give you a lift?"

"To Michigan?"

"If you'd like. I am on paid leave," she said smiling and revealing a dimple.

"All right. I'll take a lift." He saw disappointment in her eyes. "I mean, I'd love a lift, thank you."

She smiled.

"But not to Michigan," he told her, "only to West Wendover so I can get another car."

In her moving SUV, he asked her again. "So what are you doing here?"

"I came for you."

He'd assumed as much. Somebody once said there are no such things as coincidences, a theory Tre prescribed to.

"I tried waving you down at the hotel and again at the pharmacy, but I guess you didn't see me."

"I don't understand why you are here. I thought you and Jamie were getting married."

"Jimmy. Yes he asked me, and yes I accepted."

"But?" Tre asked.

"But then I said no. I didn't mean to hurt the guy, but I felt pressured to say yes. Remember I told you that last day in the office that he'd asked me? Well that night he takes me out to dinner and surprises me with my parents and his parents there, as well as a few of his siblings and their kids. I'm thinking the whole meal that he's going to say something about it, but he doesn't. Then dessert comes and the prick has them deliver a strawberry cheesecake with a big diamond on the top. How could I say no?"

"He really put you on the spot."

"Exactly. The kids thing was downright low."

"How so?"

"My parents don't have any grandkids and my sister told them last month that she's gay. I'm their only hope."

"Maybe she and her partner will get a sperm donor, or adopt."

"Doubt it. My sister once described kids as Satan's little toys. So it's me or nothing."

"I see what you mean."

Silence ruled for a few miles.

"So *what* are you doing here?" Tre repeated, beginning to get a bit restless at the thought of her tracking him down.

Katie blushed and nervously tugged her dress up, so much so that it revealed she wasn't wearing granny panties.

"I came looking for you."

He understood that part.

Anxious, she rubbed her hands on the steering wheel, clenching it to the point where if it had a pulse, it'd begin to fade. She started to speak but nothing came out. Tre looked intently at her lips as they tried to find words. Suddenly, and very loudly, she blurted out, "I came looking for you to profess my love. I want to be with you." She let out a large sigh and released her death grip from the wheel.

Tre felt uneasy, and somewhat alarmed at the lengths she had gone to, but had no reply to her admission. What could he say to that? He went with a change of subject, which was the prior subject. "But how did you find me?"

"Deanna told me where you were."

John's wife, of course. She and Katie were close friends. Tre felt relief knowing she hadn't put a tracking device on his car or hired a private eye to follow him. Technically though, a private eye followed his every move. "Makes sense," he replied.

"So what do you think?" she asked him.

"About what?"

She began to cry. "I just professed my love for you, that's what!"

He didn't know what to say. "Thank you."

"THANK YOU?" Once more she gripped the steering wheel tightly, like she was trying to wring the last drop of water out of a wet rag. She swerved into the passing lane and zipped past a minivan full of family. "Typical guy answer. How about a few words that tell me how you feel?" Tears welled up above her reddened cheeks.

Tre tensed. He had had this discussion on occasion with other women, but such proclamations from a woman typically took place in bed. He would sweet talk his way out of the discussion, saying non-committal words like 'Baby, you know how I feel', or have sex again hoping she'd forget to bring it up again. Or he'd find a way to leave.

He'd always managed to avoid giving an answer with any feelings attached. Then again, he'd never had this discussion captive in a moving vehicle. A vehicle moving very quickly and erratically. He looked at the speedometer. She'd pushed it up to one hundred miles per hour and the needle continued to move to the right.

"Maybe we should slow down," Tre cautioned, trying to keep calm but betrayed by his tightly clenched hands.

She took it another way. Her crying continued, but changed. The anger had disappeared from her face and a look of pity replaced it.

"I am so sorry, Tre. That wasn't very sensitive of me. It's too soon."

Tre firmly believed he would never, ever, understand the emotions of women. He listened to her metamorphosis continue. At least the vehicle slowed, marginally.

"I know you don't want to admit it, but I can tell you were in love with Cassy. It doesn't surprise me. She was so different from all the women you constantly, and I mean constantly, banged. And I know she had a secret crush on you. She confessed to me one night after too many watermelon martinis. We both thought you'd give up on your wild ways eventually and want to settle down with a girl like one of us."

Tre could see how Katie could think of herself as the kind of girl to settle down with, at least compared to the Hollywood clientele of his practice. He listened, knowing better than to interrupt a woman in full ramble.

"Did you know that I came up to visit you in the hospital?" She glanced over and could see he didn't. "Three times, I sat by your bedside. Even snuck out one time when Jimmy had stayed over at my place. I read to you for two hours each time. They say it sparks brain activity of coma victims to hear familiar voices. Although you weren't technically in a coma, you were completely out of it. Except the last night. That's when I knew you'd be okay."

Tre waited for her to finish her thought, but after a long pause, he asked, "What happened that last night?" Tre peeked at the speedometer, relieved it had continued to slow to the point it returned to an acceptable level of speeding.

"You must have been reliving the accident. Has that happened since?"

Tre took a deep breath. "Only when I close my eyes."

Katie reached across the console and held his hand briefly before returning her grasp to the wheel. "It started with restless twitching. I thought you were waking up until I saw your eyelids flitting like hummingbirds. Suddenly, you lurched forward," and she violently threw her hands up from the wheel. "You were frantic, grasping at the air," and she mimicked the motion, "and you called out Cassy's name, over and over again."

Tre looked down at his feet, trying not to close his eyes and see the scene in his mind. "And then I woke up," he replied.

"Not that time," Katie said, surprising Tre.

"What do you mean?"

"You yelled out one more thing."

Tre waited.

"You were sitting up, both hands stretched out a far as possible, and said 'I love you, Cassy'."

Tre slumped back in the car seat. He'd never remembered that part. Why? Surely Katie wouldn't make it up after confessing her own love for him. He'd only told one woman that he loved her, besides his mother and some other female relatives. And that other woman was long ago and far away, until a few days ago.

Katie sat quiet for a few minutes, taking a sip from a bottle of water.

"I guess what I'm trying to say, is that I know you aren't a lifelong playboy, and I think you're closer to settling down than you know. I think you're ready but you're not willing to admit it to yourself."

Tre mumbled to himself, "If you think so," though contemplating what she'd said.

"What'd you say?"

"Maybe you're right."

"And I know there's more to you than playboy, dentist, and sometimes ruthless business man."

Tre smiled about the last part.

"I know there's more because I've seen firsthand." She looked him in the eyes. "I never told you why I so desperately wanted to work for you, did I?"

Tre shrugged. He didn't know she had.

"My brother was a very smart kid. Too smart for his own good at times. He managed to stay out of trouble most of his high school years, but his senior year he started to get recruited by a local gang. He had excellent grades all through school, but my parents had no money. They'd used my father's small inheritance to put me through community college and had nothing left for my brother. He didn't know what he wanted to do after graduating, so the lure of gang money was attractive."

"I never knew you came from a poor family," Tre commented.

Katie got defensive and raised her voice a notch. "We weren't poor. My parents provided for us. They just couldn't save money no matter how many jobs they worked."

"I didn't mean anything by it. Sorry. What about your brother?"

"As I said, he was smart. I felt guilty about there not being any money left for his tuition, so I looked into other ways to get him into college. I applied to every scholarship that I could find for him. Month after month, I watched as he was bypassed or turned down by each of them. Then one day, we got a call. He'd received a full scholarship to the local college."

"That's great."

"You couldn't imagine my relief! We were so proud when he was presented with it at school by the Santa Monica Young Leaders."

Tre blushed. The fund that he'd set up.

"You don't remember me from that day, do you?"

"No, sorry. I was nervous about being there. I wanted the whole thing to remain anonymous and didn't want to present the award in person."

"Humble is a side you don't show very often." She smiled. "I like it though."

He thought about her coming to work for him as a result of the scholarship. Was she stalking him even back then?

"So I wanted to work for you because I figured anyone behind such a thing had to be a good guy to work for. And trust me; most dentists are not very good bosses."

"Well I'm glad you like your job." Tre looked out the window and wondered how much further to West Wendover.

"I've loved it. At least most of the time. It was hard watching you flirt with most of your patients, not to mention knowing you were screwing half of them."

Tre cleared his throat and took a drink.

"And after we finally had sex together." She took a deep breath then bit her lip. "I mean it was the best I'd ever had, and still is. It felt exciting and dangerous. I didn't know what erotic meant until we hooked up." She squirmed in her seat as she recalled the experiences. "Your touch. Your tongue. Your breath on my skin." She closed her eyes briefly. "The things we did together. I'd never. I've never since."

He watched her expressions carefully. Her eyes lit up as she talked about their times together. Katie's body language said more than her words. He'd definitely left an impression. It turned him on listening to her and watching her movements. He'd gone a long time without sex. A very long time by his standards. Tre was tempted to tell her to pull over and ravage her, but found the willpower to resist. He lifted his bottle to take another drink and cool off, but he'd finished it. He tried to think other thoughts.

"So where are we?" he said.

"Oh," she said, lost in her steamy thoughts. She looked at the mileage marker go by. "I think about forty minutes out of West

Wendover. You know, I think I'll pull over for gas up here, before we get into town."

25 Down the Road

Stopping her car in front of the pump, Katie shut off the ignition. Tre opened his door.

"What are you doing?" she asked him, sounding like she feared he was going to run away.

"Getting out to pump the gas. The least I can do for your trouble is to buy you a tank of gas."

Katie grinned. "Thank you. I'm used to pumping my own gas. Jimmy doesn't even offer to pump, let alone pay."

"Do you mind running in and getting me a Gatorade?" Tre smiled as he asked her.

"Not at all. I need a water myself. What flavour?"

"Surprise me," he replied with a smile.

She'd surprise him all right. Katie walked into the small store and looked around. She grabbed a litre bottle of water and a grape Gatorade. After paying for the drinks, she slipped into the washroom. Placing the bottles on the counter, she fumbled through her purse and pulled out a bottle of sleeping pills. She took a gulp of Tre's drink, then dropped three pills into it and watched as they sank to the bottom. She watched them sit there, slowly dissolving. *Shit – this will take forever.* Katie violently shook the bottle and the little buggers began to melt away. Fixated momentarily by the dissipating fizz, she snapped out of it and thought about Tre's weight. She wanted to be sure. She slipped two more pills into the beverage and repeated the shakeup. Exiting the washroom, she almost bumped into Tre.

"Just paid for the gas. I'll be out in a minute," and he pointed to the men's washroom.

"See you at the car," Katie replied, short of breath from almost being caught in her act of treachery. In the driver's seat again, she opened the rental agreement that Tre had held. She called the rental company, explained what happened to the car, and where it was left. She made arrangements for a replacement car in West Wendover.

"Can I borrow your phone?" Tre asked as he returned. "I foolishly didn't bring mine on the trip."

"I can't image life without my phone!" She held it up like it was the Holy Grail. "I'd feel so disconnected from the world." She looked at Tre, who shrugged his shoulders. "Oh, I get it. That was the idea."She slid her phone back in her purse. "No need. I just called the car rental company and everything's set."

"Efficient as always," he said. "Thanks for the drink." He grabbed the bottle and noticed it had been opened.

"Hope you don't mind. I had a couple of sips. Sometimes I get tired of water and need a little sugar. Besides, we've shared bodily fluids before."

A glimpse of a smiled passed over his lips. "Sure. No problem."

Pulling back onto the interstate, Katie struck up more conversation.

"So what's it like, being with all those movie stars? Is it glamourous?"

Tre welcomed a change of conversation from Katie talking about sex, an oddity for him. "It's often more tedious than glamourous. A lot of waiting. And nobody's there to see me or grab a quote from me. I mean, it's cool to see these famous people all decked up and rub elbows with Brad and Angelina. But for me the novelty wore off pretty quickly."

"But you and Marla were pretty serious for a while, weren't you."

"Definitely hot and heavy for a while. Not long after she became famous, she moved on. I can't say that I blame her. In Hollywood you have to grab your fifteen minutes and try to hold onto them as long as you can. And dating a dentist wasn't good for her career path."

"Maxillofacial surgeon."

Tre smiled, but it morphed into a yawn before he could take a drink. As the yawn passed, he gulped down several more ounces of his sports beverage. "Excuse me. I took an Oxy back at the gas station and it's making me sleepy."

Katie looked at him and grinned, hoping the combination of his self-medicating and her help wouldn't kill him. "That's okay. I'll wake you when we get to West Wendover if you've nodded off."

"Thanks." He looked at the prescription bottle, moving it around trying to focus on the label. "Maybe this is a stronger dosage than I had last time," he said, the bottle falling from his fingers. His eyes rolled back in his head, and his head fell to his chest.

"Tre?" Katie placed her hand under his nose, checking for breathing. She was relieved to feel him exhale, knowing she hadn't killed him. Yet.

Katie drove into the hotel parking lot, pulling up under the canopy for arriving guests. She flipped down the visor, opened the mirror, and spread on a fresh coating of luxurious red lipstick. She puckered and wiped a small smudge from the corner. She checked Tre's breathing one more time, and shook him to confirm he was good and out. She pulled his wallet out of his pocket.

"I'm going to get us a nice suite, sweetie." She planted a gentle kiss on his cheek before heading to the lobby, leaving a trace of red but careful not to smear her handiwork. Katie pointed the mirror down and adjusted her breasts in her bra. Closing the mirror and pushing the visor back out of the way, she was ready.

"Checking in, Miss?"

"Yes. And it's Mrs." She smiled to show off the pearly whites between her brilliant red lips. "Mrs. Tre Brightman."

"And what type of room would you like, Mrs. Brightman?" He looked her over, quite pleased with the view.

"Do you have any suites available?"

"We do indeed. We have a very nice suite on our top floor. Do you have AAA?"

"I do, but it's under my maiden name. Just haven't had time to change it yet."

"That's fine. We get a lot of newlyweds on their way back from Reno." He reached across and took the card from her. "With the discount, the room will be $549 per night, plus taxes of course."

"That will do just fine, thank you."

"How many nights, Mrs. Brightman?"

"You better put us down for two nights. Mr. Brightman is recovering from surgery, and he needs a few days to get his strength up again."

He looked her over again, betting that her husband would need all the strength he could muster.

"Very well." He punched some info into his computer then swiped two key cards through a coding machine. "Two keys, I assume?"

"Yes, thank you."

He slid a paper across the counter. "If you could sign by the x's and initial in the circles. And how will you be paying, Miss?"

"Mrs.," she said smiling. "With a credit card." Katie placed the card in front of him.

As she leaned forward to sign the paper, he admired her cleavage. He swiped her credit card and returned it to her.

"Is there anything else I can help you with today?"

"As a matter of fact, you look like a big strong guy." She looked him over in a way that she knew he'd like. "My husband is medicated in the car from his surgery, and I could really use some strong arms to help get him up to the room."

"I'd be glad to help. Do you have much luggage?"

"Just a few bags."

"First I'll roll the courtesy wheelchair out to the car for Mr. Brightman. Then I'll make another trip to fetch a bellman's cart for your bags. Just give me a second."

"Thank you for hospitality. I'll meet you at the car." She knew he'd be watching her every move toward the front door, so she slowed her walk, her hips swaying seductively.

Five minutes later, the clerk opened Katie's hotel room door so she could guide the wheelchair carrying Tre across the threshold.

"Very nice," Katie told the man as she eyeballed the room accoutrements upon entry.

He followed her with the bellman's cart. Unloading the few bags, he pulled the cart back toward the door. "If that's everything, Mrs. Brightman, I'll be going."

"Katie," she replied. "You can call me Katie." She bent down to lock the wheelchair from rolling, her breasts strategically heaving through the act. "I know it's a lot to ask," she started, pausing to twirl a lock of hair with her fingers, "but could you possibly help me lift Mr. Brightman onto the bed? Please?"

He was a sucker for a pretty face. And a heaving chest.

"Sure, Mrs. Brightman."

"Katie," she replied with a smile.

It took a profound effort from the clerk that at times resembled a slapstick movie, to get Tre's much larger frame out of the wheelchair. Barely keeping Tre from collapsing on top of him, the desk clerk heaved a huge sigh of relief as he watched the deadweight fall onto the bed. Haphazardly flopped onto one corner of the bed, Tre appeared ready to slide onto the floor at any second. Katie grabbed one of her companion's legs and flopped it over the other to secure his position for the time being. The clerk was doubled over sucking wind, but still had the wherewithal to check out Katie's ass as she walked over to the nearby desk to pick up her purse. Katie opened her bag to find a tip for the profusely sweating man but he refused, content with the views he'd enjoyed and intoxicated by the proximity of her perfumed form.

With the desk clerk gone, Katie wasted little time. She was fairly confident that Tre would remain unconscious for at least a few more hours, but didn't want to risk it. She didn't want him waking up until everything was ready. Hoisting her small but overweight suitcase onto the luggage rack, she unzipped the outer compartment and pulled out four lengths of rope. First she tied a very firm knot around his right wrist before securing the other end of the rope to the bed post. She climbed over his limp frame to tie up the other wrist. His body needed adjustment to fasten the second arm in a likewise fashion to the bed. She knelt down on the bed and, arms around his waist, lifted him for a second and a few inches at a time toward the centre of the bed. The effort it took made up for her lack of a workout today. Satisfied that Tre lay close enough to the midpoint of the mattress, she pulled his left arm back and tightly bound it, eliciting a small unconscious groan from him. Sitting down on the bed to catch her breath, Katie looked over her knots. She let out a deep sigh upon realization that she'd forgotten to take his shirt off. Patiently she unbuttoned his shirt, admiring his chest as it became exposed in front of her. She contemplated whether to leave it that way or cut it off him. She'd decide later. For now, she wanted to get his legs tied down. She unzipped Tre's pants and pulled them and his boxers down without even the slightest movement from him. She soon had both ankles bound.

Having forgotten to do it earlier, Katie drew the curtains closed, then re-opened them on one side upon realizing nobody had a line of sight into their room from there. She unpacked both of their bags, then stripped herself and neatly folded her clothes, placing them on the ottoman in the sitting area. She turned the thermostat up a few degrees as Tre lay on top of the covers, and lay down naked beside him. She pressed herself up against him and lay with her head on his chest for a good half hour. She talked to him the entire time about her dreams and aspirations. He remained knocked out. Katie began caressing his privates and happily got a positive response. She looked intently at his face, but still no response from the neck up. She continued to stroke him to get his flag flying full. Katie carefully straddled him and closed her eyes to savour the moment. Every few minutes she opened her eyes to see if he had awakened, although she expected he'd say something if he had. She had re-entered heaven with the man she loved. She wrenched back and forth until she could feel he'd climaxed. She collapsed forward onto his chest, holding him. Everything was going to be great!

26 Waking Up

Tre was not immune to erotic dreams, especially when he hadn't had sex over a prolonged period. And waking up with an erection was a daily occurrence, whether he'd been active or not the night before. His dreams were not of women he knew, just a beautiful face or images of magnificent curves. That's why today seemed so peculiar. Today he dreamt Katie was having sex with him.

Overcome by brightness as his eyes fluttered open, he could see, and feel, a woman's hand and head going up and down on him, but he could only make out a silhouette. After all the experiences he'd had lately, had he finally died and gone to heaven? He lowered his eyelids and tried to clear his head, which was difficult with the other sensations he felt. Rationalizing the situation, he wondered if his actions over the past five years justified a place in heaven. God is supposed to be all forgiving if you have a place in your heart for Him. But Tre wasn't sure he'd made that place more than the size of a pinhead. Surely Tre wasn't in heaven.

The brilliance of the light subsided substantially as he opened his eyes again. The woman had blocked the light as she sat up and guided him into her. Long brown hair covered her face. Curious as to her identity, he went to reach up to brush back her flowing mane. That was when he realized his predicament. Rolling his head right, he saw his hand bound to the bed. Quickly and frantically looking left, the same visual greeted him. He tugged to test the strength of the knots. They weren't going to come undone without help and, if anything, his struggling made them tighter. Realizing he lay spread-eagle, Tre knew his feet were secured as well. The woman flipped back her head as she began to gyrate above him. It was indeed Katie. *Now what to do?* His next move was limited, seeing that he couldn't move.

She repositioned herself above him, leaning forward on both palms. Her soft, sweet smelling hair draped over Tre's face. She noticed he had awakened.

Panting, she spoke. "Good morning, darling." She planted a kiss on his cheek and sat up again. He couldn't help but admire her sleek body. She didn't lose a beat, and he knew he was close.

He grunted slightly, debating if he should resist finishing or just let it happen and get it over with. She wasn't going to stop until she was satisfied or he was done, so he let go. It felt good, but didn't feel like a few weeks' worth of pent-up semen. She quickly rolled off him and came to rest beside him.

"I love you sooo much," she spoke softly as she rested her head and hand on his chest.

Tre avoided his usual answer of 'thanks'. "Well, that was different. When we were together you never mentioned you were into bondage."

"I'm not really. But it was kind of fun. I'm glad you woke up this time."

"This time?"

"You weren't awake either time yesterday. I was pleasantly surprised that you responded so mightily, especially the first time. Talk about a gusher!"

That explained one thing anyway. "So why …"

Katie put a finger over his lips. "I'm going to have a shower, and then I'll come back and clean you up."

"You're going to leave me like this? I mean, you've had your fun."

"You're right. I'm not being considerate." She walked over to the door, lifted the 'do not disturb' placard off the handle, opened the door slightly, and slid it on the outside handle. Turning back to him, she grabbed the bed throw and gently laid it across his mid-section. "There. I'll be right back."

Tre thought of protesting, but figured it pointless. Something must have snapped in his assistant's mind. How could he convince her to let him go? He looked over at his knots again. He rotated his wrist to see if he could somehow get a hold of one of the ends of the rope. His work required nimble fingers, but he had no success. He repeated his attempt on his left wrist to the same result, plus some pain. If he were a sloth, perhaps he could have freed his ankles by manipulating his toes. In frustration, he pulled at all four corners at once, bouncing on the bed. That only proved to serve as a reminder that he hadn't recovered from his rib and other injuries. In desperation, he looked at the night tables for a pen or anything that might be used to leverage an escape from his binds. Nothing.

Lying there, he wondered what could have driven Katie to subject him to this. From the car ride, before he passed out from whatever she'd put in his drink, he knew she held onto a hope of them becoming a real couple. He hadn't been with her in what, a year or more? And she had dated or lived with Johnny, or whatever his name was, for at least the last six months. The guy even proposed to her. How big was the candle that she still held for him? Obviously very big, based on her actions the past twenty-four hours.

The shower stopped running and Tre could hear Katie singing and humming as she towelled off. How could he get out of this situation? Screaming and hollering would prove fruitless. He could tell she'd put them up in a very large suite. The bedroom had windows on two sides with the curtains open full on the wall directly in front of the bed, hence all the light greeting him as he awoke. This meant another full room or two sat between where he lay and the hallway. He doubted anybody outside the room could hear anything coming from the bedroom. Option two was talking completely honestly with her about his feelings – that he had none for her. Would she really free him just because he said he didn't love her? And worst case scenario, she'd pull a Lorena Bobbitt. He doubted she'd turn violent, but then again she did drug him, tie him up, and although it sounded weird to say, raped him. Multiple times. Those weren't the actions of a sane person, so who knew what she was capable of. His best option, given the circumstances, was to just go along with whatever she had in mind. He didn't have much say. He'd seldom felt helpless in his adult life, and never, ever to this extreme. Another idea was to grab hold of her hair, if he could get a good grip, and not let go until she untied him.

Katie came out of the bathroom wrapped in an oversized white towel, with another smaller towel securing her hair above her head. She held a washcloth in one hand as she sat gently on the bed beside Tre.

"Did you miss me, sweetie?"

"Thought of you every moment," Tre replied, noticing hair grabbing was out of the question.

"Awww, that's sweet!"

She flipped back the bed throw, exposing his privates to the cooler air. He hoped she used warm water on the washcloth.

"Let me just clean you up a bit," she said, washing off his vulnerable area. The cloth was indeed warm, and triggered a mild reaction. Her eyes lit up and she smiled from ear to ear. Continuing to rub the cloth on him, she leaned over him and gave him a full, passionate kiss. He went with it.

She could feel him grow under the washcloth. "You feel so good. I could go for you again right now." She pulled away the washcloth and looked down at him. "But I've got a feeling that your little guys have already done their thing." She rubbed herself below the waist. "I told you yesterday while you slept, but I suppose you don't remember. Jimmy, my ex-fiancé, wanted to have a baby as soon as we got married. So I stopped taking the pill. Funny though, I broke it off with him without having sex again. So you're my first since. I know this sounds silly, but I think I feel a new life growing inside me!"

Tre's face went pale.

She noticed his reaction and sat up abruptly, causing the towel covering her hair to fly off. Her tone changed. "You should be happy for me. No, you should be happy for *us*! We're going to have a child together. We're going to be a family."

He could see the intensity in her eyes. She looked angry and sad at once. He doubted that the anger would trigger violence, as she'd expressed the desire to start a family together. Regardless, he tried to defuse her. "You just caught me by surprise, that's all. I've never thought about being a father."

A smile returned to her face. The colour returned to his.

"I'm sorry. I'm just very emotional right now."

That was an understatement, Tre thought.

She continued. "Besides, aren't you on a journey of making amends to those you've wronged in the past?"

"Yes …"

"Well, this is how you can make amends to me. It broke my heart watching you have all those affairs after our intimate encounters. I've always known we were meant for each other, even if you didn't. So yes, this is your way of making it up to me. Giving me a baby. I know the type of man you are deep down, and you won't leave your son or daughter. And that will bring us together. And we'll have a happy family. And maybe more babies."

Tre didn't know what to say. When he'd set out on his trip, he certainly didn't have fathering children and settling down on the agenda. "It sounds like you've thought it through and have it all figured out."

"I'm a pretty good planner. You'll come to realize that."

He wondered if she'd planned to kill him a few weeks ago, but failed and changed her mind. That wouldn't make any sense. But who knew with the state of mind she was in. She could change her mind at any moment and go nuts on him. "I see that. So what's the plan from here?"

She caressed his privates again. "Doing it again is tempting, but I need to get dressed and get us some food. They don't do room service for lunch, and I bet you are starving."

"You're right about that. Do you want me to come with you to help carry stuff?"

She patted him on the chest. "No, no. You just relax here." She pulled the throw back over him. Katie got off the bed and hummed as she went back to the bathroom to get herself ready.

About twenty minutes later, she popped into the room to say goodbye then left. She seemed gone an eternity. In a perverse way, he missed her while she was gone. For some reason when she was there he didn't feel quite so violated tied up naked to a bed. He nodded off to sleep for a while, awoken by the hotel room door shutting behind Katie as she returned.

"I'm back, sweetie!"

Tre could hear the rustling of bags from the other room. A minute later Katie entered the room carrying a couple bowls of soup and two glasses of wine. "I've got some deli sandwiches too." She placed the soup and wine on the end table. Fluffing a pillow, she shoved it behind Tre's head propping it somewhat upright.

"This isn't going to be very easy to eat," Tre remarked.

"You'll be fine. Here, have some soup." She proceeded to spoon feed him, taking breaks to have some out of her bowl. "Would you like a sip of wine?"

"Is it drugged?"

"No, and I'm disheartened that you should think that."

"Sure, I'll have some wine."

"Great! I don't like to drink alone." She carefully poured some into his mouth. "Let me clear away the empty soup bowls and go get the sandwiches." She pranced out of the room and returned to place two sandwiches on the table beside him. "I assumed you'd want a Reuben, since it's your favourite. But if you want my turkey club, you can have it instead."

"The Reuben is fine. Thanks for remembering."

She fed him bites of his sandwich, taking time to give him wine between gulps. The sandwich was plump with meat, but he had no problem devouring the entire thing. He even had her pour him a second glass of wine. She got downright chatty after her second glass turned into her third and fourth. Tre got to hear much of her life story, as well as the plans she had for them and their baby, right down to birthday parties at Disneyland, cruises to specific Caribbean islands, and how they would spend Christmas. By then his attention span began to fade and he struggled to stay awake.

"You told me you didn't drug the wine," he challenged her.

"I didn't lie. I think honesty is the most important aspect of a relationship. I drugged your soup."

"Good to know you didn't lie," Tre said as his eyes closed.

She removed the fluffed up pillow from behind him and lowered his head to rest softly on the remaining firm pillow.

27 Gone, Baby Gone

A new day greeted Tre, and appeared to treat him more amicably. As he instinctively wiped the sleep from his eyes, he immediately realized he'd been released from his bindings. He also lay fully clothed. And he had to piss like a racehorse. It hadn't crossed his mind yesterday, but he hadn't gone since the first drugging. He felt an itch on his privates as he walked to the bathroom. *If she gave me something I'm going to be really pissed.* In the bathroom, he flipped up the toilet seat and stumbled to grab the counter as he temporarily lost his balance. A side effect of being drugged and tied up in bed for two days. His stance recovered, he unzipped his fly and reached in his pants, shocked to touch something that didn't belong there. Pulling out his penis, he found a tag tied to it with a fragment of the rope used to tie his wrists. No wonder it itched. On the tag, in pretty penmanship, was 'Property of Katie', and a smiley face in vibrant red lipstick. He did his business with this tag dangling and swaying from side to side. He had to go, and couldn't wait to figure out how to undo the knot, or clip it off without disfiguring himself.

Feeling relieved, but with the love tag still strapped firmly, he sat on the edge of the bed fiddling with the knot. Frustrated at his lack of progress, he surveyed the room for a sharp object. All he found was a corkscrew. Tricky business this task at hand, and not one to perform in haste. After careful maneuvering, he shredded the rope and removed the tag without any damage. He placed the corkscrew on the end table and spotted a neatly folded note with a red lip smack on the front. He picked up the note and paced as he read it.

Tre, thank you so much for your contributions the past few days. You were a real stand-up guy, so to speak.

A smiley face followed.

Just in case, I did you one more time last night before I left. You are forgiven for past transgressions. Best of luck with the remainder of your trip. When you return from your quest, we will be waiting (me and your unborn child – I think it's a girl). I look forward to starting our life together! Love forever, Katie.

X's and o's in the shape of a heart followed.

Moving into the main room of the suite, Tre saw his wallet, keys, and another note. This note also had a red lip smack on it, and he unfolded it on the table where it lay.

Hi sweetie! Here is the rental agreement and keys for your replacement vehicle. I took care of it yesterday when I ran out for food. The nice guy at the rental agency dropped it off for me. He also gave you an upgrade to a Chevy Camaro for free, for the inconvenience, he said. I think it was due to the short skirt I wore (I felt really sexy after we'd made love). The car's set up for return to LA. Love, Katie.

More x's and o's followed. At the bottom of the page, she'd written one more line.

P.S. I signed the rental agreement as Mrs. Brightman, and checked in that way too. Can't blame a girl for dreaming. Love ya!

Tre read the note over again. Then he re-read the first note. Nothing in either to incriminate Katie of anything, aside from using his surname. He imagined the discussion if he went to the police…

"I'd like to report a crime."

"What crime, sir?"

"I was drugged, kidnapped, and raped repeatedly in a hotel."

"In some seedy hotel, no doubt."

"No, in a suite at the Luxury Inn."

"By a man?"

"No! By a woman."

"Do you have a name or picture of this woman?"

"Yes, I do. She works for me as my assistant."

Tre would show the picture of her he had on his phone from an office gathering. In the only picture he had of Katie she wore a skintight short skirt, and she practically burst out of her top. She looked very hot.

The officer would look at the picture and reply, "Seriously? You're complaining about having intercourse with this woman?"

"Not just intercourse. She subjected me to oral sex."

"Oh, yeah. That's definitely a problem. You're not married, are you?"

"No, why?"

"Never mind. Anything else?"

"Did I say she repeated this four times?"

"It must have been hell. Do you have any proof of these allegations?"

"Look at my wrists. See the rope burns?"

"Where? I get a worse rash wearing the sweater my mother-in-law bought me last year for Christmas."

"But she did it to get pregnant. She wants to have my child."

"Well, now there you finally have something legitimate to investigate."

"Thank you. Finally you're taking my side."

"There are no sides. So what proof do you have that the sex wasn't consensual?"

"None. But it wasn't."

"Have you had sex with this woman before she ..." and he would crack a huge grin, "raped you?"

"Yes, but not for over a year."

"And that was consensual?"

"Yes, but that was a long time ago."

"So who's going to believe it wasn't consensual this time?"

Nobody. And Tre knew it. Worse than looking like an idiot, his luck he'd end up face to face with an idiot detective who just happened to be the triplet of the morons in Sacramento and Elko.

So no police. But he knew he needed to tell Jack.

The phone rang at the Gordon Detective Agency.

"Gordon Detective Agency, John speaking."

"John, its Tre Brightman. Is Jack there?"

"Tre! How have you been making out? Are the ribs almost healed?"

"Still kind of sore. As for how I'm doing, you wouldn't believe me."

"Try me."

"Okay, but I warned you."

Tre spent the next twenty minutes recounting the last twenty-four hours to John. The detective mostly listened, and only interjected a few one-word remarks such as "seriously?", "really?", or simply confirmed he remained on the line with the occasional "uh-huh". Tre ended his story and asked John, "Well? What do you think?"

"You're right. That is quite the story. I think it's a good thing you didn't go to the police with all that you've endured in the past week. Your credibility at this point is probably pretty low with the men in blue."

"So, what do you think I should do?"

"Not much right now. We can talk more about it when you get back to LA."

"Really? It could be another three or four weeks from now."

"Yeah, I don't think there is a hurry on this. After all, it'll be at least a month before Katie knows if she's pregnant."

Tre scratched his head in disbelief. "Well if you say so."

"Say, did you pick up a cell phone? What's the number?"

"No, I'm calling from the hotel."

"Hey, I better let you go. They're going to charge you a fortune for this call, Tre. Safe travels. Talk to you later."

Tre hung up. Somewhat in disbelief over John's lackadaisical approach to his latest information, Tre stared at the phone, trying to remember Jack's cell phone number. He closed his eyes to picture his cell phone screen with Jack's name and number on it. That did the trick. Disregarding John's concern over the cost of calls from the hotel, Tre dialled Jack's cell phone. It went straight to voicemail, soliciting a brief curse from Tre as he wished Jack's prerecorded message would pass with haste, though knowing better from having heard it a hundred times. "Jack its Tre. I'd ask you to call me back, but I don't have a phone. I bet you're laughing at me now. I'm about to hit the road again, so I will call you at my next stop. I explained my latest travails to John just a few minutes ago, so he can give you the scoop. I'm just concerned about his advice. Later."

Tre pivoted on the bed and packed up the last of his belongings. Scooping up the new rental keys in one hand and his bag in the other, Tre bid adieu to the hotel room where he laid captive a short time ago.

The man at the front desk recognized Tre, but Tre had never seen him before.

"Mr. Brightman, how are you doing today?"

"I'm doing fine. I assume that you are the one that checked-in Katie."

"Yes indeed. Mrs. Brightman is quite delightful isn't she?"

"She's something all right. But she isn't Mrs. Anybody."

"That's not what she told me, sir."

"Yes, I believe she did. So what's the damage?"

"If you just give me a second, I'll print up your receipt." The man stepped over to the computer and began navigating the screen. "Oh wait a second, I see you have some phone charges that just came through. I'll add those in a jiffy, and have your receipt for you." The man grabbed two pages from the printer and slid them across the counter to Tre.

"We certainly do like to live in style don't we?" Tre grimaced at the bill.

"Mrs. Brightman is a woman of expensive taste."

"Especially when it's my money."

The clerk chuckled, before a look of sudden recollection came across his face like a lost thought found its way home. "I just remembered Mrs. Brightman left an envelope for you!" He swivelled on his feet, plucking the letter from the corner counter beside him. "She said these would put a smile on your face."

Tre looked at the back of the envelope, trying to see if the clerk had opened it out of curiosity. The contents appeared undisturbed. "Thanks." He held up the sealed envelope. "I think I will wait for the privacy of the car to open this."

"Suit yourself. I've seen the pictures anyways."

Tre looked puzzled. He looked again at the envelope. "Did you take them out and put them in a new envelope?"

"No. It's the way she gave it to me."

"So … ?"

"Who do you think took the pictures?"

Tre had lost any appetite to view the pictures. He gave the man a stern look, but forewent any action in favour of a quick exit to the car.

After a quick stop at a gas station convenience store to load up on Gatorade and energy bars, Tre enjoyed the burst of power from his new rental as he guided it onto the interstate heading east. After five futile minutes trying to find a radio station in his wheelhouse, he gave up and settled for a country station. One of the many available for him to choose from. There certainly wasn't the choice like LA. His first rental had satellite radio, but no such luck on this one. His knowledge of country music was limited to a handful of cross-over songs and any used in beer or truck commercials. To his surprise, the next song that came on was 'Picture', by Kid Rock and Sheryl Crow. Of course, all that did was get him thinking about the unopened envelope on the passenger seat. He looked in the rear-view mirror for traffic, snatched up the package, shook the pictures down to one end, and tore a strip off the top. Glancing in the mirror again, he held the open envelope with his left hand on the steering wheel, reaching in with his right to pull the mysterious pictures into view. Only a few pictures in total, but they said thousands of words. As he looked at each snapshot, he grunted and slid it onto the dash before looking at the next image. Five Kodak moments later, Tre looked at the spread on his dashboard, and it was literally a spread. All the shots showed him and Katie in bed, naked except for the mirrored sunglasses and cowboy hat perched on his head. The hotel clerk must have got his rocks off watching Katie pose, and had to have helped her arrange Tre's limp body. Fortunately, Katie's hand, or head in one shot, covered his junk, the only silver lining he could find. At least his face was non-expressive, so perhaps he could convince someone that he was knocked out and the photos staged.

A transport trailer whipped by him blasting his horn, startling Tre as he'd lost focus on driving and had drifted too close to the middle line for the other driver. He cursed, and in anger threw the envelope at the passenger window. A paper flew out and landed upside down on the carpet in front of the passenger seat. Tre checked the mirrors again before lunging below the dashboard at the paper. Quickly springing back up, his ribs reminded him of their still-bruised presence. He flipped over the paper to a brief note.

"Miss us yet?"

Red lip marks adorned the note, apparently her new trademark. Tre plucked the envelope off the neighbouring seat and deposited the note and four of the pictures back inside. The fifth photo had slid to the farthest crevice of the front dash and lodged itself there. It reflected off the windshield, doubling the size of the contentious image. Not wanting to risk an accident, he'd endure it until stopping for gas to secure it from view. At least that was the plan. After ten minutes of the errant picture staring back at him, Tre pulled over to the shoulder and stuffed it out of sight.

28 Finding My Religion

Six minutes. Eight minutes, according to his father. The hospital records noted it as six minutes. The six longest minutes of John's life, and six he'd never remember. The six minutes before he was officially born. The six minutes it took for John to join Jack in the world. During that time, Jack became the alpha male of the twins. Not that there was ever much separating the boys. Both were very talented athletically and somewhere above average intellectually. But John knew his place from the moment he emerged second. He would compete handsomely with his older brother, but when push came to shove, or the quarterback position came to question, John would concede to his older twin. He knew it wasn't worth the pain to continue battling with Jack, as his brother would never – and he meant never – give in. John had experienced it on many occasions, and most of all, he understood it because he himself exhibited the same trait with everyone except his brother. At least until Deanna came along.

As John recalled, Jack referred to Deanna as Yoko for a short period after their marriage. John took it as an insult initially, thinking it in reference to the breakup of The Beatles. One night following a few drinks, a less frequent occasion for John following his wedding day, Jack confided that he meant well by the comparison.

"You see, little brother," Jack said as he put his arm firmly around his brother's shoulder, "the way I see it, John Lennon searched for years to find himself." Jack paused to sip his draught. "It wasn't until Yoko showed up that he achieved contentment. He may have stopped cranking out number one songs that would play for eternity, but he was happy. And in my books, you can't go wrong with being happy."

"Thanks, Jack. But I don't know if she'd appreciate the sentiment if you slip and call her Yoko to her face."

"No sweat. Deanna it is."

True to his word, Jack dropped the nickname. But now John wondered if maybe his big brother wasn't onto something. Lately, Deanna had sought her spirituality. Religion was an area that the Gordon boys had never been steered toward by their parents, and never had occasion to get involved in. John and Jack held similar views. Religion was for those dying who needed hope to hold onto.

And that perhaps was the key for Deanna. Her near-death experience on the force had ended her police career, but didn't seem to have any lingering impacts. At least that's what John had thought. She suffered the occasional screaming nightmare. The trauma was a few years in the past, and now it surfaced from some deep crevice in her soul. John initially wrote off her sudden interest in attending church service to her trying to satisfy her Catholic Mexican mother. When she started leaving work to go to weekday masses, John reacted by putting his PI skills to work following her, thinking she might use church as a cover to have an affair.

While John enjoyed going to church on Sunday, its roots came from spending time with his wife and seeing how happy it made her. While more than once a week would have been too much for him, John didn't really care how often she went. At first, anyway. When she came home one day with a pamphlet about a retreat in the mountains north of San Francisco, he became worried. He was torn – go with her and have to suffer through an entire long weekend of wall to wall religion, or let her go alone and have her involved with who knows what kind of quacks up there. He opted to go, make her happy, and keep an eye on her. Fortunately, or otherwise, the day before the retreat, the agency landed a big case and Jack insisted on John sticking around to investigate. Deanna went off alone. She came back armed with reading material and with a different look in her eyes. At first John thought his wife was stoned, maybe from sitting in a circle and toking over the scriptures all weekend. There was more to it, though. She immediately began holding John to a higher moral standard. No more drinking with the guys, in spite of his pleas that even Jesus got together with the guys for drinks. She thought John should limit the bad influences of some of his single friends, meaning Tre and his brother, Jack. It had an instant impact on the rhythm of their marriage. He tried to get her to go to counselling, for their marriage and for post-traumatic stress disorder. She refused, stating she received counselling from the ultimate authority, God.

John bent over backwards to accommodate Deanna, hoping it was a phase of her recovery and that she would find what she searched for and return to normal (although he regretted the use of that word one long afternoon). He enlisted Deanna's best friend, Katie from Tre's office, to try and talk sense into his wife. Katie didn't really try, but she did take some of the burden off John by going to church and related functions a few times with Deanna. After a few weeks, Katie said she had issues of her own to deal with and couldn't commit the time to help Deanna 'further her journey'. Or some such nonsense.

Work had been a good escape from 'the church lady', as he internally began calling his wife, in spite of working side by side with her. She seemed focused at work, and maybe even more vigilant in tracking down leads to 'shine an ominous light on the sinners of this town'. John, conversely, became less productive. He dwelled on what she said, interpreting every word to have some hidden religious connotation. His effectiveness at research went down the toilet. He still found what he needed, but not with the lightning speed that he, and Jack, expected. And he made mistakes. Such as not passing on messages, or not clearly writing down his findings and wasting time repeating his searches. He longed for Deanna to snap out of it, or tone down her spiritual dial. Instead, she began running off every few weekends to another retreat. He was losing her to Him, and it was hard to fight an omnipresent being. Marriage was one of the few things he'd beaten Jack at since those fateful six minutes and now John was losing at that.

29 The Long Road Ahead

Road trips were not a new experience to Tre; as a kid they had them all the time. When you grow up in the Midwest, you have to road trip to get anywhere. Nothing is conveniently located a subway ride away. Even more true twenty years ago. And in college, he'd made the drive from Louisville to Boston just to grab a pint in an Irish pub on St. Patrick's day, then turn around and drive back for class the next day. So a trip across the expanse of the great northern states didn't seem unreasonable when he first came up with the idea. Of course, his body was in the worst physical condition of his life, the effects of a car crash battering compounded by all the other calamities he'd encountered in recent days. The oxy extended his tolerance for pain, but the effects shortened his drive time per day compared to full health. As he thought of it, with one hand he twisted open the prescription bottle and popped a pill. Enough hours on the road had passed for the morning pill's impact to expire. This latest jolt should give him another three or four hours, provided he scored some food energy to offset the drowsiness the pill would soon unleash. The dash clock read one-thirty. He'd get to Cheyenne, Wyoming by dinner and call it a day.

With twenty miles to his destination, a yawn escaped. He slapped his face on both sides to perk himself up. Adjusting the lumbar support, he shifted in his seat, a physical trigger that the meds had worn thin. He didn't dare take one now. He could last twenty minutes, then take one with food after he found a place to park his butt for the night.

It proved a long twenty minutes. The yawns came fast and long. His eyelids weighed five pounds each. He ran onto the shoulder grids once and scared the crap out of himself. He entered the southern part of town and immediately took the next exit. Crossing the river, a brew-pub in a historic building attracted him. Tre slid a pill into his pocket to take after dinner, locked the Mustang, tucked in his shirt, and strode toward the entrance. He welcomed the fresh air.

The Cowboy Brew Pub was a book you could judge by its cover. The fantastic restored fascia centred around two oversized meticulously stained wooden doors which opened to reveal a charming and warm interior. A rich mahogany bar spanned the length of the establishment, with gleaming ornate pillars supporting upper cabinets of the same wood that semi-concealed countless bottles of liquor. Mirrors behind the bar gave the illusion of a much larger pub. Oversized uncovered windows provided light uncommon to the dark, beer-stench aroma stereotype of a pub. Or at least the pubs from back home.

The pub looked just over half occupied on this early evening. With most patrons finishing dinner, they would soon make way to the drinking crowd. Tre found the restroom sign and made as straight a path to it as he could through the randomly distributed tables. In the back corner, a slim woman with luxurious blonde hair pulled back a chair and took a seat, back to him, alone. He made a mental note to alter his return route so as to pass in front of her for a peek. As he stood relieving himself, he closed his eyes out of fatigue. An image came screaming to the front of his mind, from some memory buried long ago. A woman from some moment in his past pulling a chair out from a table. He opened his eyes as he finished his business. *It couldn't be, could it?*

Washing his hands, he again closed his eyes hoping to resurface the forgotten memory. He strained to no avail. Only one way to find out. He opened the door to exit, almost running into another customer in his haste. Circling in front of the table of the woman, he stopped in front and looked hard. She read a menu and didn't initially see him. He took a step to the left and cast a shadow in front of her. When she looked up, in spite of the blonde wig and sunglasses, he knew her.

"Meagan?" Surprised, Tre spoke with his outside voice.

"Shhhh!" She held up a finger to her mouth and anxiously motioned for him to quickly sit. "Don't use my name. And sit down."

Cautiously sitting down, trying to remember that this former flame had recently plunged a knife multiple times into the chest of her husband, he tremulously smiled. Lowering his voice to marginally above a whisper, he asked the obvious. "What are you doing here? I thought you'd be in Mexico by now."

"Good, that's where I hope they're looking for me."

"So where are you headed?" Tre inquired.

"If I tell you, I'll have to kill you, Trevor." A slight smirk squeaked from a corner of her mouth.

"Funny."

"I'm serious. I'd really have to kill you. And don't think I won't do it."

Tre sat up straight, startled. Perhaps he no longer knew this woman. A waiter walked over to the table and extended a menu.

"Sorry, I didn't see you join her until just now. Would you like a drink to start?"

Tre, still stunned by Meagan's remark, looked at the draught in front of her. "I'll have one of those."

"Great. I'll be right back with the Pale Ale, and will take your order then if you're ready."

Tre hesitated for the waiter to clear hearing range. He leaned forward and looked at her eyes, hoping she'd remove the sunglasses.

"Why did you do it? You know, to your husband?"

She took off the glasses, leaned forward and held his hands.

"He turned me into a smoker."

Tre noticed the nicotine patch on her arm. "Possibly an overreaction, I think." With a forgotten tenderness, he squeezed her hand. "No, tell me the real reason."

She pulled her hand back, nervously rubbing her fingers together. "I had to get out. I couldn't take it anymore."

Her eyes showed her internal agony.

"But why not just leave? You were a little extreme, weren't you?"

"You don't leave an abusive husband. You escape."

"He hit you?"

"Once too often." She sat back and nudged up her blouse to expose a discoloured bruised abdomen and ribs.

"That's awful! But why not just report him?"

Meagan leaned in close. "They didn't listen the first time, why would they the twentieth or thirtieth time? And you know what made it worse? I came to find out that his routine meant banging someone at the dental office after hours, then coming home to beat me."

"Surely the police would think you were defending yourself."

"Maybe I should have" – and she lowered her voice further – "gunned him down inside the bedroom and claimed I thought he was an intruder. I actually thought of it, but that morning the rage just got the best of me and I had to do it before I lost the courage. He always opened up in the mornings and I always went in for ten. That day I went into the office early to catch up on some paperwork, before either of us had appointments, and he was screwing our assistant in my office. Not his office. My office. On my desk. Do you believe it? On my friggin' desk! I fired her on the spot and sent her running out of the office half dressed. He went about his business scrubbing like nothing happened. That's when I lost it."

They spotted the waiter returning, and separated. Identical burger orders placed, they returned to whispering distance.

"You stabbed him eight times. Isn't that a bit excessive?"

A perplexed look came over her face. "It's not like I've ever stabbed someone before. I'm quite lousy at it, I found out, and it took that many times to make sure he was dead. I didn't want to leave the poor bastard there to die slowly, or worse, recover."

"But couldn't you have just left him?" Tre asked. "You know, moved out of state and started your own practice? Was he crazy enough to hunt you down?"

"Don't know what he would have done, but I didn't want to find out. Besides, he had my back to the wall." She sighed and leaned forward again. "Remember, Trevor," she said, looking deep into his eyes, "remember how spontaneous and impulsive I used to be? That's what did me in with Nate. He was so charming … a lot like you at one point. Swept me off my feet. I was on the rebound, as you know, and jumped in with both feet. We started the business while we dated and we put the business in his name, even though I put in about three quarters of the start-up money in from my grandmother's inheritance and a smallish loan. Stupidly, I signed an agreement saying it was separate property under his name and not community property under California divorce law. He told me it provided the best tax advantage for us as a couple and I trusted him. I was in love, or thought I was."

"So this is my fault, is that what you're saying?"

She looked at him, perplexed. "Why do you say that?"

"If you weren't on the rebound and vulnerable, you would have made better life choices."

"Humph." She crossed her arms. "Never thought of it that way. But let's go with that. So I spoke in haste saying we were even when I pushed you down the stairs. By the way, I hope that I didn't break anything?"

"No, just extended my healing time."

"Good." Meagan smiled. "As I was saying, I forgave you in the heat of the moment. Now that we've talked, I think you owe me for my miserable marriage and for the trouble I'm in."

Tre took the last gulp of his draught and placed the glass down. He opened his mouth to speak but their burgers arrived, larger than life and surrounded by a small mountain range of fries. They thanked the waiter, asked for another round of draughts, and each grabbed a single fry to munch on.

Tre placed the cloth napkin on his lap and returned his focus to Meagan.

"Okay, I'm listening."

"Here's the deal." She leaned forward and looked around the room before softly speaking. "I need twenty thousand to buy a new identity."

"All right. I can do that. But certainly you have cash to live on."

"I have some, but the damn feds closed in on my accounts limiting what I could withdraw in cash. I took a bunch out in Stockton to get them thinking I'd headed south. I continued south to Fresno, but when I tried to run my card for gas, it was declined. So I don't want to use more cash to buy ID."

"I'll get it in the morning, when the bank opens."

"And …"

"And, what?" Tre asked.

"And I need you to drop off my photo and half the money with the guy."

"What guy?"

"Guys, actually. Big, ugly, scary guys. Maybe the biggest, ugliest, scariest guys I've ever seen. If mobsters in Cheyenne look that bad, I'd hate to see the New York or New Jersey variety. You're a good size, and you're a guy. They won't give you the shit they gave me today. I didn't think I was getting out of there with my clothes on and my virtue intact."

"Nice. I look forward to meeting them."

They sat back and enjoyed their dinners, reminiscing a bit, and catching up. A lot had changed in a few years, aside from the obvious. Grateful for this time together, Tre knew it wouldn't last. Both declined dessert in favour of another pale ale, and Tre asked for the cheque. They could have sat all night and talked, but Meagan wanted Tre to go to his rendezvous early, so she could get the finished product back the same afternoon. She'd give him the upfront ten grand so he could go before the bank opened.

As they finished their beer, Tre looked around the now crowded bar. "Well, I should get going. I still have to get a hotel room."

"No you don't. You're staying with me."

"I appreciate the offer, but I don't think we should."

"Give it a rest! I'm not offering to sleep with you. I want to keep an eye on you."

"Why?"

She leaned forward. "I can't trust that you're not going to run off and tell the cops."

"Seriously? You think I'd tell them?"

"Sorry, but I can't take any chances."

Tre stood up, angered.

"Sit down!" She yelled as discreetly as she could, trying not to attract attention yet still get her point across.

"Why should I? I offer to do these things for you, and you don't trust me?"

"You should because I have a gun on my lap under my purse and it is pointed at your knee." Meagan smiled. "It was pointed at your crotch until you stood up."

Tre sat down in disbelief. Then quickly stood, realizing where the gun had returned to pointing. "I guess we're roommates for the night."

"That's the spirit. And I do trust you, Trevor. I just have to be paranoid in my position. And remember, no names."

"Shall I drive?" Tre asked.

"No need. I'm in the hotel across the street." She put the gun in her purse and pointed at the building looming out the window.

"Nice and close to the Cowboy Brew Pub."

"We're on the tenth floor." She wrapped her arm in Tre's and smiled at him. "You know I always wanted to look down at a cowboy."

30 The Exchange

A sweet smell blessed Tre's nose as he awoke. An aroma he'd never forget, although he'd forgotten the smile it put on his face.

"Put that thing away," Meagan said as she rolled away from Tre's spooning. "Somebody could lose an eye. Nothing happened last night and it's certainly not going to happen this morning. And what are you doing in my bed anyway? Why aren't you on the couch like you're supposed to be?"

He ignored her question. "I always liked that you didn't make me get up and brush my teeth beforehand. I hate crossing cold floors first thing in the morning. It's very deflating, if you know what I mean."

"I do, but get that out of your mind!" She paused while recalling their past. "I will admit some mornings were the best moments of our relationship."

Tre reached for her hand. She pulled it away and snapped back to the present. "You've got business to take care of."

He rolled off the bed, groaned from his aching injuries, and picked up his pill bottle. "No problem. I'm just happy to wake up without handcuffs, in the hospital, in jail, or dead."

"No wonder you have nightmares like that one last night! You never used to have nightmares. How long since they started?"

"Since the accident. They've just increased in intensity recently."

"Well, you've had a hell of a trip so far. But I bet those Oxy don't help with the nightmares. One of the side effects, in case you didn't know."

Tre looked at the bottle as he set it down. "I don't think these are the problem. Too many bad experiences lately."

"If you say so. How about you keep 'getting shot' off that list of bad experiences, and get your sorry ass moving?"

"You say the sweetest things in the morning. Can I at least have a shower?"

"Just make it quick."

"Then you won't be joining me, I assume."

"Better make it a cold one, cowboy."

Twenty minutes later, Meagan had re-donned her wig and shades, Trevor had showered and dressed, and they'd looked up Tre's nearest bank for after his meeting with the fake ID guys. Meagan swapped her new Jeep for a cheap sedan in Modesto, making the car dealer very happy, before doubling back north. She drove her 'new' car to the location to buy the fake ID, which also served as a small used car lot, Trust Worthy Motors. She'd driven by the dump the night before her first meeting. The 'T' had burned out in the sign, leaving it to say 'rust Worthy', surely a huge enticement for potential buyers driving by, she laughed to herself at the time. The small lot had no more than twenty cars crammed on it. A few even looked like they might make it around the block. A couple sat up on blocks. If any place looked like a front for illegal activity, it was here. She stopped short of pulling in the entrance, turned to Trevor and handed him an envelope.

"Ten grand. Go into the sales office, the small trailer at the back, and say the secret phrase, 'I'd like to buy a '57 Impala'."

"Great secret phrase. What if someone actually wants a '57 Impala?"

"They didn't make them until '58. Tell them I stopped in the other day and you're just dropping off the pictures and the deposit. Tell them you need them by four, then get out of there as quick as you can." She looked at Trevor with the concern of a mother sending her kid off to their first day of school.

"Got it. Are you going to give me your gun?"

"So you can shoot yourself? They patted me down, so you should expect the same. Except they may not take as long doing it."

"Great."

Meagan pulled the car into the lot and stopped, leaving it in position for a quick getaway. "All set?"

"Ready or not," and Trevor stepped out of the car.

Two large men stood, arms crossed, outside the sales office. These guys weren't into subtle. They weren't even in the same county as subtle. Tre glanced at their faces, and Meagan was right. They were ugly, with emphasis on the ugh. They looked him over, determined him not to pose a threat and watched him enter. Before the door could swing closed behind him, one of the goons clutched it and followed Tre into the office.

A short, scruffy man with receding greased-back hair looked up from a desk. No papers cluttered the desk, just a coffee and newspaper folded open to the crossword puzzle.

"Do you see something out there that you like?"

"No, I'm looking for a '57 Impala."

The man stood up and Tre could see the extent of his vertical challenge. The term fubsy came to Tre's mind, as the salesman could play Danny Devito's body double. The man put his fingertips on the desk to support himself as he stood on his tiptoes to lookout at Meagan's car.

"You came with the broad from the other day?" He motioned to the bodyguard, who began to frisk Tre. "Too bad she didn't come in. Leroy here very much enjoyed patting her down. Maybe we should bring her in, just to be sure."

"Can we just get down to business?"

"In a minute, after Leroy clears you."

Leroy stopped his frisking at Tre's left ankle. He rolled up the pant leg to see the cast boot. Satisfied, he tugged it back down and backed away, nodding to his boss.

"Sure. Do you have the twenty G's?"

"Ten now. Ten later." Tre tried his best to ooze confidence. Truly, he oozed fear.

"All right. That's fair."

Leroy held out his hand for the exchange, looked inside, then passed it to his boss.

"Aren't you going to count it?" Tre asked.

"I don't think Leroy can count that high. And if it's not all there, I'll get it, plus interest when you come to pick up."

"That's fair." Tre handed four pictures to the man. "I want them back by four."

"Same day service, huh?" He folded the money envelope and stuffed it into his front pants pocket. "You know we're doing primo work here. Driver's licence, passport, work ID, and even a fake profile on the internet, including a Facebook account. Same day will cost you extra."

"How much?"

"Two thousand."

Tre looked at him, for a millisecond debating negotiating. Thinking better of it, he nodded agreement. Not wanting any trouble and with everything done, Tre seized the opportunity to bolt out of there per Meagan's advice. Grabbing the door, he felt a large hand on his shoulder pull him back.

"Leroy has a present for you, to remind you to not do anything stupid, like bring the cops or protection."

Tre looked up at Leroy, who smiled, then delivered a very strong blow to the dentist's right ribs. It doubled Tre in half, but hurt a hell of a lot less than if the fist had targeted his left side. Leroy sadistically laughed at the message he'd conveyed.

"Got it," Tre said, gasping for air and grabbing his side as he pushed through the door. The boss yelled out to Tre as the door closed behind him.

"Say hi to the chick for us. Tell her Leroy misses her." A deep raspy laugh turned into a hacking cough, threatening to bring up a lung.

Back at Meagan's car, Tre got in and simply said "Go."

She squealed the tires in her haste, likely making the boss laugh again, but they didn't look back. Halfway down the block, Meagan turned to Tre and asked if he was okay.

"I'm fine," he said wincing as he lied. "You were right, though."

"About what?"

"That is one ugly bunch of guys."

"I know, huh? They even make you look cute."

"Funny. They asked for two thousand more to have the stuff done today."

"I hope you told them no!"

"You are kidding, right?"

"It wouldn't have hurt to ask."

"Normally, I agree with the philosophy of 'it never hurts to ask', but in this case, it would have hurt. That's the most painful punch I've ever received, and I didn't say anything."

"I'm sorry," she apologized, uncomfortably squirming in her seat.

"Makes me look forward to four o'clock," Tre sarcastically replied.

"They've likely had their fun. You'll be okay."

"Easy for you to say. You'll be sitting across the street in the car."

"I'll come in with you then," she proclaimed.

"Not going to happen." He waved his hand to cut her off. "I'm in this to make amends for past failures. I'm not going to add putting your life at risk on my list or my conscience."

"Fine. Then take my gun."

"They'll pat me down, find it, then use it to kill me."

She parted her legs and pulled her purse up from the floor in front of her seat. Handing it to Tre, she said, "In the side pocket."

Tre took the colourful bag and slid his hand in the side, pulling out a very small handgun. "This is your gun? It's pink! You mean I trembled in fear over this little pea-shooter?"

"It's called a Pink Lady .38 Special. Don't be fooled, it would have scrambled your eggs if I hit you under the table. It's made for self-defence from an up-close attacker, not for gunning someone down across the street."

"I'd look gay carrying this thing."

"What? Do you plan on walking in there waving it around? It's perfect because you can conceal it."

"Hide it? Where? They frisked my crotch, and I think Leroy enjoyed it."

"There," she chuckled as she pointed to his foot. "In your soft boot."

He looked at her, at first like she'd lost her mind, then he realized it might just work. "Leroy saw the boot and just flipped my pant leg back down. If I had this little beauty stuffed in there, he'd never check."

“I’m sorry, what did you say?” Meagan beamed at her bright idea.

“You’re right. It’s a good idea. Happy?”

“Thank you.” She grinned at him. “Now put it back in the side pocket. This is your bank. I don’t want you wearing it going to get the cash.”

Tre handed her back her bag. “Be right back.”

As he walked in front of the car, she called out to him. “Don’t forget the extra two thousand.”

He nodded, and limped off, trying to stretch out the muscles around his newly injured ribs.

Ten minutes later, Tre returned to the car, a bulge in his front pants pocket.

Meagan turned down the radio as he buckled up. “I assume that you have the money, and that you’re not just happy to see me.”

He laughed. “I was happy this morning and you didn’t want anything to do with me.”

She looked at him and put her hand on his thigh, caressing it. “That was this morning.” She leaned over close to him and seductively whispered in his ear. “How about we go back to the hotel and I’ll do what I did for you in New Orleans?”

Tre’s eyes looked like they would pop out of their sockets.

“Seriously?”

“No.” She pulled away and turned the key in the ignition. “Just messing with you. Let’s go get lunch. You’ve got a big afternoon, and I’d hate for you to die on an empty stomach.”

31 The Deal Goes Down

Having checked his watch every two minutes since lunch, Tre's anxiety built to the point he almost jumped out of his chair when his watch alarm sounded three forty-five P.M. He and Meagan had spent the past few hours going over all the possible outcomes of his pending rendezvous. The worst case scenarios dwarfed the positive outcomes and overwhelmed him. He never backed out on a commitment or a promise, though he habitually avoided making them to women, and he intended to keep this one, as he deemed it necessary on his road to recovery.

Meagan drove her car to an alley a few minutes from Trust Worthy Motors. Obscured from public view, Tre took care to edge the pink handgun into his soft cast.

"I'm sure there's nothing to worry about, but I do want to thank you for doing this. You really didn't have to."

"You were going to shoot me."

"That's true, I was. But I still want to thank you. Many opportunities for you to split have presented themselves, yet you always came back. So, thank you."

"You're welcome, but this isn't goodbye. I'll be in and out of there in five minutes and we can say our goodbyes then. Okay?"

"Okay." She leaned over and hugged her former boyfriend. He reciprocated, briefly.

"We really should get moving," Tre said.

Meagan pulled away, wiping a small tear from her reddened eyes. Tre pretended not to notice, but felt a lump in his throat over the possibilities.

"Remember the plan," she said, putting the car in gear. "I stop a block before the place and drop you off instead of using their parking lot. You walk from there. I will circle the block and pull up kitty-corner to the dealership so I can see the front door, but hopefully not get noticed by the goons at the door. That'll keep me from getting boxed in by them too. As soon as I see you coming out the door, I race to the front of the lot, pick you up, and we take off."

Satisfied with the plan and that he'd hidden the pistol well, he gave Meagan the okay to proceed. A block from the car dealership, Meagan pulled over to the side of the road and put the car in park.

"Good luck, Trevor."

"See you in five." He slammed the door shut.

She watched him quickly hobble down the street, then drove away to get into position.

The pistol hidden in his cast aggravated Tre to the point his limp became more exaggerated. Fortunately the walk was short and his delay insignificant. Crossing the street while approaching Trust Worthy Motors, he saw the two bodyguards towering next to the sales office door, arms still crossed in their menacing pose. Close to the door, a twisted smile came over Leroy's face, like he looked forward to administering another beating. Surprisingly, Leroy held the door open for Tre, who replied with thanks.

"Mr. … what did you say your name was?" The boss picked up an envelope from his desk as he stood.

"I didn't say."

"Well what should I call you?"

"How about Rusty?"

"Okay, Rusty. Leroy's going to check you out so we can conclude our business."

Leroy began his pat-down, hesitating briefly at the cast before standing up and giving the all clear sign to his boss.

"Excellent start to this afternoon. Came alone and clean. Now let's see the rest of my money."

Tre pulled a folded envelope out of his front pants pocket and held it out. Leroy grabbed it and handed it to his boss.

After a quick count, the boss seemed satisfied and gave Leroy the package with the documents. Tre pulled them out and began to check them over, passport first. It looked real, from what he could tell. He saw holograms and image refractions when he tilted the small book. The picture looked good too. He read the name out loud.

"Karen Feeding."

"Yeah, I think she looks like a Karen, don't you?"

"Sure, but Karen Feeding?"

"Check the other docs. She's a freelance nurse specializing in elderly care. I think the name fits."

"It fits too well. Sounds a little suspicious."

"Relax. I see it all the time where the name fits the profession. For example, Leroy's last name is Basher."

"Can't argue with that one." Tre looked through the last couple of documents and found all the pictures, names, and dates in order. "Looks like we're all set." He took a step to the door. Leroy took position blocking the door, and much of the light coming through. "What's the problem? I thought you counted the money."

"I did, but money's the problem."

"It's all there."

"Yeah, I know it was. But I got to thinking. You didn't complain at all when I jacked up the price by two grand. All the locals here would have freaked out on me. They would get Leroy's knuckles, but they would have protested."

"So?"

"So, I figure you got lots more where that came from." He sized up Tre. "I'm guessing you're a lawyer, or maybe a doctor. A job where money doesn't matter much. Definitely not a politician – not slimy enough. So here's what we're going to do, Rusty, or should I say Dr. Rusty. We're going to go out back and Leroy will help you into the trunk of a very nice Chevy we have back there. Then we'll drive you to this out-of-the-way ATM we know of and you're going to take out as much cash as you can, and then we'll let you go. How's that sound?"

"I'd rather just go."

The boss laughed. "He's funny, isn't he Leroy. Why don't you help Dr. Rusty get into a position where he'll fit nicely into that trunk?"

Leroy put his arm around Tre's shoulder then deftly punched him in the abdomen, doubling him over.

"There! Now you'll fit nicely." The boss laughed again. "Let's go."

Sucking wind, Tre thought of reaching for the concealed handgun. With Leroy's large hand clenching Tre's collar though, he deemed it unwise to try anything now. He'd wait until they opened the trunk at the ATM and then let the cretins have it.

The black Chevy stood ready at the door, trunk already open in anticipation of its intended occupant. Leroy pushed Tre toward the cavity and told him to get in. Tre gingerly stepped in. Having already spent time in a trunk on this trip, he didn't look forward to a repeat appearance. He obviously took too long for Leroy, and the large man pushed Tre down hard into the car, gashing Tre's head on the way down. Grabbing his skull to check for bleeding, he brought his bloody hand up to his face just as the light disappeared with a slam. He heard the car start up and begin to creep toward the front of the lot. Next he knew, all hell broke loose.

32 Stuck

The Chevy began to pick up speed through the potholed landscape of the parking lot, bouncing Tre around in the trunk. He struggled for anything to hold onto to reduce the impacts but didn't find it in time. Sirens blared, spilling into the air from all directions. The Chevy screeched to a forceful halt, throwing Tre hard into the support bars holding the back seat. The car violently reversed course and spun wildly as the boss tried to evade capture from the police. Tre's face flew flush into a tail light housing, eliciting a scream that surely no one heard above the mayhem outside. Muffled yells from the car's occupants led Tre to believe their situation was dire. Seconds later the Chevy smashed into a vehicle on the right side, the sound of mangling metal reverberating through his now tinier cell. A barrage of gunfire followed, instigated by Leroy and the vehicle's other passengers. Amidst their assault, they screamed at each other, their plight heightening as the police returned fire. Tre lay damaged and helpless. His anxiety escalated as he heard bullets pierce the light-weight automobile shell. A military grade Hummer this wasn't.

Leroy, or whoever drove, attempted to reverse out of trouble again. Tre could feel the car quickly accelerate backward, but no spin came. Instead, the car slammed into an immovable object. The trunk buckled around Tre, but didn't open. The shooting stopped.

At first, he only heard the car engine retching to its death. After some distant yelling, rapid footsteps approached as the police secured the vehicle. Tre imagined no survivors. He barely felt like he'd survived. The back of his head was gashed, his nose felt broken from smacking the tail lights, and he felt a new pain in the back of his leg. Reaching down, he felt more blood, and a hole. An errant bullet.

The police outside, presumably in full SWAT gear, began to holler to each other about the state of the occupants. All were dead. Tre almost yelled out for help, but fortunately thought first. Fortunate for himself since he lay in possession of forged documents and an illegal weapon, but also for Meagan, who they would surely capture and send to prison for life, or death. So he zipped it, even with the pain mounting. He tore off his sleeve and made a small tourniquet for the bullet in his leg. Then he waited.

Most of the excitement had died down within an hour and a half. Tre fell asleep briefly at one point. Fortunately, his watch illuminated for periodic time checks. After a further twenty minutes, Tre heard voices very close to him, followed by the beeping of a vehicle backing up. He could hear the men talking. A tow truck hooked up the Chevy to haul to the police station. There was no getting out now. He'd have to escape from inside the impound lot, or wherever the car ended up. He just hoped it wasn't headed for a crusher – certainly they'd keep it for evidence for a while. He began to think about how he would escape then realized he still had the pistol. If he couldn't jar the trunk open, perhaps he could shoot his way out. So long as the bullets didn't ricochet. Perhaps he needed to think about it more.

As he thought about the pistol, he thought about Meagan. She must have witnessed the whole crazy shortest police chase on record from her proposed vantage point. She must have been horrified, and he assumed she thought him dead. He doubted she stayed around long enough to see that Tre's body was not pulled from the wreckage. Or she didn't have a sufficient vantage point and assumed the worst. Either way, he'd have let her down unless he could successfully escape his metal tomb and get the documents to her.

The tow truck stopped and he heard an electronic gate beep as it rolled open. Seconds later, the tow truck had finished maneuvering the Chevy into place and unhooked it to await further inspection. Tre checked his watch again. Seven thirty P.M. He felt secure that no one would investigate further tonight. He would wait till midnight to make his escape. In the meantime, he'd try to figure out just how to do that.

There was no longer any noise outside the car, and there hadn't been for a few hours. He felt sure the impound lot was locked up tight for the night. At least to outsiders. Optimistically, Tre assumed that upon freeing himself from the trunk, he could locate a freely accessible gate control inside the impound lot.

The Chevy did not have an internal trunk release – too old for that. He twisted his body around to try a jarring kick at the trunk lid. On his left foot, he had an ankle cast with a gun shoved in it. On his right leg, he had a fresh bullet wound. He wondered which would hurt less if his kick didn't free the trunk. Pulling the pistol out of the cast, he pulled his left knee to his chest. Then counting to three, he rapidly thrust his left foot at the trunk. He sucked back an agonizing scream as his foot bounced back without the least bit of success. Time for Plan B.

Being a hatchback, Tre hoped one of the seat releases remained in working condition. He started by pulling the handle on the side of the car that had not fallen victim to ramming into other cars in the Trust Worthy Motors lot. Nothing. He tried again. And again. And again. Each time pulling as hard as he could while trying to will it open with his mind. Now sweating and panting from his failed trials, Tre wiped his brow with a remnant of the sleeve he'd used to wrap his leg. He deemed success unlikely on the accordion-looking side of the Chevy, but never one to discount all avenues he contorted his body to achieve an angle to pull the other seat release. Inhaling, he clasped the handle on the bent rod and yanked it. A faint sound met his ears. He tugged at it again, and on the third swift jerk of the handle, the seat popped open. Well, partly anyway. It came free of its latch, but the vehicle's damage restricted its movement. Tre leaned forward and pounded on the seat back, first with his right hand, and once it started to budge, he brought both forearms to bear. The shiver of pain on contact reminded him of his injured left arm, but the fresh, cool evening air that greeted him as the seat gave way was most welcome. The opening would have been quite comfortable for a child, or maybe even Meagan to slip through. It was anything but for the six-two dentist. He picked up Meagan's handgun from behind him and placed it into the backseat. Tre outstretched his right arm to clutch the front seat headrest and haul the rest of his body through the opening. A sharp, jutting piece of rear quarter panel gashed his side, leaving an eight inch long surface cut that annoyed him more than added pain, at least for now. Falling into the open back seat, he righted himself and ducked below the windows. A glance around showed the area deserted as speculated. Tre first peeked at the fence to see if scaling it was a viable option, but the barbed-wire looked imposing. The car rested in a location beneficial to his escape. He'd only have twenty feet to run to the gate release, thirty feet if he wanted to mostly avoid the camera focused on people entering the gate. A slight loop would allow him to avoid detection to the point where he had to push the gate release. At that point, he'd be fair game. While the gate opened very slowly, he'd just need it to open a foot or so to slip out. He took off what remained of his shirt and created a makeshift hood. It would shelter his face from the camera. He'd planned on tucking Meagan's handgun into the back of his belt to allow him to run unimpeded, but with no shirt, it'd show in plain sight. Palming the small weapon, he slid it into his front pant pocket, out of sight.

Ready to go, Tre inhaled deeply and slowly released it. He ran through the plan again in his head, including which direction to run once free of the impound lot. He lifted the door handle. It didn't budge. He tried again, nothing. He reached out the shattered window and tried the handle from the outside. Still no luck. Clambering into the front seat, he tried the passenger door next. Same result. Then the driver's side, also to no avail. The front windows remained intact, so back into the rear seat he awkwardly clambered. Back at the door he'd first tried, he plucked out the remaining fragments of glass to the point where the bottom ledge became clear of any obstructions. Last thing he needed was a torn-up ass, or worse, from climbing out the window. He imagined it very difficult to run with glass in his ass. Not that he would move too swiftly anyway, with a cast on one foot and a bullet in the other leg. But Tre was a determined man.

Clear of the window, Tre hobbled as quickly as possible in the evasive loop pattern he'd planned. In seconds he pushed himself flush to the wall, sliding along into position to release the gate. Looking around the outside of the lot, he spotted no foot traffic. The impound lot lay to the side of the station, improving his confidence in his plan. A quick slap of the release pad and the gate came to life – complete with the beeping sound that Tre had forgotten about. As he slid through the expanding opening, the impound lights came on, the police alerted to his presence by the gate. But bad leg and all, Tre had already darted into the night beyond the limits of the lights.

33 Now What?

The day had run on forever for Meagan, and the night headed in the same direction. Her insides drank a horrible cocktail of anxiety and sorrow. Anxious that her escape plans had crashed down in a gunfight today, and woeful for Trevor's demise doing her dirty work. She sat, beer in hand, staring at the ceiling.

She really had no idea what to do without her new identification. A remote Mexican village seemed out of reach, as well as her other thought-out destinations of Comoros, Madagascar, Cape Verde, or Sao Tome e Principe – all due to their lack of an extradition treaty with the United States, their cool sounding names, and equatorial island geographies. Dirt cheap to live in as well, and she held no predisposition to any lofty standard of living in spite of her recent lifestyle. The only viable option she could think of now was Canada. She knew the border was stricter than before 9-11, but surely she could find someplace along the expansive border due north where a person could cross undetected. Besides, if she did manage to settle down and get caught weeks or months later, Canada's extradition treaty would prevent her from returning to California to face the death penalty.

She flipped open her laptop to search online maps, causing a paper to flutter through the air and onto the floor beside her. Picking it up, she unfolded it to uncover a note.

I hope as you are reading this note, it's because I've secured your papers and we've gone our separate ways, and not because I've been killed by those incredibly ugly thugs.

A little smiley face dotted the end of the sentence. She tried to catch a harsh exhale, but failed. A flow of tears followed. Using the back of her hand that held the letter, she brushed the wet drops aside, only to have fresh ones appear. She lowered the letter and continued to read.

I can't put into words how happy I was to be able to help you out, and make some small amends for past wrongdoings. I truly am sorry that you were driven to such desperate action, and that I played a role in pushing you to that point.

"Oh, Trevor. You're too hard on yourself." She felt the need to express herself out loud, as though that made it real versus just thinking it. Once more, she brushed back tears.

I was immature and scared, but mostly, I was wrong. Wrong to leave. Wrong to leave without a note, without an explanation, without giving you a chance to allay my fears. I apologize – you deserved better. You deserve better.

"After all these years, the bastard finally apologizes." She took a long swig of beer and flapped the letter in the air. That was when she noticed a small note on the back.

P.S. You weren't really going to shoot off my drill, were you?

Meagan laughed amidst more tears. Finishing her beer, she leaned back and looked straight up, perhaps hoping that would quell the flow of water from her eyes. Trevor could make her laugh, and he always seemed to have the right words. Until that day he'd left and had no words. For some odd reason, she wished she'd had sex with him last night. Like the last meal for a death row inmate. Given the choice, Trevor probably would have picked sex over a last meal.

Grabbing two beers from the hotel bar fridge, she plopped back down in front of the laptop and scurried to Google Maps. Due north it curiously looked like Montana highway 191 ran to the Canadian border and stopped at the imaginary line. Zooming in, she could see the road actually went somewhere into the neighbouring country. The border crossings looked spread about twenty to thirty miles apart. *Certainly somebody could walk across somewhere in between?* Meagan picked at the label of her bottle while surveying the routes. A scroll to the right showed much of the same through the rest of Montana, all of North Dakota, and into Minnesota. Back to the west, things looked more interesting. Mountainous terrain with National Parks. Drive in and ditch the car, then set off on foot. She'd just look like another hiker. With that much territory, she surely could blaze a trail to freedom. She typed Cheyenne, WY and Glacier National Park, MT to get directions, and spit out some beer when it returned 856 miles and thirteen hours and fifteen minutes. She dragged the end point around the map. She could get to Chicago in about the same time. And Juarez, Mexico in two hours less! Maybe there was no clear way across the ditch they called the Rio Grande, but Arizona was a big place. It was also a hell of a lot warmer place to try to make a run for it. Of course, there was no cover in the desert, unlike the mountainous north. Plus the Federales would ship her sorry ass back to California and to death row to await her fate. Canada it was. Besides, they loved their beer up there, and it was really good beer too. Speaking of which, she needed another one.

Nearing the mini fridge, she heard a knock on her door. She almost dropped one of the empties. She looked at her watch. Two A.M. – that narrowed down the possibilities. No righteous hotel staff would come around at this hour. The knock seemed too normal for cops. They would pound on the door and summon her to open immediately, or more likely, just break the door down. Quietly approaching the peephole, she nervously leaned forward, closed her left eye, and looked out.

"Shit!" She excitedly fumbled to unfasten the chain and unlock the deadbolt. She flung open the door and cried out to her late visitor. "Trevor!" Meagan lunged forward and embraced him. He returned the hug, cupping the back of her head in his hand.

"Let's get inside," Trevor replied.

She nodded and pulled him across the threshold and closed the door, bolting and chaining it. "How?" she asked.

"I was in the trunk of the demolition derby car."

"My God! I saw the whole thing. The car looked riddled with bullet holes, like aluminum Swiss cheese. I waited around for a while but couldn't see them pull any bodies from the car. I saw them march a couple guys out of the office, and none were you. I wanted to wait around but got too anxious about being spotted. I assumed you were killed in the car."

"No, thank God. But I thought my number was up."

She noticed the moist red cloth dripping down his leg. "You're hurt!" She reached out again to him.

"Yeah, have you got tweezers?"

"You've been shot?"

"Through the trunk."

"Better than in your junk in the trunk," she said, laughing at her own joke.

"That reminds me." He reached into his front pocket. "I've got your little pink handgun here."

She smiled for a second before another thought came to her. "What about my papers? Did you get them?"

Trevor slipped his hand into his back pocket and pulled them out. "Here you go, Karen."

"Karen? That's my new name?"

"Yes, Karen Feeding, RN."

"Seriously?"

"You betcha. Do you think you can put those care and feeding skills to use to care for my leg and feed me some grub?"

"Absolutely." She tossed her ID on the counter then re-embraced her ex-boyfriend. "I'm so glad you're okay. I was so worried!"

He partially pulled away from her grasp and looked at her eyes. "Did you cry because you thought I was dead?"

"I'm not going to lie. I did cry." She paused and looked over his familiar but sadly absent-for-too-long face. "I cried because without those papers, I thought I'd have to run away to Canada. And it's cold in Canada."

34 Nice to Know You

Considering he'd slept on a couch and endured his nightly flashback of horror, Tre woke well rested. Still in body pain, but his mind was rested. Perhaps it had relaxed with the knowledge that he'd done some good and made a difference to someone who truly mattered to him. He rolled over and called out.

"Good morning!"

As his foot hit the ground while sitting up, his eyes opened to what his ears heard – nothing. No Meagan. Actually, no sign she had ever been there. The place looked like the maid had come in and worked around him. He checked his watch. Nine o'clock. Wow. He had slept. Rubbing his eyes quickly, he stood, buckling at the pain from the gunshot wound. Tre turned to the small desk where he'd left his meds, snatched the small canister and deftly spun it open. As the last two pills slid down his tongue, he spotted the note. Yanking Meagan's letter from the table, he walked to the washroom and unfolded it in stride. Tre tucked the note under his arm as he cupped his hands to gulp some water from the sink. Another handful of water invigorated his face. He snapped the hand towel from the rack and partially dried his face. Haphazardly he tossed the used cloth toward, but missed, its original hanging place. One step to the left, he pulled down his boxers and stood to relieve himself. With one hand keeping his trunks down, he flapped open Meagan's letter and began to read it.

Dear Trevor, it was so nice to spend some real time with you. You brought back a million memories, most of them good. I was truly heartbroken when you left me in Louisville, especially the way you left. I'm glad to finally hear your explanation, but it saddens me. During our *time together, I felt that I was always there for you. I stood beside, and behind you when necessary. I always thought I was your rock, grounding you with a stable support system away from home. I didn't realize that instead of your rock, I was simply a stepping stone. I wanted to be the one you could lean on, the one who was there, no matter what. I'm sorry if I scared you off, or smothered you. If only we could have talked about it.*

Tre had finished his business, but remained in the same position. A solitary drop splashed in the bowl below him. He used the back of his hand to wipe across his eye. He began the next paragraph.

I really appreciate what you've done the past few days to help me out. In spite of our past, I knew I could trust you, and it felt good to do so again. I still want you to feel bad about how you treated me, and beg you not to ever do that to anyone else again. I do forgive you, wholeheartedly accept your apology, and free you from any additional obligations. While you may want to keep this note as proof in case I come back at you later, you must destroy it completely when you finish reading it. Flush it or something – knowing you, you're sitting on the can reading it now.

Tre laughed and pulled up his boxers.

P.S. If anyone asks about the bullet wound, tell them that I shot you to keep you from going to the police. And no, I wouldn't have shot your lovely drill.

A smiley face followed the first P.S.

P.S. 2 Hotel is paid through tomorrow – my treat!

Instead of her name, she ended the letter by saying, '*Nice knowing you! XOXO*'.

Tre stood in a trance as he fastidiously reread the note. Finishing, he folded it multiple times and shredded it into the toilet bowl. Pausing to stare at the remnants floating, he wished he'd read the note one more time in spite of memorizing it. Sighing, he flushed her last words beyond his reach, but not his memory.

A hot shower made most of his tattered frame feel better, but opened afresh his recent wound. Usually his morning shower cleared Tre's head and got him thinking of the day ahead. Today, his mind clouded with those million memories Meagan had mentioned.

Fully dressed with a redressed leg, Tre scoured the kitchenette for food. Meagan had carefully cleaned up any traces of her. Even the garbage had been emptied and disposed of. He looked around the hotel room and felt lonely. He never felt lonely. He missed Meagan. He missed Cassy. He didn't miss Katie – she reminded him of the hell he'd faced on this trip. Tre decided to break down and pick up a cell phone. A burner phone anyway. Nothing permanent, just a device to call Jack, or to use if aliens plucked him from his car. Sliding a hotel key card from the table into his wallet, and stuffing that in his back pocket, he spun his car keys on his index finger and glanced around in case he'd forgotten anything. Not much to look at as he reached for the door, aside from yesterday's boxers hanging halfway out of his backpack.

Tre examined his new phone as he sat at a small sandwich and sub shop to eat his lunch. He wondered what the opposite of a smart phone was, because he had it. The phone came with two options. Make calls and hang up. The display wasn't even backlit for seeing at night. With the last bite of his veggie pita, he dialled Jack's cell phone.

"Jack here."

Tre attempted to disguise his voice with a Scottish brogue.

"Guid mornin! Hou's aw wi ye?"

Silence met his greeting. Tre chuckled to himself before continuing.

"Can ye gie's a haund?"

"You need some help, is that what you need?" Jack struggled with the accent.

"Can ye spaek slowly?"

"Do … you … need … some … help?"

"Ay, a misst ye sae muckle!"

Again momentary silence on the other end.

"Who is this? Bobby, is that you?"

Tre laughed into the phone. "Bobby's Scotsman isn't that good. It's Tre."

"Tre, man! Haven't heard a peep out of you in, what's it been? Almost a week?"

Now it was Tre's turn to silently pause. "Didn't you get my message from John?"

"Not a peep from my brother, brother."

"Really? I laid some *pretty* serious shit on him last time I called."

"Nothing. I asked him and he just shrugged. He hasn't been himself lately. I think Deanna's going off the deep end and pulling him into the abyss with her. He's not doing the religious retreats and all that, but she's got his head so screwed up, he doesn't know if he's coming or going. He's doing F-all with your file. How about you fill me in, then I'll give you the few nuggets I've been able to get from John."

Tre spent the next ten minutes relaying the Katie story, to which Jack responded by telling Tre to write everything down so he could read it as a deposition upon returning to LA.

"Also," Jack added, "something else that didn't make sense at the time but completely does now."

"What's that?"

"The car rental company called, since you gave them my number, and said you owed them a grand to clean the gas tank."

"Clean the gas tank? That's got to be their fault, isn't it?"

"There was so much sand in it that a game of beach volleyball broke out. There was so much sand they opened a golf course around it. There was so much sand that Sports Illustrated shot a swim suit edition. There was … "

"Okay, okay! I get it."

"You sure? I've got a good one about crabs."

"Save it, please! I get there was a lot of sand in it. Obviously intentionally put there to make it break down. And Katie conveniently comes along and saves me from my roadside plight."

"I'm not sure she saved anything. Sounds like she put it all out there for you."

"Thanks for your support. Did you take care of the rental company?"

"Put it on your tab, buddy. Any chance you can get me a payment, while I think of it?"

"Sure, I'll wire you some money today."

"Anything else I should know about?"

Tre hinted at his exploits in Cheyenne, mentioning an errant bullet, but careful to leave out any mention of Meagan.

"That's it for me," Tre concluded.

"Can you take a day off from mayhem? I hope this whole making amends business is worth it."

"I'm finally seeing some positive results."

"That's good, because my God you've been through the wringer!"

"That reminds me," Tre replied. "I need a refill on my script."

"Already? You filled it last week. That last one should have lasted you three weeks."

"I've been through the wringer, remember. And I've never been shot before. Shot at, yes, but never shot."

"I'll see what I can do. Are you near a pharmacy?"

Tre gave him the address of one near his hotel in Cheyenne.

"Now tell me what you've found out," Tre asked.

"Not much, like I said. John's been like tits on a bull, as you would say."

"Good to see you listen to me sometimes."

"Hang on every word, buddy. Anyway, John's narrowed the SUV down to three out of, what was it, forty-something? Most likely it's a rental from LAX."

"Smart, make it look like an out-of-towner."

"My thought too. Trying to throw off our scent. I'm sure John will confirm that car tomorrow by eliminating the other two, but he's not getting far with who rented it. The rental agreement indicated it was used by someone named Pat Burns. They didn't get an address; just that the licence was from Jersey."

Tre laughed.

"What's so funny?"

"I don't suppose the name of a late hockey coach means much to a guy from Sacramento."

"Should have known that'd end up a dead end, too. They used a pre-paid Visa card to pay for the rental and John's trying to run it down, but it's not likely to lead anywhere."

"I've been thinking about why this nutcase hasn't made another appearance."

"Why's that, Tre? Does he think you're just going to do yourself in?"

"Funny. No, I'm wondering if he's tied to a job in LA and can't get away to chase me down."

"What about shooting at us in Sacramento?"

"Wasn't that on the weekend?"

"You may be right, but I'm not sure how it will help, aside from eliminating the independently wealthy. You know what we really need is another lead."

"I suppose you'd like me to come back to LA to draw him out?"

Jack now laughed. "Would you mind? It would make things so much easier. Maybe you can buy a spot on 'Dancing with Celebrities' announcing you're back in town."

"You know that I'd love to help you out, but you've got to do something to earn all this money I'm paying you." Tre paused for a moment. "Then again, the billboard might cost less than paying you two buzzards."

"Three buzzards. Don't forget Deanna."

"Oh, you've got her on this case too, have you?"

"She's been doing a few hours a week on it. You know we're all in for you, buddy."

"All in my wallet, I'd say. Let me give you this number. Call me if there's anything I need to know. Tell Bobby I said hi, but please don't give him this number. Or give it to anybody but John, okay?"

"Sure, no sweat." He took down the number. "Where to next?"

"Just going home. Two days, tops and I'll be there. I'm looking forward to seeing my mom, that's for sure. It's long overdue."

"And your dad?

"He's on my list."

35 The Feds

Entering the hotel foyer, Tre observed some not-so-inconspicuous men in suits milling about. He'd seen enough cop shows and movies to recognize their intent. Tre limped past them to the elevator, wondering if they'd somehow made him from his midnight escape out of the police impound lot. No, they would have sent uniform officers after him if that was the case, and they would have acted in the lobby upon spotting him.

With the final ding of the elevator, the doors opened to his floor and glancing left ahead of turning right, Tre spotted a third suit leaning up against the wall reading a newspaper. Stopping in front of his door to remove his key card, a second look left detected the suit touching his ear and talking. Not a good sign for him, but he entered his room to await the impending declaration from whichever branch of law enforcement these gentlemen represented. He'd carried home a small bag of drinks and snacks for the room, and stuffed them in the small bar fridge, bag and all. He placed his wallet, cell phone, and keys on the table so that his pockets became empty. Less than a minute later, a pounding came on the door.

"FBI. Open up."

"Coming," Tre replied. He hadn't bothered to latch or bolt the door. He turned the handle and pulled open the door, raising his hands as he did so.

"Step back, sir."

Tre complied. One of the now-vested men took Tre, and in one swift motion, had him hands on the wall, spread-eagle. The other two men burst past Tre, weapons drawn as they cleared the small room and bathroom.

Slapped into cuffs and pushed over to a pulled out chair, they unceremoniously planted Tre on it. The treatment brought out the pain in numerous places, emitting a wince.

"Where is she? When's she coming back?"

Feigning aggravation, Tre answered. "By she, do you mean Meagan Winters, that sick freak?"

"That's exactly who we mean. Answer the questions."

These guys came off as all business, definitely a different breed with superior training from the boob brother police detectives he'd encountered. "I don't know. I don't think she is."

The questioning agent looked around, watching the other agents tear the place apart. There wasn't much to search, but if there was anything hidden, Tre had no doubt they would have found it. They knew what they were doing and one of them handed the questioning agent Tre's new prescription bottle. The agent knew the drug on the label.

"Oxy, huh? What's this for?" He angled his weapon at Tre as an intimidation tactic.

"I was in a car accident recently, not to mention your suspect pushed me down a very long staircase in El Dorado Hills."

"I'm aware of your involvement, Dr. Brightman. Are you going to try and tell me that you happened to run into Meagan Winters, a thousand miles from Sacramento, in of all places Cheyenne, Wyoming?"

"I know it sounds unlikely, but that's what happened."

"It does sound unlikely. Sounds more like a rendezvous than an accident. I think you've aided and abetted our fugitive."

"I'm headed home to Michigan, and I-80 is the best route. I pulled off the road at Cheyenne due to my meds making me tired. I picked out the Cowboy Brew Pub to eat at because it looked interesting."

"And she happened to be there."

"Hey, I was as surprised as anyone!"

"And why did you not contact the authorities?"

"She pointed a gun at me!" Tre was getting agitated.

"And if I go to the bar, people will tell me that?"

"No, because she had it pointed at me under the table."

"Sounds like you're making that up too."

"Roll up my right pant leg. The bitch shot me after we left the bar!" Tre stood up violently from the chair, causing it to thunder to the floor. The second he did it, he realized it wasn't the brightest thing to do with three heavily armed FBI agents interrogating him. One of the secondary agents righted the chair, and with a firm hand on Tre's shoulder, slammed his ass down on it.

The lead agent leaned forward and menacingly glowered up close to Tre's face.

"Don't do that again!" The man took the snout of his automatic rifle and tugged up Tre's pant leg, exposing a bloody strip of gauze and tape. He pulled back from Tre and nodded to the other agents. Grabbing the other chair, he spun it around and sat backwards on it, careful to flip his weapon around the back of his shoulder.

"Okay, I believe you." He motioned to the agent standing behind Tre to uncuff him. "We've looked into your background to confirm the Sacramento force didn't miss something by letting you go. There's nothing to connect you two since you abandoned her over six years ago." He pointed at Tre's shot leg. "You know, if I was her, I would have shot you too. I mean the way you left? Cruel."

Tre raised his eyebrows at the level of information they'd gotten on him.

"And why'd you change your name, anyway?"

"It's too long of a story, but nothing illegal."

"Oh, we know that." The agent stood up from his chair. "Do you know anything about her whereabouts now?"

"I think she's headed to Canada."

"Why do you think that?"

"When I woke up, she had her laptop open, working on it. I got to within five feet of her before she noticed. She slammed down the lid, picked up her pistol, and waved it at me to sit down and mind my own business if I didn't want another hole in my body."

"That's helpful. We know what's she's driving, so we should be able to track her down." The agent extended his hand and shook with

Tre. "If you see, or even hear from her, please call me immediately." He handed Tre a card with just a phone number. "And take care of that wound. You wouldn't want it to get infected."

"Yes, sir."

Tre followed the men to the door, and secured it with the latch and deadbolt. He pulled a Gatorade from the bar fridge, twisted it open and took a long drink. He popped a few of his new pills, took another guzzle of sports drink then flopped on the bed, eyes closed. He'd done Meagan one last favour, and finally felt that chapter of his life could close.

36 Catching Up

Aside from the now standard 3:45 A.M. wakeup, Tre's conscience let him sleep soundly. At least his nightmares managed to find a schedule in this insanity of a road trip. He'd gotten used to waking with dry mouth as well, a side effect of the Oxy that he would acknowledge. He had a couple of long days of driving ahead of him. Before the accident, he'd have easily made the remaining seventeen or eighteen hours in a single shot. He knew his current limits would prevent that, so he set more realistic goals. Des Moines tonight, home tomorrow night. Hopefully incident free.

Equipped with time to think as he drove, Tre set his mind to daily check-in calls with Jack. Tre also committed himself to give Bobby a long overdue call. There was nothing his friend had done to deserve the silent treatment. Tre needed to deal with his demons on his own, and knew Bobby would offer all kinds of advice that he'd rather not hear. Sometimes the value of knowledge is only truly appreciated if you come to the conclusion on your own. Bobby sometimes extended the orthopedic part of his title beyond the spine to trying to straighten Tre's head. Tre felt certain Jack had given Bobby the 50,000-foot updates, and Bobby would thirst for absolute details. Tre would have to find a happy medium or stay on the phone for four hours.

The hours and miles flew by, and signs harkening Des Moines and all of its attractions became frequent. Happy to find a quiet hotel and put his feet up, Tre ordered a pizza, sometimes a reckless folly while on the road, then dialled Jack before Bobby.

"Jack, its Tre. How's it going?"

"Why don't you tell me? When I hear from you two days in a row I get nervous."

"No new disasters today. You can relax. Just looking for an update on my stalker."

"John did confirm it was the black SUV from LAX. The other two checked out. He also tracked the prepaid Visa to a pharmacy in Hollywood, within a mile or so of your office."

"Katie?"

"She certainly looks good for it, with that whole psycho-chick thing she pulled on you."

"I'm not so sure," Tre said. "Why try to kill me one week, then force me to impregnate her a few weeks later? Why wouldn't she just kill me on the side of the highway?"

"Did you miss the part about psycho-chick?"

"Yeah, yeah. I suppose she could be the one, but I don't see it. What's John's next step with the SUV?"

"I think he's at a dead end. The pharmacy has video but it cycles every week, so it's gone. The prepaid Visa was paid in cash and was the sole item on the receipt, so nothing there either."

"Doesn't sound promising."

"John's changed his focus to trying to track down the gun, but it's a bit of a needle in a haystack too. Working with the police, they're certain the shot came from a Remington 700P, based on the calibre of the bullet and the range of the shot."

"Sorry, Jack. I know squat about guns."

Jack laughed. "I guess it'd be like you telling me about the latest dental equipment. The rifle is standard police sniper issue."

"So it was a cop?"

"Can't say that. These things sell to civilians too for under a grand. There's a lot of them out there."

"So that's no help."

"I didn't say that. They think a solitary shot was taken, and it was taken from five to six hundred yards away at a moving target."

"So the guy's a pro."

"Definitely has some type of training. Maybe SWAT. Maybe just shoots a lot. The police are going through their files for officers that have, how should I say it, gone over the edge."

"Can't be too many, can there?"

"Not likely. John's also checking contestants at local shooting competitions. I've participated in some of them, and there are a few militia minded souls in that crowd. Maybe one of them decided to step up to the next level of live targets."

"Great. But no other shootings like this in LA since mine, right?"

"No, so it was definitely somebody who knew you or Cassy."

"Cassy? Do you think someone would want to gun her down?"

"With her lifestyle? Not very likely. My money's on you, buddy."

"Thanks. At least it should narrow the suspect list pretty quickly."

"We don't even have a list yet, so don't get ahead of yourself. John just started on this today, and the police have other priorities than hunting for one of their own. Then there's cross checking any names with your client list, known associates, dates, etc."

"Maybe you did it? Do you have an alibi?" Tre laughed.

"I wouldn't have shot you. I would have just stuffed one of your attempted layups down your throat."

"Hey, I'll be back in game shape by the time I return to LA, and we'll see who's king of the court. Speaking of which, I better let you go. Promised myself I'd talk to Bobby tonight."

"Good luck with that. Make sure you hit the can before you make that call, because you're going to be a while. That man had more questions than Jeopardy contestants when I called him last night. I had to fake another call just to get off the line."

"I'll keep that tactic in mind. Talk to you soon."

Tre's pizza arrived as he hung up, so he put the call to Bobby on hold for another twenty minutes. After eating, Tre gave Bobby the latest news, leaving out much of the painful details. Bobby had prepared a list of questions, and Tre could hear Jenny prompting his friend in the background too. Thirty minutes into the call, Tre claimed the pizza delivery guy was pounding at the door, and that he'd call Bobby back in a day or two from Michigan. His friend thanked him for calling, and told Tre he was glad that his final destination was at hand.

With his obligations for the day fulfilled, Tre popped a couple pills, closed his eyes, and waited for 3:45 AM.

37 Brothers

As much as he felt he had a legitimate gripe related to his brother's effectiveness at work lately, Jack himself was distracted. He was not the kind of guy that would fall head over heels for a girl after a date or two. Bobby was that kind of guy back when he was single, but not Jack, nor his brother John. And certainly not Tre. But Paula had somehow touched that nerve. From the time they met on the plane from Sacramento, he'd felt a connection that he couldn't describe. Jack cleared his calendar for the coming weekend in the guise of a visit back home to his parents, so he could see her again. The 'L' word wasn't part of his vocabulary, but it had recently burrowed a hole into his subconscious. John's recent marital distress, however, hung like a black cloud over Jack's psyche.

Entering the detective agency office, Jack saw his brother alone at his desk. Deanna was nowhere in sight, again.

"Hey, John. How's it going?" Jack greeted his brother, avoiding mention of the third member of the agency.

"Good," John replied, looking up from his computer. Feeling the need to explain the absence of Deanna, he elaborated. "Deanna's picking up supplies at Staples this morning. She'll be in about eleven."

"Cool. I'm running low on elastic bands to zing you with." He paused for a minute. "I don't want to pry, so tell me to shut up if I'm out of bounds, but is everything okay with you guys?"

John stood and stretched. For a split second, Jack tensed, sensing his brother about to throw a punch at him. John must have detected the flinch, and laughed.

"I'm not going to hit you, although I'm sure I could think of some reason why you deserve it."

Jack came down off his heels and grinned.

"Deanna and I don't have the same goals in life anymore. I don't have a desire to run off and join a commune to find my inner spirituality. She can't get enough of that stuff."

"Sorry, man. I think she's still traumatized from the accident."

"It wasn't an accident, Jack. Someone shot her on purpose while she was trying to do her job. Someone who didn't know her tried to kill her."

"Did you suggest she see the force's trauma counsellor?"

"Of course I did. And both times ended badly. She's convinced God is the answer."

"Maybe, but isn't she taking it a bit far? I mean these weekend retreats are happening with greater frequency." Jack sat on the corner of Deanna's desk.

"She's headed to another one tomorrow. Four days."

Jack shook his head. "Are you going to be okay this week? I mean with me heading up to Mom and Dad's?"

"You mean to Sacramento to visit Paula, where Mom and Dad just so happen to live?"

Jack blushed. “Busted, huh? Is it that obvious?”

“Naw, you’ve been cool about it. Hell, Bobby would have talked my ear off about it by now. Remember what he used to be like?”

“Yeah,” Jack laughed. “Remember how Tre used to call him Gossip Girl?”

John laughed too, the first time in too long. “You go do what you’ve got to do. Don’t let my marital problems put a damper on your love life.”

Jack turned to pour himself a morning cup of joe. “Say, why don’t you come home with me? I’m driving up. It’d be good to have some company.”

“I think I’d be lousy company this week.”

“You’re lousy company anytime and I’ve never let it bother me.”

“Funny, but I’ll stay here. I want to keep on top of Tre’s case.”

“You can do that from anywhere with your laptop. Besides, Mom would be glad to see you.” He knew that would get his brother.

“All right, fine. But no singing, even if the Killers come on.”

“Harsh, bro. That’s what I do best. Nail the killers!”

38 The Chase

With Des Moines more than an hour in his rear-view mirror, Tre and his bright orange Camaro hit the outskirts of Iowa City. He'd noticed a black SUV in his rear-view about twenty minutes earlier, and kept an eye on it as it methodically closed the gap on him. Surely if it was someone out to kill him, they wouldn't have taken so long to catch him. He wondered if Katie had sabotaged his gas tank again and lay in wait for his car's engine to seize up. Paranoia or not, he was about to find out. The black SUV had come to within thirty or forty feet and pulled out to pass. Tre checked his rear-view again, but the trailing vehicle straddled the dotted middle line, remaining a car's length back in his blind spot. Tre increased the pressure of his foot on the gas to regain a safe distance. The black SUV followed suit. Tre sped up another ten miles per hour. His shadow kept pace.

Tre cursed out loud. "If you're some stupid kid playing a prank, I'm going to be really pissed!"

As if the other driver heard him, the other car slowed down and pulled in behind the Camaro. Instantly, Tre knew why. A highway patrol car whizzed by, not stopping or even slowing for Tre's twenty miles per hour over the speed limit. Clocking at a hundred and ten miles per hour or faster, the officer had bigger fish to fry than Tre's induced speeding. The police car grew smaller on the horizon in front of him, a combination of the cruiser's continued speed and Tre's natural reaction to slow down at the sight of one. Comfortably registering eighty on the speedometer, Tre took another look back, just as the black SUV shifted back onto the centre dashes. He was about to curse again, but didn't get the chance. The other car suddenly accelerated, slamming into the driver's side rear bumper of the Camaro. The orange vehicle roared over the rumble strips, sending the shoulder's accumulated stones flying and creating a small cloud of dust, stunning Tre as he panicked to get his new ride under control. Fortunately, the black SUV had backed off and not hit Tre with a second shot, or the Camaro would have gone barrelling off the paved surface and into the depths of the nearby ditch. Squealing tires guided the fishtailing car back over the rumble strips and onto the highway. He buried his foot on the gas pedal, the engine exceeding his expectations with the new found thrust. The black SUV fell behind until the Camaro got caught behind a transport passing another. Tre contemplated passing on the left shoulder, but a quick glance showed debris ahead. He fidgeted the Camaro back and forth looking for an opening or encouraging the trucker to make haste with his pass. Both proved fruitless. The SUV grew large in Tre's mirror. As the eighteen-wheeler signaled to complete his pass, another firm bump from behind greeted Tre. This time, however, the dentist expected it and the effect was minimal except to encourage a slight swerve onto the left shoulder to accelerate past the transport as he completed his lane change to the slow lane. The SUV followed suit.

Bracing for the second bump, Tre tried to glimpse the face of his pursuer, but could see little due to the height difference of the vehicles. All he could tell was that the crazed lunatic was male with sunglasses.

Tre scanned the traffic ahead, looking to avoid another incident with a passing transport. He had a feeling that the next time, his stalker would just push the Camaro right into the back of the transport. As they neared Iowa City more by the minute, the traffic picked up. The two cars weaved between slower vehicles, Tre's blood racing as fast as his car. Finally an opportunity presented itself. Tre slowed, hoping the SUV would pull up beside him to more effectively run him off the road. His hunch was right. As the other vehicle began to pull up beside him, Tre nudged the accelerator, trying to stay ahead. He looked ahead. He only needed a few more seconds. Which was good, because the black SUV almost pulled even with him. Tre glanced over, but the tinted side windows prevented a look at the driver. The passenger window of the SUV began to lower and Tre knew what came next – the muzzle of a gun. But Tre had timed it perfectly. He pulled hard to the right on the steering wheel, bouncing over the beginning of the divider for an off ramp, but catching his pursuer off guard. Tre heard a shot ring out, but heard no contact to his car. He looked over his shoulder to see the black SUV race by above on the highway. Tre slowed going down the off ramp as he saw a stop light closing in. He planned to hang a quick left and double back on the highway, hoping the black SUV would think Tre would try to hide on the city streets.

Not wanting to come to a complete stop, Tre drifted to the light, gauging the crossing traffic to determine if it was possible to run the red. The sound of a few car horns startled him, and he looked to the sound. Straight in front of him, on the ramp going back onto the highway, the black SUV swerved the wrong way through oncoming traffic, headed right toward Tre. Jumping the light, Tre sped left under the highway and bolted through the turn back onto the westbound highway. He looked back, praying the SUV hadn't seen the turn and had gone straight. His prayer went unanswered.

Tre pounded the steering wheel with both hands and cursed. He needed a new plan. Entering the highway, he jumped lanes to the left, slammed on the brakes and turned onto the grass median. As he floored it to cut across, grass ripped up behind him. It seemed like a good idea at the time, but he'd forgotten about the short posts protruding every ten feet to alarm drivers who may have fallen asleep. He clipped one with his front passenger side wheel, and a second with the driver's side rear wheel. It scared the crap out of him, but it could have been worse. One of those rods under the chassis could have left him in serious trouble.

A loud blasting horn snapped Tre back to reality. A transport truck raced up behind him. Tre knew he had no time to get up to speed, so he scooted to the right shoulder, gladly exchanging the vibrations of the rumble strips over a transport causing a wreck. As the transport stormed by, horn still blaring, Tre looked back across the highway. The black SUV had slammed on its brakes, drawn to the truck's horn. The driver waited on the opposite shoulder, judging traffic for a break long enough to pull the same maneuver across the median.

Tre sped away from the shoulder at the same time his pursuer gunned it across the highway and into the grassy stretch separating eastbound from westbound. Foot to the floor, Tre saw sparks fly from the SUV as it re-entered the highway. The distance between the cars was a mere hundred feet but smoke began to appear from under the

SUV. Tre considered using the same off ramp to elude the shooter until he spotted two police cars coming up the ramp the wrong way. As Tre whipped by, followed by the closing SUV, he could see the cruisers' lights go on as they set up to block further traffic. Tre knew that meant one thing – more police cars waited ahead. Good for him he thought, provided he could avoid getting shot – by his stalker and the police.

The Camaro slowed in anticipation of the blockade, but mindful of the chasing black vehicle. As it turned out, he needn't have worried. The smoke under the SUV darkened and thickened. The car slowed, but not due to its driver. Tre slowed to stop about fifty feet from the parked cruisers, shut off the engine, tossed the keys out the window, and put his hands on the steering wheel in plain sight. He sat still, hoping his tactics would prevent bullets from heading his way. Focused on what lay in front of him, he almost forgot about the instigator of the car chase. Peeking into the mirror, he saw the man roll out of the smoking stalled car. The man sprang to his feet and began running full tilt toward Tre's car, raising his gun as he neared. A shot rang out. Followed by three or four in quick succession. The first bullet pierced the skin of the Camaro, resonating through the car. Two of the other bullets incapacitated Tre's hunter, causing his gun to go bouncing across the pavement out of his reach.

39 Now We're Getting Somewhere

A few weeks ago, Tre would have been nervous walking into a police station, unless accompanied by Jack or John. Now, walking into a jail versus waking up in a cell made him happy.

A truck driver had radioed in that Tre's Camaro had been shot at by a black SUV, and an officer in an unmarked car had witnessed the SUV's wrong way pursuit of Tre's car. So instead of waiting, cuffed in a cell, he sat free at a detective's side chair relaying his account of the incident. Tre had already spoken to Maury, who cautioned his client about saying anything without him there or until he could find a closer associate to address the matter. Tre told Maury that he'd endured enough and wasn't going to risk getting thrown in jail for a few days for not cooperating. Hearing a very short account of the day, Maury advised Tre not to specifically mention how fast he had driven or other motor vehicle offences, but simply state that he'd been pursued by a person who had made an attempt on his life. Tre took the advice to heart and his statement focused on what the assailant had done to him, and not what Tre had done illegally in his attempt to escape. Before giving his statement, Tre bargained for, and received, the name of the attacker. Although the name meant nothing to him, he hoped it would light a bulb for Jack or John. Tre remained at the station for over six hours while the detectives sifted through his other recent incident reports, shaking their heads at what he'd sustained in such a short time.

Tre left the station in the pitch black of night. He looked at the bullet hole in the Camaro, but even with the lights of the police lot, it was hard to see the damage to the rear quarter panel. He found a hotel and called Jack. Maury had already briefed Tre's detective friend.

"Good thing you found this guy, or should I say he found you. We've run into dead ends everywhere, pal. The sniper rifle was a needle in a haystack. I guess now we won't have to have the guy put a slug in you to get a match."

"I don't remember volunteering."

Jack laughed. "It's too bad your car chase today didn't happen a day earlier."

"Why's that?" Tre asked.

"We had a black SUV following us for a while today, but it turned out to just be a family on vacation. The dad wasn't too thrilled about us cutting him off and pointing our pistols at him over the hood of our car."

"Bet he won't forget his vacation," Tre chuckled.

"And you got your guy's name from the police? That was clever thinking on your part. I'm not sure my connections run all the way to Iowa City, but I'll see what I can do to see what they find out. In the meantime, I'll get John on this right away since it's early evening here in Sacramento."

"What are you doing back there? Is everything okay?"

"Yeah, it's cool. John needed to get away for a while, if you know what I mean."

"Sure, I do. You mean you're trying to cosy up to that new girl of yours."

"Guess I'm as obvious as your cross-over dribble."

"I'm happy for you. She sounds like a keeper."

"Like you'd know one if you saw one," Jack laughed.

"I did," Tre sighed.

"Sorry, man. At least you can put this whole thing behind you now."

"Wish it were that easy. But I am glad they caught the lunatic and I can finish my trip in peace."

40 End of the Road

The sign welcoming Tre to Monroe, Michigan felt long overdue. What a long strange trip it'd been. He'd fallen into a Grateful Dead song. Maybe he did need to lay off the Oxy. Anxious to get home to address his greatest act of regret, he had a minor stop to tend to first.

The Monroe Diner had been around for many years. In Tre's high school days, it was *the* hangout. He owned a plethora of memories from that place, most of them good. Today was the day to make up for a bad one.

Walking in the door, the bell overhead tinkled to announce a new patron's arrival. The regulars, accustomed to the bell, paid no heed to it; only the owner behind the counter did. Although the years had added grey to his mane, Mr. Henry looked much the same. A warm smile accompanied the gentle nod of acknowledgement from the owner. The man looked like he still enjoyed running the diner, a trait Tre admired after all the years.

"Brickman!" A boisterous greeting came from a red leather booth on the right side of the establishment. A tall young man stood, adorned in a worn, and snug around the middle, jacket, emblazoned with the Monroe Trojans' logo. Other heads turned at the proclamation. "Is that really you, Brickman?"

Tre looked the man over as he approached, looming a good six inches over Tre's six-foot-two-inch stance. "Stretch? Stretch Williams?"

"Sure as shit!" Stretch extended a hand to shake. As Tre closed his hand, the towering former teammate pulled him into a bear hug. "Man, it's good to see you."

"You too, man." Tre replied as he stepped back from the welcoming embrace.

A petite woman came to the right of Stretch and reached up to put her hand on his belt loop.

"Oh, shit. Where are my manners? Trevor, this is my girl, Vicky. She moved to Monroe about a year or two after you left."

She extended her hand to Tre. "His wife, Vicky." She rolled her eyes. "Two years – you'd think he'd be used to it by now."

"Two years, wow!" Tre smiled. "Any little Stretches?"

She looked up at her man. He smiled back and nodded. She replied in a whisper. "Well, Simon, I mean Stretch and I haven't told hardly anyone, but I'm two months."

"Congratulations. Both of you. That's great."

Vicky smiled, trying to contain their secret and her excitement. "Well, we know you haven't settled down yet. Simon pointed you out at the Golden Globes a few years ago, with Marla Main. And then we saw you again last year at the People's Choice awards with what's-her-name."

"Yeah, what was her name," Tre laughed.

"Must be cool banging all those Hollywood babes," Stretch said, followed by a punch on the arm from Vicky.

"I think that means time to change the topic." Tre smiled at Vicky, trying to determine her height. At most she stood five-one, with the modest heals she wore, meaning a seventeen to eighteen inch difference in height between the couple. That'd be like him dating someone four-feet-eight. He shuddered at the thought. But as long as she made Stretch happy, who was he to argue?

"You want to change topics, let's talk about that last game."

"Man," Tre shook his head, "I've apologized for that so many times. I think Chris Webber's had an easier time about calling that time out when he had none."

"Maybe. But he didn't throw up a brick from five feet away in the last second to lose by one."

"Is that why you call him Brickman?" Vicky asked.

"Has a ring to it, doesn't it?" Stretch replied.

"I liked Gunner better," Tre answered.

"That was before the big brick, man."

"I swear," Vicky added. "Why is it guys are permanently stuck in high school? Trevor, what are you doing back in town?"

"Going to visit my folks. It's been too long. And I've got a few other things to take care of."

"Like what?" Stretch asked.

Vicky laid another shot on his arm. "Mind your own business, Simon."

"No, it's no problem. It's actually why I'm at the diner. Excuse me a minute."

Tre walked over to the counter, putting his head to his chest for a second and taking a breath. He pulled a thick white envelope from his front pocket.

"Mr. Henry?" Tre said to the man cleaning up from a recently departed customer.

"Yes. Is that really you, Trevor?"

"Yes, sir. It is."

"Well, you've certainly made a name for yourself around here. Mr. Hollywood, some of your old gang calls you."

Tre blushed. "My fifteen minutes of fame, I suppose."

Mr. Henry spread out a couple of new place settings between them on the counter. "What can I do for you, Trevor?"

"I came here to apologize and ask for your forgiveness."

"What in the world for? You were always a perfect gentleman when you came in." He looked over at Stretch. "Unlike some of your high school pals."

"Remember the water damage you had late one summer?"

"How could I not? It closed my place for a week. I used all my savings to fix the place while I fought with the insurance for months to pay up. They accused me of negligence and even at one point of intentionally causing the damage." His reddened cheeks displayed his horrible memories. "You're not saying you were involved in that, are you? Weren't you gone off to college?"

"I was involved. I left the next day. I didn't mean it to happen, and didn't even know about it until a week or so later."

"How could you?"

Tre sat down on a stool at the counter. "I didn't mean to, honest. I was playing a gag on Stretch." He jerked his head in the direction of his high school chum. "He had the runs and was stuck on your toilet while they passed. I thought it would be funny to soak his feet, so I put a rag over the drain, plugged the sink, and ran the cold water. When he came out with a soaker, I figured he'd at least shut the tap off, if not unplug the sink. He came out so angry with me, he'd forgotten to do both. You already had your coat on and hurried us out so you could lock up the place."

"I'm not sure what to say." Mr. Henry stood unconsciously wringing the dishcloth in his hands.

"I came to pay you retribution, and ask for your forgiveness." Tre slid the fat envelope across the counter. His face wore the expression of a young boy who'd lost his puppy.

The diner owner hesitantly grabbed the envelope and flipped the unsealed flap open, finding it stuffed with hundred dollar bills. He thumbed through them, not counting, but amazed at the stack. Before he could reply, Tre added one more thing.

"I didn't realize the difficult situation it put you in, and the hassles the insurance company gave you. My buddies all just laughed it off, saying you'd fixed it up with the insurance money and that it was the best thing to happen to the diner. I truly am sorry."

Mr. Henry glanced at the envelope again, once again flipping through the bills. He bent the flap over and stuffed the envelope into his apron pouch. Thinking twice, he retracted the envelope and slid it behind the apron and into his pants pocket. He looked up at Tre, tears in his eyes.

"All I ever wanted was to know who did it. I knew it wasn't my fault, but I even began to doubt myself as the whole thing dragged on. Do you know what it's like to close your eyes and have the same nightmare every night for months?"

"I'm afraid I do. I have the guilt of someone's death that I deal with nightly. And like you, when I'm awake I know it wasn't my fault. Closing my eyes though brings out the demonic thoughts. So if you choose not to forgive me, I will understand."

"It took five years for me to let your buddy Stretch back in this place, because I was convinced it was his fault. He never confessed or asked forgiveness, but I forgave him. You didn't need to walk in here out of the blue and tell me any of this, let alone give me any money for damage that happened so long ago. But you did, and to me that speaks to your character. So, yes, I forgive you."

41 Home at Last

Tre started to turn into the driveway of his parents' home before course correcting and parking on the road. His father got aggravated by another vehicle blocking the drive when he wanted to get out. Tre sought no additional quarrel than the one he'd started and avoided all these years.

From the passenger seat Tre scooped up the bouquet of fresh cut roses and carnations he'd picked up at Deb's Flowers. He got out of the car and locked it. Pausing to catch his breath like a teenager on a first date, he calmed his nerves and strode across the street and up to the door. He felt odd ringing the doorbell, having spent the majority of his life under the roof of this modest two-storey home. Before the door opened, Tre could hear his mother squeal with excitement and begin hollering his father's name. He wasn't the only nervous one, as his mother fought with the deadbolt to open the wooden door.

"Tre!" She lunged forward and hugged him like he'd returned from the dead. He felt tears leak through the shoulder of his cotton shirt, his mother on her tiptoes. She pulled back and wiped away the sentimental flow with the cuff of her sleeve. "Sorry," she said as she sniffled. She turned and bellowed to her husband, "Howard, your son Tre is home!"

From a room at the back of the house came a gruff remark. "I don't have a son named Tre."

"Never mind him. He's so stubborn sometimes I just want to scream." She put her hand on Tre's arm. "Come in, son. Do you need help with your bags?"

"I'll get them later, Mom. Here are some flowers for you."

She smiled as she took the flowers, started to cry again then hugged him one more time. "You didn't have to." She looked at the wrapper. "Oh, Deb's! You remembered."

"Nothing but the best for you, Mom."

"Come to the kitchen. I want to get these into water."

Tre walked through the hallway toward the kitchen. Not much had changed. Same pictures on the wall, same carpet, same wallpaper. That is, until they entered the kitchen. What used to be a cosy, but oft crowded cooking space had been transformed into a modern kitchen with a new sunlight and an additional two hundred square feet of dining space, complete with floor to ceiling windows.

"Wow! Mom, this is gorgeous! When did you get this done?"

"Just finished last month. You like it?"

"It's amazing. You must be so happy to finally have your dream kitchen."

"Every morning I come out, start my coffee, and just look around, smiling."

Tre lowered his voice. "I'm surprised Dad sprung for this. It must have cost a small fortune."

"It was a bit dear, that's for sure. I had to remind your father that his heritage is British and not Scottish."

"And that did it?" Tre was surprised such a simple trick would work.

"Not at all," she smirked. "I have other tricks too."

"Mom, I don't want to hear if you threatened to withhold sex."

His mother laughed. "Like that would do it. I told him I had talked to you and that you were going to send me the money to do it. Your father is a proud man and would have none of that."

Tre smiled as he looked up at the new sunlight. "Glad I could help, even if I didn't know anything about it."

"Let's just keep that our little secret." She poured Tre a very tall glass of apple juice and looked up at the wall clock. "I better get dinner started. You know your father if his meal isn't on the table precisely at six o'clock."

"I'll leave you to it and go get my bags. Is my room still available, or did you turn it into an observatory or butterfly sanctuary?"

"Still as you left it. Come back when you're settled in and we'll talk a spell while dinner cooks."

"Sure thing. See you in a few."

Tre's mother wasn't kidding. The room looked exactly as he'd left it. A thin coating of dust covered the desk and his memories, so his mother must have cleaned it periodically, just not lately. A picture of his high school sweetheart lay face down on the desk, turned down after his first trip home from college. He didn't have the heart to throw it out at the time, nor the heart to look at it for the first few times back. After that, he decided to leave it down as a mini shrine to his high school days. His mother knew the significance and had left it untouched. A few other reminders harkened back to high school. He chuckled at a faded newspaper clipping of a game-winning three-pointer earlier in his senior year playoffs, but overshadowed by the 'brick' that Stretch had painfully recalled. Unzipping the side pouch of his bag, Tre pulled out a small toiletries bag and tossed it on the dresser. He unzipped the main compartment of his backpack, held it over his bed upside down then shook it to spill out all of its contents. He stuffed a few clean items back into the bag before he tossed it onto his desk chair. He rolled the dirty clothes into a ball, wrapped his arms around the bundle, and headed downstairs to do some laundry. He managed to slip down to the basement laundry room without his mother spotting him and telling him to leave it for her to do. Tre knew she had her hands full with his father, one month into his early, and forced, retirement.

Returning upstairs, he found his mother standing at the top of the stairs, shaking a spatula at him.

"You know I would have done your laundry for you."

He took the plastic weapon from her hand. "Mom, I didn't come home to have you do my laundry. What do you think? That I've bought new clothes for the past ten years every time mine got dirty?"

"No, just took them to get laundered." She smiled at her boy and swiped back her spatula. "And don't think you're doing any cooking while you're here. There's no way in hell you're messing up my kitchen. I barely let your father step foot in it, and he's a clean freak compared to you."

He protested, "Mom, I'm not a messy high school kid anymore." His mother's eyes shot daggers at him. "Got it," he whimpered. "No touching the kitchen."

After thirty-five minutes of catching up on the neighbours, their kids, and grandkids, the stove timer beeped a reminder that dinner was ready. Tre's mother sliced the meatloaf into monstrous pieces for him and his father, and a morsel for herself. She extracted golden cobs of corn from a pot of recently boiled water, and finished loading up the plate with baked potatoes the size of bricks. Pouring milk into the glasses she'd set out, she gave the table a once-over then yelled out her husband's name.

Tre's father entered the room, the two exchanging glances for the first time in forever. His father's hair had lost all signs of its dark brown heritage, but looked as thick as ever in its white reincarnation. The similarly six-foot-two former CEO had developed a bit of a hunch over the years, making his son appear taller. His father shot a fleeting glance before turning to assume his spot at the head of the table.

As Tre's mother said grace, his father gently grunted at the mention of blessing the Lord for the safe return of their son. After uttering his amen, Tre's father kept his head down and dug into his food. Tre looked at his mother, who shrugged and smiled back.

"Pass the salt please, Elaine."

The salt sat right in front of Tre, but his mother began to reach for it. Tre grabbed it and held it up in the air. His dad finally looked up.

"Dad, I've been through a lot the past few weeks."

"What does that have to do with me getting my salt?"

"Nothing, except it may be the only way to get your attention."

"You've got it." His father laid his utensils down on his plate and straightened up.

Tre had seen this focused look from his father before, and he imagined how his employees must have feared that view across the boardroom.

"As I said, I've experienced a lot and it's caused me to reflect on my past life decisions. I've made some good ones, like my profession, and I've made some bad ones, specifically how I've treated people. Or in your case, how I ignored your wishes."

His father's gaze stayed fixed. Tre wondered if the man ever blinked.

"Dad, I did what I did to be successful in LA. It's a cut-throat ruthless business environment, even for a dentist."

His father corrected him, "Maxillofacial surgeon."

Tre smiled recognition of his correct profession. "You of all people should understand what it takes to succeed in business. I'm sure it was a tough road to CEO."

"If only you knew."

"Someday you'll have to tell me. But it's different when you work for yourself. In LA, a name can make or break you."

His dad's voice expressed his agitation. "There was nothing wrong with your name."

"When you gave it to me, there wasn't. It's not like I wasn't proud of my name. I just needed a name that would attract attention. Positive attention."

"It's not your fault, what your cousin did," Tre's father stated emphatically.

"I know that, Dad. But what was I to do? I had the same name as him and he'd been arrested."

"I expected you to make it on your own merits, like you did. You could have added your middle initial or name to your signature," his Dad replied.

Tre's mother sat quietly listening to the back and forth, but staying out of it. Her husband continued, "I'm sorry you ended up with the same name as your cousin. It wasn't planned, you know. I hadn't seen or talked to my brother in five years, and had no idea he'd gotten married let alone had a kid. Both of us named our boys after your great grandfather. Shit happens."

"Well shit certainly did happen with Dr. Trevor Brockman, didn't it? Becoming a drug addict and raping those patients with his assistant."

"Language please! We're at the dinner table," Tre's mother objected.

The two men both mumbled an apology.

His father's voice raised another level, to the chagrin of his mother who shrank in her chair. "It still wasn't right. Your lineage goes back to a knight in England. It's a history that you should feel pride in, not ashamed of."

Tre put his hands up, palms towards his father, moving up and down in a calm down motion. "Look, I'm sorry for changing my name. Very sorry. I know that I can't make up for the anguish I've caused you, but when I return to LA, I will no longer use the name Tre Brightman."

His mother sat up. "You're going back to Trevor, son?"

"Yes. Dr. Trevor Brockman."

42 Life's Lessons

Cleaning up following dinner was no longer a chore at the Brockman household. Trevor couldn't believe that his father had finally talked his mother into getting a dishwasher after all these years, especially after he'd forked out big bucks on the renovation and a new stainless steel fridge and stove. She'd rejected the notion saying washing dishes provided her solitude and time to reflect. Yet she would complain about how dry her hands felt all winter. Tonight, cleaning up meant loading the dishwasher, an easy wash of the pot used to boil the corn on the cob, and adding some soapy water to work on the caked-on remains in the meatloaf tray.

Trevor grabbed a clean glass from the cupboard and half-filled it with tap water. Reaching into his front pocket, he pulled out his pain medication.

"I'm going to have a cat nap after I take my meds." He spilled two pills into his cupped hand.

"You have a prescription for pain pills?" His mother picked up the bottle from the table and read the label. Her eyebrows furrowed. She reached over and closed her hand on Trevor's before he could ingest the pills. "You can't take these anymore!"

"What?"

"You must know how addictive these things are! You're already two-thirds through this bottle and it's only a few days old!"

Trevor didn't dare tell her it was the third bottle. "But I've gone through a lot." He didn't want to worry his mother, but he felt the need to justify taking a couple more meds. "I've been in a car wreck, thrown down a staircase, and shot!"

His mother's eyes opened wide at her son's pronouncement, temporarily though. Quickly her look returned to concerned mother. "Trevor William Brockman, I'm sure your body is not used to that pain, but I will not allow a drug addict in my house."

"Mom!" He protested, but knew he was in trouble from the use of his full name.

Her hand flashed up to make a stop sign, and her other hand plucked the pills from Trevor's palm. "Your father has plenty of Ibuprofen in the medicine cabinet. Help yourself. And take some of his whiskey if you need it."

Trevor didn't have a response other than the 'yes, Mom' that he'd been programmed to say from his youth and the firm smacks to the back of his head from his father when another response was uttered.

His mother took the bottle of pills and dumped them down the sink, followed by the two in her hand. Trevor let out a reserved sigh.

"You'll thank me for this in a few days," his mother stated, tossing the empty pill bottle into the garbage after confirming the label indicated no refills.

"I hope you're right, because I feel like hell now." He stood from his chair, noticing the pain more now that she'd removed his crutch. "I'm going to get some of those Ibuprofen and grab a cat nap. See you in a bit."

With four Ibuprofen tablets taken, they were only 200 mg after all, Trevor tried to nap on the couch. He'd grown up grabbing pre-dinner cat naps on the same couch. His father was not allowed to sit on that couch unless company came by, but Trevor'd had carte blanche to nap on it since high school. This evening, he did not fall into a deep slumber upon laying his head down as accustomed. Instead, he tossed and turned, which led to more shooting pain, which led to more discomfort and restlessness. After forty-five minutes of the opposite of rest, Trevor started to his room in hopes of finding a leftover oxy in his pants pockets. Halfway up the stairs he remembered he'd already thrown them in the washing machine. He continued up the stairs to seek his mother's other suggested pain reliever, the one that came in liquid form.

Twilight had come to southern Michigan. Tre enjoyed the mid-summer nights back home. The heat and humidity edged down to a tolerable level that made sitting outside extremely enjoyable. His father sat on a padded wicker chair, feet up on the matching ottoman, reading his Kindle. His father looked up for a second and went back to reading, before his mind registered what his eyes had spotted. He slapped shut the Kindle cover and placed it on the small table beside him that held an empty highball glass. The burgundy and wood case that his son carried in his arm put a smile on his face.

"If you feel obligated to bribe me with Glenlivet 21, who am I to object?" He presented his empty glass to his son.

"Thought you might like this. I hedged on the 25, but thought you preferred the 21."

"Good memory, Trevor." He purposefully used his given name. "Besides, your mother saw the price of the 25 that time I brought it home and it almost gave her a stroke. And she just finished filling my head with a lecture of your oxycodone use, which is somehow my fault."

Trevor hung his head slightly. "Yeah, that." He raised his line of sight to make eye contact again. "So I'm taking her advice and going to drink my way through the pain."

His father laughed. "It's a cure that's worked for countless generations of Brockman men. I see no practical sense to ending a tradition now."

Trevor removed the sleeve from the wooden box holding the twenty-one-year-old single malt scotch. The bottle itself was a beautiful thing to behold for the two men. The amber liquid poured tantalizingly into his father's empty glass – no ice allowed in this family's scotch!

After silently consuming the first round amidst quiet satisfaction, Trevor refilled their glasses.

"So tell me about your life, son. I try to puzzle it together based on bits and pieces from your mother."

Trevor nodded. "I truly am sorry that I haven't stayed in touch."

His father shook off the apology. "It goes both ways, son." He set his drink down. "I let my stubbornness get to me. I know some people would say I let my pride get in my way, but there's a big difference between pride and stubbornness. They only belong together when the quality of one's work is at stake, or a fundamental value is at risk. I am very proud of our lineage, but I'm more proud of the person you've become and your accomplishments."

Trevor raised his glass to toast, "To the death of stubbornness."

They clanked glasses. His father leaned forward in his chair. "I assume that you are still unattached, I mean coming all the way across the country by yourself."

Trevor looked away into space before answering. "Yeah."

His father spoke. "I was late to settle down, especially compared to your grandparents. My father was married and had two kids by the time he was twenty-one, and your grandmother was a year younger."

"Wow. I can't imagine getting married that young, let alone having kids."

"It was different back then, that's for sure. Not much birth control, for sure." His father laughed. "Of course, when I was young, it was such a big deal to buy condoms. I remember buying a bunch of crap I didn't need at the pharmacy to make it look like the condoms were just another item."

"Now it's a big deal not to buy them."

"I think you and I have a lot in common when it comes to our love lives at that age. I was a free spirit back then. Best of times, worst of times, as they say. Had a blast, but always felt something was missing."

"Know what you mean," Trevor said. "I've dated all these Hollywood celebrity types and had a great time, but seldom did any of them inspire thoughts beyond getting them in bed."

"Did I ever tell you how I knew?"

"How you knew what?"

"That it was different with your mother?"

"No."

"We were on our second date. We went canoeing, stopping for a picnic. She was so different from most of the women I'd known. For one, she didn't bat an eye at jumping in a canoe. And when she spoke, she had purpose to her conversation. She was interesting to listen to, and made me think. At the end of the date, I drove her home, kissed her at the front door, and said goodnight. It was like a movie from the fifties. Pathetic, huh?"

"Sounds like a chick flick." Trevor laughed.

His dad burst out laughing too. "You're right. To me, a second date meant a lot more than a peck on the cheek. Guess I was a bit promiscuous, but I wouldn't likely call again if sex wasn't involved."

"Or call again if it did," Tre added.

A sigh came from his father. "You're not too far off." He paused to sip his scotch. "It's funny how meeting your mother turned me on a dime. No more desire for the chase." Mr. Brockman finished his scotch and handed the empty glass to his son for a refill. "So, what about you, Trevor? No ah-ha moment for you yet, I assume?"

Tre looked away. "I thought so ..." He looked in his father's eyes before Trevor's head sank in sombre reflection.

"What happened?"

"She was the one …" Trevor fought to get out the words as much as he fought the moisture building in his eyes. "The one in the crash."

"I'm sorry, son." His father put a consoling hand on Trevor's shoulder.

"Why did it take me so long to realize it?" He didn't expect his father to answer. "I mean, I worked with Cassy for years. Why didn't I see it?"

"I knew your mother for a few years before we went on our first date. It takes the right circumstances, I guess."

"What if she was the one?"

His father straightened up. "I've never believed in" – and he made air balloons with his fingers – "the one'. I mean, I believe there are people that we match perfectly, and your mother is one for me. Does that mean that I believe if I hadn't met her I would have been doomed to a life of misery and loneliness? I don't think that at all. I think a lot of people settle for less than they need, less than they deserve in regards to the respect and treatment they receive, or less than will make them happy. It doesn't mean that patience wouldn't have allowed that to occur because 'the one' got away."

"Thanks, Dad. I'm sure you're right. You usually are."

His father chuckled. "What do you mean, usually? Haven't I always given you good advice?"

"I remember some of your better ones," Tre laughed. "One that I remember as odd the day you told me, but came in handy later. Never date sisters..."

His father joined in to finish, "Especially at the same time."

"There's another good one I've used so much I've lost count. Change the subject immediately if your partner asks any of the following questions – does this make me look fat, which outfit do I look best in, or my favourite, what's wrong with my mother?"

"Good to see all my pearls of wisdom haven't gone to waste. I still practice most of those, except the mother one, God rest her soul."

"Any other new nuggets to share?"

His father cleared his throat. "Well, never call the Chairman of the Board an asshole at a board meeting where they have the power to force you into early retirement. Even if everyone at the table knows you're right, they will still support the asshole in a vote to terminate you."

"So that's what happened. Mother never said."

"She only knows that the Chairman and I no longer saw eye to eye, and that I got a nice separation package. It did teach me something though."

"What's that?"

"Never take for granted what you have at this moment in time, and don't expect it to last forever. My entire career was propelled by change and my ability to predict and manage it. But this change has been hard. I'm not accustomed to idleness."

"It's that A-type personality."

"It's the scotch getting to me, I mean making me reflect. I always lived life on my terms when I was younger. At work, I had little regard for what or who I left drowning in my wake. It took a while, and the help of your mother, to learn that I had to temper my aggressiveness outside of the office. She taught me that running a Fortune 1000 company was different than dealing with family, friends, neighbours, or the guy at the hardware store. Her father told her to treat everyone like some day your life was going to be in their hands."

"Good advice. Hard for us A-types, but I see the point."

"Exactly. It was hard. But think of it. I mean, what are the odds that you could count on someone to help you out if you can't be bothered to call them by their name, or even know their name? Or worse, treated them like shit because you thought you were better than them?"

"Like Mom says, treat people like you want to be treated."

"Yes, but much more than that. Treat them better than you expect to be treated in return, and they will someday surprise you in the most unexpected ways." His father finished another scotch and set the glass down. He picked up the almost half empty bottle. "Almost forgot how good this stuff was. And how much it goes to my head." He stood up. "I'm heading in for the night."

Trevor stood up and hugged his father. "Thanks. For everything. Always."

They separated and looked at each other, his father seeing a younger version of himself in his son. "Glad to have you home, son."

"Well, now that you've got time on your hands, you can come visit me in LA."

"Your mother would like that."

43 Checking In

The flow of Glenlivet all night had Trevor forgetting any need for pain pills. The conversation with his father had likewise lifted a burden from his aching soul. A temporary feeling of normalcy engulfed him, leaving him satisfied. Halfway up the stairs to his childhood room, his cell rang. He contemplated answering it, opposed to his normal reflex of answering immediately. He couldn't see Jack giving the number to anyone else, and couldn't envision any bad news, so he answered.

"Tre, did you make it home today?"

"Indeed I did. It was a good day and I'm Glenliveted out."

"Is that a word? Good to hear anyway, my friend."

"Before I forget, I'm changing my name back to Trevor. But no sweat if you want to stick to Tre."

"No problem, Trevor," he said, elongating the last syllable. "Just don't get pissed when I slip up though, bro."

"How's John holding out?"

"Not so good. Deanna's on some week-long retreat. I had to get John away from the office so he wouldn't sit there staring at her empty desk. He needed a change of scenery something bad and some pampering from our mom. John's wondering if she's going to even come back. It took him until Stockton to change the subject, poor guy. But he was good about meeting Paula at dinner with our parents."

"So you took the big step, did you? Good to hear, buddy."

"Yeah, pretty cool, huh? I've just had a feeling about her since we met on the plane. It was different, you know what I mean?"

Trevor reflected on the conversation with his father. "Yes, I do. Good for you."

"Sounds like we've both had good days. I don't think what I'm going to tell you will ruin your day, but it won't make it better."

"Lay it on me."

"Your guy in Iowa City confessed to trying to kill you in Iowa City and in Sacramento, when he shot at us in the Mustang."

"I'm sensing a but."

"You are correct. But, he says he didn't shoot at you on Highway 1, doesn't own a sniper rifle, and doesn't know how to shoot one."

"That doesn't make sense."

"It does when you add in that he says he was hired to kill you and he wasn't hired until the day you were arrested in Sacramento. He's a small-time thug from LA. His name is Quinn. Turns out John arrested the guy a few years back. Some police detective thought the guy was good for a couple shootings, but all they could pin on him was the mugging that John nailed him for. So the guy did short time and was out."

"I don't suppose this Quinn said who hired him?"

"Not that easy, bro."

"So we're back at square one."

"Not exactly."

"Why? What aren't you telling me?"

"The person who hired him was a woman."

44 Morning Glory

Trevor awoke in pain. A slight hangover, but mainly craving his meds. Though, at ten in the morning Mom's alternative of booze didn't seem practical. Slipping on a fresh shirt and shorts, he rationalized that food and water would help. Bounding down the stairs in a fashion that would surely bring memories back for his mother, he steered straight to the cupboard where he'd found the cereal for his midnight snack the night before.

Chowing down on a Jethro Bodine-size bowl of cereal, Trevor looked up as his father entered the kitchen. He had to put a hand in front of his mouth to catch the food spewing out of it. With his hand coated in damp cereal bits and milk, and his mouth full of food, he blurted out a garbled statement.

"What the hell are you wearing?"

"What?" His father looked down at his morning garb. "What's wrong with this?"

"What is it?"

"It's my tool belt, what did you think it was?"

"I can see it's your tool belt, but what the heck is in it?"

"These?" He slipped a squirt bottle free from a loop. "This is glass cleaner," and he re-holstered it. "And here is a squeegee, a red rag for wiping up drips, and on this side," and he spun the tool belt around forty-five degrees, "a Dustbuster. Pretty cool setup, don't you think?"

Trevor shook his head. "My father. CEO and ergonomic household engineer."

"Hey, this saves me a lot of time. You know how many times I'd put down the Windex and have to hunt around for where I'd last set it down?"

"I'm sure it's a model of efficiency, Dad."

Trevor's mother walked in the room, refilling her glass with water from the fridge dispenser. Dressed in stylish, but modestly worn workout clothes, her brow perspired. She took a red cloth and patted dry her forehead and cheeks. Finishing, she spotted the red cloth on her husband's modified tool belt.

"Howard! What have I told you about the red cloths?"

Trevor's father looked at him, signalling for him to pay attention.

"Red cloths. Red cloths. Let me see … they are for cleaning, right?" Trevor's father grinned.

"No, no, no! You know better. The red cloths are for my workouts. The white cloths are for drying dishes, the blue cloths are for housework, and the brown cloths for messes."

Mr. Brockman looked again at his son. "And you laugh when I wear a tool belt to organize things." He turned back to his wife. "Yes, Elaine. I know the cloth colours. But I needed a cloth this morning for cleaning and all the blue ones are buried somewhere in the laundry hamper. Trevor's washing his clothes and left a heap in there."

She looked at her husband, not quite sure what to make of his excuse. She looked at her son, who just shrugged his broad shoulders. "All right, I forgive you this time." She refilled her now half empty glass. "Back down to the workout room for ten minutes to cool down, then I'll come up to help."

After she was out of earshot, his father spoke.

"She runs a tight ship, that mother of yours. I could have used a few more like her on my leadership staff. I just wish she appreciated how much I help out around here. I mean, neither my father nor hers lifted a finger around the house unless it meant nailing or tinkering with something. Certainly not cleaning anything. That was the woman's job."

"Get over it, Dad. Those lines don't exist anymore."

"I get it, but sometimes it seems humiliating going from CEO to getting yelled at for using the wrong colour rag to clean. You could have spilled a gallon of milk on the kitchen floor and my father would have walked around it for days without even thinking to mop it up."

"Try being self-employed. The first few years were hell, back before I could afford to pay for someone to do my taxes, pay my bills, order supplies, or clean my offices because the hygienist wouldn't do it. I could have used that tool belt back in those days!"

"Well, you may need my tool belt today. Your mother was on the phone all night and morning calling relatives and friends to come by late this afternoon for a get-together to celebrate you coming back to town."

"Cool! That will save me running around to see people. Please tell me that you are barbecuing your fantastic Louisiana style spare ribs?"

"Called Mac at the butcher shop this morning and had him put aside a bunch of slabs for me. I'm picking them up in an hour so they can marinate all day."

"My mouth's watering already. Just tell me what to do around here."

"I think your mother wants you to finish your laundry first then set up the long tables and chairs outside. I'm sure she'll have more lined up for you by the time you're done that. She's got a grocery list the length of my arm for me to pick up when I get those ribs."

A few hours of frenzied cleaning and setup whisked by. The scotch came out as Trevor learned how to make his father's tantalizing rib sauce. The rub applied to the ribs and set aside to marinate, Trevor poured a second drink as the front door was knocked on then opened. The youngest of four of Howard Brockman's sisters entered, followed by four teenage girls, all carrying a dish for dinner. Their father trailed the group by a few steps, struggling to carry a stack of lawn chairs.

"Trevor! Come help your Uncle Ralph with these chairs."

As Trevor approached the front door, twin girls accosted him, screeching questions at him.

"You have to tell us about Marla Main! Is she as nice in person? Is she as tall as she looks on 'Hot Singles'? Are her boobs real?"

Trevor's eyebrow went up with the last question. "You girls really have grown up, haven't you? Let me help your dad, then I'll answer any questions that are appropriate."

The girls excitedly squealed, dropped their dinner dishes on the hallway bench, and both began frantically texting their friends.

Trevor rolled his eyes before moving through the doorway to meet his uncle. "Let's take these around the side, Uncle Ralph."

"Thanks, Trevor." He set down the stack of chairs and Trevor snatched up half of them. "I feel sorry for you today, Trevor."

The statement surprised Trevor. "What do you mean?"

"Normally, the girls whine and complain every time we're asked to go to any family get-together, but as soon as they heard their famous movie star-dating cousin was going to be here, they were pushing us out the door to come. The whole way here they yacked about what to ask you about different starlets."

"So I see. It's cool. Man, they've grown. I think Maddie wore diapers last I saw her."

"We were talking on the way over. I think it's eleven years, and Maddie's the youngest. She would have been two or three."

"Caroline's the oldest, right? She's got to be, what, eighteen?"

"Nineteen, next month. The twins just turned sixteen."

"You've got your hands full, I bet."

"It's all good. At least now since I put in a toilet in the basement."

As they finished setting up the chairs, the twins came out the back sliding glass doors, each carrying a drink.

"Thank you, girls," Trevor replied. "Now, what do you want to know?"

Their father warned them. "Girls, take it easy on your cousin. He didn't drive all the way across the country just to tell you Hollywood gossip."

The girls gave their father a look like, 'of course he did'.

Trevor laughed as he opened his laptop. "Let me show you some pictures of when I went cliff diving with Marla in Negril, Jamaica."

The girls leaned forward in attentive silence.

By six o'clock, all the guests had arrived and dug into hearty platefuls of ribs, corn on the cob, barbecue-roasted potatoes, and numerous salads and side dishes. Boisterous talking and laughter filled the back yard, and eagerly scooped seconds and thirds nearly depleted most of the serving dishes. Each relative took their turn talking to Trevor, with the twins interrupting on several occasions to ask new questions they'd thought up or a friend had texted them. Darkness soon arrived, and the senior Mr. Brockman lit a bevy of torches around the yard. Half the group went inside, not wanting to take their chances that the citronella would actually keep the often ravenous mosquitos at bay. Within ten minutes, everyone had moved inside, as a quick storm rolled through, dousing the torches and raising the humidity to an unbearable level in spite of the darkness.

The new kitchen came in handy for such an occasion, and as usual at parties, the majority of the group crowded into its four walls. Trevor was surprised he heard the doorbell over the rowdy kitchen scene, and hoped that a missing favourite cousin stood on the porch. Opening the door, Trevor's face lit up and he heartily laughed. Before him stood a minister, topped off with a Detroit Tigers baseball cap.

"Zachary! So good to see you."

The cousins hugged in the doorway. Trevor took a step back. "Is this your casual look? Full minister's gear and ball cap?"

"Naw, this is what I wear to service. Only I wear the hat backward at mass."

Trevor laughed. "Come in. Let's catch up."

The two men turned into a small den at the front of the house, partially closed the French door, and sat on a couple of locally made Lazyboy recliners.

"So, last we spoke I was pleased to hear you were about to embark on your quest to make amends. I see you've made it all the way home. Did it turn out as you expected?"

Trevor thought about the question. He explained how he certainly hadn't expected all that he'd been through. He'd naively thought he could just talk to people, ask for forgiveness, and move on. He discussed in detail all the trouble that he'd fallen into, and how at times he'd felt like he moved backwards toward the abyss instead of into the light.

"You set out on a goal that was more complicated than you thought, but it was simpler than you could ever imagine."

"What do mean, Zach?"

"It's impossible to know what you would be required to do to obtain forgiveness from each of the people on your list. And, frankly, they may not be willing to forgive you. Not now, or ever. We all see the world through our own unique lenses, and we all have our own way of perceiving our treatment in any given situation. What you may have seen as a terrible atrocity to another human being, they may not have given a second thought. And conversely, something that you dismissed offhand as silly, may be a friendship killer or trust breaker to someone else."

"You could have told me that before I set out." Trevor ran both his hands back through his hair above his ears, pulling his face tight as he did so.

"You had to learn your own lessons, I'm afraid." Zachary sat up in his chair. "So was it worth the effort?"

"It was, but I have to say that I only batted about five hundred."

"Nobody bats a thousand, Trevor. And it is foolish to think that you would on such a difficult quest. You can only control what you can control."

"What do you mean?"

"I mean, the one thing that you can control is how you feel about what's gone on in your life. Have you forgiven *yourself*?"

Trevor sat speechless.

"Trevor, we all make mistakes. Most of the time we can't take them back, no matter how much we want to or try. We can just learn from the mistake, adapt, and move forward. Too many people dwell on their mistakes and can never move forward."

As Trevor pondered his cousin's advice, he heard a commotion at the front door. As he stood up, a noise unfamiliar to his home made his heart sink. A gunshot rang out and silenced the kitchen sounds.

45 Hunter at the Door

Beyond the French door to the den stood a small gunman, head to toe in black, with a hoodie obscuring their face. Trevor opened the door and Zachary stood up beside him, an inch or so shorter than his cousin.

The gunman waved the gun around and hollered demands. "Everybody just shut up! Now! Don't make me use this on anyone."

Trevor's father snaked gingerly through the crowd to step in front of everyone. Aware of his emergence from the crowd, the gunman barked another order.

"Not another inch closer," and the gunman pointed the weapon at Mr. Brockman.

"I'm Harold Brockman. What can I do for you?" He looked calm, as if addressing his management team.

"Tre Brightman. Where the hell is he?"

"I'm his father. What do you want with him?"

"I'm not looking for your son. I'm looking for Tre Brightman. From Los Angeles."

"That is my son. He changed his name."

"No shit! I don't care what you call him. Just get his sorry ass out here."

Trevor stepped out of the den, with Zachary in his shadow. "Here I am."

The gunman pivoted to face Trevor, turning the gun to point directly at his head. The movement revealed the face under the hood.

"Deanna?" Trevor said, startled. He fixated on the muzzle of the gun, wondering if this was the end.

"You know this woman, son?"

"She's the wife of one of my best friends," Tre replied, visibly shaken.

"You didn't …"

"No, Dad. I didn't." Tre turned back to Deanna. "Why? What did I do to you?"

"You are not a good man and you must atone for your sins." She pulled out a pair of handcuffs and looked at Tre's father. "Come put these on your son," she barked out to him.

Zachary stepped out from behind Tre. "This is not the way to solve your problems, my child."

Deanna spotted the collar. "I'm not your child, Father." She paused to think over her words. "I'm a child of God, not some priest in small town Michigan."

"Surely the Lord does not want you to act with violence."

She tossed the cuffs at Zachary. "Just be quiet and put those on Tre."

Zachary continued to press for a peaceful resolution. "You must see the error of your – "

Bang!

Zachary fell to the ground in front of Tre, clutching his shoulder as he lay writhing on the ground. Tre bent down to look him over.

"Get up, Tre. And pick up those cuffs and toss them back to me."

Tre followed her orders, and she in turn flipped the cuffs over to Tre's father. "Put those on your son now, unless you want to join the Father on the floor."

Mr. Brockman walked over to his son, who held out his arms.

"No! Behind the back. Turn him around and put them on behind his back."

Tre turned to allow the cuffs to be secured. His dad whispered 'I'm sorry' and stepped away when he'd finished.

"Let's go. Out the front." Deanna motioned to the door and followed Tre out, keeping one eye on the stunned crowd in the house. She looked back at Tre's dad. "Wait five minutes before you call an ambulance for the Father."

46 In Peril

Deanna opened the back door to her rental sedan and pushed Tre headfirst into the vehicle. She slammed the door, hopped in the driver's seat and double checked the child safety locks on the doors and windows. She hit the gas and peeled away from the curb, looking at the front door of the house as she went.

"You're a hard man to kill, apparently." She looked in her rearview mirror at Tre as he straightened up.

"I can't believe it's been you all along."

"It wasn't a couple of times. The Molotov cocktail was me, and the car accident was me. But I contracted out the rest. I should have known better than to hire that loser Quinn to get rid of you. I thought that if he was smart enough to avoid those other murder raps, he'd handle this easily. Twice he had you in his sights and let you get away." She sat up as straight and tall as her five-foot-six frame would allow, trying to strike a righteous pose. "But I won't let that happen again. I'm going to take care of you myself!"

Tre sweated profusely in the back seat. The car was warm and his nerves were worn.

"Just tell me why. I don't get it."

"You've left a trail of destruction in your wake."

"Yeah, I get that part. The accident brought that into focus. I thought Katie would have told you all about my trip to make amends."

"Oh, she did. And I heard she got what she wanted out of you."

"And?"

The car accelerated through a turn, throwing Tre to the side of the car.

"And you never even thought of putting me on your list, did you?"

Tre was flummoxed. "I keep telling you, I don't know what I did to you, so why would I put you on my list?" He thought back to Zach's comments.

In the mirror, Tre could see tears streaming down her face. The car bounced as it left the road and entered the parking lot of a hotel. She hopped out of the car and ordered Tre out, her gun obscured from everyone's view but his. She led him around the side of the hotel to an entrance door left unlocked by a band of duct tape she'd put in place. She led him to the elevators where she motioned him to the back then punched the button for the top floor. Exiting the elevator, she directed him to the nearby stairwell. As the door swung open, Tre could see a 'Roof Access' sign.

"Up you go, Doctor."

Once again, the door had been jimmied open. They walked out into the open air, revealing a view of the town that Tre had never seen.

"Walk over to the side."

As he reached the side, she ordered him to stop.

"Remember I have a gun and know how to use it," she told her prisoner. She held the gun with one hand while turning the key of the handcuffs with the other hand. As they clicked unlocked, she quickly backpedalled and raised the gun to eye level.

"You still haven't told me what I did to you," Tre said, rubbing his freed wrists.

"Up on the ledge first," she motioned.

Tre looked behind him. There was a foot-wide ledge all around the roof. He stepped up, and couldn't help but look down. Five storeys never looked so high, or so far down. He was not afraid of heights, but he couldn't help but think what she had in mind.

"Are you going to tell me now?" he said, his legs feeling uncharacteristically like rubber.

Though looking angry, tears fell from her eyes.

"You really don't know, do you? I guess that shows how shallow you are."

Tre still awaited a clue.

"You killed my sister, you prick!"

"What? What the hell are you talking about? I've never killed anyone."

"You don't even remember Juanita, do you?"

"Juanita?" Tre's eyebrows furled as he thought. "What's your maiden name? Flores, isn't it? Juanita Flores?" Tre closed his eyes to think. "No, I'm sorry, I don't remember."

"It wasn't Juanita Flores. It was Juanita Ramirez."

"I'm sorry …"

"We all called her Juany."

That sparked a memory in Tre. "I've only met one Juany before, but I can't say I really knew her. If I remember, she interviewed for the job Katie got."

"So you do remember!"

"I'm sorry. I heard she died, but I don't know what makes you think I killed her."

"When she got home from the interview, she was devastated. She'd been turned down for hundreds of acting roles. She'd been fired from her waitressing job, and had been looking for weeks to get a new job. When she got home from her interview with you, she told me she was certain she'd bombed on the interview. She went to her room in our eighth floor apartment, wrote a note that simply said 'goodbye' then jumped out the window." She gasped as she finished the sentence.

"But …"

"That's why I left you that 'goodbye' voicemail on your cell phone."

"Oh …"

"So I blame you for not hiring her."

"And you become best friends with the girl that got the job?" Tre looked puzzled.

"It wasn't poor Katie's fault that you discriminated against my sister."

"I did no such thing."

"Then why didn't she get the job?"

"Because she was dead. Do you know how I found out she'd died? I phoned to ask her to start the following Monday. Someone told me she'd died. I was shocked and didn't ask how, but simply said sorry and hung up. I called Katie shortly after and gave her the job."

Deanna stood stunned. Then she lost it. Looking skyward and spreading her arms up towards the heavens, she let out a blood-curdling scream. Startled, Tre instinctively took a half step back before recalling his perilous position.

She brought her arms down and retrained the pistol on Tre.

"Even if what you say is true, it doesn't matter. Something you said or did triggered my sister's collapse."

Tre nudged forward on the ledge, "But – "

Tre's objection was cut off by the sound of a gunshot and a piece of concrete near his feet exploding into dust around him. He stepped back from the safe edge of the ledge.

"Now, you are going to suffer the same fate as her. You are going to jump to your death."

Tre glanced over his shoulder.

"I'd rather not."

Deanna took a step forward. "You can jump, or I'll shoot you and you'll fall backwards over the edge."

"Go ahead, kill me. It'd be better than falling to my death."

"Yes, it must be a *horrible* way to die." She put both hands on the gun. "So I'm going to shoot you, but only wing you. You'll still be alive on the way down."

She'd moved close enough for Tre to see the madness emanating from her eyes. She was definitely certifiable. He weighed his options. They looked bleak. He could try to jump her, but she was still a good ten to twelve feet away and a trained marksman. By the time he took one step, he'd be wearing a bullet somewhere, if not two or three. What would be worse, bleeding out or falling to his death? They say most people don't die from the fall, but from a heart attack on the way down. He'd hate surviving to live in a paralysed comatose state.

'Bang'!

Tre almost jumped out of his skin. She'd fired a second shot, this one striking the ledge between his feet.

"C'mon, Tre, time to jump! Now!"

And it was. Tre nodded slightly, turned his back to his assailant, took a long stride along the ledge, and jumped.

47 Pursuit

It didn't take John long to put together the pieces. While Quinn didn't know who'd hired him, he gave the Sacramento police some information that they discarded but that John found enlightening. Quinn said he thought his employee was a cop because of the manner in which everything was handled. This led John to make the connection back to his Deanna. He double-and triple-checked everything. He laid it all out for Jack and walked him through it to make sure he hadn't made any mistakes. When they were both convinced, they left their parents' home and headed for the SF airport where they could get a non-stop to Detroit.

The twins pulled up to Tre's house as Deanna sped away. Jack ran inside the house and found chaos, but that things were under control. An ambulance and the police had already been called. Jack got back in the car and the men sped off in pursuit. John had installed tracking software on his, Jack's, and Deanna's phones as a precaution in case a stakeout or case went south. With Jack behind the wheel, John activated the tracking software on his cell.

Along the way, they discussed what they might be headed into. Trained to formulate a plan and contingencies before entering any situation, the twins discussed the probable tactics of a very familiar opponent. Her training would lead her to a well thought out plan and multiple escape routes. Reducing her alternative means of escape would enhance their chances of successfully capturing her, although that likely meant she'd already accomplished her goal and killed her target. They pulled into the hotel parking lot a scant few minutes behind her. John and Jack argued about Deanna's intended method of execution of their dentist friend. Jack's mind envisioned torture. She could have simply walked in the house and shot Tre, but she wanted to make him suffer. For what, he didn't know. Conversely, and John didn't know the reason, nor could he explain why he suspected it other than gut feeling, but he was certain Deanna was going to make Tre jump off the roof.

The two detectives scanned the roofline of the hotel, but saw no one. John again pleaded his case to his older sibling to trust him that she was headed for the roof. As Jack opened his mouth to protest, they heard a gunshot. They quickly glanced up again then ran into the front door to the lobby.

Jack continued straight to the front desk where he momentarily flashed an obsolete LAPD badge to a startled clerk. "We have reason to believe there is an armed and dangerous person on the roof of your hotel. We are going to put the elevators in fire mode to prevent her escape."

"Her?" The clerk stuttered, shocked by the officer's approach.

John had already brought the elevators down with the fire service button and returned to stand at his brother's side.

"Which staircase leads to the roof?"

"The left – "

"Thanks."

"But you can't go up there!"

"Are you threatening a police officer?" Jack stood tall and straight, hand going to his sidearm.

"No sir!"

Jack thought the man wet himself. "And don't even think of touching those elevators until I return. Got it?"

"Yes sir!"

Jack looked at John and they exchanged smirks. "You take the left staircase, little brother, and wait for me on the top floor. I'll take the right."

Both men stood, guns drawn low to their sides. John looked at Jack, his stern action face somehow penetrated by a look of sadness. "Please only disable her."

Jack put his hand on his brother's shoulder. "Promise."

48 The Roof

Navigating their respective staircases without incident, the brothers stood briefly at the last set of stairs between them and Deanna.

"Ready?" Jack asked.

"Ready. On your lead?"

Jack nodded. He stepped out from under cover and pointed his gun up the stairwell. After a two- count, John ascended the first flight. John then stepped out and pointed his weapon upward for cover as Jack rounded the stairs and stopped at the top step, to the side of the open door. He glanced out the door and gave John the all clear to join him.

Both men took a deep breath. They smiled at each other, a silent acknowledgement, then emptied out onto the hotel rooftop, guns firmly in front of them.

They rapidly scoured the rooftop for danger. No sign of anybody around the edge, but rooftop ventilation and elevator shafts blocked part of the view.

"Over there!" Jack shouted. "See the chunks out of the ledge? Bullets struck there."

They raced over to examine it. Before they could look over the edge, a noise from behind them perked their ears. They turned to see Deanna headed through the doorway and down the stairs.

"I've got her!" John yelled.

Jack grabbed his brother's sleeve. "No you don't. I don't want you living with the guilt of shooting her if it comes to that. And I won't let you get shot by her because you hesitated."

John stared into Jack's eyes. He knew his brother was right. He nodded. "Remember your promise!"

"Promise!" Jack hollered back as he ran off.

John went to the edge and looked over.

49 Hitting the Ground Running

Jack knew what he was up against. He was pursuing a killer with deadly accurate marksmanship. And he had to be careful not to fire a fatal shot. As he raced through the rooftop doorway, he came to a sudden, paralysing stop. He looked down and counted. Twelve. Anxiety raced through his veins, sending a bone-chilling cold through his body. Sweat poured off his brow. He counted again. Twelve. *How could he not have noticed on the way up?* Too much adrenaline, he supposed, but why did it fail him now? He knew every second was precious if he hoped to catch Deanna before she got to her car. But all he could see was twelve fateful steps. Dozens of times he'd envisioned his fatal fall in a scenario just like this. Childish. Weak. Either way, he obeyed the fear, slave to his recurring nightmares. Until he heard a gunshot from down the stairwell.

Realizing that more people were in danger, Jack tentatively took his first step, then another. His foot slipped on the third step and he frantically grasped for the railing with his free hand. Balancing himself, he exhaled and took another step. Then another. He soon raced flight to flight, guarding himself as best he could without any backup. At the third floor, he came upon a teenage-looking girl squatting in a corner, a bullet hole two feet above her head. She sat ghostly white, trembling. Jack whispered a few reassuring words before turning down the next flight of stairs. At the next turn, he heard the ground level entrance door slam two flights below. Deanna had made it out of the building. If he hurried, he could still disable her car before she escaped the divided lines of the parking lot.

Hitting the sunlight with weapon straight in front of him, Jack turned to head to the parking lot. Running a few steps, he stopped dead at a commotion coming from the back of the hotel. A gate stood open to the pool area. Jack reversed direction and bolted toward the gate. As he approached the pool, an unexpected sight unfolded. Everyone had evacuated the pool and all the sunbathers had huddled into a corner of the pool deck, scared for their lives. Standing at the poolside, Deanna pointed her gun at the pool and was cursing like a trooper. In the middle of the pool, treading water, was Tre. As Jack approached, Deanna's tirade was interrupted by a voice from above.

"Deanna! Put the gun down, sweetheart. Everything is going to be okay!" John kneeled on the rooftop ledge, looking down on the scene.

"Bugger off, John. This isn't your concern!"

"You're my wife and you're trying to kill one of my best friends! How's that not my concern?"

She looked up at him. "I told you to bugger off!" She turned and fired a shot in his direction, missing.

Jack knew the miss was on purpose, and he didn't dare risk her taking another shot at his brother. And he knew his brother wouldn't quit trying to talk her down. He fired.

"Shit!" Deanna screamed as she hit the ground, dropping her gun into the pool and grabbing at her left calf.

"No!" John yelled from above.

Jack ran forward. "Sorry, Deanna." He harshly rolled her on her stomach, yanked her arms behind her back as she grunted, and cuffed her. He looked up toward his brother, but John had already begun his descent through the stairwell.

50 Capture

Trevor heard sirens as he pulled himself out of the pool. John had made a tourniquet for Deanna's wound, in spite of her kicking him two or three times with her uninjured leg.

Drying himself off as he approached her, Trevor was verbally accosted by Deanna.

"Let me free! I've got to kill Tre. He killed my sister and he doesn't deserve to live."

She struggled with her restraints. "Why Katie loves you, I have no idea. I told her you didn't respect women and it was useless chasing after you, but she insisted I keep her posted on your whereabouts."

Through the pool gate, Trevor could see four officers approach, weapons drawn. Jack and John had holstered their guns and placed them ten feet away on a table along with their expired badges. The officers holstered their guns upon securing the brothers' guns and assessing the situation. Trevor heard another siren approaching, and within the time it took for an officer to re-cuff Deanna with their own issue, an ambulance pulled up.

Trevor motioned to the officer to stop with Deanna.

"I am truly sorry for what happened to your sister. I had no idea." He paused briefly and looked down. "You took Cassy away from me, so I understand how you feel."

"Cassandra was an unfortunate casualty. It should have been you."

John walked away with the officers as they escorted Deanna to their cruiser. Jack turned to Trevor and shook his head.

"What a crazy day!"

"They don't get much crazier," Tre replied.

"Are you okay? That was quite a jump!"

Tre winced. "I'm actually so sore I can barely stand. It hurt like hell to hit the water like that."

"I wish I could have seen it," Jack stated.

"Just like cliff diving in Negril. Much easier there though. I didn't have to propel myself ten feet out on a busted up ankle, knowing I'd be dead if I missed. And the water's deeper there too." He looked down at his scraped legs. "At least I missed my head when I turned up out of the dive."

51 Visitors

A gentle hand on his shoulder startled Trevor from a short slumber. Initially unaware of his surroundings, the back pain triggered a reminder that he'd slept in a hospital room chair. His mother whispered 'sorry' to him as he straightened himself to sit up. Blood raced to his extremities as he stretched with clenched fists.

"Zachary's doing much better this morning, dear," his mother informed him.

"Thanks, Mom. How's Dad?"

"He's fine. A bit sore from all the excitement last night."

"I bet. He and Zachary saved my life."

His mother smiled, fighting back a tear at the possibility that had almost transpired last night. She returned her hand to her son's shoulder.

A tapping at the hospital room door attracted both their attentions.

"Am I interrupting?"

A welcoming smile crossed Trevor's face. "Hey, Jack."

"Hey, buddy. Say, I didn't know you had a sister."

Trevor's mother blushed.

"Mom, this is Jack. He's the P.I. friend of mine that I spoke about."

"One of the twins, right?"

"Yes, Mrs. Brightman. I mean Mrs. Brockman." He turned apologetically to Trevor. "It's going to take some time to get used to, man."

"How's John doing?"

"He's a wreck. Don't think he slept a wink all night. He feels terrible about what Deanna did, yet he's scared for her. The guy's still crazy about her, even after this and all the weird religious cult crap."

"I feel bad for him. I'm glad you're here though. Means a lot to me."

"You're like a brother, Tre. Trevor. Sorry. You're like a brother whose name I don't know."

Trevor laughed, realizing how much he'd missed his friend since he'd headed out on his trek. Talking on the phone never held the same feeling as exchanging jabs first-hand.

From across the room came a low almost indiscernible moan. Trevor's mother grabbed his arm with excitement.

"Zachary," she called out. His eyes remained closed but his arm moved in a restless or uncomfortable way.

Trevor ducked into the hallway and flagged down a nearby nurse.

The visitors all sensed relief to see the young minister awake. The doctor had earlier deemed the surgery a success, but there was nothing like feeling his eyes upon them to reconfirm what the doctor had stated.

Back at the Brockman household, John had returned from the Monroe County Jail. He broke down at the doorway when Trevor greeted him. Following a few minutes of silence sitting in the living room, John spoke of his visit with Deanna.

"She's scared. She's not sure what came over her, saying she felt totally obsessed with killing you, Trevor. The police medicated her shortly after processing last night. I didn't know it, but she'd been on quetiapine from the time of her incident on the force, until about two months ago. She suddenly stopped refilling her prescriptions. Once its effects thinned out of her system, she started to change for the worse."

"What's that medicine for?" Mrs. Brockman asked.

Trevor answered. "You've heard of Seroquel. It's a quetiapine – an antipsychotic, Mom. It's used for schizophrenia, bipolar disorder, etc. Maybe to keep away the paranoid thoughts, too."

"I can't believe that I never knew she was on it." John shook his head.

"She's a private person," Jack consoled his brother.

"Falling off the medication triggered her obsession with taking down Tre. She escalated pretty quickly from death threats to action," John said, still disbelieving his own words.

"Look on the bright side," Trevor's father added. "She may get a reduced sentence or even just sentenced to a clinic for what she did yesterday because of her medical history."

John half smiled. "I appreciate the attempt to cheer me up, but you're forgetting that she used a sniper rifle to kill Cassy. She's not going to get off with a little mental retreat and walk out in six weeks."

The room went silent.

Jack looked at Trevor, hoping his friend would once again come up with the right words to say when needed most.

Trevor looked back, lost for words. Desperate to avoid silence, he changed the topic.

"I'm flying back to LA tomorrow."

"What?" his mother exclaimed, looking abandoned.

"I'll be back in a few days, Mom. I've got to go back and sign some papers for a real estate deal that's closing."

"Can't that all be done on the internet these days?" his mother protested.

"I'll be back in a few days. Promise." He turned to Jack and John. "I don't want to speak for my mom and dad, but I will. Please feel free to stay here as long as you need to while you find out what's going to happen to Deanna. I imagine they'll send her back to California for the" - he paused to find the inoffensive words, both to John and himself – "for the thing out there."

52 Back to LA

Despite the flight taking just two hours off his watch, it felt the whole five plus hours in duration. Trevor felt exhausted from the aftermath of the last few days' cocktail of withdrawals, adrenalin, sorrow, and utter fatigue. Completely out of form, he couldn't wait to get the paperwork out of the way to clear the way to crashing in bed. His bed. Due to his last minute booking, he landed a seat in the back row of the plane, across from one of the lavatories. Even if he'd wanted to sleep, the lavatory door opened and slammed closed every few minutes. Not to mention the constant line-up of people waiting to use the washroom. So much for the announcement about no loitering to use the facilities.

Trevor knew there was no rushing to get off the plane. Unless he wanted to cause a scene, he was destined to be the last person off the plane, save the crew. He used his temporary cell phone to call his lawyer to confirm the appointment for signing. He'd be glad to clutch a new version of his own cell phone again, not for all the games and gadgets, but just because it felt right in his hand.

After watching the last of the occupants wrestle with their overhead bags, Trevor finally got up empty-handed and walked up the aisle and out the boarding door. He wasn't used to travelling with no bags at all. He usually packed light enough to fit everything in a small carry-on bag and an undersized backpack. It felt like walking naked down the street. Disembarking and walking uphill through the jet bridge, the waiting throng of the next flight's passengers jammed the gate area still congested with confused travellers from his flight. He knifed his way through the crowd until he noticed a group of people had peeled away from the main crowd and stared transfixed at the hanging LCD television. Instinctively, he slowed to look. The television played at its usual annoying loud level, often causing the overhead public address system to sound muffled and incomprehensible, but in this case allowing Trevor to hear the story.

"Remarkably," the announcer said with a small image of a young lady in the corner of the screen, "this is a picture of the woman as she was found wandering through the woods."

The small picture resembled many of the homeless Trevor had encountered. He turned his head and began to walk away. A beeping horn stopped him dead in his tracks; he hadn't noticed the extended golf cart hauling passengers to the nearby gate. A minute later, he found himself grateful for the delay.

The television announcer continued in the background. "The police immediately could tell she wasn't a homeless drifter. She is in excellent physical condition for someone who looks like they've been lost for many weeks. The police believe she is a foreign exchange student from one of the local colleges. So far she has only spoken French to the officers. Here's how this pretty young lady looks all cleaned up." The image swapped in the background and expanded in size to fill half the screen. "If you have any information, please contact the LA police and ask for Missing Persons."

Trevor looked up at the screen and his jaw dropped. He began running through the terminal, his heart and mind both on the brink of exploding. Catching a cab, he asked them to step on it to the police station. After slipping the driver a couple of fifties, he complied.

Taking the steps two at a time, Trevor ascended the stairs to the old police station.

"I know the girl," he panted, short of breath and long on anxiousness.

"You and half the city, by all the calls we've gotten."

"No, I really do know her," he said, doing his best to make himself presentable after his sprinting. Out of the corner of his eye, he could see her through a glass door in the room next door. He ran over to the door and fruitlessly yanked on the knob. He pounded on the glass to get her attention.

He got it. She jumped out of her chair and limped quickly to the door, which failed to open on her side as well, but sounded an alarm on her attempt. An officer restrained her as she pounded back on the window. The officer then swiped his badge on the security pad to terminate the alarm and release the door. She twisted herself free, ploughed through the door and flung herself into Trevor's arms.

"Tre! Tre! Tre!" she exclaimed over and over.

"See," said the officer that greeted Trevor. "She's a crazy French girl."

Trevor hugged her and rubbed her hair, then turned momentarily to the officer. "She's saying my name. My name is Tre. Her name is Cassy. I thought she died in a car crash over three weeks ago."

53 The End

The shortening days of summer in southern Michigan were a portent of the not-too-distant arrival of fall. The humidity had lessened with the length of daylight, making the evenings in the back yard most enjoyable.

Trevor Brockman carefully poured another scotch into his father's glass. He turned and filled Jack's glass, and held the bottle up to the others circling the fire pit. All others declined, some with a look of disgust at the thought.

"I'd like to make a toast," Jack said as he stood.

Everyone stood and lifted their glasses.

"Here's to Cassy and Trevor. May nothing keep them apart again!"

Clanging filled the air as glasses saluted the toast.

"So tell me, Cassy," Jack asked, "why did they think you were a foreign student?"

She smiled at him, only recently feeling like herself. "I'd been in survival mode for quite some time. I'd broken my leg and arm in the crash and had to splint myself using my clothes and what Mother Nature provided. They said I suffered some form of shock and could only utter one word. I kept saying Tre over and over. I guess they tried speaking to me in Spanish, thinking I was saying the Spanish word for three. But when I didn't respond, and since I don't look Hispanic, they figured I must be French. Tres is also a French word meaning very. And even though I didn't respond to the French translator, they thought I looked more French and stuck with it."

"But to survive for that long? That's amazing. And with broken limbs." Jack's girlfriend Paula looked in awe at her new friend Cassy.

"All that nature girl stuff saved her life," Trevor said, pulling Cassy close with one arm around her shoulder.

"It's not the only life she saved," added Jack.

"What do you mean?" Mrs. Brockman asked.

"It kept Deanna off death row in California. John says she's responding well to new medications that she's on in the minimum security prison she's at."

"It's too bad he couldn't make it," Trevor replied.

"He's where he needs to be right now."

"We all are, Jack." And Trevor raised his glass for another toast.

Did you love this novel?

Let the world know!

I appreciate every honest review of my work on Amazon, Goodreads, or your favourite book lover website.

For an Independent author and publisher, this is the best advertising that I can receive.

Thank you,

Dale J. Moore

Other books by Dale J. Moore

UbiquiMed: We're Everywhere, For You!

The world had changed. A violence Plagued nation, torn apart by a financial crisis, struggled to find its way back. Disease and poverty were rampant. Government assistance led to government intervention. Thus emerged Ubiquitous Medical, a federally funded health organization designed to fill every need of a desperate public.

*"**UBIQUITOUS MEDICAL** is a fast paced ride that will keep you guessing. Twists and turns keep you on the edge of your seat, while the characters grow and deepen with every page. Dale J. Moore's voice shines through in this unique tale of a chilling future."* **Gemma Halliday, award winning author of the High Heels Mysteries**

Trials of Katrina Series

"I enjoyed Friends of the Deceased by Dale J Moore tremendously, a novel with all the right ingredients to thrill, chill, and keep the pages turning! Witty dialogue, likable--and dislikable!--characters. Katrina keeps moving forward, and I look for more in this line of books."

Heather Graham, New York Times and USA Today Bestselling Author

Check out the FIRST book in the series,

Life of the Party

Maureen P. Moore

'Outgoing? Gorgeous? Enjoy P/T evening work? Good fun! Good pay! THIS IS PERFECTLY LEGAL!' The ad in the Toronto paper sounds just about perfect for Katrina. Except for the 'outgoing' part. Desperate to escape a creepy roommate and a scary landlord, she must find some way to supplement her meager café salary to flee to a new apartment.

Eye-popping beautiful but woefully shy, when Katrina is hired as a professional guest (aka PEST) for a company called Life of the Party, her nerves get the best of her. Before she can make a total fool of herself and lose her new job, she's saved by a dashing and mysterious stranger who vanishes into the night.

With the help of her newfound friend and fellow PEST Cathy, Katrina tries desperately to find her mystery man. Her search, and her life, gets disrupted by the nefarious affairs of her roommates, landlord, and new boss. Along the way, Katrina learns that she may be shy - but she's certainly no wallflower.

The Second book in the series,

Friends of the Deceased

Dale J. Moore

How does a small town girl end up investigating crime at a funeral home in Toronto? Drop-dead gorgeous Katrina is trying to run her new salon and take her relationship to a new level. The unexpected death of a client and struggles with her salon lead her to the Shady Rest funeral home.

As she stumbles her way through the personal problems that plague her world, Katrina ends up immersed in the world of preparing people for the next world.

With the help of a ruggedly handsome police detective, some old friends, and a few new ones, will she get to the bottom of what's going on, or end up buried by it? One thing is certain; when Katrina gets involved, chaos and comedy will ensue.

"Friends of the Deceased features Katrina (Kat), a heroine who refuses to be daunted by lies and treachery and finds a silver lining because of her kindness." **Carolyn Hart, Author of the Death on Demand series.**

"Behind-the-scenes hijinks at a funeral home will have you cheering for hairdresser Katrina and her gang when they delve into stolen goods, fraud, and charity scams. Katrina has to unravel the mysteries before the next ultra luxury casket is made for her." **Nancy J. Cohen, Author of the Bad Hair Day mystery series**

The Third book in the series,

Days of Wine and Tomatoes

Dale J. Moore

Katrina is back for her third chaotic adventure! Trying to revive a struggling relationship with her detective boyfriend, they're off for a long weekend to wine country along the shores of Lake Erie. Customary to Katrina's exploits, trouble crosses her path like a black cat, altering the idyllic getaway.

As the town of Leamington holds its annual Tomato Fest, the summer waterfront party atmosphere is disrupted by a kidnapping. Mixing the enjoyment of the lake front wineries with sleuthing and rooting out clues, Katrina missteps from one mishap to another while solving mysteries in her unique way.

Having been the Life of the Party, and after surviving Friends of the Deceased, Katrina's latest escapade has barrels of wine and laughs. Mix in a bushel of tomatoes, a misfit crew, and the summer sun, and you've got Days of Wine and Tomatoes.

"A rollicking respite perfect for a lazy spring afternoon."
Deborah Coonts, Author of the Lucky O'Toole Las Vegas Adventures

www.ingramcontent.com/pod-product-compliance
Lightning Source LLC
Chambersburg PA
CBHW071220250626
47163CB00001B/58

* 9 7 8 0 9 8 6 8 5 3 4 1 8 *